Rugged, sexy and too hot to handle!

These protectors need taming— who is up to the challenge?

He'll investigate her past, catch her heart and protect her future… all she has to do is say yes!

D0528384

*Harlequin, Harlequin Duets and Colophon are
trademarks used under licence.*

*First published in Great Britain 2001
by Harlequin Mills & Boon Limited,
Eton House, 18-24 Paradise Road,
Richmond, Surrey TW9 1SR*

HER PROTECTOR © Ellen James 1998
HER BODYGUARD © Peggy Nicholson 1999

ISBN 0 373 04813 0

20-1101

*Printed and bound in Spain
by Litografía Rosés S.A., Barcelona*

HER PROTECTOR

Ellen James

&

HER BODYGUARD

Peggy Nicholson

HARLEQUIN®

TORONTO • NEW YORK • LONDON
AMSTERDAM • PARIS • SYDNEY • HAMBURG
STOCKHOLM • ATHENS • TOKYO • MILAN • MADRID
PRAGUE • WARSAW • BUDAPEST • AUCKLAND

For my dad—we miss ya, Jake.

Her Protector

by

Ellen James

THE WOMAN WITH the gun was beautiful. She was also scared, and doing her damnedest not to show it.

Mark studied her. She had russet hair cut short, but not too short—a few stray tendrils had been left to curl against her cheeks and at the back of her neck. Her eyes were a clear hazel, but Mark could see a shadow of fear in them. He also saw just a hint of desperation. He was good at reading subtle little signs like that. After thirteen years of being a cop, he was very good at reading people.

He was the one who'd placed the gun in her hand a few moments ago. Now she gazed down at it, her expression changed to one of mingled disgust and determination.

"Second thoughts?" Mark asked casually.

She gave him an unreadable glance. "I came here to learn how to shoot. And that's just what I intend to do."

He wondered why she needed a gun. What was she afraid of? As a police detective, he'd often seen

the results of fear, the things people could do when
they were pushed to the brink. He shook his head.
Not his problem. At this particular point in time he
wasn't a police detective—not officially, anyway.
He was on leave from the department, whether he
liked it or not. To keep from going stir-crazy he'd
signed on here at the local shooting range, and that
meant he was currently an instructor in the fine art
of using firearms. So why wasn't he instructing?

"Maybe that's not the right type of weapon for
you," he told the woman. "Maybe you'd like to try
out something a little…smaller."

She frowned at the Beretta automatic in her hand.
"It'll get the job done, won't it?"

"Depends on the job," he remarked.

An oddly bleak expression flickered across her
face. "I've never held a gun before now," she said
in a low voice. "But if it's to keep a promise—"
She broke off abruptly. He could see the obvious
effort she made to conceal all emotion behind rigid
features. "Anyway, I just want to find out if I can
handle this thing. *Can* we get on with it?"

Mark positioned her at a lane, and began setting
the target: the standard outline of a human figure.
Then, after a second's thought, he changed the target
to a plain old bull's-eye. It seemed more benign
somehow. Not that there could ever be anything benign about shooting a gun. He became aware of the

ache in his leg, a reminder of the bullet that not too long ago had just about sheared his femur...the bullet, in fact, responsible for his enforced absence from the police force. No, there was nothing benign about guns.

He waited until the woman had the sound dampeners over her ears. Only then did he load the gun for her, sliding the clip into place.

"Now," he said, "use your left hand as a support. Arms fully extended...that's good. No, don't squint. You're not going to pull the trigger. Just squeeze it..."

She held the gun for so long it seemed she'd changed her mind, after all. She didn't say a word, didn't move, and an uneasy waiting filled the air.

Then, without giving any warning, she fired. The shot went wide.

"Try to visualize where the bullet will hit," Mark told her. "It's not enough to look down the sight. Shooting is a mental exercise, as much as anything else. You're squinting again...that's better."

After an initial shakiness, she settled in. She focused closely on his instructions, a resolute calm seeming to take her over. One shot, then another and another. She was an able student, and she possessed a natural skill at the endeavor.

Mark stepped back to let her try it on her own. She seemed to have forgotten his presence, all her concentration focused now on that bull's-eye. Robyn Myers, that was how she'd introduced herself when she'd first walked in here. Once again he wondered what had made Robyn Myers pick up a gun for the first time in her life. He noted the tense line of her shoulders, the effort she put into holding her arms absolutely steady. In the short time she'd been practicing, her aim was improving rapidly. A natural, all right.

At last Mark brought the target forward, the bull's-eye swaying back and forth as it drew closer. "Not bad," he said, observing the smattering of bullet holes.

She set down the gun and pushed off the ear protectors. "I think I'd like to get out of here," she said, her voice brittle. Without waiting for his response, she hurried through the door and toward the front reception area.

Mark caught up to her. "Have a seat in the office," he said. "I'd like to talk to you for a few minutes."

She gave him a skeptical glance. "The lesson's over, isn't it? I got a passing grade, didn't I?"

"Yes on both counts. But I still think we should talk." He ushered her into the office and pulled up a chair so she could sit in front of the cluttered desk. He sat down behind it, grimacing a little as the pain flared in his leg.

"What's wrong?" she asked.

"Let's just say I'm recovering from an on-the-job injury." He debated how to start; something told him that Robyn Myers wouldn't take kindly to what he wanted to say. Meanwhile, she leaned forward and picked up the photograph displayed at one side of the desk.

"Nice family," she said. The photo showed a smiling brunette and two young boys.

"Afraid I can't take any credit," he said. "That's Benjamin's family." At her inquiring look, he added, "Benjamin's the one who owns this place. He's a friend of mine from way back."

"I see. And he doesn't mind you appropriating his office." Her tone was sardonic.

"Just as long as I don't make a habit of it." He gazed for a few seconds more at the photograph. "My own kids are pretty much grown up," he was surprised to hear himself saying. Robyn Myers gave him a considering look this time, and he figured he was getting offtrack.

"Ms. Myers," he said, "for somebody who'd never shot a gun before, you did good back there. Surprisingly good."

She shrugged wearily. "It's not something I want to be good at. Before yesterday, it's not something I'd even have considered."

He let a pause settle between them, and then he spoke. "What happened yesterday?"

Immediately she was on her guard again. "Nothing that concerns you, Mr. Stewart."

Maybe she was right. Then again, being a cop meant you poked your nose into other people's troubles. And Robyn Myers was in trouble…he didn't have any doubts about that much.

"So," he said. "You came in here today because you're thinking about getting a gun."

"That's the general idea. Tell me, Mr. Stewart, do you grill all paying customers this way?"

He tried a smile on her. "Actually, I hadn't come to the grilling part yet."

She didn't smile back. "What's your point, Mr. Stewart?"

"I can tell you're in some kind of fix, Ms. Myers," he said. "Believe it or not, that's probably the worst time to think about getting a gun. You're scared. And scared people don't always make the best decisions about things like firearms."

She stood, her cheeks turning a slightly indignant pink. "It really *isn't* any of your business, is it, Mr. Stewart?"

He could tell her he was a cop, but some instinct warned him not to. "It wouldn't hurt to talk about it," he said. "Whatever it is that's bothering you."

It was there again in her eyes, the shadow of fear.

She stood in front of the desk, and he thought she was going to confide in him, after all. But then she withdrew behind that rigid mask, just before she turned and walked out the door.

"HOW IS HE, Mom?"

"He's sleeping at last," Nina Myers said anxiously. "That's a good thing, the doctors say. But how can anything be good right now? You go sit with him for a bit, Robyn. If he wakes up, it will help him to see you."

Robyn looked her mother over. Nina appeared utterly exhausted, her usual cheeriness and optimism defeated by the events of the past few days.

"You need something to eat," Robyn told her.

"I haven't been hungry, not since this terrible thing happened to your father..." Nina bent her head as she sat there in the hospital waiting room, as if she simply had no energy left. Even her silvery hair seemed to have lost its luster, falling in limp strands against her cheeks. Always in the past Nina had been the take-charge type, managing the family and the family enterprises with skill and confidence. For Robyn, one of the worst things about this crisis was seeing her mother falter.

"Mom," Robyn said gently. "You really do need to eat something. At least go down to the cafeteria."

Nina stood. "Yes, I suppose I should. But you go to your father, dear."

"Mom...be careful."

"What could happen to me?" Nina asked with a hint of the old spirit. "It's your father we have to be concerned about."

"Just be careful," Robyn said, knowing how inadequate the words sounded. She waited until her mother had stepped onto the elevator. Then she slipped into her father's room, her stomach tightening in apprehension. She'd already undergone the worst, she knew; yesterday she'd had the first shock of seeing how badly hurt her father was. Yet, every time she'd come into the room since, she'd felt disbelief. *That* couldn't be her father, lying so helplessly in the bed, bruised and battered almost beyond recognition. One eye was swollen shut, a deep gash sliced into his cheek, several ribs, as well as his left arm, broken. There had been ominous talk about the possibility of a punctured lung. Although it had turned out to be a false alarm, and although the doctors had patched up Cal Myers as efficiently as possible, a sense of dread still churned inside Robyn. Who had done this to her father? And, dear God, why?

She sank into a chair beside the bed, propping her elbows on her knees. She listened to her father's slow, rasping breath as he slept. Robyn supposed the pain medication had kicked in again. It was a relief to know he could rest.

Robyn gazed at him, hating to see him so vulnerable. Her father had always been such a strong person—confident and decisive. Growing up, she'd known that she could go to him with any problem, and he would have the answer for her. He'd made her feel safe and protected. And, over the years, he'd encouraged *her* to be strong, to have faith in her own abilities. That was one of his most precious gifts to her.

In an echo of her mother's posture a few moments ago, she lowered her head. She felt the prickle of fatigue all through her body, and no wonder—she'd hardly slept at all since arriving in Santa Fe yesterday. She and her mother had taken turns staying with Dad. Aunt Janet and Uncle Greg had taken their own turns, of course, but the entire family was feeling the strain. The night before last, someone had entered Cal Myers's art gallery and brutally attacked him. So far the police had no suspects.

Robyn heard a rustling sound from the bed and glanced up. Her father had awakened and was staring at her. His bruised face had worked into an expression of anguish.

"Dad," she said quickly. "You shouldn't get agitated. That's what the doctors said." She reached to press the buzzer for the nurse, but he took hold of her arm with his free hand. His grip was disconcertingly strong.

"Did you do it?" he asked, laboring to make each word distinct.

"I promise we'll talk about it later. You have to rest—"

"No! Tell me, Robyn. Did you do what I asked?"

She hesitated, but realized he would only grow more upset unless she answered him.

"I don't have one yet, Dad. It takes time, what with filing for a permit and everything. But I went someplace, to see if I actually had it in me. To see if I could actually make myself use a gun…well, I used one, all right. The man at the shooting range told me that my aim was surprisingly good. Those were his exact words, 'surprisingly good.'" She hadn't liked hearing that—it wasn't a talent she wanted to have.

Her father only seemed to grow more distressed, his grip on her arm tightening. "It's not enough! You have to get a gun—now, Robyn. I can't ask your uncle Greg to do it—after his heart attack, he can't take this kind of stress. It has to be you, Robyn. You have to protect your mother. Yourself."

"Tell me *why*, Dad," she said, starting to feel frantic. "Who attacked you? What makes you think they'll come after us, too? Give me something to go by—"

"Just do it. Before it's too late." His hand finally loosened from her arm, falling back on the bed.

"Dad, the police will be questioning you again. Tell them what you know…tell them exactly what happened. If you're really worried about Mom or me being in danger, you have to tell the police—"

"No." The despair in his voice was raw. "I can't. I was warned not to involve the police. If I do, something even worse will happen. And you mustn't tell your mother! Not a word about the gun. Just get it, and watch over her. Do you understand, Robyn?"

A chill seeped through her. "I don't understand anything," she whispered. "Oh, Dad, why can't you trust me enough to tell me the truth?"

She might as well not have spoken. Already he had slipped back into that drugged sleep, leaving her with all questions unanswered. How quickly the life of her family had shattered out of its normal, ordinary routine. The vicious, unexplained attack on her father…the distraught phone call from her mother…Robyn's last-minute flight out of Denver…and then her father's frightening demand. *Get a gun, Robyn. You have to do this. Get a gun, and protect your mother. Protect yourself. Promise me that you'll do exactly as I say.*

At last she'd promised. How could she have refused him anything as he lay there hurting? How could she ignore the fact that danger suddenly threatened her family? But a gun…

She hated guns—she hated violence. As a high-school teacher, she'd seen too many kids get caught up in violence. She'd told her students over and over that it was never an answer to any problem. Yet, this very afternoon, she'd gone into that shooting range, driven by her promise to her father. She'd been driven, too, by anger and frustration and by the unreasoning conviction that perhaps it really *was* up to her to keep anything terrible from happening again. She'd held a gun in her hand and fired it, and tried desperately to believe she could keep herself and her family safe.

But then Mark Stewart had sat her down in that chair and told her she was scared, almost sounding as if he was accusing her. He'd been all too percep-tive, that much was certain, and Robyn had imme-diately gone on the defensive with him.

Now she went restlessly to the window and looked out. A brilliant New Mexico sky arched above, tinged gold from the late-afternoon sun. She told herself there was no sky like it anywhere else, stretching limitlessly over mountain and mesa.

She tried to concentrate only on the beauty of it, tried to give herself some measure of peace. The effort was useless.

A nurse came into the room to check on her father, and Robyn went back to the waiting area. She sat down and leafed futilely through a magazine. A few moments later her mother stepped off the elevator, carrying two plastic cups of coffee.

"Is he all right?" Nina asked breathlessly. "Maybe I shouldn't have left—"

"He's fine." Robyn paused. Her father had been so adamant—*Don't tell your mother. Just watch over her.* But didn't Nina have a right to know as much as possible? "Mom...he did wake up for a few moments. And he said he was worried about us."

Nina attempted a smile. She sank into a chair beside Robyn and handed her a cup. "That sounds just like your father. He's always done his best to take care of us. I'm sure he can't bear the thought of us taking care of *him.*"

Robyn sipped her coffee without really tasting it. She marveled that even in a time of crisis familiar patterns asserted themselves. Cal Myers was a man of vision and imagination. He knew how to see the hidden talent in the work of fledgling artists, knew how to encourage that talent and make it flower. He'd helped many, many artists go on to prestigious careers, and in the process developed his own reputation. He was not, however, a man who liked to concern himself with the day-to-day requirements of running a business or a family. Nina was the one who'd taken care of the Myers clan over the years. She'd always kept things going—ensuring that investments were well maintained, bills paid, obligations met. Even so, she perpetuated the illusion that her husband was looking after things.

"Mom, Dad thinks we might be in danger. You…and me."

Some of Nina's usual matter-of-factness seemed to reassert itself. "That's nonsense," she said. "An awful thing happened to your father, but it's over. It was something horribly random. Someone breaking in, trying to rob the gallery. We need better security, that's all."

"Nothing was stolen," Robyn said, still speaking as gently as possible. "All those valuable paintings, and not a single one is missing."

Nina's expression grew stubborn. "Your father is a brave man. He stopped whoever it was before anything *could* be stolen."

"Robbery wasn't necessarily the motive," Robyn persisted. "The police said there were no signs of a break-in. Maybe Dad let the attacker—or attackers—into the gallery."

Nina gave a frown. "What are you implying, Robyn? That your father would be foolish enough to open the door to suspicious strangers, when it was practically the middle of the night?"

"Maybe we're not talking about strangers. Maybe he opened the door to someone he knew."

"Your father would never associate with…with *criminals*," Nina said. "And only a criminal could have attacked him in that savage way." Nina's loyalty to her husband was impressive; her entire life seemed to revolve around Cal Myers. How awful it must be for her, knowing that someone had assaulted him in his very own gallery. But the questions could not be evaded.

"Mom, why was Dad at the gallery so late? That doesn't make any sense, either."

"He often works late," Nina replied. "That's part of being self-employed. A stranger broke in and attacked him. We're just lucky that your father's going to be all right." Despite the firmness of her voice, worry lines had etched into her face, along with the telltale lines of age. Nina had recently turned sixty. While still a pretty woman, today she showed every single one of her years. Robyn reached over and clasped her hand.

"Mom, you have to listen to me. I don't want anything to happen to you. If Dad thinks you're in danger, then he has a reason. Even if he won't tell us what it is—"

Nina withdrew her hand. "Your father would not deceive us. He's already told the police that he doesn't know who attacked him. He has undergone an ordeal. All he needs from us right now is our support.''

Robyn saw her mother's shuttered expression. This was Nina all over again, refusing to admit that her successful, talented, charismatic husband could be anything less than perfect, anything less than aboveboard. Robyn, however, had to be a little more realistic. Much as she admired and loved her father, she believed that he was hiding something. Why else his demand that she obtain a gun?

Robyn was on the verge of telling her mother about Cal's urgent request. *You have to do it, Robyn. You have to protect your mother, and yourself…*

But there was the other part of the request to consider. He had been so insistent that she *not* tell her mother. Why? Always that question, over and over, resonating in Robyn's mind.

''Robyn,'' said her mother, ''everything has been so chaotic we haven't even had a chance to talk. I want you to tell me about Denver, about the high school and all the rest of it.'' Obviously Nina would rather make small talk than confront any uncomfortable discussions about her husband's plight.

''Mom,'' she said, ''about teaching…the fact is, I'm considering taking a leave of absence. I'm not sure it's what I want to do anymore.''

''Nonsense, dear. You've always loved your job so much. And you do so much good—''

"It doesn't seem that way," Robyn said heavily. "I don't feel like I'm making a difference at all. There are lots of reasons—"

"Oh, honey." Nina patted her shoulder. "Of course you make a difference. You know what's wrong? You're just getting over a divorce, and of course that's traumatic. I'm sure it tends to color the rest of your life, and you mustn't let it."

"My second divorce," Robyn couldn't help reminding her. But it wasn't a comfortable thing to admit. Not once, but twice in her life, Robyn had fallen for the wrong man. She now had two ex-husbands as proof of her dubious judgment. "Anyway," she went on, "my personal life doesn't have anything to do with teaching—"

"Give it time," Nina said consolingly. "Another man will come along. This time he'll be the right one."

Robyn would have laughed if she'd had any energy for it. Her mother, the perennial optimist. The fact that her only child couldn't stay married didn't seem to daunt her in the least. And Nina persisted in believing that true happiness could only be found in partnership with a man. Didn't her own life with Cal Myers prove as much? Forty years of marriage...forty years of devotion, forty years of believing that nothing really bad or unpleasant could ever occur. But now something bad *had* occurred, to Nina's very own husband.

Nina rose from her chair, her attention already retreating from Robyn. "I need to be with your father. Everything will be all right…as long as I'm there with him. I just have to be there."

Robyn watched her mother go down the corridor. Then she stood and walked the length of the waiting room, the turmoil inside her threatening to overflow. It struck her that every aspect of her life was in disarray. The inescapable doubts about her career, the debacle of divorce number two…and now this, her father lying defenseless in a hospital bed, unseen danger threatening her family. Robyn clasped her arms tightly against her body, but that didn't stop the sensation engulfing her—the sensation that, any moment, she would shatter completely.

CHAPTER TWO

MARK READ the notice in the newspaper for possibly the third time, telling himself it had to be some other Kerry Stewart. Yeah, right, he mocked himself. There had to be a lot of twenty-one-year-old girls with his daughter's name, announcing their engagements in the *Santa Fe Gazette*.

Mark held up the engagement notice, studying the picture that accompanied it. It was his daughter, all right—and she looked so mature, so sure of herself. She also looked very happy, clinging to the arm of a spindly young man Mark had never seen before. Frederick Graham, the paper said, a recent graduate from the University of New Mexico with a degree in finance. Who the hell got a degree in *finance?* The kid didn't even sound as if he had a job yet. And why the hell was his daughter marrying some guy named Frederick? What was she going to end up calling him? Fred—or, even worse, Freddie?

Mark knew what was really bugging him: the fact that his youngest daughter was getting married and she hadn't even bothered to let him know. The sensation he felt now went way beyond regret. Had he failed his children so completely that this was how it had to be? Reading about them in the newspaper instead of being a part of their lives?

Someone stepped into the office. Still immersed in painful thoughts of his daughters, he glanced up reluctantly. A woman stood before him…the woman who'd come by yesterday, wanting to learn how to shoot a gun. Hazel eyes, reddish hair that curled just a bit against her cheeks, name of Robyn Myers. She was still beautiful. And something told him she was still scared.

He nodded at the chair in front of the desk. "Have a seat," he said.

"Don't you think you're pushing things a little with your friend Benjamin?" She glanced around the small office.

"Benjamin's glad for some vacation time. But I didn't think I'd see you again, Ms. Myers."

"Why not?"

"Maybe I'm wrong, but you didn't seem to like coming here."

Even now, he had the feeling she was about to turn and walk out of the place. After a moment, though, she sat down. Her hair was a little rumpled, as if she'd driven over here with the windows rolled down, allowing the breeze full rein with her. She held her hands loosely in her lap, obviously trying to disguise her tension. Her eyes were shadowed by any number of emotions.

She sat there and gazed at him as if she still couldn't figure out what she was doing here.

He glanced down at the newspaper. "My daughter's getting married," he said.

"Congratulations," Robyn said.

"Don't be too happy for me. If I hadn't been catching up on the local news, I wouldn't even have known. It's not like she sent me an announcement herself or anything."

Robyn Myers didn't answer, nor did she look sympathetic.

"My daughters have a stepfather they call Dad. Nobody to blame but myself, though. I guess you could say I haven't been the most involved father."

Robyn Myers continued to appear less than sympathetic. As far as he was concerned, that made her a good audience.

"My ex-wife says I was a lousy father even before the divorce. She says my job was always more important to me than my family. So she remarried, and provided a stepfather my kids seem to worship." That was the hardest thing for Mark to admit—that his efforts to be a better father over the years had been met by his kids' undoubted preference for their stepdad. "Now I just keep asking myself—is it too late to make things right? And who the hell do I think I am, imagining that I *can* make things right?''

Robyn didn't seem to have any answer for these questions, but she'd settled back in her chair.

''I wonder why I'm telling you any of this,'' he said dryly.

''I don't know,'' she remarked. ''Maybe you think I'll be encouraged by your…candor. Maybe you think I'll open up in return, and tell you what's wrong.''

He nodded thoughtfully. ''Any chance of that?''

She stared down at her hands, and now they tightened in her lap. She took a ragged breath. ''I only came here so I could have another lesson,'' she said.

''Are you sure that's the only reason?''

Her head came up. ''*Yes*, Mr. Stewart. Much as I'm fascinated by your personal travails, that's all I want—to learn how to shoot.''

He folded the newspaper and set it to one side. Then he led her back to the shooting range. He set the target again, got her positioned with the automatic. She was definitely a natural; she remembered everything he'd taught her yesterday, holding the gun straight out in front of her with absolute steadiness. This time she didn't try to squint. She looked down the sight as if imagining exactly where the bullet would hit.

Just like yesterday, however, she didn't shoot

right away. She stood there with her feet angled slightly apart, her shoulders set in a tense, rigid line. And then, almost convulsively, her finger pulled back on the trigger.

She didn't stop there. She held on to the gun and aimed one bullet after another at the bull's-eye. The expression on her face was one of absolute fury and pain. He had seen that look before, with people who felt trapped and panicked. Shot after shot she fired. He knew better than to touch her or try to calm her. He just let her empty the clip. She had started to shake, but her finger seemed to move with a will of its own on the trigger.

Even when she'd run out of bullets, her finger kept pressing the trigger. Only after a moment did she loosen her grip and drop the gun. She yanked off the sound dampeners and tossed those aside also. When she turned, the look she gave Mark was one of horror and dismay. Then, tears brimming in her eyes, she fled from the shooting range.

ROBYN LEANED FORWARD and put her head against the steering wheel. Her cheeks were wet, but she barely took note of the fact. She didn't care that she'd made a fool of herself in front of Mark Stewart. That seemed inconsequential. The way she'd felt when she'd held the gun—that was tormenting her.

What was wrong with her—where had the terrible rage inside her come from?

She closed her eyes, but the tears kept coming. She felt herself trembling.

There was a tap at her window. Reluctantly she opened her eyes and saw that Mark Stewart had followed her. She rolled down the window a fraction.

"Please leave me alone," she said through clenched teeth.

He didn't argue with her. He just opened her door, took hold of her elbow and deftly maneuvered her from the car. She tried to resist him, but he wouldn't let go. Before she knew it, he'd guided her across the parking lot to a sturdy old Land Cruiser. The tears continued to spill onto her cheeks no matter how often she wiped them away. Mark opened the passenger door and put her inside, even reaching across to fasten her seat belt. Then he walked around the vehicle and climbed in the driver's side.

"I wish…I wish you'd just leave me alone," she said.

"It's not hard to see something's troubling you," he said imperturbably. "You came back today because you needed to talk to someone. I'm a good listener. So that's what we're going to do. You're going to talk, and I'm going to listen." He started the engine and pulled out of the parking lot.

"I don't want to go anywhere with you," she began.

"I'm not kidnapping you, Ms. Myers. I'm just taking you down to my favorite coffee shop. We're going to sit in a booth...perhaps have a doughnut or two...and perhaps you'll tell me what has you running scared."

Five minutes later they were, indeed, sitting in the booth of a small coffee shop. Mark had placed their order, and it arrived promptly: steaming mugs of coffee and two large cinnamon rolls. Robyn couldn't have imagined that she'd ever feel hungry again, but the cinnamon roll enticed her.

"Take a bite," Mark said. "A good bite."

"Do you always commandeer people this way?" she asked irritably. The tears had finally stopped and she'd blotted her face with a tissue, but her eyes ached and still threatened to leak at the corners.

"I do what's necessary," Mark said. "Right now it's necessary to feed you."

She tore off a small piece of cinnamon roll, nibbled a bite or two. She worked on another piece, then a little more. Before she knew it, she'd eaten half the roll. Then she sat with her hands wrapped around her mug of coffee. She gave Mark a grudging look, wondering why she'd allowed him to take over like this. He seemed the type of man who was used to taking over. She searched for flaws in him.

By no means could he be called a conventionally handsome man. He had too many rough edges for that—a face that looked as if it had seen too much, dark untidy hair, gray eyes, which she suspected could all too easily turn cold and hard. Mark Stewart gave the impression that he would be able to handle himself in any situation. It struck Robyn then: no matter how strong her father had always seemed to her, if Mark had been the one in that art gallery, and an attacker had entered, the outcome would have been much different. She gave an involuntary shiver.

"Mind telling me about it?" Mark said.

She took a spoon and stirred her coffee. "I hate what happened back there," she said in a low voice. "At the shooting range…the way I felt…"

"Like you could kill someone?"

Robyn pushed the coffee away. "No! Yes…I wasn't thinking coherently. Everything seemed to descend on me all at once. The anxiety of these last few days…and everything else, too. The frustrations I've been having with my teaching career…oh, Lord, even my ex-husband." She pressed her hands against the table. "I picked up that gun, and everything engulfed me. I wasn't in control, don't you see? I started firing the damned thing, filled with that anger. I didn't know I could be like that. So…so…"

"Out of control?" Mark suggested.

She closed her eyes briefly, the shame of those

few moments haunting her. "Worse than uncontrolled. It was…unreasoning. Just all that hateful anger. I couldn't stop. I didn't know how to stop." Miserably, she opened her eyes. Mark Stewart was regarding her calmly.

"Look at it this way," he said. "You didn't take the gun and try to hurt somebody else. You shot at a target. You didn't turn your anger anyplace it could do harm. Deep down, you *were* in control, you were thinking."

She wanted desperately to believe the logic of his words, but she couldn't forget the way she'd felt. "I didn't know a human being could ever feel that vengeful," she muttered.

"Is it your ex-husband?" Mark asked almost conversationally. "Is he the reason you wanted to learn how to shoot?"

"My ex-husband…" She gave a bleak laugh. "Brad and I may not get along anymore, but he's not capable of driving me to violence." She looked at Mark, saw the expression in his eyes that seemed to say nothing in this world could surprise him. Suddenly she found herself telling him everything.

"Three nights ago someone came into my father's art gallery and attacked him. It was vicious and seemingly senseless. Except that now my father's in the hospital, and he's made me promise to get a gun. He thinks whoever did it will come after my mother, or me. He won't say why. And he won't tell the police what really happened. Today, when I held that gun...I really wanted to hurt the person who hurt my father.''

She had run out of words. The problem was still hers; it hadn't gone away. But she'd shared it with someone who didn't seem about to go into shock or fly off the handle. No...Mark Stewart definitely wasn't the type who'd fly off the handle.

His expression had grown intent. ''Was anything stolen from your father's art gallery?''

''Nothing. That's just it—there were no signs of a break-in, not a single painting stolen. They're quite valuable paintings, yet they didn't even tempt whoever attacked my father. There has to be another reason for what happened, but Dad won't say what it is. He just seems so...so *distraught*. I don't know how to explain it, except that he's suffering in spirit as much as he is physically. That's not like him at all.''

''Robyn,'' Mark said, ''has your father ever had any enemies? Not just recently—I want you to think back. Anything from the past, anything at all that might indicate someone with a grievance against him.''

She considered his question for several moments, but finally shook her head. ''My father is one of the most generous people you'll ever meet. Although he's a talented artist himself, he prefers to focus on other people's careers. He's helped any number of artists to make names for themselves, and they're all very grateful to him. He has friends, not enemies. I can't think of anyone who'd wish him harm—for any reason. That's what's so puzzling."

"He runs an art gallery...any chance he could be involved in something illegal? Forgery, for example."

"Of course not!" she said defensively. "I know my father. He couldn't possibly do something illegal. He doesn't have it in him."

"Maybe you don't know your father as well as you think. Obviously there's something he's not telling you. Obviously he has at least one enemy—a pretty serious one, at that."

Robyn stared at Mark. "Do you always look so quickly for the underside of things?"

"Occupational hazard, I guess." He drank some of his coffee. "I'm a detective."

She struggled to understand. "Like a private detective, you mean?"

"Police. Homicide, to be exact."

She stared at him. "I don't get it. You teach at a shooting range."

"Temporarily. I'm on leave from the department—recovering from a tussle with a bullet. Nothing too serious...but my boss thought I needed a little extra downtime.'' Mark gave a slight grimace. Robyn, however, wasn't interested right now in any problems he had with his boss. She stood up, only to find that she was shaking again.

''Thanks for the coffee, Mr. Stewart,'' she said, surprised at how normal her voice sounded. ''And the cinnamon roll, too, of course. But maybe you'll understand why I can't stay and chat. My father has made it very clear that involving the police any further could be dangerous for my entire family. Goodbye.'' Robyn walked out of the coffee shop, the door swinging shut behind her.

She was halfway down the street before he caught up to her.

''Robyn,'' he said. ''Never listen to anyone who tells you not to go to the police.''

''What's this, Mr. Stewart—a little P.R. work for the department? You're not exactly unbiased, are you?''

''The police are the only people who *can* help you.''

''Fine,'' she said. ''I'll take that under advisement. But you said you were on leave from the department, didn't you? So, officially, I don't have to tell you a damn thing.'' She quickened her pace. In response he lengthened his stride easily.

''Okay, you're ticked because I didn't happen to mention I was a cop the first time we met.''

"It does seem you've been operating under false pretenses," she said acidly.

"I have a habit of following my instincts," he told her. "They warned me that you wouldn't talk to me at all if you thought I was a policeman."

She had a wild desire to run. Instead, she forced herself to talk to him. "Your instincts are highly accurate. What are they telling you now?"

"That you need somebody to help you. That you want to trust me, but you're still scared. That you know you should trust me."

Suddenly she stopped walking. She leaned against the side of a building.

"Mark," she said. "I don't know anything for certain. Maybe my father's right. Maybe talking to the police is the surest way to bring more harm on my family. Or maybe *not* talking to the police could be our biggest mistake. I don't know. All I know is that I haven't slept at all the last few days, I haven't eaten much except half a cinnamon roll and...I'd just like to be on my own for a little while."

"Robyn...you need help."

"Let me guess," she said. "You have a little spare time on your hands, nothing much going on down at the shooting range."

"Maybe my motives aren't so bad," he answered. "Maybe this is the kind of thing I do on the job.

Maybe it's the kind of thing I've been missing. And maybe I just want to help.''

He made it sound as if she'd be doing him a favor by leaning on his shoulder. Granted, it appeared to be a broad, competent shoulder, and she was sorely tempted to lean. But she couldn't forget her father's warning. *Don't tell anyone, Robyn. Don't involve the police.* She'd already gone way too far by opening up to Mark Stewart.

Purposely avoiding any glance in Mark's direction, she began walking again. ''Look, I'm sorry you're…laid off from your job—''

''On temporary leave,'' he reminded her as he kept pace.

''Anyway,'' Robyn said, walking a little faster, ''two very nice police officers talked to my father in the hospital. If necessary, I'll contact them.''

With just a touch on her arm, he compelled her to stop. ''Look,'' he said. ''What I told you before is true. I miss doing my job. I've been going damn stir-crazy during my so-called recuperation. There'd be nothing wrong with me providing a little unofficial help on your case.''

The anger flared in her again. ''Is that how you look at people—as *cases?* Someone's life is falling apart, but meanwhile it's just an interesting *case* for you to solve—''

''It's what I'm good at, Robyn,'' he said quietly.

"Personal relationships…yeah, I'm lousy at those. But work is something else."

She felt saddened by his words. Mark Stewart seemed to have closed himself off in some essential way, focusing only on the job that was so important to him. But her instincts warned her that she had to handle this on her own. For her parents' sake, she had to be strong. Until she knew more, she had to listen to her father's warning. It might be the only way to keep her family safe.

"No, Mark," she said. "Just…no. I can't accept your help."

CHAPTER THREE

MARK HAD CHOSEN the best restaurant in town. At least, he thought it was the best restaurant in town. He wasn't all that sure what his daughter would think. The place was small, low-key, on a narrow winding lane some distance from the plaza. The adobe walls had been plastered thickly over the past century or so, the layers swirled like frosting on a cake. Overhead the time-weathered beams known as *vigas* had been left exposed, and the deep-set window frames had been trimmed in a satisfying blue-green color. It was the food, of course, that gave the place its reputation, an offering of dishes unabashedly southwestern: green-chile stew, blue-corn soup, pinto-bean pie.

Mark sat at a table in one of the window alcoves, nursing a tequila sour. He could no longer deny that his daughter was late. Not exactly eager to see the old man, it seemed. When he'd called and asked her to join him for lunch, her voice had been decidedly cool over the phone. She'd agreed only with reluctance.

He shifted in his seat, trying to get comfortable. Some days his leg ached more than others. Lord, at forty-three maybe he really *was* starting to feel his years.

He shifted again, easing his leg out in front of him. Maybe it had been the wrong approach, inviting Kerry to a restaurant for dinner. Maybe he should have tried for something a little more casual and relaxed. But wasn't that the problem right there? He hadn't been casual or relaxed with either of his daughters in a very long while. Both of them treated him as if he was some sort of inconvenient relative—like a distant uncle they had to be polite to.

Did he have anyone to blame but himself? Sure, his ex-wife had played her part—after the divorce, she'd found plenty of subtle little ways to keep his daughters occupied and away from him. Perhaps it had been her payback for all the years when he'd been a distant husband. But there was no point in allocating blame. Only one question remained: Where the hell did he go from here?

He signaled the waiter. "Any calls for me?"

"No, Mr. Stewart. Still no calls."

Thinking about his daughters made him feel a failure. He far preferred the way his job made him feel—convinced that he was making a contribution, doing something useful. Getting back on the job, that was what he needed. Being assigned a case, following leads, working out the puzzle set before him. Lord, he missed that right now. And, because he missed it, he'd done some unofficial poking into the Cal Myers case. Forget the fact that this morning Robyn Myers had categorically refused his help. Mark had gone right ahead and put in a few calls to the station house, gotten the update on Robyn's father. It was pretty much as she'd said. Cal Myers claimed to have been attacked by someone he didn't know—someone he'd never even seen before. No, he couldn't provide any description. The attacker had been wearing a mask, and it had all happened very quickly. No, he didn't have anything else to tell the police.

But meanwhile, according to Robyn, Cal Myers had asked her to get a gun. And he seemed afraid that whoever had attacked him would next turn on his daughter, or his wife. His fears were something that couldn't be dismissed.

This morning Mark had given Robyn a few pointers on looking out for herself, advice that would probably do her a whole lot more good than a gun. Little things, like making sure she didn't go anyplace alone, and always being aware of what was happening around her. There was a certain watchfulness that became second nature if you practiced it long enough, a watchfulness that would keep you out of the most basic kinds of trouble.

"Hello, Father. You're a million miles away, as usual."

Mark rose to his feet and gazed at his daughter.

She looked so polished, so poised, nothing like the little girl who had once loved to play softball and skin her knees in the dirt. This Kerry wore an expensive silk dress. Her hair was swept up in some kind of twist, saved from bland sophistication by a brightly beaded clasp stuck in as if at the last minute. Mark smiled a little. Kerry had a habit of dressing conservatively, but then she'd add some colorful, individual detail that would betray a rebellious spirit. He wished she would let the rebellion out more often. It was what made her unique and special, her ability to see when the rules ought to be broken.

Now Mark wondered how to greet her. He supposed that most fathers would give their daughters a kiss on the cheek, but tonight Kerry had a don't-touch air about her. A handshake? You didn't shake hands with your kids, not if you were on speaking terms.

"You look great," he said inadequately. "I guess being engaged agrees with you."

"Frederick and I are both very happy." The response was automatic, no doubt the standard reply she tossed off for strangers and acquaintances. Mark pulled out a chair for her and a few seconds later they were sitting across from each other at the table. Kerry ordered a brandy cocktail, and then gave Mark a reassuring glance.

"I am twenty-one, you know. I'm allowed to drink."

"Of course." He'd worked hard six months ago to find just the right gift for her coming-of-age birthday—a silver and turquoise necklace that had set him back a month's salary. She'd accepted it the way she'd accepted all his birthday presents over the years—with a friendly but careless thank-you. It was as if she couldn't even bother to be angry with him; he'd become that insignificant in her life.

"Kerry," he said, "it's…great that you're getting married. Really great."

"If you say 'great' one more time, you'll make it sound like it's not so great, after all." Now there was just the slightest edge to her voice.

"I guess I'm still having trouble getting used to the idea," he said. "It seems like only yesterday…"

"I know. It seems like only yesterday I was a little girl in pigtails."

"You never wore pigtails," he said. "You hated them."

"Really? Imagine you remembering something like that." She opened her menu and began to peruse it. "I've never eaten here before, but I hear the food's good."

Mark rubbed the back of his neck. They could go on like this all night, exchanging meaningless comments. Or they could be real with each other for once.

"Kerry," he said, "when I saw that announcement in the paper…it really hit me. How far apart we've grown."

She didn't even glance up from her menu. "We see each other all the time," she said.

"Every few months or so. That's not all the time."

Usually when he called his daughters, they had some excuse why they couldn't see him. Gettogethers with their *real* family, previous commitments with friends. They were always civil about it, always gracious, promising that next time things would work out. Mark would tell himself how glad he was that his kids were busy and happy. But then he would let more and more weeks go by before he contacted either of them again. Was he worried that one of these times they'd reject him for good? Or was he just proving his ex-wife right, after all—he didn't know how to put family first? Either way, he knew that he hadn't tried hard enough to break down the barriers between himself and his children.

"I'd like things to change," he said. "I'd like us to see each other more often. I know I've been at fault—"

"It's not anybody's fault," Kerry said hurriedly. "I spend most of my time in Albuquerque these days, what with school."

"Albuquerque's not very far away at all," Mark said. "We should be able to work something out."

"We're having dinner together now, aren't we? Hmm...I haven't had *posole* in a while."

Obviously she wasn't going to let him apologize for his failure to keep in closer contact. Maybe that was the ultimate brush-off, letting your father know that you would not dignify his regrets by giving them any attention whatsoever.

He tried a different tack. "How is school, anyway?"

"Fine. I'm taking a wonderful writing class. I think it's really helping me to branch out."

He wasn't too sure what she meant by "branch out," but it didn't seem appropriate to ask. "Still writing poetry?" he ventured instead.

"Of course."

How did he talk about his daughter's poetry, especially when she'd evaded all his requests to see some of it?

For all he knew, she was a brilliant writer. Too bad she wouldn't let him find out.

Just then a young man approached their table with a confident stride. Kerry lifted her face to the man, and he kissed her. It took Mark a couple of seconds to recognize this guy as the one in the engagement photo—none other than Frederick Graham, college graduate in finance.

"I asked Frederick to meet us here," Kerry said. "I hope you don't mind—I just thought you'd welcome the opportunity to meet him."

Mark shook hands with his daughter's fiancé. This wasn't what he'd had in mind at all. He'd wanted some time alone with Kerry so the two of them could finally start talking to each other. She'd expertly thwarted *that* attempt.

"Mr. Stewart," said Frederick Graham, "it's an honor to meet you."

Honor? Since when was it an honor to meet your girlfriend's father? The guy was laying it on a little thick.

Not only that, but Mark didn't like the looks of him. He seemed too damn young, for one thing, with the gangly limbs of someone who hadn't fully settled into himself. How could he be a college graduate when he looked as if another growth spurt was just around the corner?

All three of them ordered dinner, and then Frederick Graham gave Mark an overly assured smile. "Sir, I understand you're with the police. Must be a fascinating career. I'd like to hear all about it."

Sir? Now it was *sir?* "Why don't we talk about your plans instead," Mark suggested. Even from across the table, he saw the way his daughter stiffened. But he was only trying to find out if this…this youngster would end up having a decent job.

Kerry was the one who jumped in. "A lot of firms want to hire Frederick. He's in a very good position."

Frederick grinned, and put his arm around her. "Let's not exaggerate, Kerry. I have a few decent prospects, Mr. Stewart. Rest assured, I'll be able to support your daughter."

"Kerry, fortunately, believes in supporting herself," Mark said. He thought for sure he'd score points with that one—the enlightened father, expecting his daughter to make her own way as a woman. Turned out he was wrong.

"Frederick doesn't have any problem with the fact that I won't be making a lot of money," Kerry said. "Or maybe not any money at first. As soon as I get my degree, I'll be writing poetry full-time."

"Poetry…full-time? What happened to your internship with the publishing house?" Mark asked.

"Oh, I quit that ages ago. Poetry is what I've always wanted to do. Frederick is behind me a hundred percent."

"You'd better believe it, Mr. Stewart. It's my prediction that someday Kerry is going to be a very well-known and respected writer."

His daughter, the poetess. Most likely the penniless poetess. Mark wondered if Kerry had thought this through. Did she expect to keep up her expensive taste in clothes, her love of travel? Not to mention little things like *eating*. Now Mark wondered what his ex-wife had to say about all this. Andrea couldn't be overjoyed that her future son-in-law didn't even have a job yet—and that her youngest daughter was going to devote herself solely to poetry.

The conversation was dying, and Mark made an effort to prod it back to life. "So," he said, "how did you two meet?" He couldn't think of a safer question, but Kerry frowned.

"It's too involved a story, and I'm sure you're not really interested—"

"I'll tell it," intervened Frederick. "It happened at school, Mr. Stewart. Kerry was studying really hard for an exam in psychology, and she fell asleep at the library. That's the first time I saw her—fast asleep with her head on the desk, and she was actually snoring. A very delicate snore. Pretty endearing, actually—"

"Frederick. You don't have to go into this much *detail*." Kerry seemed to be growing tense. Her fiancé, however, cheerfully ignored her, and went on at length about the fated meeting at the library and a subsequent rendezvous at the student union. All Mark had to do was sit back and listen.

Frederick Graham seemed perfectly content to ramble on, heedless of Kerry's discomfort. Mark saw the way she creased her napkin over and over, the way she glanced toward the door as if longing to escape. And he knew there was something more going on here…something more than mere embarrassment over having the details of their courtship revealed. Maybe this engagement wasn't going as well as Kerry insisted. Maybe she wasn't really that happy with Frederick Graham. Mark didn't like the thought of his daughter not being happy, for any reason. He found himself scowling at the boy, enough so that Frederick began to wind down.

"Well, sir…anyway, that's how I met Kerry, and we've been together ever since. I promise you I'll do everything in my power to make her glad she agreed to be my wife." The kid was definitely laying it on thick. Kerry seemed to agree; she scooted her chair just a little bit away from Frederick. That didn't faze him. He managed to lean toward her, keeping his arm draped around her shoulders. Again she scooted her chair away.

"Sweetie, you okay?" Frederick asked.

"I'm fine," Kerry muttered. "I wish—I just wish the food would come."

"You don't seem okay," Frederick insisted. "You seem a little uptight. You can tell us what's wrong. I mean, you're here among friends—''

"Stop." Kerry pushed back her chair and stood. Two bright spots of color burned in her cheeks, and she seemed about to cry. She looked from Mark to Frederick then back again. "This was a mistake," she said. "A very big mistake. Seeing the two of you together, side by side…the man I'm supposed to marry, and my *father*…it makes me wonder if I even want to go through with the wedding!"

For once Frederick seemed to lose his assurance. He stared at Kerry. "What are you talking about?" he asked. "I know you've been nervous about getting married, but that's natural. I'm nervous, too. Why can't we just be nervous together?"

She clenched the back of her chair. "It's more than that. Something's been bothering me, and I didn't even know what it was." Kerry gave Mark an accusing glance, after which she gave her fiancé an accusing glance. "Then you came in, and it all clicked. I saw exactly what could happen…how easily it could happen. The two of us getting married, Frederick, but ending up exactly like my mother and *him*. Unhappy and miserable and *divorced*. I can't let it happen! Don't you see? I just can't let it happen." The tears spilled over. Kerry suddenly seemed aware of the people at other tables who were trying not to watch her. With a small cry, she turned and made her escape.

Mark rose to go after her. He didn't know how

to offer her comfort, but he had to try. Frederick, however, shook his head. "It's better if I take care of it, sir. She'll talk to me when we're alone, and she'll tell me what's really going on. I'm sorry about what she said just now. She didn't mean it, you know. I'm sure we'll get it cleared up in no time. Anyway, very nice meeting you, sir." Frederick pumped Mark's hand, his smile forced this time, and then he loped after Kerry.

Mark sank back into his chair. For a minute there he'd almost felt sorry for Frederick Graham. The kid was trying so damn hard to make everything right: portray himself as the mature adult with everything under control, get along with his fiancée's father, smooth over his fiancée's outburst. That was a lot of work for one person.

The waiter arrived bearing a tray with three plates of food, and gave Mark an inquiring look.

"Change in plans," Mark said. "But go ahead, set it down—I'm paying for everything."

He'd been paying for his mistakes a long time, it seemed. Years ago, when his daughters had been younger, he'd believed firmly and idealistically in the value of his work—chasing down the bad guy, trying to make the world a little bit safer. That had meant days and nights away from home, absorbed in one case after another. It had also meant efforts to keep his family remote from the inevitable seediness and harshness of his job. And, in the process, he'd ended up keeping the people he loved remote from himself...

He gazed at the three plates of untouched food now set before him. One fact alone seemed paramount: His youngest daughter was unhappy, and he was the cause.

ROBYN PACED through the art gallery one more time. A few paintings were propped against the wall. She tipped one toward her and peered at its backside. Nothing unusual—just ordinary framing, with the canvas stretched over it. Certainly there was no clue that would explain the vicious attack on her father. She felt a bit foolish. What had she hoped for—a note left behind by the perpetrator, conveniently explaining everything? But she'd combed the gallery over and over, searching for something, anything, that would help her understand. She hated the helplessness of *not* knowing.

A knock came at the door, startling her. She'd made sure everything was locked and bolted after letting herself in, reassuring herself that she would be quite safe that way. Now she went to the door and peered warily through the glass. She saw Mark Stewart standing outside.

She hesitated a few seconds, then unlocked the door and swung it open.

"Hello," Mark said.

"I don't suppose it's any surprise," she said, "you managing to find me. Doing your detective work, are you?"

He stepped inside the gallery and glanced around. "You told me you wouldn't go anywhere alone. Now here you are, back at the scene of the crime."

She folded her arms against her body. "Why did you come here, Mark? I told you that I would be very careful, and I have been. I'm practically developing eyes in the back of my head, making sure no one sneaks up on me unawares."

"I guess I expected you to come for another lesson today. You turned down my help, but I figured you might want a few more pointers on handling a gun. When you didn't make it to the shooting range, I got a little concerned."

"I've decided to pass on buying a gun," she said. "After my experience yesterday…it just seems like it's not for me."

"You didn't do anything wrong," he told her. "Okay, you got mad, but you took it out on the bull's-eye. You didn't lose control."

"I *felt* out of control, that was bad enough." She didn't feel particularly on top of the situation right now, and that bothered her. For some reason Mark's presence in her father's art gallery was too uncomfortably dominating, too unsettlingly potent. Perhaps it was his sureness, his way of assuming command. Perhaps it was also his dark hair, his definite features, his unequivocal masculinity. But did he really think he could come in here and take over, the way he'd done yesterday when she'd lost it at the shooting range? Couldn't he stop being a police detective, not even for a minute?

She looked around the gallery, trying to regain some equilibrium. This was a large, airy place, striking in its simplicity. All superfluous details had been pared away so that only the work of the artists would stand out. The floors were a glossy oak, the walls a clean white. Several of the paintings displayed were evocative southwestern landscapes: a field of chile peppers glowing red in the afternoon sun, aspens turning to gold in the Sandia Mountains, a view of multitiered Taos Pueblo. There were a few stark portraits and other paintings in a bold abstract style. Altogether it was a startling but effective mix.

"Dad's always been one to take chances," she murmured, almost to herself.

"Maybe he took a chance he shouldn't have," Mark suggested, "and that's why someone beat him up."

Robyn felt a murky swirl of anger and irritation that Mark Stewart seemed to inspire in her. "I meant that he takes chances on artists. He'll see the potential in someone's work, when no one else can see it. He'll gamble on that person's talent, and usually he wins.''

Mark didn't answer, but his expression was skeptical. He looked around the gallery one more time, as if he would find some secret she hadn't revealed to him.

"Thinking the worst about people," she said. "That's what you do, isn't it?"

His gaze returned to her. "Not always," he answered.

They stared at each other, and Robyn's emotions felt murkier than ever. She tried not to let her gaze travel over him, but wasn't successful. She noted the way his khaki shirt fitted across his chest, the way his jeans conformed to the length of his legs. Then, quickly, she glanced upward, and was caught by the slate-gray of his eyes. Mark gave a slight frown, as if some disturbing thought had occurred to him.

"You shouldn't have come here alone," he said gruffly.

"I told you—I'm being careful. I came from the hospital with my uncle Greg. He and Aunt Janet are right next door. They run the Chocolate Shop." The Myers family had always been close-knit. Years ago, Cal Myers and his younger brother, Greg, had pooled their resources to buy this lovely courtyard of shops in the heart of Santa Fe, just far enough off the plaza to be ultrachic. The family enterprises included Cal's art gallery, as well as a store that sold hand-painted cards and one-of-a-kind gifts, another store that offered rare and antique books, and of course the Chocolate Shop, where delectable candy could be purchased. Each business did very well, and by now the Myers clan had a decades-long reputation for supplying excellence.

"I'm still concerned about you," Mark said.

"I can take care of myself," Robyn answered. But then, once more, she found herself unable to look away from Mark. Part of her said that he was the type of man you'd want protecting you. Another part warned that a woman might need protection against Mark himself. She sensed something unreachable in him—as if Mark Stewart might risk his life for you, but not his heart.

They gazed at each other, unsmiling. The moment might have gone on, but then someone pushed open the door to the gallery and a light female voice intruded.

"Robyn, I...oh. Excuse me. I didn't mean to interrupt!"

CHAPTER FOUR

ROBYN TURNED AWAY from Mark and surveyed the woman who'd just entered the gallery. At twenty-six, Emily Parkman, the young woman who managed the gift shop for Robyn's parents, was flat-out gorgeous, with large green eyes and unusual tawny streaks through her hair.

"I really didn't mean to interrupt," Emily said as she walked across the gallery, coming to stand practically between Mark and Robyn. "Two's company, and all that."

Robyn didn't answer. The truth was, Emily Parkman grated on her nerves. The woman was too full of herself—irritatingly poised, excessively confident. But, then again, maybe Emily couldn't help it. Her figure was statuesque in all the right places. Her skin was creamy, her hair gleamed. Everything about her seemed to shine. Every woman would love to look like Emily Parkman…and Emily Parkman knew it. Whenever Emily smiled, she seemed to be congratulating herself on her own good looks. Wearing that little smile now, she glanced from Mark to Robyn.

"Oh, dear. You really wish I hadn't barged in here, don't you? Not that I blame you." Now Emily gave Mark a frankly admiring gaze, and she spoke to him in a conspiratorial tone. "Robyn doesn't like me," she said. "She's only known me a few days, but already she's decided I'm far too outgoing."

Robyn stifled a groan. True, she had known Emily only a few days, but she'd had more than enough exposure to the woman. As if being knock-down gorgeous wasn't enough of an attention-getter, Emily would say the most outrageous things to make certain everyone knew she was in the room. Now Robyn studied Mark to see his reaction. But his expression remained impassive, and it was impossible to tell what he was thinking.

"Robyn, you *are* going to introduce us, aren't you?" Emily asked.

"Why not," Robyn said dryly. "Mark, this is Emily Parkman. She runs the gift shop next door for my parents. Emily, this is Mark Stewart. He's…a friend."

"A friend," she murmured. "Well…hello." She offered her hand to Mark as a gift, but he gave it only a brief shake. Emily seemed aware that she wasn't having the desired effect on him, and her manner changed subtly. She threw in a little inno-cence.

"I came over to see if you're going to reopen the gallery," she told Robyn in a well-meaning tone. "Your poor dad—maybe that's what he'd want, business to go on as usual."

"I was just checking on things," Robyn said. "I doubt my father's thinking about business right now."

"I suppose not." Emily addressed Mark again. "Robyn's parents have been great. They treat me like family. Nina has agreed to several of my ideas for the gift shop. She's even going to let me revamp the place. Nina trusts me. Robyn's the one with res-ervations." Emily gave another smile, showing how pleased she was with her insights.

Emily had been working at the gift shop less than six months, but already she acted as if she owned the place. And she was right—Robyn did have res-ervations.

Mark's expression still gave nothing away. "How many stores does your family have?" he asked Rob-yn.

"Only the ones along this courtyard—four alto-gether. Everyone in the family's carved out a niche. Dad handles the gallery, Uncle Greg and Aunt Janet make chocolates, Mom spends most of her time with the bookshop, and—"

"And I run the gift store," Emily finished. "A cozy little *family* operation." She gave Robyn the most patronizing of looks. "Well, I am supposed to be on the job. Give your mom a hug for me, Robyn, and tell your dad to hang in there. Mark...very nice meeting you." She gave him a dazzling smile this time, then went back out the door.

The gallery suddenly seemed quiet without Emily's presence. No doubt that was exactly what Emily wanted...to be remembered after she'd left the room.

Robyn studied Mark, but as usual it was impossible to tell what he was thinking. Had he been attracted to Emily? Robyn didn't like the niggling jealousy she felt. Lord, she was thirty-seven, and here she was envious of a girl in her twenties.

"My mother's delighted that she found Emily," Robyn said. "She was having trouble getting someone reliable to manage the gift shop. The two of them hit it off right away." Whenever Emily was around Nina, she took on the attitude of the grateful protégée, listening attentively to everything Nina said, offering her own suggestions in a respectful voice, seemingly anxious to gain approval.

Mark regarded Robyn thoughtfully. "You never wanted to run one of the family stores yourself?" he asked.

"As a child it was all I wanted. These four shops

seemed so magical to me—full of life and beautiful things, and full of people who cared for me. But my father always encouraged me to go out in the world and find my own niche."

"So you became a teacher," he said.

"I don't remember telling you that—"

"Yesterday, in the coffee shop. You said you'd been feeling frustrated with your teaching career."

"Do you always remember extraneous details?" she asked.

"When they seem to matter," he answered.

She found herself gazing at him again. This time she made a special effort to glance away. "I imagine you're wanted back at the shooting range."

"Benjamin pretty much lets me put in the time I want."

"Everyone should have such an understanding friend, I'm sure. But I've told you, Mark—I'm being careful. You don't have to watch out for me, or whatever it is you're doing here."

"Robyn," he said gravely, "whatever happened to your father isn't going to solve itself. Why don't you just accept my help?"

His offer was tempting. But she'd already let her father down on one promise. She'd refused to get a gun. Could she ignore his other plea? *Don't involve the police, Robyn, or something even worse could happen...*

"No, Mark. I can't," she said in a low voice.

MARK SAT on one of the benches at the plaza, doodling. The designs he'd made on the notepad appeared random, but he was thinking, sifting through what he knew so far about the Myers case. Of course, he'd read the police report, talked to the officers involved. He knew the basic facts. But it was the information he'd gleaned from Robyn that interested him most right now. Her family had obviously done very well in Santa Fe. Until a few days ago, the Myers clan had seemed to lead a charmed existence. Wealthy, successful—and, judging by Robyn, intensely loyal to their own. But now Robyn's father was in the hospital, which made you wonder about the charmed-existence bit.

Meanwhile, if Robyn kept turning down Mark's help, why didn't he just give up, forget about it? Okay, so he missed his job—missed it like hell—but that didn't give him the right to take over the Myers case. Besides, he had his kids to think about. He should be spending his time trying to rebuild his relationship with them. He gazed down at the notepad and drew some more random lines.

"Hello, Father. Busy as always."

Mark stood up and confronted his eldest daughter, Debbie. The perusal she gave him was cool and reserved.

"Thank you for coming to meet me," she said formally, as if he were the CEO of some important company who'd finally agreed to an interview.

"Debbie, you know I'm always glad when you phone." Something of an overstatement, since she hardly ever phoned.

"No one's called me Debbie in a very long while," she told him.

"Right…Debra." He remembered when she'd been happy to be "Debbie." She'd been an exuberant child, more fearless than Kerry. Over the years, she'd learned to focus her exuberance, concentrated her enthusiasm on achieving her goals. She'd won admittance to a private, very select college, graduated with honors and immediately landed a reporting job with an Albuquerque newspaper. The transformation had been complete then: adventurous, joyful Debbie had become intense, focused, ambitious Debra.

He motioned toward a wrought-iron bench. "Have a seat," he said. "Tell me what's new."

They sat down together, and Debra glanced around the plaza. "Nothing changes," she said. "Still too many tourists."

Mark glanced around the plaza, too. Sure, it was crowded, but his daughter didn't seem to see the grace notes he appreciated—the early-spring grass showing itself along the flagstones, the trees starting to bud, the ornate old lampposts, the weathered soldiers' monument rising in the center. A dog chased a Frisbee, a boy and girl walked with their arms wrapped tightly around each other.

Debra swiveled toward Mark. Now she stared at the notepad where he'd been doodling. "Nothing ever does change," she said. "You used to do that all the time, when I was growing up. You'd be working out your cases on a piece of paper. You'd crumple up one piece then start on another."

"You do the same thing," he said.

"No, I don't—"

"Sure you do. Ever since you were a kid…when you wanted to puzzle something out, you started drawing. Except that you were always a better artist than me. You drew animals and clouds, that type of thing."

"Really. How interesting. I use a computer most of the time now." She paused. "What's the case this time?" she said. "I thought you were still on leave."

"It's not really official," Mark answered. "Just someone who needs a little help…but won't admit it."

"You've always had a soft spot for 'someone who needs a little help,'" Debra said with the lightest of irony. Something about her demeanor suggested *she* would never be so foolish as to need his help. Mark felt it all over again—the sense of having failed both his daughters. He studied Debra, wishing somehow he could make things right with at least one of the girls. But how did you come to terms with a twenty-three-year-old who'd decided long ago she had no more use for her father?

"Anyway," Debra said, "this isn't a social call. Mom sent me to talk to you."

Something told him he wouldn't like hearing the rest of this. "Your mother knows she can phone me herself anytime—"

"She thought it might be better to have a sort of…arbitrator." Debra lifted her shoulders as if to express a neutral position. "She's ticked at you— she blames you for the fact that Kerry's scared about getting married."

Mark recalled his youngest daughter's tear-streaked face last night. And he remembered the exact words she'd used, her fear at ending up "unhappy and miserable and divorced." He swore a little under his breath.

"Debbie, the last thing I want is for either you or Kerry to feel bad about anything—"

"Well, Kerry definitely feels bad. It seems that last night she blew up at Frederick and told him he reminded her far too much of you."

Weren't daughters supposed to look for husbands just like their dads? Unless, of course, they were fed up with their dads. But there was another wrinkle to all this. Try as hard as he could, Mark didn't see any resemblance between himself and Frederick Graham.

"Maybe if I talked to her," he said. "Maybe I could find out what's really going on."

"I think she's made it pretty clear," Debra said. "She's scared to death of ending up like you and Mom."

"Okay," Mark acknowledged, "we didn't give her the best example. But your mother and Len have been happily married for quite a few years now. Doesn't that tell Kerry things can work out, after all?"

"Mom and Len *have* been a good example," Debra said. "They really care about each other, and they're proof that two people actually can get along. That's exactly what Mom's been trying to tell Kerry. But since last night, Kerry's been insisting she hasn't chosen a man like our stepfather. She says that instead, she's chosen a man like *you*. She won't explain to us exactly what the similarities are—she just gets upset and refuses to discuss it anymore."

"I'll talk to Kerry," Mark repeated. "I'll try to straighten this out."

Debra got a beleaguered look. "You really don't understand, do you? The reason Mom sent me...it was to ask you *not* to speak to Kerry. Not to get involved anymore. Just to leave it alone.''

''My own daughter's having problems—problems that are supposedly all my fault, and I'm supposed to bow out—''

''Mom thinks you'll only make things worse. Listen, maybe she's overreacting, but I think it would be wise for you to…keep a low profile. At least for now. At least until things settle down.''

''Keeping a low profile with my own family,'' he said, his voice heavy. ''That was the mistake I made all along, wasn't it? Not being there when you needed me. Sometimes things do change. I'm trying to change, anyway.''

''I'm sure you have good intentions,'' Debra said, her tone almost soothing now. It had come to this, his kid trying to placate him.

''The way it seems to me,'' he said, ''Kerry already had some doubts about this marriage—''

''Of course she's had doubts. She wouldn't be normal otherwise. Nobody goes into marriage without wondering what the heck they're getting themselves into.'' Debra's voice had sharpened. ''It's only when you're on the other end of things—when you can't even get a *proposal*—it's only then you think getting married would be the most marvelous thing in the world. Just shows how *stupid* you can be.'' Debra stopped this uncharacteristic outburst, as if already regretting it, but it was too late. Mark had a pretty good idea they were now talking about Debra herself…not her sister, Kerry.

"So," Mark said as casually as possible. "You still seeing that guy? Trevor, wasn't it?"

"Yes, I'm still seeing Trevor," Debra said, sounding very strained now.

"Debbie, tell me what's wrong—"

"*Will* you stop calling me that? And nothing's wrong! Except that my little sister's throwing away her chance to marry someone decent, and meanwhile, Trevor positively cringes every time *I* so much as mention a walk down the aisle." Debra scrambled to her feet, as if appalled by the words that had spilled out of her. She made an obvious effort to compose herself. "Forget I said anything, all right? Whatever's going on, I'll work it out."

His adventurous, ambitious Debbie…breaking her heart over the guy. Mark had never met Trevor, but already he didn't like him. He didn't like anybody who could bring that sudden look of misery to Debbie's face. Suddenly he wished both his daughters were kids again, nowhere near even thinking about things like marriage.

"Listen," he said. "Don't let this Trevor ruin your life—"

"Oh, stop." She looked truly miserable now. "You're only making it worse. Don't you see? You can't do Kerry any good right now—and not me, either. It's like we're both *cursed* somehow. Neither one of us knows how to make things right with a man. And you can't help. You just ought to leave both of us alone!" And then, without even a good-bye, Debra went hurrying off across the plaza.

THE HOSPITAL had a walled garden where visitors and patients could go to find a semblance of normalcy. The flower beds had been recently tended, although no blooms had yet made their appearance. The daffodils were only now beginning to push their way out of the ground, too early perhaps; the weather had been unseasonably warm but frost was still a possibility. As Robyn followed her mother along the brick walkway of the garden, she felt sorry for the plum tree that had started to bud too optimistically. Snow could yet fall in the Sangre de Cristo Mountains, blanketing the town in winter once more.

Robyn glanced around warily, and saw a few other people strolling through the garden. There was nothing outwardly menacing, nothing that hinted at danger. She hated feeling like this, as if she had to look underneath the most benign of surfaces, searching for hidden threats.

Nina Myers sat down on one of the wooden benches, and waited until Robyn settled beside her.

"Isn't this lovely?" she asked. "I'll be glad when your father's well enough to take a walk with us here. It's such a peaceful atmosphere."

Robyn didn't think her father would be ready anytime soon for garden strolls. In addition to his physical injuries, he seemed emotionally broken. That hospital bed had become something of a refuge to him. Before this, Cal Myers had always embraced life, always surmounted with confidence whatever difficulties faced him. But it seemed he had now encountered difficulties he didn't know how to battle. If only he would tell Robyn the truth about the attack. Maybe then they could battle the problem together...

"I don't like leaving Dad," Robyn said.

"I don't either," Nina murmured. "But your aunt and uncle promised they'd sit with your father as long as we're away. Everything will be all right...you'll see." In the past day or so Nina had obviously been struggling to regain her old optimism. It seemed the only defense she knew: insisting determinedly that everything would be all right, trying to deny the worry and heartache that showed in her eyes. "We're all jumpy, dear," she said in a forced voice, "but I brought you down here on purpose so you could relax. And so you could tell me about the new man in your life."

"Mom, what on earth are you talking about—"

"Emily told me all about it," Nina said relentlessly. "How she saw you earlier today at the art gallery, with a very nice man. And how the two of you were gazing into each other's eyes."

"Mom!"

"It's true, isn't it? Why deny it? There's nothing wrong with having a boyfriend. It's exactly what you need."

"Mom," Robyn said. "Mark Stewart is not my...boyfriend. I've only just met him, and besides—how could I possibly think about a man at a time like this?"

"Your father doesn't want your life to come to a halt. He would be happy if he knew you were interested in someone."

Nina had it all wrong. *She* was the one who thought her daughter couldn't exist without a man. Cal Myers had always wanted Robyn to be independent.

"Mom," Robyn tried again. "Mark is just...an acquaintance. Why do you have to make it into something more than it is?"

"Emily was clear about it. She said you and this man were looking at each other quite fondly. It's true, of course, that Emily has romantic notions. I wish I could find someone for her."

Nina was the one with romantic notions. "Mom, I have the feeling that Emily Parkman is perfectly capable of finding a man on her own. She's not exactly shy."

"Don't let Emily fool you," said Nina. "She puts on a lot of bravado, but underneath she wants the same thing all of us do. A real home, a family that's whole and happy."

Nina refused to think anything but the best of Emily. Seeing the best in others…that was one of Nina's special talents. Although Robyn loved her for it, being on guard now and then wasn't such a bad idea.

"Mom—just don't let Emily make too many changes at the gift store. Business was pretty good before she came along, remember?"

"Yes, but at the same time business can always be improved. That's been the attitude in this family all along—we've never grown complacent."

Robyn sighed. Yes, she knew all about the family search for excellence. That was why the shops had always done so well. But she doubted Emily Parkman could contribute any real improvements. Emily seemed more interested in advancing her own interests than anyone else's.

"You've switched the subject on me," Nina said. "We were talking about romantic involvements. Specifically, your own. Or lack thereof—"

"Some women like the thought of being unattached," Robyn said.

"Nonsense. Your father and I have been together for forty years, and I can't imagine any other type of life. You'd agree with me, if only you'd admit it."

Forty years of making a man the center of your life…that was what Nina had done. There was something poignant about it, but Robyn didn't know if she could ever do the same thing. Maybe one of the reasons she'd made such a botch of her own marriages was her fear that she'd become too much like her mother. The doting wife… Maybe, in reaction, Robyn had gone too far in the other direction. Maybe she hadn't doted enough.

She stood. "Let's get back up to Dad," she said.

A mysterious look came over Nina's face. "Wait, dear. We can't go yet. I've asked someone to meet us—someone who needs your help."

"Mom, what are you talking about—"

"Very well, I never could keep a secret." Nina rushed on. "It's Emily's brother. I did tell you that she has a brother, didn't I? Young Joshua. Only nine years old, and very much in need of someone who can tutor him. He's having trouble at school—and no wonder, considering everything he and Emily have been through. Both their parents gone, the two of them trying to struggle along as a family on their own. It hasn't been easy…but now we can help them. *You* can help, Robyn. You're a teacher."

Robyn listened to this flood of words with a dreadful sinking feeling. "Mom, I told you…I'm not at all sure about teaching anymore."

"That's just the point, isn't it?" Nina asked. "You need something that will help you realize how very much you *are* a teacher. So I asked Emily to drop Josh off here today. Why…here he is now."

Robyn turned around slowly, her apprehension about this situation deepening. She saw a young boy approach, scuffing his feet along the path. He wore jeans and running shoes and a well-used San Francisco Forty-Niners T-shirt. Robyn would have recognized him as Emily's kid brother right off—he had the same green eyes, the same distinctive features. He also had the same tawny hair, made unruly by a cowlick right in front. But this little boy seemed to have none of Emily's brazen assurance. He looked altogether too solemn, and he also looked ready to bolt at the first opportunity. He kept his eyes glued to the ground, but then, a moment later, he lifted his head, as if his curiosity had gotten the better of him. He gave Robyn a quick, searching look, just before ducking his head again.

CHAPTER FIVE

LATE THAT EVENING, Robyn stood inside the art gallery and flicked the switch to turn on her father's computer.

Then she glanced over at Mark Stewart.

"You're making me crazy," she said.

"All in a day's work," he answered.

Robyn sighed. "I keep telling you that I can't accept your help. That, in fact, it could be dangerous for me to accept your help. And you keep showing up anyway."

"What's that old saying about a bad penny always turning up again?"

She gave him a closer glance. The only light came from the track lighting in the front of the gallery, shadows deepening all around. In this atmosphere, Mark looked mysterious and forbidding, a man not easily reckoned with, the enigmatic expression in his eyes giving nothing away.

He had called her on the phone a short time ago, suggesting that she go through the art gallery's records to see if there was anything that might explain the attack on her father. It was a logical idea, one that she had considered herself. But she'd resisted it until now. It hadn't seemed right, invading her father's privacy.

"You were so damn persuasive on the phone," she said to Mark. "Pointing out that my father isn't being fair to me…that he's in trouble of some kind, but he won't tell me what really happened…so of course I'm justified in trying to find out everything I can. Believe me, it all makes sense, but I still feel rotten about doing this. And I feel rotten about letting you…a policeman…come over here—"

"Detective," he said imperturbably. "And I didn't give you much choice. It would be pretty foolish for you to do this by yourself, considering your father's warning that you could be in danger. Besides, it's not like my dance card's full."

Robyn frowned at him. "Mark, let's get this straight. Why are you really here? Is it just because you miss doing your job and this is the closest you can come to working on a case?"

Now he seemed uncomfortable. "Besides the obvious fact that you shouldn't be alone, there are two reasons I came. The first is, I don't like vacations…never been good at them. I sure as hell need something useful to do." He stopped.

"You said there were two reasons," she reminded him.

He looked at her. He still seemed ill at ease, but he said nothing. She flushed under his gaze.

"Mark," she began.

"Take it easy, Robyn. Maybe I'm attracted to you, but I'm not in the market for a relationship. I botched things with my ex-wife, not to mention my *two* daughters. I'm not looking to botch things with anybody else."

Now all Robyn could do was stare at him. He'd said he was attracted to her, but he'd made it sound like an inconvenience. Well, she certainly hadn't invited the man into her life. She hadn't asked him to feel anything about her, one way or the other. He didn't need to act as if *she* was putting *him* out, for goodness' sake.

"Look," she said, "it's not like I'm searching for a new relationship, either. My family's going through a crisis, and that's the only thing on my mind." She didn't know why she felt worked up. "Besides," she went on, perhaps more forcefully than necessary, "it's not just my family situation. There are plenty of *other* reasons I'm not looking for a relationship. If you want to know the truth, I have *two* ex-husbands. Talk about botching things— I'm the expert."

Mark's expression grew interested. "So you figure you win," he said. "Your two exes get you first prize."

"It's not a damn contest—" Robyn gave another exasperated sigh.

He seemed perfectly grave. "Maybe not. But I have to tell you the part about two ex-husbands, that's an icebreaker. Makes a person want to know more."

She sank onto a chair in front of the computer. "One ex-husband you can justify," she said. "Everybody's entitled to one romantic mistake. But two, it starts to get embarrassing. You're suspected of lacking fortitude, not to mention good judgment. You know the funny thing, though? My family's never blamed me. My mother's still certain there's a mate out there for me. And my dad…well, my dad keeps telling me that my marriages were learning experiences. At least, that's what he kept telling me before he landed in the hospital." At this moment, she longed for things to be the way they'd been before—both her parents' lives going along smoothly while *her* life was the only one in upheaval.

Dismayed, she felt tears smarting behind her eyelids. Any second now and she'd be bawling. The last thing she wanted was to lose control in front of Mark Stewart. She gave him another glance and noted the careful absence of emotion on his face. Maybe that was what they taught you when you joined the police force—don't sympathize too much with the crime victims, just work on the case until you solve it.

She willed her own emotions into submission. "Mark, you've seen that I'm safe and sound here. You can leave now. I'll keep all the doors and windows locked, and I'll call Uncle Greg to come pick me up when I'm finished. I'll be fine."

He sat down in a chair next to her. "Someone attacked your father here only a few nights ago," he said. "I'm staying."

Now he wore what she'd already come to identify as his implacable look. She knew she wouldn't be able to pry him out of that chair. And she had to admit one thing. She didn't really want to be alone, not here at her father's gallery, where the attack had happened.

She pulled her chair closer to the computer. "I'm going to do it," she muttered. "I hate being a spy, but I have to do something to find out the truth." She clicked the mouse to bring up the financial software. "When it comes right down to it, I'm spying on my mother as much as on my father. She does the bookkeeping for both the gallery and the bookstore, and she's taken to computers, big time. She's always up on the latest technical developments. Dad and I are the only ones besides her who know the password to get into these records." Her fingers paused on the keyboard.

"I won't look," Mark said.

"It's not that," Robyn said. "I just feel like such a *snoop*. Mom only told me the password in case of an emergency."

"Maybe this qualifies as one," Mark said.

Robyn felt the all-too-familiar chill seeping through her. Quickly she tapped out the password: Carmel. It was the place where Cal Myers had proposed to Nina more than forty years ago. Trust Nina to be able to combine romance and business.

Robyn pulled up the financial records for the current year, scanning debits and credits. Mark didn't talk. He didn't move, didn't give so much as a twitch. He must be really good at a stakeout, she thought. Ever-watchful during long hours. She made a genuine effort to forget he was here, tapping a key to bring up more information. For a little while she was almost successful as she concentrated on the task before her. But then…it was impossible. You just couldn't forget the presence of a man like Mark.

Her gaze strayed over to him. "So far I've learned that my parents throw even more business parties than I remembered. Art exhibits always call for a party, of course, and my folks have always known how to do it right. Best entertainment, best caterers in town."

Mark appeared thoughtful. "Any chance your

parents have been spending beyond their means, getting into financial trouble?''

"Not according to these figures. Mom always says to be lavish with the important stuff, then economize on what doesn't matter so much. It seems to work out.''

"According to those figures,'' Mark said.

"What are you implying?'' Robyn asked indignantly. "That my dear sweet innocent mother has cooked the books, and we'll find her out?''

Mark didn't offer so much as a smile, and Robyn stared at him in frustration all over again. "You act as if it's really a possibility,'' she told him. "One of my parents capable of doing something illegal.''

"I didn't say anything,'' he remarked mildly.

"You don't have to say anything. It's your whole attitude. You seem like the kind of person who wouldn't be surprised to find out your own mother has been up to something nefarious.''

He shrugged. "*Nefarious* isn't exactly a word I'd use. But, no, I guess nothing surprises me.''

Robyn propped her elbows on the desk and rubbed her temples. She still hadn't had a decent night's sleep since arriving in New Mexico. "Maybe that worries me is that I'm becoming a cynic, too,'' she said. "I met this little boy today…a nine-year-old who needs some tutoring. He doesn't seem too sure of himself, doesn't seem too sure about school, either. He could use a boost as much as any kid, I think. But that didn't make me want to agree to the job. Maybe I've stopped believing I can make a whole lot of difference in any child's life. What does that tell you about me?''

Mark settled back in his chair as if he surmising this would be a long story. Robyn frowned again.

''Okay, so I gave in anyway,'' she said. ''I agreed to be his tutor. English, math and history, three times a week. And this is right after I called my principal in Denver and told him I needed at least a month off—time to be with my family, not a nine-year-old boy who's falling behind in his studies. Am I crazy, or what?''

Mark gave her a measuring look. ''Maybe you figure he's worth the effort. Maybe you're a teacher, and you can't resist.''

She shook her head. ''Oh, sure, I used to think I was going to march into a classroom and inspire kids to change their lives. I was so convinced that being a teacher was my calling. But then...'' She told herself not to make any more confessions to Mark. But she couldn't seem to stop herself. He sat there as if he really *was* on a stakeout, and he didn't have anything better to do than listen to her. So she talked.

''Everybody gets so damn apathetic. The students, the administrators...hell, too many of the teachers themselves. It just starts beating you down until you even wonder if *you* care anymore. Budget cuts, one after the other. Parents who don't seem to give a damn about their kids, much less their kids' education. You start losing faith. You wonder if you're trying as hard as you should. And that's when you wonder if maybe you should get out.''

Mark seemed to be listening to every word she said, but he still didn't show any emotion. She stood restlessly.

''Anyway,'' she said, ''as far as the nine-year-old who needs a tutor…his name is Josh, and he happens to be Emily's brother. It seems my mother has founded the Emily-and-Joshua-Parkman Improvement Society, all on her own. And now she wants me to jump on the bandwagon.''

At last Mark shifted position, and Robyn saw him give a slight wince. ''The conversation's that painful, is it?'' she asked, trying for a light tone.

''Actually, it's my leg. They got the bullet out, but it did some damage. Nothing that a little time won't fix, though.'' He sounded matter-of-fact, as if he were recovering from some ordinary ailment.

''What happened?'' she asked. ''Who shot you?''

Once again his face took on that hard, unreadable mask. ''It wasn't anybody you'd care to meet,'' he said. ''Let's just say I finally managed to track down someone wanted on a murder charge from a couple of years back. My aim was better than his.''

Robyn shivered. "You…killed him?''

"No," he said. "I told you—my aim is good. I don't shoot to kill unless it's absolutely necessary.''

His words implied that if necessary, he *would* kill. What was it like, having a job where that was always a possibility, knowing you might be forced to take someone else's life? Perhaps it accounted for the aloneness she sensed in him.

"Mark," she said, dreading her own words. "Have you ever had to…kill someone?''

He waited a few seconds before answering. "Yes," he said, no emotion in his tone. "Once. There was no other choice.''

She didn't want to hear any more. "I hate it," she said fiercely. "I hate that in a few short days my life has come to this. Wondering if *I'd* have what it takes to shoot someone. Wondering where the threat's going to come from. Talking about things like this, things I've never even thought about before—''

"Talking about them with a detective," Mark added. "That gets to you, too, doesn't it?''

"Yes," she said. "It does. I can't help it—my father begged me not to involve the police, but here you are. Off duty or not, you've made it very clear you're always a cop. You're so darn intense about it."

"Exactly what my boss says." Mark's tone was wry. "He thinks I need a break for a little while...need to 'kick back' a little. I tend to disagree—being a detective is what I do. If there's one certainty in my life, it's my work." He spoke with what appeared to be an unshakable conviction. Robyn envied him that. Nothing in her own life seemed very certain at this moment.

She sat in front of the computer again. "Mark...oh, hell. Let's get on with it."

During the next hour or so, they went through all the computer records, and afterward examined the receipts and invoices that Nina kept neatly stacked in a metal box. But there was nothing out of the ordinary, nothing that didn't add up, nothing that hinted at the reason Cal Myers had been so brutally attacked.

Robyn finally pushed away a bundle of receipts. "This is useless," she said. "We don't even know what we're looking for."

"It was worth a try," Mark said. "And don't give up yet. Maybe there's still something hidden in these records, and we just have to figure out how to look for it."

"My family isn't the secretive type. We don't *hide* things—"

''Your father's obviously hiding something,'' Mark reminded her. ''Whatever happened that night, right here in the gallery, he's not talking about it.''

Her gaze strayed unwillingly around the gallery, and she imagined the violence that had taken place here so recently. Had there been one assailant, perhaps more? She didn't even know that much.

She pushed back her chair. ''As long as we're at it, we should look at everything. Come with me.'' She led the way into a room at the very back of the gallery. Reaching up, she pulled the string that turned on the overhead light. ''This is the official storage room,'' she said. ''All the records from past years are kept in the boxes along that wall. And there are some other boxes that look positively ancient—who knows what's moldering away in those. Maybe we'll find something, after all.'' She tried to sound optimistic, and then the irony struck her: She was hoping to find something that would incriminate her father.

Before she could hesitate any longer, she began hauling one of the dusty old boxes into her arms. It was heavier than she'd bargained for, however, and she ended up swaying backward. Mark immediately put his arms around the box, anchoring the load. They were now standing very close together.

Robyn looked into his eyes and an unsettling ripple of awareness went through her. She clung to her end of the box, as if that would steady her against the bewildering sensations that had suddenly flared in her. Mark gazed back at her. His eyebrows came together, as if he was puzzling out a particularly vexing problem. He drew the box away from her, set it on the floor and turned back to her. They were still standing too close to each other. Robyn told herself to step away, but somehow she couldn't move. Mark continued to gaze at her with a slight frown. Then he bent his head and kissed her.

At first it was the lightest of kisses, Mark's lips scarcely brushing hers. Robyn was taken by surprise. She knew that all she had to do was step away from him. She knew that was what she ought to do. But she stayed where she was, her face tilted toward Mark. And then, ever so slowly, the kiss became something more. Mark deepened the contact between them. And, with the taste of his lips on hers, everything terrible that had happened these past few days seemed to recede. It was as if she suddenly found herself gliding over a beautiful lake, far from threatening shores. She felt a warmth spread through her. It seemed the most natural thing in the world to let him take her in his arms. She moved her hands inside the light baseball jacket he wore, seeking yet more closeness. Her fingers bumped against cool metal…the metal of a gun. Mark was carrying the thing in a shoulder holster.

All the terrible events came flooding right back. How had she allowed herself to forget? Her family needed her—needed all her attention and concern— and she was kissing Mark Stewart! She pulled away.

"Robyn," he said.

She made the mistake of gazing into his eyes. She saw the way they had darkened to a cinder gray.

A sound came from the main room of the gallery. It was a faint rustling, as if a breeze had quivered over the receipts and other papers left on the desk. But Robyn knew that all the windows in the gallery were shut, both doors locked tight. She'd checked them herself.

Already Mark had slipped his hand inside his jacket and brought out his gun. He inched his way from the storeroom, moving without making a single noise. Heart thudding, Robyn stayed close behind him. Stealthily they moved into the main gallery. Robyn drew in her breath when she saw the front door standing wide open to the night—the very door she had bolted so securely only a short time ago. She glanced around wildly, wondering who or what she would find. But no one else was here...all she saw was a few receipts that had drifted from the desk to the floor.

Mark gripped Robyn's arm. "Stay with me," he said in a low voice. He didn't have to ask twice—

she wasn't going anywhere on her own. Together they slipped out the door of the gallery and made a quick scan of the courtyard. Robyn strained to see through the darkness, all too well picturing someone lurking in the shrubbery or around a corner. But it didn't appear anything could take Mark unawares. He seemed to glance in all directions at once as he and Robyn went round the back of the shops. They made a full circuit, only to find no sign of anyone.

Inside the gallery once again, Mark thoroughly checked the main area, the washroom, the storage room, Robyn right at his side. She found her teeth beginning to chatter, and she had to speak.

"I'm—I'm glad you kept me with you. I've seen too many of those movies, you know, the ones where the hero tells the heroine to wait for him, and then he comes back and of course she's not there anymore…"

"It had to be someone who has a key to the gallery," Mark said, responding to queries of his own. "We should have heard the door being unlocked…of course, we were preoccupied at the time, at the back of the gallery, and whoever it was obviously decided to be careful. We didn't hear anything until he—or she—reached the desk. And then, to be able to leave again so quickly and silently…it was someone who knew exactly what he was do-ing.''

He…or she. Either way, Robyn hated the thought of someone invading the gallery with such silent, skillful intent.

"We were preoccupied, all right," she said grimly. "Way too preoccupied. Believe me, I'm the first to say we shouldn't have been doing what we were doing—"

"Who else has keys to the place, Robyn?" he said, ignoring her remark.

Trembling, she went to the front door, locked it again, checked the bolt twice. She checked the back door, too, even though she knew how useless the effort was. She could not rid herself of that eerie image: the door open wide to the night, those re-ceipts scattered from the desk onto the floor. Now she bent to pick them up.

"Both my parents have a key," she said. "My aunt and uncle, too, of course. Everyone in the fam-ily has access to all the shops. No one else that I know of."

"Think, Robyn. Any friends of your parents who might have been given a key? Former employees?"

"I don't know. I suppose it's possible—"

"Does Emily Parkman have a key?"

Robyn wished he would stop grilling her, making

her feel vaguely guilty, as if somehow *she'd* been handing out keys left and right.

"Emily...I don't know," she said. "Mom might have asked her to keep an eye on things while the gallery's closed. But Emily doesn't seem the type to sneak around."

He made another quick tour of the gallery, his expression intent. There was a remoteness to him now, as if all that concerned him was the problem at hand.

A knock came at the front door, and Robyn almost jumped. Mark, still holding his gun at the ready, went toward the door and peered through the glass. Robyn followed close behind, peering out, too.

"It's Uncle Greg," she said, undoing the lock and swinging the door open. Mark slid his gun back inside his jacket, but still his watchful stance said he was ready for anything.

Greg Myers stepped over the threshold. "Are you all right?" he asked Robyn. "I was driving by when I saw the lights on, and thought I'd better check things out." He gave Mark a suspicious once-over, obviously ready to defend his niece. Since he and Aunt Janet didn't have any children of their own, he'd always looked out for Robyn as if she were his own daughter. Uncle Greg was a large, burly man.

Robyn had always marveled that a man with such big, sturdy fingers could make such delicate chocolates. And she'd always loved the delicious aroma that surrounded her uncle. While some men smelled of tobacco or aftershave, wherever Uncle Greg went he carried with him a whiff of chocolate, a hint of toffee. Unfortunately, Uncle Greg could no longer eat the very candy he made. After suffering a heart attack less than a year ago, he'd been under strict orders to change his diet and to stay away from stress.

"I'm fine," Robyn assured him now. "But apparently someone broke in here a few minutes ago— well, it wasn't exactly a break-in, since whoever it was used a key." She listened to herself, amazed that she could sound so conversational. "Anyway, Uncle Greg, this is Mark Stewart, a...friend of mine."

Mark didn't wait for any more social amenities.

"You just happened to be driving by?" he asked. Robyn wondered if he knew how to pose a question without making it sound like a police interrogation.

Uncle Greg ignored Mark. "What's this break-in you're talking about?" Her uncle had on his combative look. It was a family saying that in another lifetime, Greg would have pursued a career of military glory. In this lifetime, he'd contented himself by becoming an expert on military history; he could tell you anything and everything you wanted to know about the Napoleonic Wars. Robyn had many childhood memories of perching on a stool at the Chocolate Shop while Uncle Greg explained the Battle of Leipzig or Waterloo, marshaling candies into opposing armies.

"Are you sure you're all right?" he asked Robyn now.

"We didn't even see who did it, Uncle Greg. We were...back in the storeroom. When we came out, the front door was standing wide open." She waved the receipts she continued to hold in one hand. "Apparently whoever broke in was curious about these. The whole thing just gives me the creeps. And it doesn't make any sense. Whoever it was must have known we were in here—we had the lights on. So why did they pick this particular time to make an entrance?"

"Maybe someone wanted to make a statement," Mark said. "Maybe someone didn't want you to start feeling too safe, Robyn."

Now she felt a chill so deep inside she wondered if it would ever leave. "You're saying it was a message..."

"One I damn well don't like," Mark said. "First thing in the morning, you need to get the locks changed. I know someone who'll do a good job. Meanwhile, I'll call in a favor and get a patrol car over here to keep watch on the place. It could be that the intruder was looking for something specific...maybe something they don't want anyone else to find. If that's the case, we have to make sure we find it first.''

"Just who are you, Mr. Stewart?" Greg asked. "You sound like a professional—"

"Robyn can explain as little or as much as she wants about me."

Robyn didn't want to explain anything at the moment, and she'd completely lost her taste for detective work. "I'm going home," she said. "I've had enough for one night."

Mark intervened. "I don't think you should be alone tonight. If this was some type of scare tactic, it means you could be in real danger."

"He's right," said Uncle Greg. "You'll stay with me and Janet again tonight. Of course, we'd planned on being with your mother at the hospital, but we can change that—"

"No need," said Mark. "I'll stay with Robyn."

"Just who are you Mr. Stewart?" Greg repeated. "What do you have to do with all this?"

"Enough," said Robyn. "I'm just going home."

"And I'm going with you," Mark said. "Someone has to make sure you're safe—and that's all there is to it.''

Robyn just didn't have enough energy to argue. She looked into Mark's eyes, something that was always a mistake. As usual, she couldn't look away. And this time his gaze told her she didn't have any choice.

He would be her protector tonight.

CHAPTER SIX

STRETCHING LUXURIOUSLY, Robyn pressed her face deeper into the pillow. Wonderful, contented sleep…it was something you didn't appreciate until you'd been deprived of it for a few nights. She nestled up to the pillow. If only she could go on resting…

But then, with dawning wakefulness, everything came flooding back.

Robyn sat up in bed, fully awake now. She listened intently for a moment. She didn't hear anything from the rest of the house, but she knew Mark was still here. She could feel his presence, as surely as if he were standing in front of her. Last night, after the incident at the art gallery, he'd brought her here to her parents' house, and he'd commandeered the sofa for himself. Uncle Greg hadn't been too happy about the setup; he'd wanted to take charge of her himself. Robyn hadn't wanted *anyone* to take charge of her, but at the time she'd been too tired to argue, her nerves too jangled. She'd given in to Mark.

Now she felt herself tense all over again. She slid out of bed, went to the half-open door of her room and looked out. No sign of him. She grabbed some clothes and ducked into the bathroom. Several minutes later she emerged. Teeth brushed, hair combed, fully clothed in jeans and T-shirt she felt a little more in control of the situation.

She went out to the center patio—the *placita*—of her parents' home. Nearly a century ago this house had been a girls' school, and it retained the charm of its former years. A low-slung rectangle of a place, rooms that had once been dormitories and classrooms all faced the patio garden. That was one of the most delightful things about this house—the garden flourishing in the inner courtyard, sunshine spilling down upon it. At its peak, it was always something to behold: the grapevine twining over the trellis, the beds of tulips, phlox and daisies, the little pots brimming over with moss roses and petunias, the snowy white alyssum working its way into every cranny. Long ago, Robyn's mother had instituted a tradition. Whenever Robyn's birthday rolled around in May, Nina would plant something special to commemorate the occasion. A patch of forget-me-not, perhaps, or a border of gentian. It was always a surprise, and as a child Robyn had delighted in running out to the garden first thing on a birthday morning, eager to see what she would find.

Usually these memories made her feel happy and loved, but now they only made her heart ache. The house was too empty without her parents.

Robyn went across the *placita*. She paused in a doorway, looking in at her father's studio: the easel propped up with a canvas upon it, the clutter of oil paints, the bottle with brushes jutting out willy-nilly, the morning light streaming in at just the right angle. The place looked as if it was just waiting for Cal Myers to come in and take up one of those brushes. Robyn wrapped her arms tightly around her body.

She heard footsteps behind her on the patio tiles, and then Mark's voice. ''Good morning,'' he said quietly.

She didn't turn to look at him. She just kept her arms wrapped around herself and stared into her father's studio.

''When I was a child,'' she said, ''I wasn't supposed to go into this room. It was my father's private place, where he painted. But the forbidden drew me. One day, when I thought for sure no one could see, I sneaked in and got into my dad's things. I started finger-painting on a canvas, and I made the biggest mess. When my father came in and found me like that, I thought for sure he was going to chew me out something awful. Instead, he just looked at what I was doing, and after a minute he started dipping his fingers into the paints, too. We finished the canvas together.'' She willed the tears not to come, told herself she wasn't going to lose it in front of Mark Stewart. And, after a moment, she was able to go on, her voice steady.

"That's something I've never understood about my dad. For as long as I can remember, he's painted. He's an artist himself, you can see it, but he never exhibits his own work. Absolutely never. It all stays hidden away here. He's never explained why he promotes the careers of other artists…but not his own.''

Mark didn't answer.

"I guess there's a whole lot I don't know about my father,'' she said. "That's what scares me the most. He's shut himself off from me, and from my mother.''

At last Mark spoke. "I've had that feeling, too…with my daughters. The sense that I'm being shut out. It's not a good feeling.''

She was glad he didn't try to comfort her. From what she knew about him so far, Mark Stewart was not a man to give comfort freely.

Finally she turned around and faced him. In spite of the fact that he'd spent the night on the couch, he looked as alert as always. Perhaps his hair was a bit more untidy than usual. That and the stubble of beard showing along his jaw added to his virility. He'd taken off his baseball jacket, but the gun in its shoulder holster was still very much in evidence. Robyn wondered if he slept with the thing.

"Look, Mark," she said, "I appreciate that you stayed over last night. Really, I do. But I have Uncle Greg and Aunt Janet. I can stay with them whenever I need to. It's not necessary for you to stick around."

"So you keep telling me."

She took a deep breath. "After everything that happened last night…it's more important than ever for you *not* to be involved. Someone coming into the gallery like that, when the two of us were there—maybe it was a warning for me to stay away from the police. And there's the other thing, too. The…kiss." The word dangled awkwardly, but she could tell that Mark wasn't going to help her out. He stood there, waiting for her to go on.

"I've been thinking about it a lot," she said determinedly, "and I've figured out what happened. I was vulnerable last night. Hell, I've been vulnerable since this whole thing started. Anyway, last night…I was using you to escape. I was trying to blot everything out."

"That's funny," Mark said. "I thought we were just necking."

His attitude definitely wasn't helping.

"Look, Mark," she said again. "So I ended up kissing you. Not exactly a good idea, any way you look at it. I'm telling you that I made a mistake. I don't want it to happen again. I have a habit of getting too close to men under…well, under certain situations. I met my first husband soon after I moved away to college. I was excited to be on my own, but I was scared, too. And because of that, I started depending too much on Anthony. Before I knew it, we were married, and living not so happily ever after. As for Brad, my second husband…no need to go into that, I suppose. But it was another mistake.''

Now he was getting a dissatisfied look. ''Robyn, I didn't mean to kiss you, either…certainly didn't plan it. It was a mistake for me, too. I've already told you—I'm not in the market for anything.''

''Well,'' she said. ''We're in agreement. Neither one of us wants it to happen again.''

''Seems that way.''

They gazed at each other. Then, with an effort, Robyn turned from him and studied her mother's garden: forsythia almost ready to flame golden yellow, reddish leaves uncurling on the rosebushes. Spring, a time meant for joy and promise, not this swirling fear and confusion.

''Mark, as far as your getting involved any deeper in my family's problems—the answer is still no.''

''I've arranged for a locksmith to meet us at your father's gallery.'' He spoke as if he hadn't even heard her. ''And, after that intruder last night, your father has to start telling what he knows. I've already talked to Al Donovan, the detective handling your dad's case. I've told Al that your father knows more than he's saying, and that he needs to be questioned thoroughly.''

Robyn swiveled angrily toward Mark. "Dammit, I keep telling you what my father said. Involving the police further means something even worse could happen! You had no right to do this—''

"There isn't any choice. Not after what happened last night. But I informed Al of the circumstances. I told him to be very discreet. He's a good man. He'll know how to handle it.''

The anger inside Robyn churned all the more. Mark had taken charge as if this really *were* his investigation. She despised being so out of control. She hated everything that had happened these past few days...and yes, that meant she hated Mark Stewart's presence in her life.

"Dammit," she repeated under her breath. She had a lot more to say, but the doorbell rang just then. She went to answer it. Mark came with her, as if he couldn't let her do even this much on her own— answer the blasted bell.

She yanked open the door, and Aunt Janet stepped over the threshold. Janet was a petite woman who looked much younger than her fifty-eight years. The bright jewel tones she liked in clothes—turquoise, ruby, jade—contributed to this impression, as did the fact that only a few graying strands had woven into her strawberry-blond hair.

This morning Janet carried a shoe box in front of her. "The little guy under the lid is a sparrow," she said. "I was on the way over here, and found the poor thing sitting stunned in the middle of the road. He was probably flying too low and bounced off a car." She carried the box to the patio and set it down. Then she knelt beside it. "Can you hear anything?" she asked. "I think he's moving around."

Robyn knelt down, too. This was nothing out of the ordinary for her aunt. Janet was always rescuing disabled creatures—not just birds, but the occasional cat or dog, or even turtle.

"Listen," she said. "I can hear him starting to hop around in there—can't you?"

"Yes," Robyn said, smiling. "He sounds downright antsy."

Janet inched back the lid of the shoe box, and the little bird immediately poked his head out. Janet sat back. "Just you watch," she said. "He'll be fine…he'll fly away in a minute."

She removed the lid entirely and the bird flapped his wings. Very gently, Robyn's aunt tilted the box so he could hop out. And, indeed, a second or two later he flew into one of the rosebushes. From there he soared into the open sky, and over the roof of the house.

"That was an easy one," Janet pronounced. She stood, and now she gave her attention to Mark. "Mr. Stewart, isn't it? My husband told me all about what happened last night. I was going to come over right then, but he seemed to think you two might want to be alone."

"Aunt Janet," Robyn said firmly. "Mark is just…a friend." She was getting a bit weary of introducing him that way, but didn't know how else to do it. "In fact, Mark is leaving right now—aren't you, Mark?"

"If you'd like me to meet the locksmith on my own, that'll be fine," he said. "You can give me the keys and I'll head over to your father's gallery right now."

She'd almost forgotten about the locks. She wished she could argue with Mark, but changing the locks at the gallery was definitely a good idea.

"Very well," she said reluctantly. "We'll go there together. And *then* you'll be on your way."

Mark had a talent for remaining impassive. Meanwhile, Robyn became aware that her aunt was watching her a little too intently. Growing up, Robyn had felt as if she had two sets of parents—Greg and Janet, as well as Cal and Nina. At times she had objected to all the adult attention, but she'd also learned to appreciate it. Her aunt and uncle had very much wanted children of their own. It had been difficult for both of them when no babies appeared, and Robyn had provided at least some outlet for their parental yearnings.

"Anyway," Janet said, "I'm about to pick up your uncle at the shop, and we're headed over to the hospital. I thought you might need a ride, but it sounds like you'll be busy." Janet gave Mark a considering glance, as if still debating whether to trust him with her niece. At the same time, Robyn noticed the strain in Janet's expression, the lines of fatigue. It had been a difficult time for everyone in the family.

"Are you getting any rest at all?" Robyn asked. "You and Uncle Greg have been at the hospital almost as much as Mom."

"We're holding our own. Don't you worry." But then another shadow seemed to cross Janet's face. During the last year, Janet had often got that lost expression. Robyn knew why. Some eighteen months ago, her aunt and uncle had gone through troubles in their marriage. Uncle Greg had even moved out for a time, to his own apartment. After his heart attack, he'd moved back home—the health crisis had seemed to draw Greg and Janet together again. Neither she nor Uncle Greg spoke about what their problems had been, but the sadness lingered with Janet. Janet, who took such care with wounded creatures, now seemed to harbor a deep wound of her own. Robyn had to resist the urge to hug her aunt. She knew from experience that Janet preferred that no one acknowledge her unhappiness.

"I'll be on my own way," Janet said, and then she went back out the door.

NINE-YEAR-OLD Joshua Parkman sat at the desk in the Myers's family gift shop, his sneakers dangling just above the floor. A tuft of his hair stuck straight up in front, exactly like yesterday when Robyn first met him. He wore the Forty-Niners T-shirt again; it appeared to be a favorite. His expression unremittingly solemn, he glanced at Robyn now and then from the corner of his eye. Meanwhile, his sister, Emily, presided nearby, refusing to leave the two of them alone.

"Josh is bright," Emily said in a tone that implied any relative of *hers* would have to be enormously gifted. "I've helped him with his homework before, and I've seen how smart he is. All he has to do is apply himself a little more. He has a great deal of potential."

"The sooner we start then, the better," Robyn said, hoping Emily would get the hint. But Josh's sister stayed right where she was.

"I'll admit I wasn't convinced when Nina first

suggested this tutoring idea,'' Emily said loftily. ''But if it'll give Josh more incentive—fine. Just be sure you give me your bill, Robyn. Charge me the going rate. Your mother seems to think I'm in need of charity, what with raising my little brother and all, but she's got it wrong. We do very well for ourselves.'' Emily paused dramatically, smoothing back some of her gorgeous tawny hair. ''Our parents died,'' she went on. ''An accident, three years ago. Their car was hit by a drunk driver. Sure, that was hard to take, but Josh and I have handled it.''

Josh ducked his head as if he didn't want to hear any more. Emily gazed at him, and something in her expression altered. The look in her eyes was now unmistakably one of love and concern.

''Bad things happen sometimes,'' Emily said, as if to herself. ''You deal with them, that's all.''

''You try, anyway,'' Robyn said, thinking about her father.

Emily gave Robyn a shrewd glance. ''I'm surprised you agreed to a tutoring job. I imagine you have enough to do. You're certainly keeping *busy* with Mr. Mark Stewart.''

Robyn gritted her teeth at Emily's tone. The truth was, however, that she couldn't seem to get rid of Mark. This morning, after they'd met with the locksmith, Mark had pointed out that they needed to go through all the boxes in the gallery storeroom. That

was something Robyn had planned to do herself...but somehow she'd ended up doing it with
Mark. It had been a frustrating endeavor. All they'd
found were old business records, family scrapbooks
and photo albums that Nina had compiled, newspaper clippings on several of Cal's artists who had
made it big. Mark, as always, had looked for the
underside. He'd wondered if it was possible that one
of the artists had a grievance against Cal. And he'd
also asked her to identify every single friend or acquaintance who showed up in family photographs.
Could one of them have a grudge? Robyn had begun
to wonder herself, despising the way she now had
to distrust every person ever associated with the Myers family.

Emily had drifted to the window and was gazing
out. "Of course, I heard all about the excitement
last night from your uncle Greg. Good thing you had
your Mark around. My, my, there he is," she said,
"still watching out for you after your little scare.
How sweet."

Robyn ignored Emily's snippy tone. "What—
Mark's *out* there?" she asked. She went to the window. Sure enough, that was Mark Stewart's Land
Cruiser parked at the curb, with Mark sitting inside.
He hadn't told her he was going to keep tabs on her
while she tutored Josh Parkman. He'd just gone
ahead and done it. Didn't he think she could take

care of herself for one minute? He appeared to be reading a book as he waited out there, but Robyn knew him well enough by now. She knew that no matter how absorbed he might seem, he'd be on the ready.

Robyn stayed at the window. Mark glanced up and across at her. He didn't seem surprised to see her there. He gave her a small, mocking salute with one hand then returned to his book. Robyn felt herself flushing, and Emily studied her with a knowing expression.

"He really is something, your Mr. Stewart. If I were you, I'd look for lots of excuses to have him protect me. I'd use whatever strategy I needed to keep him coming around."

"Strategies," Robyn echoed. "I may be a total failure with men, Emily, but I don't use 'strategies' to manipulate them."

Emily's expression turned oddly brittle. "It's better to manipulate than the other way around, isn't it? Besides, all you have to do is figure out what a man wants, and then provide it. After that, the rest is easy. Take your Mark Stewart, for example. I can tell he's into helping people. Protecting them. So it's simple. All you have to do is make sure you're someone who needs protecting."

"He's not 'my' Mark Stewart," Robyn said.

"And I don't want to manipulate him. I certainly haven't *asked* for his help—"

"Whatever you say," Emily remarked. She strolled off to attend to a customer who'd come in. Robyn still felt rankled, but she went to sit beside Josh. He continued to slouch in his chair, moving his feet back and forth, his face resolutely blank.

Robyn fished through her tote bag and took out a small paper sack from the Chocolate Shop. There were two candy bars inside, made from Uncle Greg's special recipe. She set one in front of Josh. His gaze flickered toward it, then returned to unblinking status.

Robyn took a bite from her own candy bar. "You're missing out on something good," she said.

He looked at the chocolate she'd placed in front of him, and a debate seemed to go on behind that young face.

The candy bar won. Josh reached for it and took an impressive-size bite. Then, apparently, he remembered his manners.

"Thanks," he said grudgingly.

"You're welcome. My aunt and uncle made these, you know. They're the best."

They ate their chocolate in what was almost companionable silence. After they finished, Robyn put a piece of paper in front of Josh, along with a pen.

"This is a writing exercise," she said. "So...why

don't you write down how you feel about school. You can be completely honest, because I'm your tutor, not one of your teachers.''

He regarded the piece of paper quizzically, as if it might reveal something to him. Robyn waited. At last Josh took the pen, scribbled a few words and pushed the sheet toward her. She picked it up. SCHOOL IS FOR NURDS, he'd written in big letters.

"Fair enough," she said. "Articulate. To the point. Only one misspelling." She pushed the paper back toward him. "But I think you could be a little bit more specific if you tried. What exactly don't you like about school?"

For a moment he poised the pen over the paper. But then he dropped it as if in defeat. He gazed at Robyn.

"I'm no good at school," he said. "But someday I'm going to play football, so I figure it doesn't much matter."

It was the most he'd said to her so far. "Even football players have to study," she remarked.

"I don't think so."

"Really, they do," Robyn said. "When I was in college, I had a friend who was an all-American. But he was majoring in economics and he worked hard at that, too. He used to joke that he was studying economics so he could manage all the money he was going to make as a professional athlete.''

Josh didn't seem impressed. Robyn tried again. ''Okay,'' she said. ''I have a confession to make. I don't know a whole lot about football. Maybe you could explain the game to me. You know, like draw a diagram, and maybe tell me some of the rules.''

This time he took the sheet of paper and began drawing X's and O's on it with considerable concentration.

''This guy here, he's the quarterback,'' he said in the kindly tone of one dispensing knowledge to the less informed. ''He calls all the plays. This guy's the tight end—he catches passes over the middle. These other guys are wideouts...''

Josh got so involved in describing the finer points of the sport, the hour seemed to fly past. At the end of it, Robyn had a very detailed diagram.

''This is great,'' she said. ''Just what I need. You know how it is—you go to a game with somebody, and you hate to act like you don't know anything. It's kind of like school in a way. You want to feel like you know the rules, at least.''

''I guess,'' he said. ''But I'd rather go to a football game.''

''You know what?'' Robyn said. ''You tutored me today, instead of the other way around. Next time maybe you can let me tutor you.''

"Maybe not," he said. He slid off the chair and went to his sister. "We're done," he said.

Emily put a hand on his shoulder. "That's fine, Josh. You can go outside now and play in the court-yard. Just don't wander off."

"I never do," he said.

"I know, I know," she said. "You're a model citizen, right?"

"Right." He grinned at her, and she smiled back. Then Josh went dashing out the door.

Emily turned to Robyn, and immediately reverted to her usual condescending self. "How clever," she said. "In between waiting on customers, I noticed what you were doing—getting Josh to talk about what interests him. But can you get him interested in his schoolwork? That's your job, after all."

Robyn didn't bother to answer, and Emily became defensive.

"Things have been hard on Josh, that's all, what with losing our parents. A boy as young as he is, it takes a long time to get over something like that."

Whenever Emily talked about her parents, her tone changed slightly—just enough to make Robyn take notice.

Robyn went to the window again and gazed out. She saw Josh kneeling down, digging in a patch of dirt with a stick. Mark had climbed out of the Land Cruiser and had bent to speak to the boy. The two of them seemed involved in a man-to-man conversation.

"Your Mr. Stewart is still out there, like a guardian angel," Emily said caustically.

Mark Stewart, an angel? Hardly. He was a man who'd made it clear he'd seen a little too much of the seamier aspects of life. But there he was, talking to a little boy and at the same time ready to protect Robyn.

The worst part was knowing that, deep down, she was actually starting to enjoy it...she was starting to enjoy Mark Stewart's presence.

CHAPTER SEVEN

TWO DAYS AFTER that mysterious intrusion at Cal Myers's gallery, Mark was still looking for answers. His search had finally led him to a hotel some blocks from the plaza. Standing in the empty lobby, he took note of the unwieldy leather armchairs, the dark moldings everywhere, the immense brass chandelier lurking above. The only other person there was the clerk, a fellow who presided over the registration desk with an air of boredom. He yawned as he studied the photograph Mark had handed him.

"Yeah, he looks familiar," said the clerk. "Guess he could have been in here."

"Think a little harder," Mark said. "When was he here? Who was he with?"

The clerk yawned again. "Nobody's memory is that good. I can't even remember what I ate for lunch three days ago. Can you?"

"Grilled salmon," Mark said. "Take a closer look."

The clerk propped his elbows on the desk and took a long hard look at the photograph. "Yeah," he said. "I'm pretty sure I did see this guy a couple of times...we're talking maybe a couple of months back. I remember because of the woman he was with."

"Can you describe her?" Mark asked.

"No—that's just it. She was wearing a hat and she kept her head turned away."

"Age? Hair color?"

The clerk sighed. "I'm trying to tell you. The only reason I remember her is because she was trying so hard to make sure I *didn't* see her. She kept her back turned, and she was cloaked inside this big coat she was wearing. It was almost a joke—she might as well have worn a sign—Conducting Illicit Affair."

Mark took the photo back, and tucked it into his pocket. "Thanks," he said. "You've been a big help."

"Gee, you've really made my day, too," the clerk said sarcastically.

Mark left the hotel and walked the short distance to the Santa Fe River. Not that it looked like much of a river here—only a glimmer of water along the sandy bed. It had been a dry winter for New Mexico.

Mark leaned against the railing that skirted the riverbank. Legend had it that this was the place where, a century and a half ago, wagons from Missouri had come to rest after completing their journey along the Santa Fe Trail. He tried to imagine the wagons creaking to a halt, mule and oxen teams jostling each other, the weary but excited travelers scrambling to the ground. But then all Mark could think about was the news he had to give Robyn. It seemed her father had been having an affair.

Mark didn't relish the thought of telling her. He almost regretted having found out as much as he had. He knew Robyn was at the hospital right now, visiting her dad. Her mother was with her, as well as her uncle. But Mark had to tell Robyn that maybe she really didn't know her father so well. Maybe he could get her alone for a few minutes.

"Mr. Stewart...sir," intruded a voice. "Thanks for agreeing to meet me here. It means a lot."

Mark turned his head and regarded Frederick Graham, his youngest daughter's fiancé. "Hello," he said without enthusiasm.

Frederick leaned an elbow against the railing. He looked younger than ever, in a spindly, undernourished way. He needed a couple of good meals, not a wedding ring.

"Mr. Stewart, I'll get right to the point. I asked you to meet me so we could talk about Kerry."

No big surprise there. "I'm listening," Mark said.

"Mr. Stewart, the upshot is...she's talking about calling off the wedding. She won't even discuss it with me. She'll only say that she's not ready. But then she gets this look like she's about to burst into tears, and she slams the door in my face. That's the worst part, knowing that after she closes the door she's going to start crying. I never knew a girl could cry so much.'' Frederick sounded puzzled, and maybe even miserable. Mark was almost starting to feel sorry for him. Most of all, though, he hated the thought of Kerry being miserable.

"Fred...Frederick,'' he said. "Believe me, I wish I could do something to help—''

"Maybe you *can* do something,'' Frederick said. "That's why I'm here. I want you to talk to her, Mr. Stewart. Find out exactly what's wrong. She won't talk to me, but you're her father. If she's going to talk to anyone, it'll be you.''

Mark shook his head. Frederick obviously had not been paying attention to the dynamics in the Stewart family. Amendment: the dynamics in what had *once* been a family.

"Look,'' Mark said, "I'm not a favorite with Kerry. The last thing she'd do is confide in me. She barely takes my phone calls.'' He didn't like admitting as much, but he owed some honesty to this kid who loved his daughter. He was certain about that— Frederick Graham did love Kerry. Why else would he be desperate enough to turn to Kerry's father?

"You're probably relieved that she doesn't want

to marry me anymore,'' Frederick said with unexpected dourness. ''You probably think it's the best thing that could happen.''

''I think Kerry's too young to get married, that's all,'' Mark answered.

''No—you have something against me in particular. I'm not dumb, Mr. Stewart. Give me a little credit.'' Somehow, gangly Frederick Graham managed to look dignified all of a sudden.

''You don't have a job,'' Mark said, deciding it was time for some more honesty. ''And Kerry wants to devote her life to poetry. You can see how maybe I'd be worried about the economics of your relationship.''

''I'll get a job soon,'' Frederick said. ''It's just a matter of time. But what good will it do me if she calls off the wedding? You have to talk to her, Mr. Stewart.''

''Kid, you don't get it—''

''I'm not a kid,'' Frederick said. ''And I do get it. The reason Kerry's scared of marriage has everything to do with you, Mr. Stewart. Not her mother, not her stepfather…you. So I've come right to the source. You're the only one who can figure out what's going on with her. Are you going to help me, or what?''

Mark thought it over. His older daughter had asked him specifically to stay out of his younger daughter's problems. Don't get involved, Debra had said. Maybe she was right.

Mark studied his daughter's fiancé. Frederick still looked way too young. But he had a determined set to his features, something that hinted at the man he would one day become. Maybe that was why Mark found himself giving a reluctant nod.

"I'll help," he said, even as he knew he would regret those words.

ROBYN SAT beside her father, reaching over to smooth his pillow. "You're getting better," she said. "You're healing. Even though you act like you've given up, you *are* getting better. Just imagine what would happen if you put a little effort into it."

Cal Myers gave her a look that could only be called bleak. It pierced Robyn.

"Dad, you have to remember how much you love the gallery," she persisted. "And your painting…don't forget about that. You're the one who taught *me* to find the passion in life. It breaks my heart to see you give up like this."

Her father's expression didn't change. "I'm tired, Robyn. I'm tired all the time."

"That's just it, Dad—you *have* given up. But you can't get back on your feet until you show a little fight."

"I'm carrying such a burden, Robyn. You don't

know… And why haven't you done it?'' he asked. ''Why haven't you tried to protect yourself and your mother? A gun, Robyn…it's the only way I can see.''

She debated how she could phrase her answer. *You see, Dad, instead of a gun, I've somehow ended up with an off-duty detective who thinks you should tell the truth. By the way, I happen to agree with him.*

''If I knew what I had to protect myself from,'' she said, ''it would make things a whole lot easier. Especially after what happened when I was at the gallery.'' Yesterday she'd told her father about the incident at the gallery. Cal had been more distraught than ever, yet he had confided nothing to Robyn.

''A gun,'' he repeated now, stubbornly.

Robyn battled her frustration. ''I know that detective—Mr. Donovan—came to talk to you again. You have to cooperate—''

''No police. I was told…no police. That's all you need to know.'' He moved his head almost frantically on the pillow, seeming to feel he'd already said too much. ''Your mother…I want her to be all right. I'm worried about her.''

''She's out in the waiting room with Uncle Greg. I've made sure that neither one of us is ever alone, Dad, just in case…'' In case of what? That question had stretched her nerves to the snapping point. She paused, wondering how much to tell her father about Mark.

"Dad, you have to trust me. Why can't you do that much?"

Her father's eyes held a look of despair. "It's gone too far, Robyn. If only I could turn back...do you know what it's like, wishing with all your heart that you could turn back? And knowing you can't, not ever again."

"Nothing is that bad," she whispered, clasping his hand. "Nothing."

"Yes. It is." His words evoked a terrible finality. Robyn tightened her fingers around his, as if she could pull him back from the darkness that seemed to be engulfing him. But just then Mark appeared in the doorway.

Mark, who had a way of taking over a room, didn't have to say anything, didn't even have to make an effort. Robyn let go of her father's hand and stood up.

"Dad, this is Mark Stewart...a friend."

He came into the room. "Mr. Myers," he said.

Cal regarded Mark with a suspicious expression. "Who are you?" he asked abruptly.

"Dad, I told you. His name is Mark Stewart, and he's a friend—"

"Robyn, what have you told him?" Cal asked,

his voice very quiet. "I want to know who this man is."

"I don't mean your daughter any harm, Mr. Myers," Mark said. "I'm just here to help. You keep saying your wife and daughter could be in danger. But unless you do everything possible to protect them—for instance, tell who's putting your family in jeopardy—you're responsible if anything happens."

Cal struggled to sit up, his bruised face turning red with anger. "You have no right to judge me. You don't know what the hell is going on. And I don't know who the hell you are—"

"Dad," Robyn intervened. "Mark's an off-duty detective."

"Dammit, Robyn! I told you not to involve the police."

"I didn't purposely involve Mark. You told me to get a gun. I was only following your wishes, and Mark happened to be the instructor at the shooting range."

"Lord, Lord," Cal said, sinking back on the pillow. "This isn't good. It's not the way things were supposed to happen. Nothing is the way it should be…"

"Dad, we're trying to help. Everybody's just trying to help."

"You need to cut the bull, Mr. Myers," Mark said, "and tell us what's really going on."

Cal turned his head away. Suddenly Robyn couldn't take anymore.

"Mark, this isn't working," she said decisively. "You're going to leave, and I'm going to…to get some damn coffee, and my mother's going to come in and sit with my father."

Mark gave Cal another look. "You're responsible," he repeated. "If you don't tell the police what's going on, you're making a big mistake." He turned and left the room.

Robyn left, too. She could feel herself shaking as she walked past the waiting area, but she didn't even glance at her mother or Uncle Greg. Instead, she kept walking until she reached the elevators. She punched the down button.

Mark, inevitably, was right beside her.

"I'm really furious at my father right now," she said in a low voice. "Except that I'm so tired of feeling this way. Angry at whoever attacked him, and angry at him for keeping everything locked up inside."

"Angry at me, too, I'd guess," Mark said.

The elevator doors slid open, and she stepped inside. Mark stepped in beside her. There were other people on the elevator, and Robyn didn't speak again until she was headed down the main corridor of the hospital.

"Yes," she told Mark. "I'm really ticked at you. Was it absolutely necessary to speak to my father that way?"

"Being kind about it hasn't gotten you very far, has it?" he countered. "Somebody has to make your father come to his senses."

She just kept walking down the corridor. And Mark kept pace beside her.

"Are you serious about the coffee?" he asked.

She took a deep breath. "Yes," she said. "That's exactly what I need. A major dose of caffeine."

Mark placed his hand at her elbow and guided her to the hospital cafeteria. He managed the tray line as adeptly as he managed everything else: in a matter of only a few moments, he and Robyn were seated at a table next to the window, with coffee and a doughnut apiece.

"Caffeine," Mark said, obviously trying for normalcy. "Growing up, caffeine was a dirty word in my house. Sugar, however, was another story." He picked up his doughnut.

It occurred to Robyn how little she knew about him. "What kind of childhood did you have, Mark?" she asked almost reluctantly. She was still mad at him, but right now she needed something to center on.

"Like I said—lots of sweets. In my family, dessert was an art form. A kid's heaven, actually. You could chart the week by our desserts. On Sunday nights it was banana splits, Monday you could count on fudge brownies."

"Seriously," she said.

"I *am* being serious. My mom and dad were very responsible people who always made sure we got to school on time, did our homework, did our chores. I guess they figured all of us needed a little outlet every day—something that wasn't quite so responsible. Enter the ice cream and chocolate syrup."

She was unwillingly intrigued by this glimpse into his past. "Sounds like you have brothers and sisters."

"One of each. And we all still have a sweet tooth—my mother and father included. It's too bad I grew up in Deming instead of Santa Fe. My family would have loved your uncle Greg's chocolate shop."

Somehow she couldn't avoid another question. "Mark...were your parents happily married?"

He appeared to give this considerable thought. "I always believed they were," he said at last. "They never argued, or if they did, they made sure my brother and sister and I never heard. So it came as a shock to me when I was about twenty, and found out my parents had once gone to a marriage counselor because they were thinking of splitting up. They're still together, though, and I guess that counts for a lot."

"I used to think that counted for a lot too…" She trailed off when she saw Mark's look of concern. "What's wrong, Mark?" she asked.

"Robyn…there's something I have to tell you. And it isn't pleasant."

She watched as he took a photograph out of his pocket and placed it in front of her. She recognized the photo right away. It had been taken a few years back, and showed her father in front of the art gallery. How carefree he looked, all his charm and vitality showing through. Robyn wondered if she would ever see him like that again.

"Mark, what are you doing with this picture?" she said indignantly. "I realize we were going through all those photos together—"

"I only borrowed the one. I needed it to do a little investigating."

"You could have asked for it. You didn't have to *lift* it, for crying out loud."

"Let's just say I borrowed it. I didn't want to bother you with the reasons unless it became absolutely necessary."

"I see. You wanted to protect me—is that it?" she asked. "Or maybe you just wanted to railroad in and handle this *case* all on your own. Do you always have to be such a damn policeman, Mark? If there was a good reason you needed this photograph, you should have told me, and then—''

He gave her an almost pitying look. ''You're not going to like what I have to say, but here goes. I started making inquiries about your father in some of the other stores near your family's. I was hoping I could find a witness who might have seen someone threatening your father—that type of thing. What I found instead was a shop owner who saw your father going into a hotel several times with a woman—a woman who wasn't your mother. That's when I decided a photograph would help me out.''

''My father—going into a hotel—''

''I showed the photo to the hotel clerk. He said he remembered your father coming in a few times with a woman, and paying for a room.''

Robyn tried to take in what he was saying. She tried to tell herself this wasn't happening. She wasn't sitting here with Mark Stewart and hearing that her father had betrayed her own mother.

''No,'' she said flatly. ''I don't believe it. This clerk of yours is mistaken.''

''It's possible,'' Mark said. ''A lot of people pass through the place.''

Somehow the fact that he didn't try to argue with her dismayed Robyn most of all. She picked up the photograph, held it closer as if she could learn a message from it. But all she saw was Cal Myers's engaging smile, his straightforward gaze into the camera. She could discern no dark shadows, no hidden life.

She dropped the photo onto the table. "No," she repeated, but her voice was less sure this time. "Even if he *was* at this hotel, there has to be some other explanation. The woman he was supposedly with—what about her? Who is she? My aunt Janet?"

If she'd hoped that Mark would acknowledge the humor, the absurdity of the whole situation, she was disappointed.

"Neither the clerk nor the storekeeper could identify her," Mark said. "It seems she was wearing a hat, and trying very hard not to be recognized. Could it have been Janet?"

"Don't be ridiculous. I was using the most farfetched example I could think of..." Her voice trailed off as she remembered something. "Oh, Lord," she said.

"What is it, Robyn?"

She didn't want any more of Mark's questions. She didn't want to have him watching her with that sympathetic but resolute expression—the expression that said no matter how much he sympathized, he would do his job and find out the truth.

"Dammit, Mark," she said. "Can't you let up, at least for now—"

"It will be easier if you tell me," he said.

In spite of her doubts, she found the words spilling out. "What I remembered just now, it can't possibly be relevant...but my father dated Aunt Janet, back when the two of them were pretty much teenagers. Janet wanted to be an artist at one time, so she signed up for a class. My father was one of the other students. The way she tells it, when she saw how good *he* was, she knew her own art didn't have a chance, and she decided she'd better find a different field of work. Anyway, they dated for a while. I don't know how serious they were about each other, but after they broke up, Janet started going out with Uncle Greg. She says that was when she found her true love, because nothing could compare to the way she felt about Greg. They got married when Janet was only eighteen. Of course that's right about when my father met my mother, and they got married, too...it's all just family history."

"What you're speculating," Mark said, "is that maybe there's still something between your aunt and your father."

Robyn felt angry again, and she welcomed the anger—it was a way to defend herself against all these wretched suspicions. "No, Mark. *You're* the one speculating." She stood. She couldn't be near him right now, not after what he had come to tell her today. "I have to do something, and I have to do it alone," she said. "Don't come with me. Please...just don't."

She walked out of the cafeteria, not looking back at him. And, for once, Mark didn't try to follow.

CHAPTER EIGHT

ONLY A FEW MOMENTS LATER, Robyn stepped off the elevator and walked back down the corridor to her father's hospital room. Her mother and Uncle Greg sat beside Cal Myers's bed, making obvious efforts to cheer him.

"Honey, you heard what the doctor said. They could discharge you as early as tomorrow," Nina was telling her husband. "I can't wait for you to come home so we can put all this behind us. Isn't that right, Greg? We'll just put it all behind us, and go on."

"Sure," said Greg in a reassuring tone. "All of us want things back to normal." He looked big and solid and comforting as he sat there. Cal, however, had a bleak expression.

"I shouldn't go home," he said. "It's not the best thing."

"Of course it is," Nina said. "All I want is to have you with me...back in our own house together, where we belong."

Robyn couldn't bear to listen to any more. She

took another step inside the room. "Mom, Uncle Greg," she said. "I'd like to talk to Dad alone, if you don't mind."

Nina glanced up. "Nonsense, dear. What do you want to say that we can't all hear?"

"I'd just like to have some time alone with Dad."

Nina seemed about to protest again, but Greg stood up. "Come on," he told his sister-in-law. "It's well past lunchtime and we're both hungry. Let's go to the cafeteria and see what we can find." He managed to shepherd Nina toward the door. As he passed Robyn, he gave her an encouraging glance. So many times Uncle Greg had been a second father to her, but she couldn't lean on him now. What came next she had to do entirely on her own.

She watched until both her uncle and mother were well down the corridor. Then she closed the door and went to stand beside her father's bed. The bruises on his face still looked mottled. He kept his face turned away. She tried to feel pity for him, but the emotion failed her.

"Dad," she said. "Please tell me the truth. Did you…are you having an affair?" She was surprised at how easily the question slipped out. She waited for him to convince her that it couldn't possibly be true. Instead, he turned his face slowly toward her, and she saw his expression: more sorrowful than she had ever known it.

"No," she whispered, still praying for a denial. But her father, it seemed, would not reassure her with lies.

"It's over," he said heavily.

"Who was she?"

"It doesn't matter, Robyn. It's over."

"Of course it matters," she burst out. "Dad, you have to tell me. This…this affair of yours, and the attack on you. Are they related somehow?"

He gazed at her with that sorrowful, defeated expression. "Promise me, Robyn," he said. "Promise that you won't tell your mother. She mustn't know. Dear God, she must never know."

ONCE AGAIN, Robyn and Josh sat at the desk in the gift shop. So far today, every tactic Robyn had tried had met with quiet but stubborn resistance. Josh had made it very clear that where school was concerned, he was not about to make any effort at all.

"Let's talk about the history of New Mexico. Tell me, Josh, what do you know about the Wild West?" Robyn opened another book.

"Wild West…that's just in the movies, and television. 'Bonanza,' 'Gunsmoke'…I've seen all those." He put a foot on his chair and fiddled with his shoelace.

"That stuff really happened," she said. "In New

Mexico there were cowboys—and cowgirls. And real outlaws like Billy the Kid.''

Josh stared at her. ''Come on. There's no such thing as cowgirls.''

''Sure there is—right here in New Mexico. Girls are just as good as boys at wrangling horses and rounding up cattle. This book tells all about it.''

Josh stared at the book she held.

''Maybe you're not interested in the Wild West,'' she said. She could tell from the expression in his eyes that he was dying to leaf through the book, but he was not about to give in.

''Well, I'll tell you what I'm going to do,'' she said. ''I'll leave the book here, on loan. You can look at it whenever you feel like it.''

He shrugged. ''I don't care.''

Robyn sat back. She suspected that Josh's resistance had to do with a lot more than school. Last night she'd questioned her mother for more background on Emily and Josh Parkman. But Nina herself knew only the few details Emily had shared: the senior Parkmans had died in a car crash three years before, and ever since Emily had done her very best to support both herself and her little brother. Meanwhile, Josh's school performance had gone from mediocre to deplorable.

Robyn wished she could think of the right thing to say to this little boy. Admittedly, however, her concentration wasn't what it should be. She had a hard time thinking of anything except her father's affair. The very word seemed impossible to relate to Cal Myers: *affair*. But he'd admitted it. He refused to say who the woman was, but he'd admitted that he'd been unfaithful to Robyn's mother. And then he'd asked Robyn never to tell Nina.

What a terrible burden—knowing something like this, and not having any idea what to do with the knowledge. Half the time Robyn wanted to blurt out the truth to her mother. The other half of the time, all she wanted was to keep her mother from ever finding out. Nina Myers had dedicated her entire life to her husband. Learning that he had betrayed her, could well destroy her. Robyn pressed a hand to her stomach. Just the thought of her father's betrayal sickened her. She needed to lash out at someone. Even though it was illogical, she resented Mark Stewart for being the one who'd discovered this wretched secret.

Mark had gone down to Albuquerque for the day, to see one of his daughters. Before he left, he'd made Robyn promise all over again that she would be careful—stay out of danger. He'd seemed reluctant to go. Mark Stewart, always the policeman: discovering secrets that could destroy her family, and at the same time trying to protect her. The irony didn't escape Robyn.

She thought about all these things as she watched Josh continue to fiddle with his shoelaces. "You know," she said, "you really are smart, Josh. Would it be so bad if you tried to prove it?"

The obstinate expression was well in place. "I don't need to prove anything."

"Maybe not. But it must really annoy you when all those other kids get good grades, and you know you're just as smart as they are."

Not a blink. Just then Nina came hurrying into the gift shop. She looked agitated.

"Robyn...Robyn, I need you to come with me at once!"

Robyn shoved her chair back. "Has something else happened—"

"Just come with me."

Emily turned from assisting a customer. "Nina, what's wrong? Can I do anything to help?"

"No, Emily. Just stay where you are. Tend to business." Nina disappeared out the door again. By the time Robyn caught up to her, she was already halfway across the courtyard.

"Mom, what on earth is the matter? I thought you were with Dad and Uncle Greg." Cal had been released from the hospital only yesterday. He'd seemed very reluctant to go home, and Robyn could guess the reason. Now that at least one person close to him knew about his affair, being with his family could only be discomforting. Of course, he might also be afraid that his attacker would put in another appearance. Robyn had certainly considered that possibility. Just as Mark had made *her* promise to keep safe, she'd exacted the same promises from her parents: they were to stay with Uncle Greg and Aunt Janet so they would not be alone.

"Your father is fine," Nina said in a wooden voice. "He finally got to sleep, and I started going through some of the mail that's been piling up. I found something..." Nina sank onto one of the small carved benches that adorned the courtyard as if her legs would not hold her upright anymore. Hands trembling, she opened her purse and brought out a folded sheet of paper.

"It's a statement from one of our savings accounts," she said. "It's an account that your father and I aren't supposed to touch. You see, we always called it our dream account. We opened it a long time ago and started putting away money for the trip we've always talked about taking. A trip to England and Spain, when things aren't quite so busy...just the two of us, spend weeks exploring, meandering...our own romantic adventure. That was what we talked about, anyway." Nina's hands tightened on the paper, crumpling it. "Apparently, though, your father has withdrawn all the money from the account. You can see for yourself, if you'd like."

Gently, Robyn extricated the statement from her mother's hands. She smoothed it out and saw that three withdrawals in the amount of five thousand dollars each had been made from the account in the past month or so.

"Your father is the only one besides me who has access to that account," Nina said. "So of course it has to be him. Fifteen thousand dollars…oh, it won't really hurt us financially. It represented a dream, that's all." Now her voice wavered. "Obviously he wanted to keep this a secret from me. He never handles our finances, so he probably forgot that a statement would come in the mail sooner or later. But why would he need this money? And *why* would he keep it a secret?"

Robyn put her arm around her mother, trying to think of the right thing to say. How could she tell her mother about her father's betrayal? How could she break her mother's heart? On the other hand, how could she *not* tell Nina? Wasn't it about time for the members of this family to stop hiding truths from each other?

Promise me, Robyn's father had begged. *Promise me you won't say anything to hurt your mother.*

Robyn simply tightened her arm around Nina, offering what wordless comfort she could, her heart aching even more than before.

MARK WAITED for his daughter outside Becker Hall on the university campus. The building looked the same as when he'd taken classes here himself, more than twenty years ago. It had been built in what was loosely known as the Pueblo style, multitiered with rounded edges everywhere, roof beams jutting out artistically. Sycamore trees still clustered around the building, cutting down on the sunlight that filtered inside; Mark knew from experience that when you took a class in there, you often felt as if you were floating sleepily in green shadows.

Nothing much had changed about the place. Mark scanned the university newspaper and saw that students were still upset about tuition hikes and that there was still a movie theater in the basement of the student union. He and Andrea had gone to that small theater on their first date, and they'd eloped not too long afterward. A whirlwind courtship, he supposed it could be called. Two college students who'd been young and foolish, and who hadn't had the sense to slow down and find out if they were really in love. Miraculously, both of them had managed to finish school, but the two babies had come quickly. Little by little after that, Mark and Andrea had grown apart.

Now Mark walked restlessly in front of the building. He was beginning to understand something. Maybe what scared his daughter Kerry was seeing the similarities between her courtship and that of her parents. After all, Kerry had met Frederick at school. They'd fallen in love quickly. Maybe Kerry thought those kinds of repetitions were bad luck. Certainly the last thing Mark wanted for his daughter was a repetition of her parents' disastrous marriage.

When it came right down to it, he blamed himself for the failure of his marriage. He was the one who'd gotten too wrapped up in his job, who'd spent more and more hours away from his family. Andrea had been left pretty much on her own, juggling work and efforts to make a home. But how did you make a home for a husband who wasn't around? And how did two children forgive a father who hadn't been there for them?

Students began trickling out of the building. Mark glanced at his watch; according to Frederick's time-table, Kerry would be emerging any minute from her computer-science class. Mark glanced at the faces passing by, yet he didn't really see them. He was thinking about fathers and daughters. Take Cal Myers and his daughter, Robyn, for instance. Cal had done something pretty unforgivable. He'd had an affair—betrayed his wife, destroyed his daughter's trust. But Robyn hadn't stopped loving him. She'd told Mark as much, only yesterday. She'd confessed that she wanted to hate her father, but she couldn't. Her loyalty—and her love—gave Mark new hope. If she could still love Cal, couldn't there be a chance for Mark and his own daughters? He'd never betrayed their mother. He'd simply made himself too absent from his family. A big enough sin, assuredly, but maybe one that could be forgiven.

"What are *you* doing here?" Kerry had come out of the building and now stood a few feet away from Mark.

"Hi," he said, trying to sound casual. "Thought I'd surprise you."

"It's a surprise, all right," Kerry said acidly. "How did you know to find me here?"

"Frederick."

Now another look went across her face. Uncertainty tinged with sadness. "I don't see what Frederick has to do with anything—"

"He thought maybe you and I should get together, have a talk."

Kerry started walking briskly toward the university mall. She didn't invite Mark to accompany her, but he did. Today his daughter wore designer jeans and a denim shirt, along with a *concha* belt of hammered silver circles. Mark wondered again how she planned to keep up her wardrobe on a poet's salary—make that a poet's *nonexistent* salary.

"So," Mark said as he walked beside his daughter. "Computer science. Sounds like an interesting subject. Computers…wave of the future, and all that.''

Kerry stared straight ahead. "It's just a stupid requirement. I'm not all that interested in it. The only thing I use a computer for is my writing.''

"You write poetry…on the computer?" Mark asked.

"Of course. You can't turn in scribbled pieces of paper to a poetry class, even though that might fit your stereotypical idea of a writer a *whole* lot better than somebody who uses a keyboard.''

"Hey," said Mark. "I'm glad you know how to use a computer—''

"So I can go out and get some *boring* job typing for people? Is that why you're glad?''

Mark tried again. "If you got a job with computers, it wouldn't have to be boring. You could be a programmer, something like that.''

"Oh, right," she said. "Anything, so long as I'm not a poet. Is that why you came all the way to Albuquerque, Father? To smear my choices all over again?''

Okay, so he hadn't said the right thing. But he wished his daughter wouldn't call him "Father" in that derogatory tone. Anything would have been better. Dad, Pop. He could have gone for either one of those.

"What do you say we call a truce?" he asked.

"Maybe we could spend a few minutes together…being relaxed. Enjoying each other's company. According to Frederick, you have a whole hour before your next class."

"Who does Frederick think he is, my social secretary? I haven't even seen him the last few days, but now he's arranging meetings behind my back. I wish both of you would just leave me alone!"

"Truce," Mark repeated. "For the next hour, anyway."

She didn't answer. They reached the mall, where a few kids on skateboards dodged among the students.

"Let's go sit by the duck pond," Mark said. "I haven't been there in a while."

At first he thought she would refuse, but she relented with a shrug. "I can give you half an hour," she said. "That should be long enough."

Mark led the way up the grassy slope surrounding the duck pond. Sunlight glimmered on the water. Mark didn't see any ducks, but he saw one of the cantankerous geese that were noisily demanding food from the students. There were sparrows, too, alighting wherever anyone was willing to scatter crumbs.

In spite of her expensive jeans, Kerry plopped onto the grass, swinging her backpack down beside her. Mark sat, too, although his leg protested as he settled on the grass.

Kerry brought her knees up and wrapped her arms around them. ''What do you want to talk about?'' she asked in a cool voice.

''About you and Frederick, I guess,'' he said.

''It really isn't any of your business, is it?''

''Frederick seems to think it is,'' Mark said.

''So you're telling me you wouldn't be here today if he hadn't suggested it. I mean, you wouldn't have come to see me just because…just because you *wanted* to see me.'' She seemed to be making a special effort not to look at him.

''Of course I would have come,'' he said too heartily.

''Knock it off. You wouldn't have come on your own.''

He couldn't deny it. He was tired of being snubbed by his daughters so these days he didn't try as much as he should. He didn't make the extra effort to get past the rebuffs and the rejections.

''Kerry,'' he said. ''When you and Debbie were kids, all I wanted was to keep the two of you from being tainted by the type of things I dealt with on the job. I tried to distance you from my career—but in the end I distanced you from myself.''

''Sounds good,'' she said. ''But aren't you just making excuses?''

"I don't think so. Maybe I cared about my job too much, and maybe I was always looking for a way to get more immersed in it. But I also cared about you and your sister—"

"You don't need to tell me any of this," she said stiffly. "Haven't we been over it before?"

"When your mom and I divorced, it shook me up to realize how far apart you and I and Debbie had already grown. I told myself I couldn't let it get any worse. I tried—" No, this wasn't a good tack, either. Right after the divorce, his ex-wife had done everything she could to minimize his contact with his daughters. Andrea had been understandably hurt and resentful, and she'd taken it out by trying to turn the girls against him. Mark wouldn't bring that up with Kerry, though. No matter Andrea's mistakes, his own were far worse.

Now he watched as a sparrow hopped near. It reminded him of the bird Robyn's aunt had rescued the other day. The Myers family…a lot of love going on there, but a whole lot of problems, too. Did any family ever get it right?

Kerry opened her backpack and took out a sandwich. She tore off a piece of crust and set it on the grass. The sparrow pecked at it, and then another sparrow landed almost on top of the bread. A brief scuffle ensued.

"Kerry," Mark tried again. "Maybe the reason

we can't move on is that you never tell me how you feel. Sure, you make it pretty obvious that you're disgusted with me, but you don't let it out, not in so many words.''

At last she gazed at him, her face solemn. ''You want me to tell you exactly how I feel—okay, I can do that. It's easy. When I was growing up, all I ever wanted was for you to be with me. I mean *really* be with me. Really pay attention to what I was saying or doing. But whenever I was lucky enough to get you in the same room with me…you weren't there. Not really. Your mind was always somewhere else.''

''I'm sorry—''

''I could forget about all that,'' she said, not letting him finish. ''I could forget about what happened years ago. I don't like carrying a grudge. But you're still doing it. Even today—even right now—you're doing it. You're off somewhere else. You're not *here,* with me. I came out of my class, and supposedly you were waiting for me, but you were just looking off into the distance. And I could tell, before you'd even spoken a word, that you didn't actually want to be here. You were only going through the motions. Just like always.'' Her voice shook a little. She zipped up her backpack and scrambled to her feet, sparrows scattering as she moved. When she glanced down at Mark, she wore the disdainful mask that she seemed to have perfected just for him.

"At least you're not bothering to deny it," she said. "But you know what's really funny? Frederick is exactly like you that way. He'll seem to want to be with me, but then he's not really *there*. He'll just stare off into the distance, too, like he's completely forgotten about me. Well, you know what? I don't want that in a father. And I sure as hell don't want it in a husband. I'm not asking for every single minute of somebody's attention. Just a little bit of focus, that's all. Is it so bad, wanting that?"

"No," he said. "It's not so bad." Ironically she'd accused him of being distracted today, yet the whole time he'd been thinking about his daughters and how to get closer to them. He didn't think Kerry would believe that. She was too used to his failings in the past to give him any credit now.

CHAPTER NINE

ROBYN GLANCED AROUND the living room of Mark's apartment, asking herself for the tenth time why she'd given in and come here tonight. Sure, she'd had one hell of a day, but now it was late and the last thing she needed was the company of Mark Stewart, off-duty detective. Yet he'd called her on the phone, and now here she was.

"How was Albuquerque?" she asked, trying for a conversational tone.

Mark was in the small kitchen, rummaging for drinks.

His voice came muffled from behind the refrigerator door. "My daughter despises the very sight of me."

So maybe he'd had a hell of a day, too. "I'm sorry," Robyn said.

He shut the refrigerator door and emerged with a couple of cans of beer. "Not exactly champagne at the Ritz," he said, handing her a beer and indicating the surroundings.

Robyn accepted the beer and evaluated his apartment one more time. The architectural details were pleasing enough: high ceilings, arched doorways, the kind of old-fashioned phone nook one rarely saw anymore. The 1940s atmosphere was pervasive, and Robyn liked it. However, Mark's decor left a lot to be desired. No paintings on the walls, a futon frame with no mattress or cushions, and floors with no rugs. The place was characterized most of all by the absence of things.

"This place looks barely lived in," she said. "How long have you been here, anyway?"

"About six months," he said. "I just can't seem to find the right place."

Robyn sat down in the one armchair, a surprisingly comfortable item, and Mark set up a folding chair for himself. Turning it around, he sat so that he could prop his arms along the back of it, and then he studied Robyn.

"So," he said. "Tell me what happened."

When he'd called her a short time ago, she hadn't been very coherent over the phone. She'd informed him only that the Myers clan had suffered an unprecedented blowup, and then she'd all too readily accepted his invitation to get away.

"Let's not talk about it," she said. "For a few minutes, at least, let's pretend the crisis in my family hasn't gone from bad to worse."

Mark sipped his beer and went on studying her.

She found herself gazing back at him…at his soft dark hair, his gray eyes, the strong line of his jaw. Then she found her gaze lingering on his mouth, and she remembered the touch of his lips.

Maybe it wasn't such a good idea to try forgetting her family problems, after all. Robyn sipped her beer, and then she spoke quickly.

"Here's how it went. Today my mother told me that my father has cleaned out one of their savings accounts…Without informing her, he withdrew fifteen thousand dollars that was supposed to be for a dream vacation of theirs. She was understandably hurt. It wasn't the money—it was that he would tamper with their dream. Anyway, after she told me, we went to confront my father. She broke down and started crying. But then…she started yelling. That was the real shocker—my mother yelling at my father."

Mark didn't look surprised by this turn of events. He just wore what Robyn had come to term his "waiting" expression.

"So anyway," Robyn said. "My dad blew up, too. He said it wasn't any of my mother's business why he'd withdrawn the money. He said she just ought to trust him. And she said how could she trust him if he was going to do something behind her back. Since they were both getting pretty worked up, Uncle Greg and Aunt Janet couldn't help overhearing—we're staying at their house, after all. Aunt Janet tried to be a sort of mediator, but then she ended up getting ticked at my father, too. She said that lying was the most despicable thing in a marriage. And Uncle Greg didn't say a thing, just stood there looking terribly sad... Oh, the whole thing was a mess." Robyn paused for breath, and meanwhile Mark took another swallow of beer.

Robyn stood and walked restlessly to the other end of the living room. Her heels made a hollow clicking sound on the bare wooden floor. "I don't think I've left anything out," she said, "except that Aunt Janet finally left the room as if she couldn't take any more. I followed her... I asked her if her anger was covering up any other emotions toward my father. After all, they'd dated all those years ago. It wasn't an easy subject to bring up, but I had to do it. Janet gave me a stricken look and said old feelings for my father were positively the last thing on her mind. Maybe she was thinking about Uncle Greg and the problems they'd had in their own marriage...I don't know, but I guess that covers just about everything. The Myers family, coming apart at the seams."

Mark set down his beer. "The part about your father cleaning out the savings account, let's start there."

"No, Mark. Let's not start anywhere. I already

told you what happened. Now I just want…I just want to forget about everything. My father's affair, and all the rest of it.''

He stood and came over next to her. ''I'm sorry,'' he said simply.

She gazed at him, and she could think of one way to forget. If Mark would take her into his arms, and kiss her again…

How could she be so weak? But she felt as if she'd been standing in the cold for a very long while, and now the promise of warmth was before her. She felt herself tremble, and Mark hadn't even touched her.

He frowned a little, seeming to question why he'd come to her. But then he lifted his hand and ran a finger ever so lightly across her lips. It was only the briefest touch, but the warmth went through her. And yes…she needed more. She was the one who took a step closer to Mark. And she was the one who lifted her face to his.

The kiss was inevitable. Mark framed her face with both his hands, brought her closer to him. At first his lips were gentle upon hers, but then gradually became more insistent. She responded eagerly, taking what she needed from him, what she craved. But the hunger would not be satiated. Instead, it flared into a deeper longing.

At last some shred of will allowed her to pull

away. "No, Mark," she said, her voice shaking. "We can't do this." She moved away, seeking to put a safe distance between them. It didn't help; she felt as if he had left an imprint of warmth upon her, and she wanted more. "I know what's happening," she said. "It's like I told you...when I'm feeling vulnerable, I tend to lean on a man. It's a bad habit, and I have to stop giving in to it."

Mark ran a hand through his hair. "So this is about your ex-husbands," he said.

"In a way, yes." It seemed important to explain. "My first ex and I had been divorced for a couple of years when he showed up in my life again. He convinced me how much things had changed...how much *he* had changed. So we began seeing each other again...even discussed the possibility of re-marrying. Only he ended up walking out on me all over again. That was a low point for me—very low. I was ashamed and embarrassed, and that made me way too susceptible. So that was when I met husband number two and married *him.* Let me give you a clue, Mark. Never marry anybody when you're on the rebound. Chances are, you'll soon have another ex."

"Are you on the rebound now?" he asked.

She began pacing again. "I don't know—yes. Maybe. Divorce number two became final only five months ago. And now, all this with my family...it would be so easy for me to lean on someone, my judgment is probably off." She knew what she ought to do now. She ought to walk out the door and go back to her uncle and aunt's house, no matter how much she wished to stay right here.

"Robyn, I've already told you I'm not looking for anything more in my own life. I'm no good at relationships."

Something in his tone put her on the defensive. "Believe me, Mark, I'm not envisioning a relationship, either."

"What do you want, Robyn?" His voice was very matter-of-fact. She looked at him, and somehow knew she had to be completely honest.

"Dammit, Mark…I want you to hold me. I want you to kiss me…and yes, I want you to make love to me. But I know it's wrong. I know we have absolutely no foundation for such a thing. We've met under all the wrong circumstances. And when I look at you, Mark…all I have are questions. Am I just trying to escape everything that's happened in my family? Am I just looking for solace, for comfort? And how can any of that be a good reason for making love?"

"I don't know," Mark said. "I don't have the answers. And hell, I've got enough problems without adding anything else to the mix. But that doesn't change one thing, Robyn. I want you, too."

They stood apart, just looking at each other. Robyn prayed for the strength to turn from him and walk out the door before it was too late. Her prayer went unanswered. Instead, she stayed put, yearning for the forbidden, watching how his eyes darkened, how his muscles tensed.

This time she didn't know which one of them made the first move. It didn't really matter, because she was once again lost in his embrace. All her arguments had done no good. All she had was this...the longing that flamed inside her, refusing to be denied. She clung to Mark, twining her fingers in his hair, molding her body to his. His arms tightened around her.

The kiss might have lasted one minute, or several. Robyn lost track of everything but the heat of Mark's touch. And when at last they separated for breath, there was a question deep in his eyes. They gazed at each other for what seemed a very long while. The question remained in Mark's eyes, and at last Robyn gave the slightest of nods.

She held on to him as he guided her down a short hallway and across the threshold of another room. A glimmer of lamplight from the living room managed to reach here, enough for her to see that the main piece of furniture was a bed, its sheets and blanket rumpled. Mark paused inside the doorway, as if to give Robyn time to change her mind. Maybe he didn't realize that she'd gone way past the point where she could change anything about this night. And so it was she who took the final few steps to the bed.

Together they sank down upon the mattress. Robyn brought her arms around Mark. He bent his head and kissed her throat. Then he caressed her, his touch achingly warm even through the cloth of her blouse. Only little by little did each caress become more bold, more provocative…Mark's hand ever so light upon her hip, her own traveling over his chest…

Finally she tugged at the buttons of his shirt. The need inside her was flaring, demanding yet more fulfillment, carrying her yet further away. Impatient, she managed to get his shirt open. She moved her fingers over the swirl of hair that tapered down toward his jeans. Now he fumbled with her buttons, and with the zipper of her skirt. She arched upward, trying to help him. He gave the slightest of groans. When he spoke, his voice was husky with desire, but she detected something else as well.

"Just my leg," he said. "The damn wound. Forget about it…" Together they slipped off her skirt, her blouse. Mark pushed up the flimsy material of her camisole and trailed his lips over her skin. She gasped with the response that went through her body, the heat gathering deep inside her.

"Mark…"

With both hands, he eased her panties away from her hips. She arched toward him again. She'd never known this sense of abandon with anyone, never known such recklessness. He lifted himself over her, and she heard the acceleration in his breath. "Robyn…" His voice was strained. "I probably have something around here somewhere…a condom…"

She didn't want to stop, but at least some remnant of common sense made her still her hands on his chest. He got up and went to search through a bureau drawer…then another one. At last he found a condom, and came back to her. A moment or two later he began to caress her again.

He took it slowly this time, every touch a deliberate prolonging of sensation. Robyn followed where he led, a captive to each kiss, each gentle tantalizing stroke. It seemed that every part of her came alive to Mark, in ways she'd never known before. He awoke in her feelings almost too keen, too intense to bear. And so Robyn opened herself to Mark, drew him into her with a yearning that made her gasp again. Now it was she who incited with her touch, her own caresses urging him to hold nothing back.

They moved in a rhythm they found together. At last Robyn cried out with the exquisite intensity that burst inside her. And then Mark added his own sounds to hers, as if the sensations between them could not possibly be contained in silence.

The silence descended afterward, when Robyn slowly came back to reality and realized what an absurd position she was in. She lay tangled with Mark, her undies dangling from one foot, her camisole twisted up around her neck. It was the position of someone who had thoroughly indulged in every aspect of sex. Oh, yes, she'd managed to escape her problems—but only for a few impetuous moments. Now everything came rushing back, this time accompanied by dismay.

She separated herself from Mark, but she could feel the dampness of his sweat on her skin—another imprint he had left upon her. "Oh, no," she said.

He lifted onto one elbow. "I was thinking more along the lines of 'oh, yes.'"

She yanked her camisole back in place, pulled up her panties. Then she began searching almost frantically for her skirt and blouse. "This was a mistake, Mark. We both knew it from the start."

"I didn't know this was going to happen tonight," he said, his voice completely serious now. "I didn't count on it, didn't plan it. But, Robyn...even if it was a mistake, we can't pretend it didn't happen."

"I wish I could pretend," she said, her voice low. "I wish I could pretend so many things hadn't happened.'' At last she found her skirt and slipped it on. After that she fumbled with the buttons of her blouse, and finally she was fully clothed.

Yet she still felt more vulnerable than when she had lain in Mark Stewart's arms.

ONLY A SHORT WHILE LATER, Mark drove Robyn toward her aunt and uncle's house. It was well past midnight, and he'd turned on the heater in the Land Cruiser. Warm air drifted over her. It should have felt cozy and comforting. Instead, all Robyn knew was that aching emptiness, and a coldness inside her that no amount of heat could dissipate.

The silence between her and Mark now seemed impossible to bridge, yet she found herself speaking.

''You don't have any pictures of your daughters,'' she said.

''What…?'' His voice sounded distracted, remote.

''In your apartment,'' she said. ''You don't have any photographs of your daughters around.'' She didn't know why she was talking about this. Any minute, Mark would probably tell her to mind her own business.

After a pause, though, he spoke. ''I have pictures of Debra and Kerry when they were kids. But after the divorce, I wasn't exactly around for family-photo shoots.'' He paused again. ''Maybe I'd display the pictures I do have, except that...''

He didn't need to finish the sentence. Robyn could fill in the blanks pretty well herself. Looking at photos every day would only remind him of the distance between himself and his daughters. And so his apartment remained bare, carefully lacking signs of a personal life. Why had she brought up the subject? Maybe as a reminder that neither she nor Mark was any good at a personal life.

They traveled in silence for another moment or two, and now their route took them past the Myers's family shops. Robyn glanced out her window. All the stores were darkened, locked down for the night...save one. Light blazed from the gift shop, and the front door was wide open. Nothing could have been more abnormal at this time of night.

''Stop!'' Robyn exclaimed. Her instruction wasn't necessary, for Mark had already wheeled into the parking lot. The Land Cruiser came to a jolting halt.

''Stay here,'' Mark said as he opened his door. Robyn didn't need to look to know that he'd reached inside his coat and pulled out his gun. But she ignored his command, sliding out her own side of the vehicle and staying right beside him as he moved toward the gift shop. She stared at that gaping door, remembering the night when someone had intruded on the art gallery. There had been a door open that time, too, flung wide to the darkness.

Robyn found herself latching on to Mark's coat. He reached the threshold of the shop, as always moving with skillful alertness. Robyn reassured herself that nothing too awful could happen with Mark always at the ready—

"Don't look," he said suddenly, turning to block her view. But it was already too late. Robyn had stepped over the threshold, and she saw Emily...gorgeous young Emily Parkman, lying on the floor in a pool of blood. Lovely Emily, her eyes open wide in an expression almost of bemusement. Emily, who almost seemed to have been smiling when she died.

DETECTIVE TOM GRANGER was thorough at his job. Right now he was making certain that every detail was attended to—photographs taken, fingerprints lifted, notes and reports carefully written. And Tom did all this while wearing a well turned-out suit in pinstripes. As far as Mark was concerned, there was something unnatural about a jacket and a pair of pants that matched to perfection. Mark himself had never been partial to suits.

Tom strolled across the gift shop toward Mark, adeptly skirting Emily Parkman's body as he came. "Well, Stewart," he said. "Imagine you being the closest thing we've got to a witness. All we know so far is that she was shot at medium range, .38-caliber most likely.'' Then, as if to assert his authority, he added, ''We'll get it nailed down. Meanwhile, you can get on with your vacation.''

Mark and Tom had known each other long enough for Tom to be perfectly aware just how much the term ''vacation'' would rankle. A little good-natured ribbing, perhaps, but Mark wasn't in the mood for it tonight. He gazed toward the far corner of the shop, where another detective was speaking to Robyn. Even from here, Mark could tell that she was making a considerable effort not to look in the direction of Emily's body. Robyn's face was chalky white, and she'd pressed a hand to her stomach, but she seemed determined to do what had to be done. She'd already called her family to break the news of Emily's death, she'd cooperated with the police, and now she was answering more questions. Through it all she'd moved with a dazed, haunted expression on her face, as if hoping this was a nightmare, and any minute now she'd wake up.

Two instincts warred in Mark. He wanted to stay with Tom and learn whatever else he could about Emily Parkman's death. At the same time, he wanted nothing more than to shield Robyn from learning more.

The second impulse won out. Without bothering

to chitchat further, Mark strode across the shop. "Leslie," he said to the detective who'd been speaking with Robyn. "You have enough for now, don't you?"

"Sure, Mark." Leslie gave him a sympathetic look.

Mark shepherded Robyn from the store. She didn't protest, and certainly she didn't look at Emily's body. Out in the parking lot they ducked under the yellow crime-scene tape and went past the police cars. Emily's death had set everything in motion— everyone was doing their job. It occurred to Mark that crime scenes were much like anthills, a whole colony of workers scurrying about: the patrol officers, the detectives, the technicians, the medical investigator, and of course, the inevitable journalists. Mark steered Robyn around a corner just as a TV-station van pulled into the lot.

He walked her down the street, his arm steadying her in the darkness. He could tell she was shaking, and she bent forward a little.

"If you need to be sick," he said, "it's okay."

"No," she whispered, and then her voice came stronger. "Who would do it, Mark? Who would do such a terrible thing? Poor Emily...oh, Lord, maybe I *will* be sick."

They stopped, Mark's arm still around Robyn as she pressed her hand to her stomach yet again.

"It's okay," he repeated. "I remember the first homicide I ever saw. It took me a long time to recover."

"The first..." Suddenly she sounded angry. "There have been plenty of times since, haven't there? This really *is* just a job to you, Mark! People dying, that's what keeps your paycheck coming down at the police department."

He knew that right now she had to be angry at someone, or something, and he was the closest thing available. He waited, still holding her, for her rage to dissipate. Finally, she swiveled toward him and buried her face against his chest.

"I'm sorry," she mumbled. "I know you have to do your job. But I can't stop thinking about Emily. I'll admit I didn't like her. She was always so full of herself—but..." Robyn pressed her face deeper against Mark.

"For what it's worth, I'm damn sorry, too," he said.

"Someone shot her," Robyn said. "It's almost a joke. My father wanted so badly for me to get a gun so I could protect myself, so I could protect Mom— and Emily is the one who ends up...dead. Only it's not a joke. It really happened. I would do anything to make it not happen, Mark! To go back and stop it. Stop whoever it was from lifting a gun and pulling the trigger..."

It took him a minute or two before he realized that Robyn was crying. The tears came silently, and he was only aware of them when they dampened his shirt. He wanted to go back, too, erase the fact of Emily Parkman's murder. He wanted to go back to the time, only a few hours ago, when Robyn had lain on his bed and he'd made love to her. Regret came over him. There would be no going back, not after everything that had happened tonight.

Already Robyn was withdrawing from his arms, making an effort to stand on her own. "How could I forget?" she asked. "Josh…poor Josh. I have to find him, Mark. I have to talk to him before your police friends get to him. I have to be the one to tell him about his sister."

CHAPTER TEN

IN THE END, it was easier than Mark had expected to find nine-year-old Joshua Parkman. Robyn's mother had been able to provide an address on Arvada Street. It was an upscale neighborhood, with houses sequestered behind adobe walls, fashionably weathered gates protecting the entrances. Mark had expected something a little more subdued for the Parkmans, and apparently so had Robyn.

"This can't be right," she said. "Are you sure we wrote down the address correctly?"

"This is it." Mark parked in front of a gate and climbed out to ring the bell—a real bell, a tarnished brass one hanging by a corded rope. It was the kind of rustic charm indulged in only if one had the money to afford the more modern conveniences. Yet, according to Robyn's mother, it had been a struggle for Emily Parkman to support both herself and her brother. This was not an address suggesting financial hardships of any kind.

Robyn came to stand beside Mark. "I'm not looking forward to this. Why can't I stop shaking?"

He pulled the bell cord again. Then he took off his coat and placed it around her shoulders. "The boy has to know sooner or later," he said. "It's best to do it now."

"I wish you weren't such a damn *expert* at all this." Her anger had returned.

"I'm sorry she was killed, Robyn."

She huddled inside his coat. The light from the street lamp picked out the reddish strands of her hair, but it also blanched her skin. "Maybe Josh isn't here," she murmured. "Maybe we really do have the wrong address."

Mark pulled the rope, and sent a clanging sound onto the night air once more. This time it sounded mournful. He put his arm around Robyn again. She didn't lean into him, as she had before, but she didn't move away, either.

At last a voice came from the other side of the gate. "Who's there?" It was a kid's voice, trying hard not to sound scared.

"Josh, are you alone in there? It's me. Robyn Myers. I need to talk to you."

"What are *you* doing here?" Now the voice sounded combative.

"Josh, let me in. It's about…it's about Emily."

No sound at all for a long moment. And then, slowly, the gate creaked open to reveal young Joshua Parkman in a pair of too-big pajamas. His hair was mussed, as if he'd just risen from sleep. He looked from Robyn to Mark and back again, and his expression grew more and more frightened.

"Where's Emily?" he asked in a small voice.

"Josh," Robyn said, "we'd better go inside."

The boy stared at her, but after another few moments he led the way over a brick pathway into the house. Once inside the living room, Robyn encouraged him to sit down on the sofa. Then she knelt in front of him.

"Josh," she said, her voice surprisingly steady, "there's no easy way to say this. Emily…your sister…I'm so very, very sorry, but she's—" The steadiness had lasted only briefly, after all. Robyn didn't seem able to go on.

Mark knelt in front of the boy, too. "Your sister has died, son," he said, knowing there was absolutely no way to soften the words.

Josh's first reaction was predictable. "No," he said. "Where's Emily? I want Emily."

"Josh, I'm sorry, but it's true," Robyn said. "Your sister was killed tonight."

Josh looked at her with a blank expression, apparently still refusing to believe. "Emily's not my sister," he said very calmly. "She's my mother, and I want to see her."

Robyn gave Mark a stunned glance, then turned back to Josh. "It can't be—"

The boy's lip began to tremble. "I want to see my mom. I want to see Emily!"

"Oh, Josh," Robyn whispered. "I'm so sorry…"

Josh's face seemed to crumple. He looked very young, and very frightened. Robyn sat down on the sofa beside him and gathered him into her arms.

"I'm sorry," she murmured over and over. "I'm so terribly sorry."

The boy sobbed. Robyn patted his back, and for a second or two he seemed about to collapse against her. But then, just as quickly, he straightened. He lifted his head, and even with tears trickling down his face he looked belligerent. "I think you should go away," he said. "Emily told me never to let anybody in when she wasn't here."

Robyn stayed where she was, and Mark sat down in a chair next to the sofa.

"Josh," he said. "I need your help, and I know you can be brave. Can you tell me why your mom pretended to be your sister?"

"This isn't the time," Robyn began to protest, but Mark gave her a warning glance.

The boy clenched his hands. "Emily says it's the best way. She says it's so people won't bug us. And she says someday we can move someplace different and then I can call her Mom and everything will be better."

"Josh," Mark said, "did your mom have any special friends I might talk to?"

"I don't know." Josh's face crumpled again, and Robyn gazed accusingly at Mark.

"That's more than enough for now," she said. "Please find something else to do, Mark. I want to talk to Josh on my own." Her voice held unmistakable command, but Mark was reluctant to leave. He knew that some things just couldn't wait, not when a murder investigation was involved. Mark studied the boy. Maybe Robyn was right. Josh wouldn't be able to tell him anything more right now.

Mark rose to his feet and went to one of the adjoining rooms. Now he would have a chance to go through the rest of the house, and see what more he might learn about the Parkmans. That was probably something Robyn wouldn't understand. Her natural reaction, no doubt, was to give death some respect, to back away from it. But Mark had learned all too well that you couldn't back away, not if you wanted to find the truth.

Twenty minutes later he'd made a thorough circuit of the house. All the furnishings appeared to be carefully chosen antiques: rosewood bureaus, a parquetry chest, an unwieldy oak dresser. The portraits on the walls were so dark and murky they could be nothing but originals. Mark found only two rooms that looked as if they'd been lived in recently. One, clearly, was Josh's, identifiable by the heap of clothes on the floor, the comic books stacked with unexpected neatness in a corner.

The other room was the one Emily had obviously inhabited. Here Mark saw an impressive array of clothes in the closet, while the dresser displayed an arrangement of perfumes, makeup, brush and comb. A few paperback novels were stacked on the nightstand. Otherwise there were no personal details.

When Mark made his way back into the living room, he saw that Josh was lying on his side on the brocade sofa, his knees drawn up almost to his chest. A blanket covered him, and his eyes were squeezed tightly shut as he pressed his cheek into a pillow. Right now he looked five years old. When Robyn saw Mark, she motioned him quickly into the adjoining room, closing the door.

"Josh is pretending to be asleep," she said in a low voice. "He can't deal with any more talk." Her tone hardened as she went on. "I can't believe the way you spoke to him. He's just a kid, and he'd barely heard about Emily, but you started asking him questions! What's wrong with you, Mark? Has being a policeman destroyed your emotions?"

"I wish I could make things less rough for the boy," he said. "But there are questions that needed asking. And I was the one to do it."

"He's scared, Mark. Scared and confused. He just heard about Emily being killed—"

"I feel for Josh, too, Robyn." Mark took a step toward her, but she held up her hand.

"No," she said. "Please don't. I just want to think. I want to try to find a way through all this."

She wouldn't take physical comfort from him, and he had nothing else to offer. "I'm trying to think it through myself," he said. "I'm trying to figure out why Emily Parkman pretended that her son was her kid brother."

"I ask myself what kind of mother would foist such a pretense on her own child," Robyn said. "But then I start thinking that she would have been only seventeen or so when he was born. A teenager…"

"I'd like to know how Emily could afford a place like this for herself and Josh," he said. "On the other hand, a little digging into property records could show that the place belongs to someone else. From the look of it, Emily only meant to stop here temporarily."

"From the look of *your* apartment, you only mean to stop there temporarily." Robyn placed both hands at her temples. "Oh, Lord," she said. "What's wrong with me? Listen, Mark, I know you're not the enemy. I really do know that…

She was trying too hard to convince herself, Mark

thought. Right now it seemed that the space between them was immeasurable. He experienced a sensation that it took him a moment to recognize. Loneliness.

"I have to take care of Josh," Robyn said almost to herself. "He doesn't have anyone else."

"Robyn, it's not your place," Mark told her. "Child Services will be involved immediately—"

"No," she said. "That's the last thing he needs right now." She swiveled back toward Mark, and suddenly she looked fierce. "I want to look after Josh. At least he knows me, I'm not a complete stranger to him."

He saw the intensity in her face, and suspected she needed the kid as much as the other way around. Why she felt that way, he didn't know, but he found himself responding to it.

"For what it's worth," he said, "I'll try to stall the authorities, or at least convince them that Josh is better off with you for now. But it's temporary, Robyn. Remember that."

She scarcely seemed to register the last part. "Thank you, Mark," she said formally. "Whatever efforts you can make…thank you."

The bell at the gate rang out, disturbing the stillness of the night air. Robyn gave an explosive sigh. "What now?" she asked.

"Three guesses," Mark said laconically.

"Your friends from the police?"

"That's my guess, anyway." Mark went back through the living room. Josh now sat up on the couch, his shoulders wrapped in the blanket. His eyes were red rimmed, but he managed to glare as Mark went by. A few seconds later, Mark opened the gate to Tom Granger.

"Somehow I'm not surprised to see you here, Stewart."

"Just lending a little help."

"You *are* on vacation, in case you'd forgotten." Tom stepped through the gate, straightened an imaginary wrinkle in his perfectly aligned suit jacket, and went in to take charge of the investigation.

A FEW HOURS LATER, Robyn finally got Josh settled in a spare room at her aunt and uncle's house. Closing the door behind her, she emerged to find her mother hovering nearby.

"You did the right thing bringing him here," Nina said. "When I think of poor Emily…" Tears leaked from her eyes. "Emily was the only family Josh had. I'm still trying to take in that she was his mother…but now he'll have to depend on us."

"Yes," Robyn said. "Yes, he will." If her own nerves felt stretched to the breaking point, the strain had to be even worse for Nina. "You should rest," Robyn told her. "Mark said he'd try to keep his police associates away for a little while, and you need to take advantage of any respite we get. It won't last long, I'm afraid."

"Rest...I wonder if I'll ever rest again," Nina said.

Just then Aunt Janet appeared in the hallway. She held one of her cats tightly against her—a three-legged calico she'd taken in as a stray. Lines of strain were etched into her face.

"Greg's gone," Aunt Janet said in a mechanical tone. "He's left me—just the way he did before. Only this time it's worse...so much worse."

Nina quickly went to put an arm around her. "Oh, Janet...I'm sorry—"

"He's gone," Janet repeated dully. The cat, as if sensing her despair, nestled closer to her.

Nina took charge. "Robyn, dear, will you go check on your father? And meanwhile, I think Janet is the one who needs some rest."

Robyn watched as her mother and aunt went down the hall. Janet was the younger of the two women, but she seemed to have aged in some irrevocable way. It showed in the slump of her shoulders, in the way she bowed her head. How could Uncle Greg have left now? How could he have just walked away...

The events of this dreadful day weighing on her even more than before, Robyn went down the stairs. She searched for her father, and came upon him in the den. Cal was sitting in front of Uncle Greg's desk, staring off into the distance. His arm was still in a cast, his face still bruised. He looked oddly stern.

"Dad, you have to go to bed," Robyn told him. "The doctor said you were to spend most of your time taking it easy."

Cal didn't answer. But the expression on his face became one of such grief that Robyn felt a cold dread seeping through her. She stepped toward him, then stopped.

"Dad," she whispered, "are you okay?"

He didn't answer for quite some time. But then, at last, he spoke. "She shouldn't have died," he said, his voice hollow.

Any number of thoughts raced through Robyn's mind. Her exhaustion had fled, leaving only this dreadful suspicion. "Dad," she said very quietly, "please tell me the truth. You've already admitted to having an affair. Now I need to know…was the affair with Emily?"

She prayed for his denial. She wanted him to say that he was sad only because Emily had been such a young woman, with so much of life still ahead of her. Instead, he merely stared at Robyn, and the grief in his expression told her everything.

"Dad, how could you? *Emily—*"

"You can't tell your mother," he said, his voice breaking. "Please don't tell her."

But Nina had already come down the stairs and walked into the room. "What is it Robyn can't tell me, Cal?" Her own voice was now without emotion. "I think I should hear. I think it's time I knew the truth."

THE REAL ESTATE OFFICE of Randall Garrett and Associates was a place where dreams came true, or so advertised the poster in the window. The poster displayed photographs of several "dream" houses for sale. Mark pushed open the door and went inside.

The place had expensive ivory carpeting, so pristine it made you uneasy—afraid you might be leaving a trail of dirty footprints behind you.

"May I help you?" The woman who spoke gave him a practiced smile. She wore white, too, not a smudge on her. She had blond hair and rather pale skin. Between the room and this woman, Mark could have done with some color right now. It occurred to him that ever since Emily Parkman's murder last night he hadn't been in the best of moods.

"I'd like to speak to Mr. Garrett," he said.

The blonde gave another smile. "I'm afraid Mr. Garrett is out at the moment. I'm his associate, however—Brianne Davie." She held out her hand and he shook it.

She had a limp grip. You'd think that in the real estate business, at least they'd teach you to give a decent handshake. Everything about this woman annoyed him, including her name. Brianne…sounded like some kind of fancy cheese.

"When will Mr. Garrett be back?" Mark asked, his rotten mood making him sound gruffer than he intended.

"I'm not certain. But I'm in charge of everything until he returns. I'm sure I can help you." She studied him carefully. "You rent, don't you?" she asked after a moment.

Mark gave her a dour glance that did nothing to discourage her.

"Let's see," she said, "what do you do for a living, Mr.…?"

"I'm with the police."

Even this didn't faze her. In fact, she actually seemed pleased. "Every neighborhood is happy to have a policeman in residence—did you know that? Now, I realize you don't make the most generous salary in the world, not in your line of work, but I have just the place for you." She thumbed expertly through the folders on her desk, extracted one and handed it to Mark. "Go ahead," she urged. "Take a look."

He opened the folder. It contained a sheet detailing a house out in the foothills—acreage, square footage, plumbing and wiring recently overhauled. There was also a photo attached, of a small place half buried among piñon scrub.

"What do you think?" asked Brianne. "It's a bit of a fixer-upper, but that puts it in your price range. Just think of that stunning mountain view."

"Let me get this straight," Mark said. "You're trying to sell me a house."

"Well, of course. Let me tell you, I have very good instincts, Mr...."

"Mark Stewart. Detective Mark Stewart."

"Oh, a detective—even better. Anyway, I have excellent instincts, Mr. Stewart. I know when a client and a house belong together. And you belong with *this* property." She tapped the folder with one of her glossy, colorless nails. Mark found himself studying the photo. The house had green trim and it was surrounded by a low exposed adobe wall.

"Two bedrooms," said Brianne, "with plenty of room to build an addition, if you'd like. That's a generous piece of land. All the potential for a family home, don't you think?"

In spite of himself, Mark found himself trying to put a family in the photo. But all he came up with was a vision of a slender, beautiful woman, her short reddish hair ruffling in the breeze....

He set the folder back on the desk. "I'm interested in a house at 239 Arvada," he said.

"Hmm…" Brianne flipped through the other folders on her desk. "Arvada…two-three-nine. Here it is. This is one of our most select properties." She gave a regretful shake of her head. "Mr. Stewart, it would be quite out of your price range."

"How long has the house been on the market?"

Brianne pursed her lips. "A place like that doesn't necessarily go quickly," she hedged. "One waits until just the right buyer comes along."

"Odd that you don't have a For Sale sign in front of the house," Mark said.

"Our more prestigious clients don't usually need to advertise that way. They would consider it…"

"Vulgar?" Mark supplied, deadpan.

"Yes, that's right. Vulgar."

"Maybe the reason has more to do with practicality," Mark said. "I understand the owners of 239 Arvada are in Europe right now. They wouldn't want to announce their absence with a sign out front. That would be an invitation to burglars and the like."

"Yes, well, that would make sense, wouldn't it?" she asked briskly. "Mr. Stewart, if you don't like the two-bedroom adobe, I can show you several other properties, but believe me, this is the place for you."

"Last night a woman was murdered. Turns out she was bunking at 239 Arvada."

At last it seemed he'd gotten through to Brianne. Her head came up, making her blond curls bounce. "Someone was *murdered*—in the house—"

"No," Mark said. "She was killed at her place of work, but she'd been living at the house on Arvada."

"That's impossible. Our clients trust us to take good care of their properties. We would *never* allow someone to live in one of the houses we're selling."

"Maybe Mr. Garrett knows something about it," Mark said. "You might want to tell him I've been around, and I'll check back to talk with him."

Brianne seemed about to get indignant, but then an almost pensive expression came over her. "The woman who died...who was she?"

"Someone unlucky," Mark said. "Someone very unlucky."

He went out the door, and almost collided with Detective Tom Granger. Tom was wearing another one of his suits. He gave the impression of someone who could actually afford a dream home.

"Stewart. Why am I still not surprised?"

"Brianne is the lady you'll be talking to in there. And watch out...she'll probably end up selling you a house."

Mark climbed into his Land Cruiser. He drove

homeward, intending to call Robyn as soon as he arrived. But when he pulled up at his apartment, he found that wouldn't be necessary. Robyn was sitting right on his front stoop, and close beside her huddled nine-year-old Josh Parkman.

CHAPTER ELEVEN

As MARK WENT UP the walk toward his apartment, Robyn stood and watched him approach.

"Hello, Mark," she said.

"Robyn," he answered.

Josh didn't say anything. The kid's eyes were red this morning, and Mark suspected he'd shed more than a few tears during the night. But his carefully set expression said he didn't want anyone to acknowledge the fact.

Mark's gaze strayed to Robyn. Her russet hair was tousled, her face free of makeup as if she'd had to dispense with the usual amenities. She looked beautiful.

"Mark, we have to talk." She turned to the boy. "Josh, would you mind waiting in the car for a few minutes? You can play the radio as loud as you like."

After a second or two of hesitation, Josh went to the sedan that no doubt belonged to Robyn's parents. He climbed inside, but he didn't seem too interested in the radio. He just sat there with all the windows rolled up, staring out the windshield.

"You've taken on a load of responsibility with him," Mark said.

Her features tensed. "He's just lost his mother. Someone has to look out for him."

"I wasn't accusing you, Robyn."

She gave a sigh. "We just need to talk, Mark. We have other problems. My uncle left the house sometime last night, walked out on my aunt Janet. It's not the first time, and maybe that's why she feels all the more betrayed. But that's not all. The affair my father had—turns out it was with Emily Parkman. I found out about it, and so did my mother." She paused to look at Mark. "Doesn't *anything* ever surprise you, Mark? You're listening as if all of this is just to be expected."

He rubbed a kink in his neck. "I'll admit I didn't connect your father with Emily."

"Apparently it started not long after she began working at the gift shop. My poor mother is devastated. She was the one who hired Emily, who took such an interest in her and Josh…and now to find out this. My father keeps telling my mother how sorry he is. Over and over he says it. He swears that he ended things with Emily several weeks ago. As if that's supposed to make it better. You know the funny thing about all this? I start to hate Emily for everything she did, and then I just can't anymore. In spite of everything, I know how she felt about Josh. She loved him, Mark. No matter what kind of crazy life she was giving him, she really loved him. And he loved her, too." Robyn's voice caught.

Until now, Mark had resisted the urge to touch her. He couldn't prevent it anymore, though. He took her hand in both of his.

"I've found out something, too," he said. "I did a little digging, and learned that the house on Arvada Street is for sale. The owners are away, and they've left everything in charge of a real estate firm. I spoke to one of the agents, and asked her why someone was living in the house. She didn't seem to know anything about it, but there's another guy I have to track down. A Randall Garrett— maybe he's the one who gave Emily a key and allowed her to settle in."

"None of it makes any sense," Robyn said. "I mean, who *was* Emily…really?"

"Josh might know the answer better than anyone else."

Robyn stiffened and pulled her hand away. "I'm sure Josh has some things to tell us, but I won't have you interrogating him, Mark. Not right now, anyway. He needs time—he hasn't even accepted yet that Emily is dead."

"Robyn…I understand how you feel. By the way,

I was able to pull a few strings, and you can look after Josh for now. I can't promise for how long, though—''

"It's enough," she said. "Thank you, Mark." After that, she didn't speak for a moment. "We have another problem to resolve," she said. "I'd intended for Josh to stay with my family, but that's out of the question now. My father has just admitted to having an affair with Josh's mother. I know Mom would never blame Josh for any of that, but right now she simply has too much to cope with. She doesn't need anything more. And Josh has enough to cope with, too. Having all of us stay in the same house is asking too much of everyone."

"I think you're right about that," Mark said.

"Everything in my family is falling apart," she said unhappily. "No one even knows where my uncle is right now. He didn't say where he was going…he just left. And Aunt Janet's not talking much, either. She still won't say what the trouble is between her and Uncle Greg. I'm beginning to wonder if I really know anything about my family."

Mark knew she wouldn't like what he had to say next. But he had no choice. "Robyn, we have to consider the fact that your uncle left the very night of Emily's murder. I've never been one to believe in coincidence."

"What are you implying—that my *uncle* had

something to do with it? Uncle Greg, whose only idea of violence is recounting the Battle of Water-loo? He's a military-history buff, not a criminal.''

"You said yourself that maybe you didn't know everything about your family."

She gave him a stony look. "I know my uncle Greg. He's kind and good-hearted. So just forget your damn implications."

Mark didn't pursue the subject. Josh wasn't the only one who needed time to come to terms with what had happened. Robyn had every right to be angry. But, when she continued, she spoke with an almost unnatural calm.

"It's my parents I'm trying to understand. I love both of them, no matter what's happened, but...I just don't understand them right now. Neither one of them will own up to the truth. Dad still refuses to say a word about who attacked him, or why he took all that money out of the bank. And when the police came to question my parents, Mom refused to say a word about Dad having the affair. She covered for him as usual. I wish she had more pride."

"I get the feeling you didn't tell Detective Granger about the affair, either," Mark said. "Isn't that covering up?"

"I don't know...maybe," she said irritably. "But I'm telling *you* about it, and you're the police, too."

"Fair enough." He studied Robyn, and saw the

emotions struggling across her face. Sorrow, disappointment, disillusionment…her father had let her down, big time. Yet, even now, she still loved her dad. She'd said as much, and Mark could also see it in her eyes. Mark couldn't help thinking about his own two daughters, wondering if they could ever feel that way about *him*…love him no matter what his past mistakes.

Robyn took a deep breath, as if preparing herself for what else she had to say. "Aunt Janet has begged my parents to stay on with her. Especially now, with Uncle Greg gone, she says she needs the company. Mom and Dad, in spite of *their* problems, have agreed. But that still leaves Josh. I've thought and thought about it, and I've realized I have to be the one who looks out for him. I keep seeing the look on his face, when we told him that Emily was dead…and I want to watch out for him. So that means Josh and I stick together. And *that* means we need someplace to stay, someplace safe…I thought about a hotel, but that doesn't feel secure enough. There's another option, of course. Josh and I could stay at my parents' house."

Mark shook his head. "The two of you, inside that big place…I don't like it. With that inner courtyard, the security's not very good. If someone wanted to, they could climb over the roof and get inside."

Robyn held her arms against her body. "You think that's a possibility?"

"Anything's a possibility at this point. We can't discount your father's warning about you being in danger. Your parents could be in danger, too, if the attacker decides to return. But I don't think anyone could get past all the media that's going to be camped on the doorstep. The murder of a beautiful young woman who worked for a well-to-do Santa Fe family…journalists are going to be falling over themselves around your aunt and uncle's house."

Robyn buried her face in her hands. "I don't believe it," she murmured. "Which is worse, my family being hounded by unknown assailants, or by the media… I really want to protect Josh from all this." After a moment she lifted her head. "Mark, I hate suggesting this, I really do. But Josh and I could stay at my parents' house if, well, if you stayed there, too. We'd be safe for sure then."

Mark rubbed that crick in his neck. "Thanks for the vote of confidence…I guess. But you know the press is bound to find out you have the murdered woman's son with you. No doubt they'd love to get some photos of him plastered in the newspapers— and on the six o'clock news. Are you ready for that?"

"God, no. I couldn't possibly subject Josh to that." Robyn was starting to look a little desperate.

"What on earth am I going to do? When it comes right down to it, what I really need is a safe house—I'm sure you'd call it that, anyway."

"A safe house?" he repeated.

"Okay, so maybe I've seen a few too many movies. But that's what the police always call it. And you being a detective and all, you should know about these things."

An idea began to form in Mark's mind. He considered it for a moment, then reached a decision.

"Look, there's another solution. You can stay with me."

Impatiently she pushed a stray wisp of hair away from her cheek. "Mark, I told you—it's not going to happen again. We've already made our big mistake."

"I'm not asking you to go to bed with me," he said. "I'm offering you a place to stay where the press won't hound you, and I'm relatively certain you won't be murdered in the dead of night."

Robyn looked at him as if she thought he had lost his mind. But then she looked over at Josh, waiting in the car.

ONLY A FEW HOURS LATER, Robyn had moved into Mark's apartment.

She couldn't believe it had happened. But Mark had pointed out the logic of the plan: there was really no place else for her and Josh to go. They couldn't stay with her family—not when her father had admitted to an affair with Josh's mother. They couldn't stay at her parents' house—not with reporters waiting to pounce. And Mark was not about to let them stay anywhere alone—not when there was the possibility of them being in danger. His apartment, Mark insisted, although cramped, was the only choice. And, because Mark was not officially connected to the case, the media wouldn't connect Robyn and Josh to him. Robyn couldn't argue with his reasoning.

At this moment, though, she felt overwhelmed by the twenty-four hours she had just gone through. All she really wanted was to bury her head in her hands and generally go to pieces.

She couldn't afford the luxury, though. Right after Mark had installed her and Josh in the apartment, he'd received a phone call from the police department. He hadn't told her what it was about, but his face had turned grim and he'd left. He'd told her to lock the door while he was gone, and had instructed her not to let anyone in. The lock was a solid one, and she really did feel safe here.

She and Josh sat at Mark's dining-room table. It was a card table, if she wanted to be precise about it. But she wasn't about to complain. Now she put a sheet of paper in front of Josh, along with his math book.

"Just try," she said. "The first problem, that's all."

"I'm no good at math," he said.

"Something tells me that you probably are."

"I don't have to do this," he said. "You're not my tutor anymore."

"I'm your friend, Josh."

His lip trembled, and his eyes filled with tears.

"I don't want any friends. I want Emily."

"I know," Robyn said gently. Again she felt a sense of unreality wash over her. She'd never experienced quite this sense of responsibility toward another person. Her parents had always had each other, and her husbands—well, they hadn't needed her. But Josh was totally dependent on her. She knew there were alternatives. Foster care...but she hated the thought of that. She couldn't picture Josh in a foster home, where people might not have the time or the interest to coax him out of that withdrawn manner of his. So far she hadn't been able to coax him herself.

"Try just one problem," she said now. "Just one."

"Why?"

"Because...because it's what Emily would have

wanted. Just like she would have wanted me to go on tutoring you.''

Josh blinked hard against his tears. He picked up a pencil, and for a moment Robyn thought he'd actually try to work the problem. But then he squeezed his eyes shut, and the tears spilled over. He swiped at his face with his sleeve.

Robyn glanced away. ''It's okay to show you care about her,'' she murmured.

''What do *you* know?'' His voice wavered.

''Only that something terrible happened to somebody you loved. Josh…do you know anything about anyone wanting to hurt your mother?'' She'd spoken these thoughts without meaning to. After all, she'd berated Mark for interrogating Josh.

Something about her words seemed to dry Josh's tears. Now he just looked frightened, and Robyn felt a chill deep inside—a sensation that was becoming all too familiar.

''Josh,'' she said. ''What is it? What *do* you know?''

''Nothing.''

''Why are you scared?''

''I'm not!''

''Yes, you are,'' she insisted. ''Do you know someone who wanted to hurt your mom?''

''Nobody. She had lots of friends.''

"Who are these friends?" she asked. "You mean, like girlfriends?"

"No, not girls, no," he said. "I don't know any of them. I don't know who they are."

"But you just told me—"

"They were scary sometimes. I didn't want to know them." Josh stood up so quickly he almost sent the card table toppling over.

"Josh, honey…"

He rubbed his eyes. "I'm tired," he said. "Ever since last night…I've been tired."

Robyn believed she understood. "Come with me," she said. "Mark's put out his sleeping bag for you."

She offered him her hand, and without any argument he took it. They walked together to the second bedroom at the end of the hall. Robyn settled Josh inside the sleeping bag and watched as his eyelids drifted downward. In an amazingly short time, he was sound asleep, his face still streaked with tears. Robyn wanted to smooth away the tears, but it was best to let him rest. He looked so innocent and unguarded. Robyn watched him a moment longer. Then, as noiselessly as possible, she swung the door shut and went back to the living room.

Here she confronted the futon with no mattress and no cushions. Sleeping arrangements for all of them would be haphazard at best. Mark had offered her his bedroom, and he would rough it in the living room. Certainly she and Mark wouldn't share a bed again—she'd made that perfectly clear. And Mark hadn't argued. Just because they would be living together for a few days, that was no reason for the two of them to start getting cozy.

She moaned, and sank into the armchair. Being in such proximity to Mark, after what they'd done last night…making love so impetuously…

"I don't believe it," Robyn said out loud, but the words did nothing to reassure her. She had lain in Mark's arms last night, beseeching him to blot out all the pain. In the end, she had only stirred more bewildering emotions. She had been able to blot out nothing, after all. The problems had remained, harsher ones had followed. Now Emily was dead, and a little boy was motherless.

A knock came at the front door, jarring Robyn. Mark had said not to let anyone in. Maybe if she simply sat where she was, whoever it was would go away. But after a moment or two the knock came again, and Robyn couldn't take the suspense. She tiptoed to the door and peered through the peephole. She saw a young woman standing outside, someone who looked perfectly harmless. After a second or two, Robyn unlocked the door and swung it open.

The young woman studied her. "I'm looking for Mark Stewart," she said.

"He's not here right now, but he should be back soon."

The young woman appeared to think this over. "I see. Well, I'm his daughter."

Robyn felt new interest. "Are you Kerry?"

"Debra."

"Hello, Debra. Look…why don't you come in and wait for him?"

Debra hesitated, but then she stepped over the threshold. "Why not, I suppose. And you are…?"

"I'm Robyn. There's an armchair over there—best seat in the house." Her halfhearted attempt at humor got no response, but Debra sat down in the armchair. Robyn took one of the folding chairs by the card table.

"Your father talks about you a lot," she said.

"Does he really? How interesting." Debra seemed extremely self-possessed. She settled back in the armchair and crossed her legs. Robyn looked for resemblances, and found them. Debra had the same dark hair as Mark, the same well-defined features. Her eyes, however, were brown rather than gray. She wore linen trousers that were fashionably creased, and a tailored blouse. No-nonsense but stylish was the aura she projected.

"Would you like something to drink?" Robyn asked. "There should be a few beers left…I just haven't had the time to make it to the grocery store yet. If beer won't do, I'm afraid we're talking ordinary tap water.''

"I suppose water would be fine," Debra said without enthusiasm.

Robyn poured two glasses from the tap, and found some ice cubes in the freezer. She handed one glass to Debra, and sipped from the other as she sat down again. She was still searching for a topic of conversation as Mark's daughter gave her the once-over.

"I didn't know my father was…living with anyone.''

Robyn choked on her water.

"Are you all right?" Debra asked, looking surprised.

"I'm—I'm fine." Robyn set down her glass on the card table. "I'm not living with Mark," she said, perhaps too firmly. "I'm just staying here a few days.''

"I see." Debra sounded noncommittal, even disinterested, but Robyn felt the need to clarify.

"Your father and I are just…friends.''

"I see," Debra repeated.

Robyn wondered what would happen if she told the truth: I did sleep with your father last night…

"I needed a place for a little while," she said instead, "and he offered his help.''

"How nice," Debra said.

"He's been a big help, all along.''

"That's my father for you," Debra remarked. "Always a big help."

Robyn didn't miss the sarcasm in the young woman's voice. This encounter wasn't going very well. She and Debra sat across from each other in uncomfortable silence. At least, it was uncomfortable for Robyn. Debra proceeded to open the briefcase she'd brought with her, and take out a pad of paper. She scanned some notes on the top page. With some relief, Robyn heard a key turning in the lock. Mark stepped into the room. He looked at Robyn then at his daughter.

"Debra...hello," he said.

"Don't act so overjoyed, Father."

"I am glad to see you—"

"Right," she said. "Don't look so perturbed. Robyn here has already informed me that the two of you are just friends. Not that I'd have any reason to object." Her tone implied that she'd long ago lost any interest in his personal life. "And now—no offense, Robyn—I'd like to talk to my father alone, if you don't mind."

Of course Robyn didn't mind. It didn't take an empath to feel the tension between father and daughter. The two of them really did need to talk.

CHAPTER TWELVE

MARK AND DEBRA ended up taking a stroll together down the block.

"I got the feeling neither you nor Kerry wanted to see me for a long while," Mark said. "It was a surprise to see you here today. Not that I'm not grateful—"

"Father, don't overdo it."

It seemed to Mark she was the one overdoing it, with the "Father" bit. Couldn't one of his daughters, just once, let an inadvertent "Dad" slip out? They walked on for a short time. Mark's neighborhood was composed of apartments, but they were mostly duplexes like his own, making the effort to look like a house without actually being one. There were willows and cottonwoods, neat flower beds and trim squares of grass. It was the kind of neighborhood where you lived if you were either too young or too old to buy a house. Mark didn't feel he belonged in either category. He didn't know where he belonged, that was the problem.

"Speaking of Kerry," Debra said. "I thought we agreed you should keep a low profile."

"You and your mother were the ones who agreed about that," Mark pointed out.

"Your going to see her at school didn't help. It only upset her more."

Upsetting his daughters seemed to be his new specialty.

After a tense pause, Debra spoke again. "This woman in your apartment...she's more than just someone you're helping out, isn't she?" Debra asked. "I mean, you like her, don't you?"

The question threw him a little, and he answered carefully. "Yes, I like her. But I'm not so sure she feels the same about me." No sense in lying to his own daughter. "Any advice?"

Debra only shrugged. "I'm no expert in these matters."

"How's Trevor?" Mark asked.

"In case you're truly interested, I told him our relationship either had to advance or—or it was over. He's thinking about it." She sounded upset, the way she invariably did when talking about this guy.

"Honey, if he's not good enough for you—"

"Anything you say can't help. So, please, don't say it." She made an obvious effort to regain her composure, and then she went on. "I didn't come to see you so we could talk about your romantic foibles, or mine. I'm here on the job.''

''I see.'' He didn't see at all.

''The paper sent me up here to cover the story on Emily Parkman.''

''You're not a news reporter,'' he said. ''I have a fairly good memory, and I recall you telling me that you handled local sports.''

''I do. But I'm trying to move up. If I do a good job on this story, my editor is sure to see I can handle weightier pieces.'' She drew her eyebrows together. ''Okay, I'm not really up here officially,'' she admitted. ''A friend of mine on the news staff gave me an early lead on this story, all right? There's something about it that intrigues me. I called around, talked to a few of your friends at the police department, and found out you're involved in the case...not so officially, yourself. So I came up from Albuquerque as soon as I could.'' Debra had a look he'd seen often enough, the one she wore when she didn't expect him to understand. It was a mixture of defensiveness and vulnerability, anger and resentment.

''Look, Debra,'' he said. ''I admire your initiative. I've always been proud of the way you go after things, and I want you to succeed in your career. But we're talking about the murder of a girl only a few years older than you. I hate to see you get involved with that in any way.''

''Father…I'm not a kid anymore. I'm perfectly capable of handling this. And don't give me that line about protecting me from the seedier aspects of life. I know, I know…you wanted to keep your job separate from your family, and that's why you were never there for us. I've heard it all before. But this is a good opportunity for me. I need your help.''

''What are you expecting from me?'' he asked. ''You want to use me as a source, that it?''

''I don't see why it should bother you,'' she said. ''This is a good chance for me. I've been trying to get a lead on the right kind of story, something that will get me noticed.''

He didn't care for the irony. He'd been doing his best to protect Robyn and Josh from the media, and now it turned out his own daughter was the media, pursuing the murder. And there was Debra's career to consider. He felt torn between helping his daughter, keeping her away from the sordidness and protecting Robyn and Josh. He stopped walking, and waited until Debra faced him.

''Debbie, maybe I've said it too many times before, but it's the truth. If there's one thing I don't regret, it's that I've always kept you from the ugliness of my job. I don't intend to change that now.''

''Are you saying you won't help me?'' she asked.

"I'm your father. And no father wants his daughter anywhere near a murder case."

She gave him a contemptuous glance. "Save the parental concern. What's the real reason? It's just too much trouble to help me, is that it?"

"Debbie, you know better than that." He stopped, seeing the hard, unyielding expression on his daughter's face. He wondered if anything he said would convince her. She wanted to believe only the worst about him.

Now she observed him speculatively. "This seems to be something personal to you. Is that woman in your apartment involved in the case? None of the information I've gathered so far mentions anyone named Robyn, but still...I'm just getting started."

"Debbie," he said again, "I don't want you involved in this case."

She shook her head. "You know, I thought you'd actually be pleased about this. I thought I'd finally found a way for the two of us to relate on some level. Instead, you're waving me aside as always."

"It's not like that," he said. "I want to protect you."

"Oh, sure, Father, you always want to protect somebody. It looks as though your Robyn is the latest protectee. At least you have good taste—she's very pretty."

"Debbie, there are lots of stories besides this murder case, other stories that will advance your career."

"So you won't help me," she repeated.

"No...not on this."

She gave him another disparaging look. "Maybe I shouldn't be so surprised. Maybe I should have expected as much. Foolish me, thinking my father was going to help me. Well, maybe you won't help me, but I *will* get this story. You can count on that...Father." She turned and strode away from him, swinging her briefcase as she went.

WHEN MARK GOT BACK to his apartment, Debra had already driven off, and Josh Parkman was still sleeping.

"I think he'll be out for a while," Robyn said. "It's the only defense he has." She sat down in the armchair, then stood up again. She didn't seem very much at home. "How did things go with Debra?" she asked.

"Not so well," he said. "She's decided she wants to handle the crime beat for her newspaper. According to her, the Emily Parkman case would be the perfect place to start. I tend to disagree...she tends to think I'm stifling her. Seems like nothing I do makes me popular with my kids."

Robyn gave him a sympathetic look, but she

couldn't seem to remain still. She walked restlessly around the living room. Her circuit of the small area brought her next to him. But she quickened her pace and went past, as if determined not to linger in his vicinity. She ended up next to the empty futon frame.

"We need to talk about Josh," she said. "He told me that Emily had a lot of men friends. But he also said these men could be scary. I get the impression that Emily was up to a lot more than having an affair with my father."

"Maybe Josh can tell us more."

"We have go to easy with him," Robyn said. "His well-being has to come before anything else."

"Solving Emily's murder—I'd say that has a lot to do with Josh's well-being."

"The case always comes first for you, doesn't it, Mark?" she said tightly.

It seemed that today he wasn't popular with anyone. "This isn't officially my case. That's why my boss hauled me in today. He wanted to remind me that I was on leave and that I wasn't supposed to interfere with Tom Granger's investigation." Something of an understatement. The captain had used language a bit more forceful. Then, at the end, he'd instructed Mark "to get a life" outside the police force.

"They're shutting you out, is that it?" Robyn asked.

Mark grimaced. "That's the general idea. My boss thinks I still haven't had enough of a break from my so-called 'latest incident.'"

"Let's get this straight," she said, observing him closely. "You're prone to…incidents? What exactly does that mean?"

It wasn't something he liked to talk about, but Robyn's gaze remained intent. He sat down and eased out his sore leg. "This bullet wound," he said. "I got it chasing down a murder suspect on my own. I should have waited for my partner…somehow I didn't get around to it. Let's just say it was considered a breach of the rules."

"Why didn't you let your partner in on it?" she asked.

"In my judgment, he wasn't up to the job." Mark gave another grimace. "He's a rookie, a guy who made detective before he was ready. It was for his own good, he could have got himself killed."

"So instead *you* got a gunshot wound to the leg."

"A minor injury," Mark said.

Robyn nodded slowly. "I'm really starting to understand you. A loner in your personal life, a loner on the job. Apparently, there've been other 'incidents' in the past. You don't want anyone too close, do you?"

He shifted his leg. "I already told you. My partner was too green."

"Why not just admit it? You're happiest on your own."

"That's not true." Even as he spoke the words, Mark knew Robyn was right. "Well," he conceded. "Maybe in the past, but...things could change. I could change. Who knows?"

Robyn shrugged. "People don't change, Mark. Not all that much, anyway. Maybe it's better just to accept yourself the way you are."

"Enough about me," Mark responded, not liking to hear that he was a loner. It sounded so...so *lonely*. One thing, however, couldn't change. The case did have to come first.

"Robyn," he said. "You realize, of course, that I had to tell Tom Granger about your father and Emily."

"I suppose I did expect it, deep down. Certainly I can't excuse my parents—or even myself, for not being up front with him. One of us should have told Detective Granger about the affair. But somehow I thought...I hoped *you'd* realize my father couldn't have had anything to do with Emily's death."

"Maybe Tom Granger and I don't always see eye to eye, but he's a good detective. He'll keep an open mind."

Now her expression went cold. "Dammit, Mark.

In spite of the despicable things my father's done, he would never physically harm another person."

"I'm not the one he has to convince," Mark said.

Robyn stared at him as if he were a stranger. "If nothing else, you have to acknowledge that my father had just gotten out of the hospital. He was hardly in the condition to hurt someone."

"Unfortunately, it doesn't take that much strength to pull a trigger," Mark said in a quiet voice. "But, like I say, Robyn...it's not me your father has to convince. Tom Granger will be questioning him again right away."

"Good for you, Mark. Maybe you're not such a loner, after all. Your loyalty to the police department comes through." Her back held very straight, she turned and walked down the hall. Then she went into his bedroom and shut the door.

This seemed to be the pattern of his life...women walking away from him. Always walking away.

YOUNG JOSH WOKE UP shortly after noon. He said he wasn't hungry, but Mark knew a good meal was in order. He piled Robyn and Josh into the Land Cruiser and took them out for a pancake lunch— sure to be a kid-pleaser. Josh did end up eating most of his blueberry pancakes, even though he didn't have much to say. After they left the restaurant, he sat in the back seat, looking small and miserable and defiant.

Returning to the apartment would be too oppressive right now, Mark decided. He followed his second impulse of the day, and started driving out toward the foothills.

Robyn gave him a reluctant glance. "Mind telling me where we're going?"

"It's a surprise."

She let it go at that, and gazed out the windshield again. He didn't think she would forgive him anytime soon for his part in her family's troubles. Briefly he wondered how it would have been if he'd met her under better circumstances. Would it have been any different for them? Or were there simply too many other barriers? These were useless questions, he knew, and he hadn't invited them. They just kept popping up in his head at inconvenient times.

It didn't take long to reach their destination. Soon Mark pulled up in front of the house Brianne Davie had recommended to him. He climbed out of the Land Cruiser, waiting for Robyn and Josh to do the same.

The house definitely had something special. It was stuccoed a gentle earth brown that blended into the landscape, but the light green trim on the window and door frames added just the right distinction.

The view was something else again: hills of piñon and juniper rising to meet the crystalline blue of the sky, and then, high above, the peaks of the Sangre de Cristos, still capped with snow. Imagine that, a real estate agent who hadn't overstated her case. Mark was glad that he'd taken note of the address in that folder she'd handed him.

"What do you think?" he asked Robyn.

"It's very nice," she said, but her tone was reserved. She glanced at Josh, who had wandered over by a woodpile next to the adobe wall. "Mark and I are going to have a look around," she told the boy. "We won't be going far. Can you stay right here, Josh?"

He nodded as if it didn't matter to him either way. Then he plunked himself down on the grass and leaned against the wall. He looked very much alone, sitting there, and Robyn gave him a worried frown. But apparently, what she had to say to Mark couldn't wait. She went around the side of the yard and waited for him to follow her.

"Okay, Mark," she said. "So what's this all about?"

He didn't answer her for a moment, just stepped up to a window and cupped his hands so he could see inside. Wooden floors...always a plus. High ceilings, another plus. And a rounded kiva fireplace in the corner, complete with brick hearth. During the winter months, that woodpile would get some use.

"Needs repainting, that's all," he said.

Robyn came to peer in the window, too. "Mark…what *is* this about?"

"I guess you got me thinking today. You mentioned needing a safe house. When I was a kid, if you'd asked me what a safe house was, I would've told you I lived in one with my parents and my brother and sister. A place with people I could count on. Yeah…that would've been my definition. Too bad you grow up and forget about things like that."

Robyn gave him a considering look. "What are you getting at?"

"Hell, I'm thinking about buying a house. Maybe even this house."

"I didn't know you were in the market," Robyn said.

"Neither did I," he said. "But Ms. Brianne Davie of Randall Garrett and Associates seems to think this is the place for me. According to her, she has instincts about this type of thing." He perused the house some more. It had a side porch with torn screens. If you wanted to, you could do away with the screens entirely, just let the open air come in. Or better yet, put in some glass walls, make it into a regular sunroom.

He turned back to Robyn. "What do you think of it?" he asked again.

"What I think of it isn't important right now. What we have to think about is a little boy who's just been through a terrible trauma—"

"I have been thinking about it," Mark said. "Everything that's happened has given me a hell of a lot to think about. Emily's death, the son she left behind... Robyn, you've accused me of losing my emotions because I'm a policeman. In the past, maybe that's been true. Maybe I've seen too much violence, been hardened to it. But last night, I saw a little boy's world crumble around him. I saw how it affected you, and that got to me, too. Life is short. And maybe it shouldn't be wasted."

She gazed at the house, then at him. Her expression was wary. "I don't know where you're going with this, Mark."

"Sometimes I look around," he said, trying to explain, "and all I see is the shrapnel of my life. Fragments...no real home, two daughters who don't want anything to do with me. I guess you could say I'd like a second chance. An opportunity to start over and do things right this time. There's definitely an appeal to that."

"And buying a house, that's a second chance?"

"Maybe it's a beginning," he said. "Maybe it's a statement of faith in the future. Or maybe it's only an unrealistic grab at the past. You start wanting the kind of home you had as a kid, but you don't know how to get it. I'm no authority on any of this.''

Robyn's expression grew wistful. ''I guess I know what you're talking about. Maybe that's what I've been chasing in my own life. I've wanted a home that would make me as happy and secure as the one I had growing up. Only, I haven't known how to get it. I ended up marrying two men who were wrong for me, and now…now the family that gave me so much security is falling to pieces…''

''So tell me, Robyn. Do I buy the house?''

She drew her eyebrows together. ''I certainly can't advise you. I don't know why you'd want my opinion, anyway—''

''We made love last night,'' he said. ''If I've asked a woman to share my bed, then I don't mind asking for her opinion.''

The flush came back, full force. ''Mark, we've already discussed this—''

''Right, right. It was a mistake. But I still want to know what you think of the house.''

She hesitated for a minute or two, obviously unwilling to give in. But then, at last, she turned to examine the place. Mark studied it again, too. It was definitely on the small side, but here and there a detail caught his attention: an unexpected but pleasing scallop design in the outline of a wall, the sturdy wooden columns of the porch, the rough-hewn tiles of the patio. The architectural design was a hodge-podge of styles...a little bit Pueblo, a little bit Territorial, maybe even a touch of Spanish revival. Somehow it all added up to a relaxed, welcoming atmosphere. This was a house that invited you to come in and make yourself comfortable. He wondered if Robyn saw the place the same way he did. But when she turned back to him, her expression was neutral.

"It's nice," she said. "Real nice. But you haven't even checked the inside yet. If I were you, Mark, I'd do a little comparison shopping before I made up my mind."

"You're right, of course," he said. "And I would check the interior if I had the key." He surveyed their surroundings once more, then said, "With this amount of acreage, you could build an addition. Problem is, it's the kind of place for a family. Enough room for a swing set, even an outdoor pool. Kids would love it."

"Thinking of expanding, are you?" Robyn asked lightly.

"Family...I'm no good at families," he muttered. "It's a shame to waste a place like this, that's all I'm saying." He told himself that Brianne Davie would be able to find someone else to buy the house—someone with a couple of children, no doubt.

But it didn't matter what he told himself. He kept picturing himself in this house. And somehow he kept picturing Robyn here, too. She and the house seemed to fit together in ways he couldn't explain. Definitely no logic to it. If he was considering a permanent home at all, she shouldn't be anywhere in the picture.

Mark uttered a curse under his breath.

"Shop around, Mark," she told him gently. "It's always best."

That was the problem. He didn't know what was best for himself anymore. He just knew that he was becoming all too aware of how alone he was, and he didn't like it.

CHAPTER THIRTEEN

LATE THAT NIGHT, Mark decided that sleeping in an armchair was an art he had yet to master. Stretched or scrunched, no matter what he tried, he couldn't get comfortable. And wearing jeans and a T-shirt didn't help, either. Mark was accustomed to sleeping in the raw, but with a full house that wasn't advisable. Finally he gave up even trying to doze, and clicked on the lamp beside him. The empty futon frame across the room seemed to mock him. He'd bought the thing at a furniture sale, intending to outfit it with the appropriate cushions so it could serve as a couch. Somehow he'd never gotten around to it. He'd never needed any extra furniture until now.

He glanced into the shadows down the hall, where two closed doors announced that he was not alone in his apartment. After a desultory supper of canned chili, Josh had gone to bed early. Somewhat later, Robyn and Mark had each retired for the night. There'd been a tension between them that had not vanished just because Robyn had gone into the other room and shut the door. Mark could feel it now, compounded of so many elements he hardly knew how to tell them apart. Lingering desire, discontentment, wishes unfulfilled...

Mark reached down and took his notepad and pen from the floor. Work had always been his best distraction in the past; why should it be any different now? Maybe he wasn't supposed to have anything to do with the Emily Parkman case, but following rules wasn't his forte. He read some of the notes he'd already made on the case: "Randall Garrett?? Robyn's father?? Boyfriends?" Right now nothing was falling into place. Wasn't it still a little too much of a coincidence that Robyn's uncle Greg had walked out on his wife the night of Emily's murder? For that matter, what about the attack on Robyn's father, and the way he'd wiped out that savings account? What was the connection with Emily Parkman? Again, Mark didn't believe in coincidence. Exactly what had gone on in Emily's private life? She'd had an affair with Robyn's father, but who were the other men in her life?

He heard one of the bedroom doors open, and a few seconds later Robyn appeared from the hall. She was wearing a plaid robe belted firmly at the waist, but he still saw a hint of lace at her neckline. Lace nightgown? Lord...he almost jotted that on his notepad.

"Can't sleep?" he asked.

"No." She came farther into the room, and he swore he could hear the rustle of lace. He had to keep his imagination from getting away from him.

"First night in a strange apartment," he said. "Bound to make you a little restless."

She wandered to the window, tilted the blind, peered into the darkness. "I can't believe it was only last night. I feel like I've aged a million years since then."

Maybe she felt bad, but she didn't look bad. Plaid became her. She ran a hand through her hair, and now it was more rumpled than he'd yet seen it. Rumpled became her, too.

"They always say hot milk is supposed to make you sleep," he said. "Maybe you should give some a try."

"I'm surprised you even have milk," she said. The implication remained unspoken: the bare fridge represented his solitary life all too well.

They gazed at each other in the soft lamplight, and Mark found himself looking for more hints of lace.

Robyn glanced away. "I came out here because I figured you probably couldn't sleep, either. I'm a guest in your place. Why don't you take the bed, and I'll take a turn in the chair."

"I'm doing okay."

"You're not sleeping," she said.

"Not much chance of that," he acknowledged.

She sighed, and sat down in one of the folding chairs. "I guess you haven't entertained a lot of overnight guests here."

"The relationships I've had since my divorce...they haven't gone much of anywhere. Actually they haven't even qualified as relationships."

"You and I are the opposite, then," Robyn said. "My relationships always go too far. I end up walking down the aisle, when I ought to be walking out the door."

"So...the ex-husbands," Mark said. "Who were these guys, anyway?"

She cinched the belt of her robe a little tighter. "I'm sure you don't really want to know."

"I asked, didn't I?"

Mark eased back in the armchair, stretching out his leg as best he could. He suspected Robyn had mentioned her trips down the aisle for a reason. He wasn't getting any sleep...wasn't going anywhere.

"Look," Robyn said, "when I met my first husband, it's like I told you—I was at college, away from home for the first time. I was trying to be independent and didn't really know how to go about it. I floundered quite a lot. Anthony had known forever that he wanted to be a lawyer, and his focus drew me. I found out too late he didn't have room for much of anything besides his career."

"And you're telling me this because I remind you of Anthony."

"Not in the least. I know you're totally centered on your own career, but I think you genuinely want to help people—even if your methods are a bit brusque at times. Anthony was a lot more concerned about carving out a position for himself."

Mark thought he'd been complimented…almost. He wouldn't let it go to his head, though.

"No, you and Anthony aren't alike at all," Robyn said. "What's similar in both situations is *me*. Like I told you, I get in a vulnerable position, and I just start depending too much on a man."

In spite of himself, Mark couldn't help being curious. "What about husband number two?" he asked.

"I was vulnerable all over again," she said, sounding as if she was accusing herself. "And I already told you the first part of *this* story. I was on the rebound after a bad attempt to get back together with my first husband…enter Brad. He seemed totally the opposite of Anthony. Had a decent job but wasn't obsessed by it. Relaxed, easygoing. So easygoing, in fact, that after a while he didn't see the need to put any work into our relationship. Exit Brad, some five months ago."

Mark heard the way she tried to be flippant. But he also detected the hurt underneath. "Robyn—"

"You're starting to sound sympathetic, Mark. Don't—it's a bad idea." She stood. "I'd give anything to break the old patterns. Why can't I figure it out?"

"I don't see that my helping you solve a family crisis is the old pattern—being too dependent on a man. I'm a detective, Robyn. It's my job, it's my life. Why can't you just accept my help and stop feeling bad about it?" He stood, too, and came over to her. She seemed about to step away, but then she held her ground.

"It's one thing to accept your help, Mark, but the rest of it..." Her voice trailed off. They gazed at each other again. And then, gently, he cupped her face. It was the most natural gesture...the thing that, underneath all their conversation, he'd been wanting to do.

"Mark," she whispered. It sounded like an entreaty. Did she want him to stop, or go on? She placed her hand on his chest, as if to stay him. But after a moment she ran her fingers over his T-shirt. Another moment later, she gave a sigh, a sound almost of defeat. And then she offered her lips to his...

And just then, a frightened yell came from down the hall.

IT WAS ONLY a matter of seconds before Mark and Robyn made it down the hall and into Josh's room.

Instinctively, Mark kept Robyn behind him as he flipped on the light switch. Josh was sitting straight up in the sleeping bag, breathing in gulps and looking around wildly. He was sweating, his hair damp at the forehead.

Robyn went to kneel beside him, putting her arm around his shoulders. "What is it, Josh?"

The kid stared at her, as if trying to focus on her features. And Mark saw the recognition pass across the boy's face, the moment of remembering that his mother was dead. It showed in the sudden, terrible emptiness in Josh's eyes, the tightening of his hands on the sleeping bag.

Robyn, it seemed, understood the look in Josh's eyes, too. She gathered the little boy close, holding him as if *she* longed to be his mother. "It's okay," she murmured. "It's okay. You had a nightmare, didn't you?"

Josh nodded.

"Might do you good to talk about it," Mark said.

"Somebody was chasing me," Josh mumbled.

Mark and Robyn exchanged glances. "Can you remember anything else?" Robyn asked gently. "Do you know who was chasing you in the dream?"

"No," Josh said, "but I was scared. And I started yelling, and nobody could hear."

"We heard you," Mark said in a reassuring tone. "You've got a good set of lungs on you."

"What did I say?" Josh asked cautiously.

"It was sort of a cross between a screech and a yowl," Mark informed him.

"Really?" For a minute the kid looked impressed. But then he burrowed against Robyn as if to shut out all the bad memories. She held him, and rocked him a little.

"It's okay," she repeated. "Everything's going to be okay." She and Mark exchanged glances again across Josh's tawny mop of hair. It was anybody's guess what the boy had gone through in his nine short years of life. And now, his mother was dead, and he was waking up with nightmares... No little boy should have to go through this. More than ever, Mark wished he could change things for Josh.

"Guess what," Robyn said. "I know the perfect cure for bad dreams. We're all going to have a cup of hot milk." She gave Mark another meaningful glance.

"Yeah, right," he said. "I'll get it started. Hot milk." It was a poor substitute, when he'd been on the verge of kissing Robyn. He felt a stirring of disappointment. He wondered if Robyn would give him another chance to kiss her.

Somehow he doubted it.

THE MORNING after Josh's nightmare, Robyn stepped inside her aunt and uncle's house. The place looked as homey as ever—the sofa covered with a bright, India-print spread, Aunt Janet's collection of music boxes displayed in a cabinet, one or two antiques in the process of refinishing, an elderly mutt named Pete taking a nap on the hall rug, one of the cats perched on the windowsill. With such pleasant surroundings, this should have been a place of contentment...of family togetherness. But Robyn could sense all the troubles beneath the facade.

She found her mother in the kitchen. Nina sat at the table with her hands wrapped tightly around a mug of coffee. Her brooding expression changed when she looked up and saw Robyn. As if slipping on a mask, she gave a determined tilt to her chin. "Hello, dear. It's good to see you. Pour yourself a cup of coffee and sit with me."

Mark was waiting for Robyn outside; she'd only come here to check briefly on her parents. But when she saw the sadness in her mother's expression—the sadness Nina couldn't quite hide—Robyn knew she couldn't leave right away. She poured a cup for herself and sat opposite her mother. "How are you holding up?" she asked. "I know the police have been back to question you."

"Yes...about your father's affair with Emily."

Nina spoke in a distant tone. "It's in the open now, isn't it?"

"Mom, I'm so sorry," Robyn said. "I didn't want to tell Mark about it, but I had to. And of course, he had to tell Detective Granger."

"Yes, dear, of course. You only did what was right." Nina gave a mirthless smile. "It had to come out, didn't it? Your husband sleeps with a woman who ends up murdered, and of course it must come out." Now her voice was brittle, sounding as if any moment it would break into a thousand pieces.

Robyn pulled her chair closer and put her arm around Nina for a moment. "Oh, Mom, I really am sorry—"

"Detective Granger insists there has to be a connection between the murder, and the attack on your father, and the money he took out of our savings…yes, I did tell the detective about the money. I'm not covering up anything anymore. It's your father who still refuses to tell everything."

"This must be really hard on you, Mom," Robyn said inadequately.

Nina made a visible effort to gain control of her emotions. "What about you?" she asked. "Where's poor Josh?"

"Mark has a friend with two boys of his own, and he volunteered to take Josh for the day. They're going to a birthday party at Hannett Park. It seemed like a good distraction, and we'll pick him up there later this afternoon.'' Robyn had worried about letting Josh out of her sight, but Mark had assured her that Benjamin, his friend from the shooting range, was a most competent person who would make sure nothing untoward happened to the boy. Benjamin himself had once been a member of the police force, after all. Besides, Mark had argued, Josh desperately needed to get out and have a little healthful activity. Robyn hadn't been able to disagree there.

''What a very decent man your Mark is,'' Nina said. ''I can't tell you how glad I am that you found him, particularly at a time like this.''

''Mother, he *is* decent, but it's not what you think.'' No, it wasn't what Nina thought, despite the fact that last night Robyn had almost gone into Mark's arms again.

She became aware that her mother had spoken, and was looking at her expectantly, waiting for an answer.

''I'm sorry, Mom,'' she said guiltily. ''I was…thinking about something else.''

''I was just telling you how concerned I am for Janet.''

''No word yet from Uncle Greg?'' Robyn asked.

''Not a thing. And yet…I have a suspicion Janet knows where he is. Maybe she's just too proud to go to him. What could be so bad that they can't work it out?''

"Mom, is that how you feel about Dad?" Robyn asked.

Nina's expression immediately grew shuttered. "That's between me and your father."

It seemed a lifetime habit couldn't be easily broken. Nina was still protecting Cal. And, meanwhile, secrets were still being guarded.

"Mom," Robyn said urgently. "Emily is dead. Before someone else gets hurt, make Dad tell the truth—all of it."

Nina set down her coffee cup with a thump. "Stop, Robyn. Detective Granger has questioned us over and over. I've told him as much as I know. What else can *I* do?"

Robyn's heart ached for her mother. But it was impossible to turn back now. "Mom, I know it's hard," she said, "but there's no such thing as just a little truth. Dad has to tell us everything—or there may be no way to save this family."

"He won't confide in the police. He says even less to me."

Robyn felt a growing futility. She couldn't give up, though—not yet. Leaving her mother in the kitchen, she went upstairs to the room where her father lay propped against pillows. He was awake, but he scarcely acknowledged Robyn's presence. A look of despair seemed permanently etched into his features. The truth was hidden somewhere underneath.

Robyn stepped through the door. "Hello, Dad," she said.

His gaze flickered toward her. "Robyn."

"How are you feeling?"

"I wish I'd been the one to die," he said, his voice low. "Do you know that? I wish I'd been the one." He delivered these words flatly, without varnish, and that made them all the more chilling.

Robyn pulled a chair up beside the bed. "Dad, how can you say that? You won't solve anything by just giving up. Start telling us what happened. It's the only way!"

At first she thought her pleas would have the usual effect: her father would turn his face from her, and he would refuse to say another word. But this time, after a long moment, he began to speak.

"I know what you're wondering the most, Robyn. Why did I do it? Why did I hurt your mother that way? I've been thinking about it. Trying to find excuses, perhaps. Trying to rationalize, for certain. The best I can come up with is that I'm getting old, Robyn. And what's worse, I was starting to feel old. I don't know, perhaps it was the way Emily looked at me, at least in the beginning. As if she could see beneath all the years. As if my life was just beginning again, not nearing the end."

"But, Dad," Robyn couldn't help protesting, "you're not old. And the way I remember it, that's exactly how Mom looked at you. As if you were always in your prime.''

''Your mother has been a wonderful wife. She's not to blame in any of this. The fault's in me, Robyn.''

''Did you…love Emily?'' she asked, her voice soft now, even though it was a question she dreaded asking.

''Do you love someone who makes you feel like you're powerful and strong again?'' he asked. ''I don't know…maybe, for a little while. Maybe I just loved the vision of myself that Emily gave to me. But it was never real. Emily only pretended to admire me. She was setting me up.''

''What do you mean, Dad? How could she do that—''

''Emily blackmailed me,'' Cal said. ''She was smart—she took her time about it. A pretty young woman, turning the head of a man who's scared of getting old… She waited until she had me right where she wanted me, and then she said she'd tell Nina all about the affair unless I paid up.''

The chill inside Robyn spread to every inch of her body. ''Dad, do you realize what you're saying?'' she whispered.

''I know how it sounds,'' he said. ''It sounds like I had a motive to kill Emily.'' Her father went on, his voice oddly expressionless. ''Maybe nothing matters anymore. Emily's gone, and your mother knows about the affair anyway. I don't think she can ever forgive me.''

''She hasn't left. She's standing by you—''

''No, Robyn. In her heart she's already left. What else can I expect? I never wanted her to know…I never wanted to hurt her. But I have hurt her terribly, and that's changed everything.'' He sounded as if he had traveled to some dark place from which he could never emerge. ''I don't think I can talk anymore,'' he said. ''It doesn't do any good to talk about it.''

Maybe he was right, Robyn thought. For sure she didn't want to know more. She didn't think she could bear it.

She left him, went out into the hall, and almost bumped into Janet. Her aunt seemed to have been listening at the door. She made no move to disguise the fact. She simply stood there, holding another of her cats, this one a striped kitten that she'd saved from the pound.

''What's to become of us all,'' she murmured.

''I don't know, Aunt Janet. I just don't know.'' With that, Robyn went down the stairs and outside to Mark.

CHAPTER FOURTEEN

ROBYN CLIMBED into the Land Cruiser.

"You seem shook up," Mark said. "You want to tell me about it?"

"Oh, well, let's see," she said. "I just found out that Emily was blackmailing my dad, threatening to tell my mother about the affair. And maybe, just maybe, that gave him a strong motive to kill Emily—" She couldn't go on. Mark put his arm around her and pulled her next to him.

"Hey," he said, "we'll get to the bottom of this."

"You sound the way I did last night, trying to comfort Josh after his nightmare. But when will *this* nightmare ever end, Mark?"

He didn't answer. He just went on holding her. She wished he would hold her forever…all the more reason she had to pull away.

He studied her for a minute or two, but then started the engine.

"I made a call while you were in there," he said,

nodding toward his cell phone. "You and I have an appointment."

"Where?" she asked.

"You'll find out soon enough." Mark swung out into the street. He drove quickly, and Robyn had to hold on to her seat as he took a corner. He held the wheel comfortably and easily, but he seemed intent on his own thoughts. Maybe he was considering the new information about Robyn's father. By now Robyn knew how much Mark liked working out the details of a case.

Lost in her own disturbing thoughts, only gradually did Robyn realize that Mark was heading for the foothills.

"We're not going back there, are we...to the house?"

"I didn't think you'd mind so much," he said. "We have a chance to see the inside of the place, and maybe accomplish something else at the same time."

"Mark, don't be mysterious. Goodness knows, I've had enough of that. What are you talking about?"

"Let's just see how it works out," was his only reply. In a short while, they were traveling along the narrow, winding road that led to the house. There were other dwellings scattered about, but the sense of spaciousness did not diminish. And there, tucked among the gentle hills, was the snug, topaz brown house with the green trim. With great reluctance, Robyn had to admit how much she liked the place. Everywhere she glanced, she saw the possibilities. That uneven patch of ground over there could be smoothed out and made into a generous vegetable garden. The woodpile could be restocked for long winter evenings by the fire. The adobe wall all around the perimeter should be left just as it was, although one could plant some lady's slippers and buttercups along the border...

Robyn curled her fingers in her palms, disgusted with herself for thinking this way. *She* wasn't in the market for a house. When Mark brought the Land Cruiser to a halt, she climbed out and followed him as he went along the path toward the front door. She tried not to notice the patterned bricks of the path, tried not to imagine how some wicker lawn furniture would look arranged on the porch.

"I've seen enough," she said.

"What bothers you so much, Robyn?" he asked. "It's just a house."

It wasn't just any house. It was a place that all too clearly asked to be a home.

"I would really like to get out of here," she muttered. But, even as she spoke, a large expensive sedan came down the road and pulled up behind the Land Cruiser. A man emerged from it and came toward Mark and Robyn. In his mid-thirties or so, he had a tall, heavy-shouldered build. He was handsome, if you liked the blue-eyed, sandy-haired type with features almost too perfect. First he shook Robyn's hand, then Mark's.

"Mr. and Mrs. Stewart," he said. "Glad to meet you."

"We're not married," Robyn said, perhaps too hastily.

"My mistake," the man said, not seeming particularly concerned about it. "I'm Randall Garrett, and I'll be happy to show you around. Nice house, isn't it?"

It took Robyn a second to register the man's name. Randall Garrett...the real estate agent who might or might not know something about Emily Parkman. She glanced quickly at Mark, but his expression warned her to let him take the lead. Garrett opened the door to the house and ushered her inside. Mark came in after.

The three of them walked through the place. Garrett pointed out all the details Robyn could see quite plainly for herself.

"Cove ceilings...these oak floors are in very good shape...this is what I like to call a breakfast nook..."

Inside, the house was just as appealing as outside. The master bedroom had an inviting window seat, the closets had double doors that gave a feel of airiness, and the breakfast nook more than made up for the lack of a formal dining room. Mark, while keeping an impassive expression, also seemed to note these features.

"If the two of you would like to stroll around by yourselves," said Garrett, "be my guests. I'll wait outside." The man was being admirably low-key…attempting no hard sell. But Robyn did not want to be alone in this house with Mark. She couldn't afford to allow the place—or Mark—to seduce her.

"No, thank you," she said. "I've seen enough." She went outside, and the two men had no choice but to follow her.

"I have several other properties I can show you," said Garrett. "If this one isn't exactly right, you shouldn't be discouraged."

"Mark and I aren't up for any more today," Robyn said firmly. "*Are* we, Mark?"

He retained that maddening, impassive look. "This is the house we're interested in," he said. "No need to go further. Besides, it's time to talk about Emily Parkman." He mentioned the name in an offhand manner, almost like an afterthought, but it had a distinct effect on Randall Garrett. The man froze for a second or two, losing the urbane good-naturedness he'd exhibited until now.

And then, just as quickly, he seemed to relax again. He gave Mark an inquiring glance. "Just who are you, Mr. Stewart?"

"I'm a police detective."

"I've already spoken with the police...but you must be the one Brianne was telling me about. The guy who showed up at the office yesterday, before the other police. She didn't appreciate being questioned twice. It's just too bad she didn't mention your name to me, or I might have made the connection." A certain look went across his face. *Displeasure* might be the best word to describe it. Robyn only knew that it was a disagreeable look, one that made her glad she wasn't alone with the man.

"I did talk to Brianne," Mark said, "and now I'd like to talk to you. Let's make it simple. Just tell me what you know about Emily Parkman."

"I've given the police all the information they need." Garrett's low-key manner had completely vanished. He didn't appear quite so handsome anymore, not with that unpleasant look on his face. Robyn glanced at Mark. She saw how calm he remained, yet she sensed a readiness in him, too.

"Let's try it this way," Mark said. "I'll do the talking, and you tell me if I'm right. It seems you let Emily stay at the house on Arvada Street. Who knows, maybe that's a habit of yours, letting pretty young women camp out in the homes you're trying to sell. Your clients probably wouldn't be too happy to find out about it, but maybe that's beside the point.''

''Emily needed a place to stay, and I helped her out. But I wonder just who the hell you are, and why the hell you think I have to put up with any of this—''

''Did you kill Emily Parkman, Mr. Garrett?'' Robyn found herself asking. He turned toward her with a menacing attitude, but at the same time Mark stepped protectively in front of her.

''Take it easy, Garrett,'' he said. ''Just answer the question.''

Randall Garrett stood very still for a moment. But then, unexpectedly, his muscles seemed to go lax. Robyn could almost see the fight drain out of him.

''Kill her…why would I do that?'' he said, an emptiness in his voice. ''How could I have possibly killed her? I loved her with all I had.''

LATER THAT MORNING, it seemed impossible to Robyn that all the ordinary details of life could continue. Surely events such as Emily's death and her father's betrayal should make everything else come to a standstill. It didn't happen that way, of course. Ordinary, mundane details did have to go on. Things like shopping, for instance. She and Mark had certain basic purchases to make. After a few hours, they returned to Mark's apartment not only with three bags of groceries, but with a full-size futon mattress. Most of the groceries went in the fridge, and then Mark and Robyn lugged the mattress into his living room. Mark pulled out the futon frame until it lay flat, and the mattress landed on top.

"At least you won't have to try sleeping in an armchair tonight," Robyn said.

"No, I suppose not." Mark gazed at the futon regretfully, and Robyn wondered what he was thinking. Maybe his thoughts matched her own. Sleeping arrangements all made…no possibility now that they would need to share a bed tonight…

She pushed the inappropriate thought away. "Well, what's next?" she asked briskly. "There must be something more we can learn about Randall Garrett. I think it's possible he's the one who killed Emily."

"Robyn, I have a feeling that right now you'd accuse anyone, rather than believe your father did it."

"Can you blame me?" she asked. "Maybe a lot of my illusions about my father have been destroyed, but at least let me hang on to this one. Let me believe in his innocence." If only she was convinced of it herself! But Cal could have been desperate enough to have done it. Despite his injuries, he could have made his way to the gift shop that night. And he could have pulled a trigger...

Mark came over to her. "You need a break from all this," he said. "For at least a little while, you need to forget about everything that's happened."

She curled her fingers inside her palms. "I can't forget, and I know you can't, either. The case is what matters, isn't it?"

"Yes," he said. But he looked at her as if he felt sorry for her. She didn't want his pity.

"There must be something else we can do," she said. "Something else we can check out. Other leads to follow."

Mark simply went on looking at her, and she saw another expression cross his face. Her heartbeat accelerated.

"Will you please *stop* making love to me with your eyes," she said. "We can't make another mistake. We just can't."

"Was it really such a mistake?"

"You know it was—"

"Perhaps," he said gravely. "Or perhaps we should just admit how we feel." His eyes held hers. Robyn could no longer deny the need for honesty. Recent events had torn from her the possibility of pretense.

"Dammit, Mark, of course I want to...be with you. Of course I want to forget everything else—"

"Is that the only reason?" As always, he could be relentless.

She took a deep breath. She wanted to stop this conversation right now. But honesty was a peculiar thing. Once you started, it wasn't easy to stop.

"I'll tell you what frightens me, Mark. Maybe it's not only escape I want. Maybe I'm starting to feel something else for you. And that's very dangerous. Because this is the wrong time, the wrong circumstances to start feeling anything. How can I possibly sort it out…"

He took a step closer to her. And then he kissed her.

A long moment later, they broke apart. Robyn felt her pulse beating in her throat. "It's not fair," she whispered. "You know what you're doing to me…"

"I know what you're doing to me," he answered.

Robyn was the one who reached out, running her fingers over his shirt. She felt the steady rise and fall of his breath. Then he covered her hand with his, cupping it next to his chest. An ache of longing grew inside her, and she could not deny it. She leaned close to Mark, brought her lips to his again.

They kissed for another long moment, and then another. Robyn told herself to stop before it was too late. But she knew, deep down, that it was already too late. Somehow, in all the pain and uncertainty that surrounded her, she had come to this…she had come to Mark. There would be no turning back. It was as if she had surrendered to the currents of desire, letting them sweep her where they would.

Together they sank onto the futon mattress. And now the caresses began. Mark's hands, tracing the line of her back...her fingers twining in his hair... She gave a sigh as his hand strayed across her hip, found its way beneath her blouse. Mark had worked his magic on her, and every touch bound her deeper under this spell of desire. The early-afternoon sunshine spilled over them, slanting its way in through the blinds, and this alone stirred a faint remnant of modesty inside her.

"Mark...the windows..."

"I'll take care of it," he murmured. He left her to draw the curtains over the blinds. And then he disappeared down the hall, going into his bedroom. She heard a bureau drawer open then close. When he appeared again, he brought a condom packet with him. Everything about his demeanor was matter-of-fact. The sun still managed to find its way around the edges of the windows, giving more than enough light for Mark and Robyn to see each other.

He took off his baseball jacket and tossed it over a chair back. Next came the shoulder holster—that ended up draped on a chair back, too. His shirt, his shoes and socks...

"Mark," Robyn said.

He came to lie beside her again. As he unbuttoned her blouse, and then helped her tug her camisole over her head, his gaze lingered upon her.

"You're beautiful," he said. When she tried to go into his arms again, he stopped her. "No," he murmured. "Let me look at you. Why do you turn your head away? You're not ashamed, are you? Because you really are beautiful."

She felt the color heating her cheeks. "I'm not used to having someone take time...to look."

"Anyone who didn't take the time was a fool. I want to look at you, Robyn. And I want you to enjoy me looking."

It seemed so self-indulgent, what he was asking of her. Yet, as he touched her, and as his gaze continued to linger upon her, the last of her reticence vanished. When together they had removed all of her clothing, she did not try to hide from him.

"Beautiful," he repeated, his voice husky. "Everything about you is beautiful, Robyn."

She looked at him, too, as his jeans came off, then his underwear. The lines of his body were strong and masculine, stirring her deepest response. She saw the scar left behind by the bullet, and she touched it.

"Does it hurt?" she whispered.

"Nothing hurts right now. Robyn..."

Their limbs tangled together as they lay on the

futon. But Mark refused to rush anything. He caressed her until she thought the longing would burst inside her, and he watched her face as if to savor every bit of her pleasure. And then she knew the secret of what Mark gave her. Instead of hurrying to fulfill his own needs, he took pleasure in her enjoyment. His fingers moved over the soft bare skin of her stomach, trailed below. As he touched her intimately, he gazed straight into her eyes, and he smiled as at last her longing could no longer be contained. She came with one ragged gasp after another.

She was still breathing unsteadily a moment or two later as she guided him inside her. She was amazed that the wanting could build so quickly again, but this time she desired *his* pleasure most of all. Their bodies locked together, their eyes locked, they moved in a powerful rhythm that swept both of them on a crest of sensation. Her cries mingled with his groans, and never once did they look away from each other.

It was only afterward that Robyn tore her gaze from Mark's, only afterward that she turned on her side so that he would not see her face. They ended up in the classic spoon position, her backside tucked against him. She closed her eyes tightly, as if that would make her forget exactly how reckless she'd just been.

One mistake, you could excuse. But two mistakes…for that, there was no excuse.

HANNETT PARK WAS the perfect spot for a children's birthday party. The gnarled old cottonwoods provided ample shade, and there were swings and a slippery slide. A volleyball net had been set up, and a game was in progress. Picnic tables scattered here and there provided a staging area for barbecued hamburgers, potato salad and other treats. Robyn stood beside one of the tables, watching as kids ran boisterously about. From here, she could see a short way across the park to where Josh sat in one of the swings. A little girl sat in the swing next to his, chattering away to him. Yet Josh scarcely seemed to be listening. His head was bent, and he scuffed his feet in the dirt underneath him. Robyn could only imagine what thoughts might be going through his mind. How did you cope when you were nine years old, and your world had been shattered? Even if it wasn't the most stable world to begin with…even if you had the kind of mother who blackmailed people and made you pretend she was your sister…even so, if you lost that world, just how did you survive? The kid needed someone to depend on. He'd need professional counseling too, if he was going to make it through this mess.

Mark had been talking to his friend Benjamin, but

now he came across the park to Robyn. "From all reports, Josh has been quiet and withdrawn all day," he said. "Benjamin persuaded him to join in a softball game, but Josh didn't show a whole lot of enthusiasm. I suspect he's afraid to have any fun—he probably sees that as being disloyal to Emily."

"She may have done some rotten things in her life, but she certainly inspired love," Robyn murmured. "Randall Garrett, her son, perhaps even my father for a time...I wonder who else loved her." She turned away from Mark, even as she spoke.

"Robyn," he said gravely, "you can't keep doing that. Acting as if we didn't make love only a few hours ago—"

"Stop, Mark. Please." Nobody else was near, but that picnic table under the cottonwood provided her an excellent way to busy herself. "I'm going to fix myself a hamburger," she said. "I never did have lunch, what with... I'm hungry, that's all." In reality, her appetite had deserted her, but Mark didn't need to know about that.

She went up to the table, took a paper plate and put a bun on it. Then she picked up the mustard. Mark came and stood beside her.

"I'll be glad to fix you a plate, too," she said, "but maybe you could do something else in the meantime."

He stayed right where he was. "Robyn, I thought

we were going to be honest with each other. Something's bothering you, and I'd like to know what it is.''

Robyn put too much mustard onto her bun. ''Everything is disintegrating around me—of course I'm bothered.''

''I'm talking about you and me,'' he said.

Now she squirted some catsup on the bun, finished off the job with a grilled hamburger and scattered some potato chips willy-nilly on her plate. She didn't see how she could possibly eat any of this—not with the way her stomach had clenched into a knot.

She sat down at the picnic table, and Mark sat across from her. She tried to nibble on a potato chip, but she might as well have been eating sawdust.

''Okay,'' she said. ''I'll tell you what's wrong. Back at your apartment, before we…before we made love, I told you that I might be starting to feel something more for you. I admitted it, told you how much it scared me. But you, Mark…you talk about honesty, but you've given nothing away. I don't even have a clue how *you* feel.''

''Robyn, maybe I'm just like you—trying to sort things out. Trying to figure out where we go from here. But I have a track record that doesn't give me a lot of encouragement.''

''Right,'' she muttered. ''You're no good at relationships. And neither am I. So where *do* we go, Mark?''

He didn't have an answer, and she didn't expect one. She pushed away the plate of food she'd prepared. With her family disintegrating and Josh to worry about, the last thing she needed was… confusing new feelings for Mark Stewart that she didn't know what on earth to do with.

''Robyn, there you are!'' came a voice behind her. It was the instantly recognizable voice of her mother.

She twisted around. ''Mom, what on earth are you doing here?''

Nina looked distraught as she came over the grass. ''You said you'd be picking up Josh here. I took a chance I'd find you. There's something you have to know…it's not the type of thing that can wait…''

Robyn made her mother sit down at the picnic table. Mark didn't try to intervene, and Robyn was grateful for that.

''Tell me what it is,'' she said.

Nina clasped her hands together, but she couldn't disguise the fact that they were shaking. ''Where to start,'' she said, her voice strained. ''Your uncle Greg hasn't shown up yet, but your aunt Janet broke down and told me…well, it seems Greg was having an affair with Emily, too.''

At this pronouncement, all Robyn could do was turn and look at Mark. He took the news with his usual aplomb, as if nothing in the world could surprise him.

"Was your sister-in-law absolutely certain of this, Mrs. Myers?" he asked.

"She caught the two of them together one day," Nina said. "She'd been suspecting that something was wrong, and when she saw Greg and Emily together…"

Robyn still couldn't take it in. "Uncle Greg…and Emily…where does it end?" Cal Myers, his brother, Greg, Randall Garrett. Just how many men had Emily entranced? But Nina was already going on.

"Janet says she overhead you talking with your father this morning. She was kind enough to fill me in. At least now we know what he did with the money from the savings account." Nina spoke like someone in shock. "And Janet says you and your father also discussed the possibility that he might have murdered Emily. What with her blackmailing him, and all…but now it seems he has another motive for murder, doesn't it?"

"Mom, what are you saying—"

"It's perfectly clear to me. Your father loses his head over a pretty young woman. And then he finds out that the pretty young woman is stepping out with his own brother behind his back. It seems perfectly reasonable that he'd shoot the pretty young woman." Nina's hands were truly shaking now. "That's what I told Detective Garrett, anyway," she said. "I called him on the telephone and told him that it's very likely your father killed Emily. I explained everything about your father's possible motives. I must say, Detective Granger is very efficient. He came right over to the house, but this time it wasn't just to ask more questions. He took your father into custody."

CHAPTER FIFTEEN

LESS THAN AN HOUR LATER, Mark was sitting across from Detective Tom Granger. At Robyn's request, he'd come down to the station to learn what he could about her father's status. "Please, Mark," she'd said urgently. "Just find out what's happening with my dad…please."

So here he was with Tom. This afternoon Tom wore a double-breasted herringbone suit, the kind that might have looked good if you were taking a jaunt at an English country estate. In a Santa Fe police office, it looked overdone.

"You know you don't have enough evidence to arrest Cal Myers," Mark said.

"Stewart, they ever give me any time off from this place, I'm actually going to take it. Unlike you, I know the meaning of the word *vacation*. I'm going to put my feet up, and do some fishing, and not much else."

Mark doubted that Tom Granger had ever been fishing in his life. "You don't have enough on Cal Myers," he repeated. "Not enough to arrest him."

"He's not under arrest," Tom said. "Not yet. We've just brought him in for more questioning. As far as what we do have on the guy, how's motive and opportunity sound? Not only was he doing the deceased, but she was blackmailing him, to boot. Estimated time of death is between 10:00 p.m. and midnight. Nina Myers assumes her husband was sleeping during that time, but she was in another part of the house so she can't be sure. No one else in the family can swear that he stayed put during those two hours. The guy sneaks out of the house, no sweat. He has a broken arm, but it's the left one. He can still drive, he can still pull a trigger."

"All circumstantial, Tom," Mark said, "and you know it. There are other leads to pursue. Randall Garrett, for instance, and any other men in Emily Parkman's life—"

"We have everything under control," Tom said confidently. "Even without you around, we're managing to do our job. We're not leaving any possibility uncovered. That includes Greg Myers—we're looking for him, and we'll bring him in for questioning, too. Now, don't you have a *vacation* to get on with? This isn't your case, Stewart, no matter how pretty the suspect's daughter is. Thought the captain reminded you of that."

Mark could tell he wouldn't get anything else out

of Tom, and he rose to go. He was almost out the door when Tom came up with an addendum.

"Say, speaking of daughters, that daughter of yours has been around a lot, asking questions about the Parkman case. Debra, isn't that her name? She's persistent, I'll give her that."

So Debbie was going ahead, with or without Mark's blessing. He'd expected as much, but it didn't help to hear it. His daughters wouldn't take advice from him…

They wouldn't take anything at all.

SURELY THE SIGN of a true optimist was someone who could find a bright spot in the darkest situation. If so, Robyn knew she'd proven herself a first-class optimist. Yesterday, due to lack of evidence, the police had released her father in the late afternoon. In this whole sorry mess, she seized on that one fact— her father had not been officially accused of Emily's murder. Whatever her private fears about his innocence, at least she had that much.

Now she watched as Josh wandered along the pebbly shore of Cochiti Lake. This was the one place where it seemed Josh wanted to be. Evidently, Emily had brought him here on outings several times. Only a short distance from Santa Fe, Cochiti was a man-made lake that stretched a dazzling blue under the equally dazzling New Mexico sky. Sail-boats skimmed the water like white wings.

Mark came up behind Robyn. "This was a good idea," he said.

"I hope so," she murmured. A few moments ago, she and Mark had stood at the shore and talked to Josh about Emily a bit. They'd encouraged him to speak about her, too. After that, he'd walked quickly ahead, making it clear that he needed to be alone. Robyn was keeping an eye on him, but she would allow him his solitude. That was part of grieving, after all.

"I wonder if I'll ever understand Emily," she said, her voice low. "The more I learn about her, the more upset I get. She's practically destroyed my family...I mean, did she have to go after my father and my uncle *both?* For all I know, she was trying to blackmail Uncle Greg, too. What a way to make a buck. Maybe that's why she told everyone Josh was her brother, not her son—maybe it made her blackmail schemes easier. I really could hate her. And yet, I look at that kid she produced, and I can't think she was all bad."

"Nobody's all bad," Mark said.

She glanced at him in surprise. "This is the hard-ened policeman talking?"

"Maybe I've changed my mind. Maybe I'm not such a cynic anymore."

She didn't trust his words. She was careful not to look at him right now, focusing only on the deep blue of the lake.

"I wonder how Mom's doing," she said. "I didn't like leaving her today, but Josh's needs seemed more important for the moment. My poor mother, though…she finally found a way to get back at Dad. Practically accusing him of murder, having him hauled in by the police."

Mark didn't answer. He, too, stood gazing at the lake, his profile intent. Robyn had to remind herself not to look at him, not to examine the details about him: his dark wind-brushed hair, the crinkles at the corners of his eyes, the strong line of his jaw…

She swiveled forward again.

"Robyn," Mark said. "We can't avoid talking about us." He took her hand, and they stood there close together at the edge of the lake.

"What do you see for us, Mark?" she asked after a long moment. "I go to your bed again? And then what?"

"I don't know," he said, frowning a little. "I only know that I want you, Robyn. And I'm pretty sure you want me, too. Maybe we'll just have to take it one step at a time."

She moved her fingers inside his grasp. "No, Mark," she said, her voice tight. "We can't take it any further at all. Not while everything's in such confusion around us. And besides, wanting isn't enough. There has to be something more.''

He didn't answer. He didn't offer her anything more. And, at last, she slipped her hand away from his.

ON THE WAY BACK to Santa Fe, Mark and Robyn didn't speak to each other for quite some time. Josh lay curled in the back seat. Robyn wanted to say something reassuring, but nothing came to mind. She ended up muttering something under her breath, and Mark glanced at her briefly as he drove.

''Didn't catch that,'' he said.

''It was nothing.'' She peered over her shoulder at Josh. ''You okay back there?''

''I'm fine.'' Josh sounded very adult, despite the cowlick and slightly sunburned nose.

Robyn twisted forward again. ''You know, Mark,'' she said as casually as possible, ''you do realize that my life may be rather complicated in the future. There's a certain…package I intend to hold on to, if it's at all possible.''

She knew he would understand what she meant: if none of Josh's relatives could be found, then Robyn herself would try to keep him somehow. She'd even started to hope that she might be able to adopt Josh. There was something about the little boy that got to her. Maybe it was his loneliness, and the way he tried so hard to be brave in spite of everything that had happened to him. Maybe it was just that behind his proud, withdrawn exterior was a kid who desperately needed a home. And she desperately wanted to provide one.

"Those kinds of packages are a big responsibility," Mark said.

"What's in the package?" Josh asked from the back seat.

Robyn found herself giving an unexpected laugh. "All kinds of good things, Josh. A lot of fun…but I suppose a lot of worry, too. You can't have one without the other."

"Yeah, well, that's kind of how I feel about having a dog," Josh said.

"You want a dog?" Robyn asked.

"Yeah. A Scottie."

"A Scottie dog," Robyn echoed.

"Sounds like a full house to me," Mark said.

A house…she certainly hadn't thought *that* far ahead. But if you were lucky enough to end up with a little boy and a dog, you probably did need a real home. She tried to envision it, but the only house that came to mind was the one out there in the foothills. Green trim, adobe walls…

Robyn gazed out the windshield, wondering if Mark had decided whether or not he was going to buy the house. She kept herself from asking, though.

She was relieved when they drove into Santa Fe and finally arrived at Mark's apartment.

The telephone was ringing as they went in. Mark answered it, then handed the receiver to her.

"It's your father," he said.

Immediately she felt apprehensive. She took the receiver, pressed it to her ear. "Dad—what's up? Are you all right? Where are you?"

"I'm fine, Robyn," came his voice. "But yes, in response to your first question, something's up." Cal sounded more assured than he had in a long while. Somehow, that did nothing to soothe Robyn's foreboding.

"Exactly what *is* up, Dad?"

"Your mother's not speaking to me, and there are a few things I need to tell someone, Robyn, just in case. It's time I was honest with myself. It's time I faced up to the problems I've caused."

She gripped the receiver. "Dad, you're resting, aren't you? You've been through an ordeal with the police, and you should rest—"

"I don't have much time, Robyn, so listen. I'm tired of being afraid…so very tired of it. I won't be that way anymore. Honey, I begged you to get a gun to protect yourself and your mother. You wouldn't do it, and perhaps rightly so. It's up to me to do the protecting."

"Dad—"

"You don't need to worry how. These things are actually quite easy if you have a friend who knows a friend, and so forth. The point is, I have a gun now, and I'm going to meet him. I will no longer let him endanger me or my family."

Robyn held the receiver so tightly that her fingers ached. She looked at Mark, saw the concern on his face, but she had to keep talking to her father. At all costs, that was what she had to do.

"Who are you going to meet, Dad?" she asked as calmly as possible.

"Why, the man who attacked me. The man who is still threatening to harm you and your mother. The man who killed Emily."

"Dad, this is something for the police to handle. Please, Dad—"

"You think the police are going to believe me now, Robyn? They think *I* killed Emily. Besides, I finally need to stand up for myself...and for the people I love. I have to do it on my own, or I'll never be able to live with myself."

"No, Dad—"

"I'm only telling you this in case things don't go well for me. It's a possibility I have to acknowledge. This guy's already killed once. But right now I'm going to meet him...where it all started. I love you, Robyn. Please know that. I love you and your mother very much." The line suddenly went dead.

The receiver fell from Robyn's fingers, but she scarcely noticed. For a second or two she felt a wave of sickness. She saw Mark's face, Josh's face, and they both seemed to waver in front of her.

"Where's your father going, Robyn?" Mark asked. Something about his quiet tone helped to steady her. The nausea passed, and she felt oddly composed.

"Dad has a gun, and some terribly misguided idea about proving his courage. He said he was going to meet the man who killed Emily. He said he would go to where it all started…the art gallery, Mark. That must be what he meant—that's where he was attacked in the first place. We have to get there ourselves, as quickly as possible."

IT SEEMED to Robyn that Mark broke every speed limit in the city. The Land Cruiser, in spite of its age, rose to the occasion. It surged down one street, roared down another. Both Josh and Robyn had to cling to their seats as the vehicle skidded around a corner and accelerated all the more. But time continued to pass nonetheless—the seconds stretched into minutes.

"Please," Robyn murmured over and over. "Please let us get there…before it's too late…"

Mark had already been on the cell phone, requesting backup. The Land Cruiser, however, was the first to career into the parking lot of the gallery. Barely had it jolted to a halt before Robyn scrambled out. She wished there'd been time to leave Josh somewhere else, but there was no time for anything, it seemed. As if in a nightmare, she heard the staccato sounds of two gunshots, one right after the other.

"You and Josh, stay here," Mark commanded, and then he disappeared inside the gallery. Robyn's first instinct was to protect Josh, and she held him close to her side. Only a few seconds later, two police cars screeched into the parking lot. And, meanwhile, scuffling noises came from the gallery.

Robyn could wait no longer. "Stay right here with one of the officers," she told Josh, and then she crept toward the door to look inside the gallery.

Mark had worked with impressive swiftness. Already he had wrestled a man to the floor—a man none other than Randall Garrett. Garrett's features had swollen with rage, but his cheek was pressed into the rug, his arms twisted behind him by Mark.

"I'm not the one you want," rasped Garrett. "Myers killed her—that bastard's the one who did it!"

Cal lay in a heap, his face truly battered this time. His arm was flung out, as if reaching toward the gun on the floor beside him, but he was unconscious. Robyn fell to her knees next to him.

''Dad...'' Her voice came on a sob. As if from a great distance, she heard Randall Garrett ranting on.

''She never should have looked at that bastard. What did she need him for? I could have given her everything she wanted...if she'd only given me a chance. I loved her...I didn't kill her. He's the one you want.''

Robyn leaned over her father, wishing she could force life into him. She couldn't even tell if he was breathing. And then, even as more sirens wailed in the parking lot outside, Josh knelt beside her and took her hand.

''It'll be okay, Robyn,'' he said. With another sob, she gathered the little boy close to her, and prayed that her father wouldn't die.

THE OPEN-AIR CAFÉ just off the plaza was Santa Fe's attempt at Parisian atmosphere, with brightly colored awnings and menus in French and a liberal supply of croissants. Mark wondered why Santa Fe needed a dose of Paris when the Southwest was exotic enough on its own. Then again, maybe he needed to stretch his horizons. Maybe he needed to be a little more cosmopolitan.

He sat at one of the outdoor tables and spread the Albuquerque newspaper open in front of him. The article about Emily Parkman's murder didn't show up till the third page, toward the bottom; world and metropolitan news took precedence. But the article carried the byline of Debra Stewart, and it was a well-written account that brought the facts of the case up-to-date. It appeared Debra was going to be a crime reporter—and a good one, at that—no matter what he had to say about it. He read the article for the second time.

It stated that yesterday afternoon, Santa Fe police had arrested real estate agent Randall Garrett for the murder of twenty-six-year-old Emily Parkman. It seemed, the article relayed, that Emily had developed a habit of getting men into compromising situations then blackmailing them. Although it was not clear whether eventually she planned to blackmail Garrett, he had allowed her to stay at some of the houses his agency listed for sale. When Garrett had discovered Emily's affair with Cal Myers, a local art gallery owner, Garrett had not only attacked Myers, but threatened to harm Myers's family. Apparently, Garrett had not been able to tolerate the thought of Emily with anyone but himself, and police speculated that this was his motive for killing her. Even after her death, Garrett had attacked Cal Myers a second time. And now Myers lay unconscious in a Santa Fe hospital room.

Mark could have filled in a few other details. Randall Garrett claimed that he was not the murderer. Instead, he accused Robyn's father of the crime. Yesterday, the two men had confronted each other at the art gallery, and Cal had attempted to defend himself. His gun had gone off twice. The bullets hadn't hit anyone, but Garrett had beaten up Cal in a rage and this time nearly killed him. Doctors could not say whether Cal Myers would survive.

Mark set down the newspaper. At this moment, Robyn was with her father in the hospital, refusing to leave his side. Mark had seen to some necessary arrangements, such as having Josh stay with Benjamin. Then Mark had spent as much time as possible with Robyn. Only one thing could have pulled him away from her...the one thing he had to do today.

He glanced up and saw his two daughters approaching him along the sidewalk. When they reached his table, they both surveyed him distrustfully.

"What's this all about, Father?" Debra asked.

"What could be so important that you had us drive up from Albuquerque?" Kerry added.

"Please...have a seat," he told them. "It is important—very, very important."

He waited until each of them had sat down reluctantly. Then he reached into the pocket of his jacket and took out some folded sheets of paper. They were somewhat crinkled with age, but he smoothed them on the table.

"I've never shown this to either of you girls, but these are the terms of the divorce agreement with your mother," he said. "Custody stipulations. The way things are set out, I get you girls every other weekend and one month during the summer. Those were and *are* my legal rights as your parent."

His daughters looked at him with varying degrees of disbelief.

"But, Father," Debra said, "we're not children anymore. We're adults."

"Is he feeling okay?" Kerry asked. "Maybe he's been drinking."

"No, I haven't been drinking," Mark said. "And I'm feeling fine. Here's how it is. In the past, none of us has abided by this custody agreement. Either I'd have a case I couldn't get away from, or the two of you would have an excuse why you couldn't be with me. That's about to change. I'm here—I'm a fact of your lives. No more excuses from any of us. You're my daughters…I'm your father. No—I'm your dad. And there's nothing you can do about it."

Both daughters stared at him in amazement. Neither seemed able to speak.

"I'm sorry," Mark continued. "I'm sorry I wasn't there for you. But I'm here now and I'm not going away. Thinking back, I realize there's something I haven't told you girls for a long time, either one of you. I love you. I love you both." He smoothed out the crinkled sheets of paper again, but he couldn't seem to focus on the print. "Every other weekend," he said. "One month in the summer. It was my legal right then, and I neglected it. But now, I want to be your dad."

Kerry and Debra looked at each other. Debra's face remained hard. But then, unexpectedly, Kerry burst into tears.

"I've been so unhappy," she said shakily. "I just haven't been thinking straight. I was so scared to get married, and I blamed you, and I blamed Frederick. But you know what he told me last night? He told me the only reason he's been so distracted lately is because's he's worried he won't get a job. And even *after* he told me that, I shut the door in his face! Am I a jerk, or what?"

"You're not a jerk," Mark said. "You're a wonderful girl who's had a lousy father. No wonder you're scared to get married."

"You tried to help. You tried to tell me Frederick wasn't such a bad guy. Oh…Dad!" Kerry erupted in tears again. And then she scooted her chair next to his and flung herself into his arms.

It had been so long since he'd held one of his daughters that he didn't know what to do at first. He patted Kerry's back awkwardly. He didn't care about the people looking over in unfeigned curiosity. He didn't care about anything except that one of his kids had just called him "Dad." Not Father…*Dad.*

"About those custody arrangements," he said. "I'm holding you to them, you know."

Kerry sobbed all the harder. Mark went on holding his youngest daughter, but his older daughter remained seated rigidly where she was. The expression on her face said it all: maybe her kid sister was swayed by all this, but not *her.*

Debra wasn't buying.

CHAPTER SIXTEEN

ROBYN SAT BESIDE her father's bed in the dim hospital room. A nurse had come in earlier to draw the shades, and now the afternoon sun barely trickled in. Robyn was grateful. It was better this way, her father's face cast in shadow. She could pretend that he was only sleeping, and not unconscious.

Her throat was raw from talking to him. She'd felt foolish at first. She'd watched enough of those coma scenes on television and at the movies, where people gathered at the bedside and said all manner of things to their unconscious loved ones. But now, for the first time, she understood the scenario. You had to talk, and you had to believe that somehow the talking would get through. Otherwise, you might entirely lose hope. Robyn couldn't face that—she couldn't lose hope.

And so she talked to her father. She was as honest and straightforward as she could be, too. When he'd made the telephone call to her yesterday, he'd stated that he no longer wanted to hide from his fears. And that meant he didn't want to hide from the truth. Robyn hoped he meant what he'd said.

"Mom has been at your bedside constantly," Robyn said now. "The only reason she's not here right this minute is that I insisted she go get something to eat. She's still so devoted to you, Dad—but that doesn't change the fact that she's still angry, too. You really hurt her, I'm afraid. And you'll hurt all of us even more if you don't come back to us."

She took hold of her father's hand, and chafed it between her own. "*I'm* still ticked at you, Dad," she said. "I wish you'd wake up so I could tell you just how mad I am. The first time Randall Garrett attacked you, that's when you should have told the police about him—regardless of his threats. As for yesterday, I know you thought you had to stand up for yourself and your family, and that's why you went off to meet Garrett. But why did you have to do it on your own? Did you think it was the only way to redeem yourself? Couldn't you have found another way to prove your courage?"

His hand remained limp and lifeless in hers. She had to strain to hear the sound of his breathing. "Please wake up, Dad," she begged. "Please…"

"Your dad will make it, honey," Uncle Greg said as he stepped into the room. "You have to believe that."

"Oh, Uncle Greg, you're back! Thank goodness." Robyn stood, and began going toward him.

"When you know everything, Robyn," he said quietly, "you won't wish I was back."

Something in his tone made her stop. His expression was all too familiar. It carried the bleakness she'd observed in her father's eyes.

"I already know about you and Emily," she said. "It's out in the open, Uncle Greg. But right now, all I want is my family around me again."

"It's what I want, too," Greg said. "But it's too late…far too late."

Her father had uttered those words, too. Robyn watched as her uncle sat down next to the hospital bed. He didn't seem quite so big and solid as he always had. His face was too pale.

"Uncle Greg, we were all so worried about you. Your heart, for one thing…"

"These past few days, my health has been the least of my worries. I've been up in the Jémez by myself, doing a lot of soul-searching. And I can only blame myself for everything that's happened."

Childhood memories came to Robyn: family camping trips in the Jémez Mountains, times when she'd been surrounded by the love of her parents, her aunt and uncle.

"Robyn, what I'm going to say isn't easy, but I'd just better get on with it. You're the one to hear it—you're the one who'll carry on this family, or what's left of it.''

Robyn stood where she was, arms held tightly against her body, dreading what he would tell her.

"Your aunt and I...we both wanted children so very much, Robyn. We had all the tests, did everything we could. Yet still it didn't happen. Finally we began to think of adoption, but that wasn't the solution for Janet. She felt that giving birth to a child was the only way she could prove herself as a woman. That idea had been so ingrained in her by her own parents, nothing I said seemed to reassure her. And gradually, Robyn, we began to grow apart.''

"To me, you always seemed so happy," she murmured.

"On the surface, yes, I suppose we did appear to be getting along. But underneath...Janet kept accusing herself for what she saw as her failure. She wouldn't allow it to be a burden that belonged to both of us. Because she couldn't be a mother herself, she mothered every sick and wounded creature she found. But when it came to our marriage, over the years she just kept withdrawing more and more. No matter what I said or did, she seemed convinced *I* saw her as a failure.''

"Oh, Uncle Greg, I never realized—''

"It wasn't something either one of us knew how

to share. But I finally realized we couldn't go on like that. I moved out. I felt anything was better than all the silences between us. Then I had the heart attack—and we were both shook up at the idea I could have died. It brought us closer for a time. I moved back in, hoping…but eventually the old patterns returned. Janet started withdrawing again. I didn't know what to do next, where to turn. Then your mother hired Emily Parkman to work in the gift shop. It had been a long time since any woman had looked at me the way Emily did. I even forgot I had a heart condition. I just felt alive—and wanted.'' Greg paused. ''Robyn, I'm not telling you any of this to take myself off the hook. Janet and I were having problems, but that didn't mean I had to have an affair. The damn affair that set everything else in motion.''

After that, Greg didn't speak for a few moments. Robyn sensed, however, that the worst was to come. At last he leaned forward, wearily resting his elbows on his knees.

''Janet could tell something was going on, and she started following me. She found Emily and me together. The details don't matter—they were sordid enough. But I'll never forget the look of hurt on Janet's face. I realized then that she had never stopped loving me—and I'd repaid her with the worst kind of betrayal. I could see how it must have seemed through her eyes—I'd made love to a young, beautiful woman…one who could, no doubt, bear children. Nothing could have made Janet feel more like a failure. Being the cause of that terrible hurt—I won't forgive myself for that, Robyn. Never.''

Robyn sat down on the other side of the hospital bed. She gazed at her father…still unconscious. She didn't excuse either her father or her uncle for what they'd done, but she loved them nonetheless. Her feelings toward Emily Parkman were somewhat different. Now, for the first time, she genuinely hated the woman for all the destruction she had wrought.

''Uncle Greg, did Emily ever try to blackmail you?''

''No, but after everything I've learned about her, I believe that was what she intended. She knew I'd do anything not to have Janet find out, but Janet walked in on us, and that must have changed Emily's plans. I broke off the affair right away, but of course it was too late. Janet's trust in me was destroyed, and she refused to believe I'd stopped seeing Emily. Robyn, do you remember the night at the art gallery, when someone came in and disturbed you?''

''Of course I do.'' The door, swinging wide to darkness…

''I'd gone out for a drive that night, just trying to think my way through the mess I'd made. Janet came after me, but she lost sight of my car. She did see the lights on in the gallery, and thought perhaps I was there—with Emily. She crept inside, but when she realized it was you and your friend Mark, she retreated as fast as she could. But I didn't learn all this until…until the night Janet killed Emily.'' His voice seemed to have gone hollow.

Robyn sat frozen in her chair. ''No! You have to be wrong. The real estate agent Randall Garrett killed Emily. Aunt Janet would never hurt anyone.''

He bowed his head. ''Afterward she told me that she didn't mean to do it. She only bought a gun for protection. After the attack on Cal, she was scared. She'd overheard your father pressuring *you* to get a gun, and she decided to get one herself. Then, after she learned Emily and I were having an affair, she thought she'd use the gun for different purposes. She asked Emily to meet her at the gift shop. She showed the gun, brandished it a little, and that was supposed to be all. It was supposed to convince Emily to leave me alone. Except then, according to Janet, Emily gave her a look of such contemptuous pity…and Emily said no man would want a defective wife…an infertile wife. She knew the most cruel thing to say because I had confided our problems to her. I believe Janet saw that as the worst betrayal of all…and then she pulled the trigger.''

''No,'' Robyn whispered. ''Please, no…''

"Janet was hysterical afterward, and she told me everything. But then I made the wrong choice, Robyn. I should have taken her to the police. Having Janet confess right then would have helped her case. But I couldn't do it...I couldn't bear to turn in my wife to the authorities. Rather than do that, I left for the Jémez Mountains. I had to be by myself, had to try sorting everything out on my own. Then I went down for supplies, and I saw the story about my brother in the newspapers. I read about this man Randall Garrett, and how he'd been the one to attack Cal. I realized if Garrett had known about *my* involvement, he would have come after me, too. But I don't feel lucky to have escaped, Robyn. I just wish it was me in this hospital bed, not my brother. And now I have to do the right thing for all of us. Even if it *is* too late, I'll try to make the police see that Janet's not truly to blame..."

Just then Janet herself came into the hospital room. Her face was streaked with tears.

"Greg..." Her voice wavered. "I heard everything you said. I've been standing outside, listening. I'm getting altogether too good at that, listening outside doors."

He stood and walked toward her. She reached inside her purse, pulled out a gun. Greg stopped.

Janet gave him a stricken look. "I'm not going to shoot. It's not even loaded. I just wanted to show

you I had the same idea as you…I meant to turn
myself in. I brought this along…the murder
weapon…so the police would have everything they
need.'' She gazed at the gun in her hand with a kind
of horror, then swiveled toward the hospital bed.
''But first I need to ask my brother-in-law to forgive
me. Even though he can't hear me, I have to say
it.'' Her voice trembled all the more. ''Cal, I'm so
sorry I let everyone think you were guilty. I was
terrified after it happened…after I did it. And so I
let them blame you. I'm so terribly sorry. If I'd confessed right away, you probably wouldn't be
here…'' The gun dropped from Janet's fingers, skit-
tering across the floor, and she seemed about to
crumple. It was Uncle Greg who caught her, held
her close.

   ''Somehow it will be all right, love,'' he told her.
''Somehow we'll make it all right. And I'll never
leave you again, not ever. Hush, now. I'll never
leave you…''

ROBYN STOOD under one of the cottonwoods at Hannett Park. The spring breeze drifted over her, as if
attempting to warm the chill deep in her bones. She
wondered if anything could ever warm her again.
Mark stood beside her.

   ''How are you doing?'' he asked quietly.

   ''I'll make it…I suppose.'' She gazed across the

park to where nine-year-old Josh sat on a picnic bench, flanked by a man and woman. Both the man and woman leaned toward the little boy as if they could not get enough of him...as if they marveled at his very existence. And well they should. They were Josh's grandparents, and until yesterday they hadn't even known of his existence.

After tracing through the complexities of Emily Parkman's life, the police had finally located her parents alive and well—Daniel and Luisa, residents of San Francisco, California. Upon being contacted, they had immediately flown to Albuquerque, and from there rented a car that would bring them to Santa Fe. Robyn had asked only that she be allowed to hand Josh over to them. She'd chosen to do so in the park because it was the kind of place you could imagine families getting off to a good start.

From what she could see at this distance, Josh was taking the measure of both his grandparents. It was difficult to tell if he'd decided on a verdict yet, but at least he was sitting there in dignified fashion, letting the two of them get acquainted with him.

Mark put his arm around Robyn and held her close to his side. ''Whatever you need to do right now is okay,'' he said.

''Mark, I'm not going to lose control and do something horrible or embarrassing. Even though what I really feel like doing is snatching up Josh and running away with him as fast as I can…'' She felt her voice catch, and she had to wait a few seconds before she went on. ''They seem like nice people, don't they?''

''From what I've seen—yes.''

''Bewildered people,'' Robyn said. ''I can't imagine what it would be like to have your daughter run away from home at sixteen. Not to have any clue where she's gone, and to look for her all those years…and then to find out she's been killed, and left a little boy behind.'' She took a deep breath, but it did nothing to steady her. ''Do you think Josh's father will ever be found?''

''I doubt it,'' Mark said. ''There aren't any traces so far.''

From Robyn's vantage point, she stared hard at Emily's parents. ''Dammit, Mark,'' she said fiercely. ''They'd *better* be nice people. They'd better not be the ones who made Emily so jaded and conniving!''

Mark's arm tightened around her. ''The authorities both here and in California will make certain they can provide Josh with a good home. But they're his family, Robyn—they have to be given a chance.''

She knew what he was saying was true, but it didn't change one fact. She'd been hoping all along that *she* would be Josh's family.

Josh's grandmother stood and came toward Robyn. She was a pretty woman, with features very like Emily's. Tears shimmered in her eyes, but she blinked to keep them from falling. That was like Josh. "Ms. Myers," she said, "could I talk to you for a moment?"

Robyn nodded, not trusting herself to speak. Mark stepped away.

"I'll be nearby if you need me," he said.

"I'll be fine," she managed to say. Josh's grandmother blotted her eyes with a handkerchief, and then she gave Robyn a thoughtful look.

"Ms. Myers, I can tell that you care about Josh."

"Please, call me Robyn. And yes…I do care. He's special."

Luisa smiled softly. "Yes, he is special, isn't he? Ms. Myers—Robyn. I know that my daughter did some terrible things. I understand that she hurt your family, and for that I am very sorry. But I want you to know…I don't believe Emily was a bad person, not at heart. When she was a teenager, she fell in with the wrong kind of people, that's all. We tried to stop her. We tried to help—but then she left us. We were so worried about her, and then so angry. And then we were just afraid that maybe she felt too ashamed to come home. Afraid that maybe she had traveled too far from us. If only she had known…all we wanted was for her to come home."

On impulse, Robyn reached out and took the older woman's hand. "I'm sure Emily thought about you a lot. And somehow I'm sure that she did want to go home. Perhaps she just didn't know how to find her way. And she loved Josh. I could see it every time she looked at him."

"Thank you, Robyn." Luisa gave her a tremulous smile.

Now Daniel, Josh's grandfather, came across the grass, walking hand in hand with Josh. He was a rumpled-looking man with a kindly face. Although his hair was turning gray, there were still hints of light brown here and there, almost the same tawny shade as Josh's cowlick. Right now Daniel had an aura of mingled sadness and joy. He, too, gave Robyn a heartfelt smile.

"Thank you," he said simply.

Robyn realized she had already started to trust both these people. She knew instinctively that they would do their best for Josh. Now she knelt beside the boy.

"Josh," she said, amazed that her voice wasn't shaking. "You're going to enjoy San Francisco, you know. It's a great town."

"Have you been there?" he asked.

"Yes. And I had the most wonderful time. The trolley cars, the wharves…trust me, you're in for a treat."

"Will you come to visit, Robyn?"

"Of course she will," Luisa said. "She has a standing invitation. San Francisco isn't so far, not by plane."

"Of course I'll come," Robyn echoed. "We're friends now, aren't we? I'm not just your tutor anymore, am I?"

Josh nodded.

"You'll give school a chance, won't you?" she asked.

"Maybe."

"For Emily," she said. "For your mom."

"Okay." And then he put his arms around her and gave her a surprisingly strong hug. Still holding on to him, and smoothing that stubborn tuft of hair, Robyn spoke to his grandparents.

"Did he tell you he wants a Scottie dog?"

"We told him it's fine," Daniel said, "as long as we start out with a puppy."

"That's the best way to start." Robyn tightened her arms around Josh one last time, and then she let him go. She watched as he shook hands with Mark, man to man. After that, Josh climbed into the rental car. His grandparents climbed in, too. Both Josh and Luisa waved as the car pulled away. And then they were gone.

Robyn hadn't realized she was waiting until now to break down. But almost instantly the tears began to trickle from her eyes, and she thought the ache inside her would sharpen into a pain she couldn't bear. Mark was beside her in just a step or two, his arms engulfing her. She wept into his shirt.

"Oh, Mark, you tried to warn me. You tried to tell me that I should be prepared to give him up."

"You did the right thing," he said, smoothing his fingers over her wet cheek. "You cared about him and that kid needs all the caring he can get."

"I can tell they'll give it to him. But even so, it will take a very long while for him to get over what's happened. And maybe he'll never get over it."

"Emily will always be his mother. His grandparents will make sure he knows that, and it will be the best healing he can have."

She cried all the harder, and Mark patted her back.

"I'm getting good at this," he said. "Having females cry in my arms, and all." He fished in his pocket and produced a handkerchief for her. "This time I'm prepared."

She buried her face in the handkerchief. "Your daughters…?" she asked soggily. "They're the crying females?"

"Only one of them. Kerry's forgiven me. Debra hasn't." His words revealed little, but by now Robyn realized how much he cared about his daughters, how much he needed both of them. She cried harder.

He walked her over to a picnic bench and sat her down. He didn't stop holding her, though, and after a moment he kissed the tears from her cheeks. She turned her mouth to his, and he kissed her for a very long moment, and at last the tears stopped.

Afterward she rested her head against his shoulder. "I don't know what's going to happen," she said. "Mark, what if my father never wakes up? What will I do?"

"No matter what happens, you'll come through. You'll do it for your family. The way you came through for Josh."

"My family...how I wish I could make everything go back the way it used to be. But it was never really as perfect as I thought. Uncle Greg and Aunt Janet were going through so much I never realized. Now, to know Janet will stand trial for murder...how can I bear that, along with everything else? She was so very wrong to do what she did— but she's the aunt who's cared for me almost as much as my own parents..."

Mark's arms tightened around her. "Robyn, I want you to come back to my apartment with me. I want you to stay with me."

If she did that, she knew they would make love again. Robyn would lose herself in his embrace, his caress, and for a few exquisite moments forget everything that had happened. But it would only be a temporary escape.

Slowly she withdrew herself from Mark's arms. Then she stood before him.

"It's not going to work, Mark," she said, struggling against the fresh heartache she felt. "You and I...we really met under the wrong circumstances. I've made the same mistake all over again—getting involved with a man when I'm at my most vulnerable. My career's in chaos, and my family—" Her voice caught. "My family's in tatters, and I can't think about anything else. And you...well, you haven't spoken of love, have you? And neither have I."

"Robyn," he said, "just come home with me."

"You don't have a real home, Mark," she said softly. "Maybe that's where you need to start...a home for yourself."

"I want to be with you, Robyn. And I know you want to be with me—"

"I told you before. Wanting isn't enough."

CHAPTER SEVENTEEN

TODAY THE SHADES in Cal's hospital room were opened wide. Nina insisted that her husband needed sunlight, and plenty of it. No matter that he had been unconscious for almost a week now. She'd arranged everything just as she thought he might like it. She'd brought a coverlet from home to place over his bed, and every day she arranged fresh flowers on the windowsill. This morning she'd also brought in a small painting. Robyn recognized the painting right off. It was one Cal himself had done, and it depicted a sunset over a New Mexico mesa. He'd managed to capture a mood of lonely grandeur. There was nothing bland about Cal's work. It was always bold, evocative.

Nina had propped the painting in a chair beside the bed, and now she sat down in another chair. She spoke to her husband as if he could hear every word she said.

"Things are changing. You and I have pigeon-holed each other too much over the years. I'm supposed to be the one who has a head for business, you're supposed to be the one with all the artistic vision. But, like I say...things are changing. When you see the gallery again, you're going to be in for quite a surprise. I'm right in the middle of arranging an exhibit of Cal Myers's art. Oh, I know you're going to bluster about it, and say you've never wanted anyone to see your paintings. I know your work always falls short in your own eyes. You've always had such impossibly high standards of perfection for your paintings, and when you can't meet them, you despair and shut the door. Well, Cal...I'm opening doors.''

Robyn listened to her mother with a sense of wonder. Nina Myers had found new strength from all of this. Perhaps new lines of grief and strain would be etched permanently into her features now, but she was more forceful, more determined. She leaned close to her husband, clasping his hand as if by her power alone she would will him back to wakefulness.

"We have a lot to talk about, Cal. A great deal, in fact. We have to figure out what brought us to such a point in our lives. You broke trust with me...and it's going to take you a great deal of effort to win my trust back. After that, we'll have to figure out how both of us have been to blame. Did we start taking each other for granted? Did we stop putting enough effort into our marriage? We have to answer the questions, Cal.''

He slept on. Nina leaned closer to him.

''Damn you, Cal Myers…you'd better come back to me. Because after we get through all the difficult stuff, we're finally going on that dream trip of ours. England, Spain…just the two of us. And we're going to rediscover whatever it is we lost along the way…''

Robyn went to place her hands on her mother's shoulders. ''You need a break, Mom. I'll sit with him.''

Nina stood, but she didn't leave the room. She seemed in a fighting mood. ''What about you, Robyn?'' she demanded. ''What about your own life? Have you finally made a decision about your career?''

''Mom, you don't have to worry about any of that right now—''

''Yes, I do. I've watched this family suffer enough. It's time we started seeing a little hope for the future. And you, Robyn, you're our future.''

Robyn hesitated. ''Well, as a matter of fact, I have made a decision. I'm going to teach again, but I'm thinking about doing it a little differently this time. I want to be a tutor—I want to work with kids one-on-one. That's what I discovered with Josh. He made me see that there are kids out there who need me. They don't necessarily have to be my own. Even if I never have children, I can still make a difference.''

''You'll tutor kids, and someday you'll have your own children, too. You'll do all of it and manage quite well, I imagine. Now, what about this Mark Stewart of yours?''

Robyn turned away from her mother. ''We don't need to discuss that—''

''You do love him, don't you?''

Robyn went to the window and stared out at the brilliant blue sky. ''I think so. But how can I be certain? I'm always falling for men when things are bad in my life, always making wrong decisions about love. Who's to say this time is any different? Besides, I can't possibly think about Mark when Dad's lying in that bed, and Aunt Janet is facing a trial—''

''This is exactly the time to think about love,'' Nina instructed. ''Robyn, what your family needs from you *is* hope for the future. And if your future lies with Mark Stewart—grab hold of it. He's not your first husband. He's not even your second husband. But maybe he's a whole new chance at happiness.''

''He says he's lousy at relationships,'' Robyn murmured.

''So maybe it's up to you to convince him otherwise. Robyn, I'd be the last person to tell you there are any guarantees. The older generation in the Myers family has done it wrong in just about every way possible. We allowed Emily Parkman to come into our midst and almost destroy us. We allowed her to find our weaknesses. And yet…I don't think she *has* totally destroyed us. Do you know how much I still love your father? Even Greg and Janet are clinging together in spite of the dreadful uncertainty ahead of them.''

What Nina said was true. Robyn had seen it herself: love enduring in her family despite everything.

''Robyn, there are no guarantees,'' Nina repeated. ''But you have to grab hold of your *own* future before it's too late. And that just might mean giving Mark a call.''

Robyn sank into the chair beside the hospital bed and put her head down on the coverlet. ''I don't know, Mom. I just don't know. Mark hasn't said he loves me. If I call him and he still can't say it…''

She felt a reassuring pat on her head. It was just like when she was a kid, and one of her parents consoled her over a skinned knee or bruised ego. ''Thank you, Mom, but I'm not a child anymore,'' she said. ''Life's a whole lot more complicated now.''

''Oh, my God,'' Nina said, and it sounded like a prayer. Only now did Robyn realize that her mother hadn't walked over to pat her head. The one doing the patting was her father.

Robyn nearly jumped out of her chair, and leaned over him. "Dad? Are you back?"

His eyelids fluttered, and opened. He gazed up at Robyn.

"Yes," she whispered. "Dear Lord, you're back."

With an effort, he turned his head and now he gazed at his wife. Nina clasped his hand in her own.

"You weren't getting away from me so easily, dear heart. I'm so furious at you, Cal...but you are my dear heart."

He almost managed a smile. The man and woman who had been married some forty years looked at each other, and in their silence made a new beginning. Robyn watched them for a moment, and then she slipped out of the room.

MARK HAD ALWAYS believed his daughter Kerry to be a lovely girl, but today she'd outdone herself. She was a vision in all that white tulle and lace, a veil floating down over her hair like a mist.

"I'm so nervous," she said as they stood together in the vestibule of the church. "How do I look, Dad? I mean, how do I *really* look?"

"So gorgeous Frederick is probably going to take one look at you and faint right there at the altar."

"He'd better not. He almost fainted already, when he found out he got that job at the software company. They like him, Dad—they say he has great potential. Isn't it wonderful how everything is working out?"

He thought it was wonderful how his youngest daughter kept finding excuses to call him Dad. He just wished his older daughter could find an excuse for it, too. He felt an emptiness whenever he thought about Debra.

Now the organ music was swelling with the "Wedding March." The flower girls had begun their trek down the aisle, and next went the bridesmaids, among them a gorgeous Debra who kept her face turned determinedly away from Mark. In a few seconds it would be Kerry's turn to start down the aisle. She twitched at her veil, bit her lip, and then glanced at him again.

"Give Debra a chance," she said in a low voice.

"I just wish she'd give me a chance," Mark said, his own voice somber.

"She's prickly and difficult—she always has been. But deep down she loves you, Dad." Kerry was trying so hard to make things right. But this was her big day. She deserved to be thinking about other things—such as the groom waiting for her.

"All I know is that I'm going to walk you down that aisle," he said. "Everyone will wonder how I got so lucky to have such a beautiful daughter on my arm. And I am lucky, Kerry. You didn't have to do it, you know. You have a perfectly good step-father—''

''Yes, and a perfectly good father. And fathers are the ones who walk their daughters down the aisle and give them away.'' She linked her arm in his. ''Are you ready?''

''As ready as I'll ever be.''

She took a step forward, then paused. ''I love you, Dad.''

Now they went down the aisle, Kerry seeming to float along on his arm. She gazed ahead at Frederick the entire time. Frederick, the poor guy, *did* look as if he was about to faint. But he also looked as if he'd never seen a vision as stunning as Mark's daughter. In spite of the gangliness of Frederick's limbs, and in spite of the fact that he was definitely too young to be a husband, he did have potential. His new employers were right about that.

Mark's gaze, however, strayed over the guests seated in the church. He was searching for one par-ticular guest…a woman with russet hair and hazel eyes. He'd made certain to have the invitation de-livered to her in plenty of time, but he didn't catch a glimpse of her anywhere.

He couldn't keep looking for Robyn, because now he and Kerry had reached the altar. Mark formally gave his daughter away to the waiting groom then stepped back. He was aware of his ex-wife sitting in the front pew, and her husband, Len, sitting beside her. Mark would never be buddies with Len, but he also knew the man *had* been a good stepfather. He was grateful for that.

"We are gathered to witness a pledge between two young people who love each other…" The ceremony proceeded all too quickly. Before Mark knew it, Frederick was kissing Kerry—and his daughter was now a wife.

The reception took place immediately afterward in the grand hall of the church. The place had been festooned with white streamers and countless balloons, and a rock band tuned up on the stage. Eventually Mark got a chance to waltz with the bride, but after that, Frederick monopolized her attention. Mark found himself scanning the hall over and over, looking for that russet-haired woman. She simply did not appear, and he felt a sharp disappointment. Maybe it was too late for them. Maybe they really had met under the wrong circumstances, and nothing could set it right.

Debra walked over. She seemed as remote and cool and self-possessed as always. He wondered if he'd ever find a way to reach his oldest daughter. He wanted to tell her that he loved her, that he'd always be there for her no matter how many mistakes he'd made in the past. But he'd already told her that, and she hadn't listened.

"Where's Trevor?" he asked instead, trying to be casual about the question.

"Trevor and I are no more," she said too lightly. "I gave him an ultimatum, remember? Either get serious, or walk. He walked."

Mark saw the pain in his daughter's eyes, and didn't know how to erase it. "I'm sorry, honey," he said.

"No need to be." She looked away.

"Debbie…"

"Are you going to tell me I'm too good for him?" she asked in a mocking tone.

"You're way too good for him," Mark said. "He doesn't deserve you."

"Oh, Dad—just save it, will you?"

It took him a few seconds to realize what had happened. "You called me Dad," he said. "Maybe it was just a slip of the tongue, but still—"

"Don't overreact. It's not that big of a deal… Dad." Her expression warned him not to get all sentimental. But it *hadn't* been a slip of the tongue. She'd just made that very clear.

With an effort, he remained casual. "According to the custody arrangements, next weekend's mine."

"Kerry will be on her honeymoon, for goodness' sake—"

"I'll pick you up at nine, Debbie."

She looked disgusted, as if she couldn't believe he was subjecting her to such an absurd ritual. But then she gave the briefest of nods, just before one of the groomsmen came to whirl her off into a waltz.

Mark remained where he was. He knew he had a long way to go with Debra. But they'd made a start, and that was all he asked. He searched the crowd again. And there she was, standing just inside the door. Robyn...

He went to her, took her hand, drew her into the center of the floor. Without a word they moved to the music.

"I almost didn't come," Robyn said, curling her hand inside his.

"I was waiting for you. And if you hadn't come, I would have gone after you."

She didn't seem persuaded. "How have you been these past few weeks, Mark?"

He wanted to tell her how much he'd missed her, but he knew he had to proceed carefully.

"I've been putting in time down at the shooting range," he said. "But in another week I'll be back with the department—back on the job."

"Congratulations. I know how much it means to you." Her voice was intentionally neutral.

"Being a detective still means a lot to me, Robyn.

But it's not everything anymore. That's the difference.''

She didn't seem to have anything to say to that. She'd consented to dance with him, but maybe she wouldn't consent to much else.

"How have you been?" he asked.

"I'm sure you're aware of the details. My father's slowly on the mend…my uncle has hired the best lawyer possible for my aunt, but of course she'll end up paying for what she did, one way or the other…my family is trying to hold together as best it can."

"And you, Robyn?"

"I'm holding together, too."

Maybe there wasn't any right way to go about this. Maybe he just had to say it. "I love you, Robyn."

She stiffened in his arms. "Mark—"

"Just hear me out," he murmured. He thought he was going to give her a list of arguments, all the reasons he felt the way he did. But then he realized there was only one thing to say. "I love you," he repeated. "I love you more than I thought possible. I'm just a fool for taking so long to figure it out."

She gazed at him with a frown. "Are you saying this because you think it's what I want to hear?"

"I'm saying it because it's true," he said, drawing her close.

She still didn't seem convinced. "What happened to being lousy at relationships?"

"I always thought I was. But now both of my daughters are calling me Dad, and I figure maybe I have more people skills than I realized."

"People skills," she muttered. "Oh, damn. Mark, I love you, too! But it scares the hell out of me. What if I'm just leaning on you because—"

"What if we lean on each other? What if we both have a lot to learn about relationships, and we learn together? What if we face *all* the 'what ifs' together, Robyn…"

She gazed at him for another long moment, and then her breath came on a sigh. "Mark…heaven help me, but I do love you. Turns out I love you to distraction…"

He didn't allow her to say anything more. Instead, he drew her even closer and kissed her as the music played.

"There's only one thing I have to know," he murmured afterward against her cheek.

"Oh…what's that?" She sounded breathless, as if kissing him had taken all of her attention.

"Robyn, how do you feel about a mortgage?"

"It depends," she answered seriously. "Is it for a house in the foothills, a house with green trim?"

"Yes, green trim," Mark repeated. "And adobe walls, and a great view of the mountains."

"Oh, Mark..." Now she was the one who brought him close, her arms holding him fiercely.

He found himself smiling. It felt good. "Robyn, I'm asking you to be my wife."

She started to smile, too. "They say three's a charm. And this time I'm sure I've finally got the right husband. Yes, Mark...I'll marry you. And we can start building that future my mother's always talking about."

The music enveloped them in their own private world. "Just as long as we start with the two of us, we'll be fine," he said.

"The two of us," she repeated. "I like the sound of it. But now...could you say it again?"

He knew what she was asking. He pressed his cheek to hers, and whispered it in her ear. "I love you, Robyn Stewart. I love you with all my heart."

Her Bodyguard

by

Peggy Nicholson

*SHE TRADED YOU FOR A CAR. A shiny red Mustang—
that's all you ever meant to that little lady. Now, why
would you want a mother like that?*

"I don't," Gillian said to the door she stood facing.
One of two double doors, twelve feet tall, carved from
some golden wood varnished to gleaming perfection.
They barred an entrance almost wide enough to admit
a Mustang car, shiny red or otherwise. She clenched
her hand to knock, but her arm stayed straight at her
side. *I don't want* her, she'd told the lawyer—a horrible little man—nearly two years ago. *I want the
facts. My facts.*

Like the name of her father. Whether she had any
brothers or sisters or grandparents. Whether she might
be deathly allergic to anything else besides bee stings.
Facts that it seemed, some days, the whole world was
conspiring to hide from her.

The people who'd raised and loved her, the doctor
who'd delivered her, the lawyer who'd arranged her
adoption, the woman who'd borne her almost twenty-
eight years ago—every one of them had lied or
twisted or forgotten or lost or hidden her facts. Or
simply refused to give them.

Her facts lay behind this door and she'd come to
steal them, since asking politely had gotten her nowhere.

Had gotten her much worse than nowhere. Her letter of shy and hopeful inquiry last year had earned her a stinging, contemptuous response: *"If I didn't want you when you were born, why would I want you now, Sarah, if that's who you really are? So go get a life! And stay the hell out of mine!"*

And so I will, Mother. Just as soon as I have my facts. Gillian Sarah Scott Mahler raised her fist, held her breath and knocked, then noticed the doorbell and jabbed that, too.

But of course a woman who owned a mansion in Newport, Rhode Island, a millionaire by marriage and a queen of television soap opera in her own right, didn't open her own front door. How idiotic to have expected it. Gillian blinked at the frowning older woman who swung back the door. "I..." She swallowed and tried again. "I have a ten o'clock appointment with Mrs. Corday. About the job. I'm Gillian Mahler."

"And just how did you get in here? Nobody buzzed the front gates," declared the woman.

Must be a member of the household rather than a maid, Gillian guessed, if she felt free to quiz visitors. She might even be a relative, an aunt or cousin, though Gillian could see nothing of herself in the dour and freckled face, the short square body, of her inquisitor. "I walked in," she said as the woman tapped one foot impatiently. "Someone was driving out as I arrived, and waved me through."

"Those kids!" The woman glared over Gillian's shoulder toward the massive iron gates at the end of the driveway, although the couple, a blond young man and woman in a Range Rover, were long gone.

"I really do have an appointment," Gillian insisted. She didn't care if she'd broken some unwritten rule of the household. No one was turning her back now, not when she was this close.

"Well, come on, then." Leaving her to shut the door herself, the woman marched away.

Gillian hurried after her, dimly aware of high, high ceilings, cool marble that clacked underfoot, a grand staircase that swept up to the floors above. Her mother's house. Assuming Lara Corday—Lara Leigh to her adoring fans—was really her mother. *And she is. Same birth date. Same high-school photo. Of course she is.*

So why wouldn't she acknowledge her own daughter?

Traded you for a car and never looked back, the lawyer assured her for the thousandth time in memory. *That's all I can tell you.*

If that trade had set a girl named Laura Lee Bailey on the road from a ramshackle cabin in the hardscrabble mountains of West Virginia to this palace, maybe it had been the smartest deal a girl of fifteen had ever made. But why—

"Wait here and I'll tell her you've come." Gillian's guide opened a paneled door, waved her inside and closed it firmly behind her.

"Whew!" Gillian leaned back against the door and pressed one hand to her thundering heart.

"*Damn* it all!" A golf ball rolled across the carpet before her. It bypassed a crystal vase laid on its side and disappeared under a sofa. "So much for my birdie!"

A man stood in front of the fireplace, glaring after his errant putt. He lowered his golf club and leaned on it, then turned his attention to her. "And who the devil are you to mess up a man's game?"

"I'm G-Gillian. Gillian Mahler." *And who are you?* Not Lara Corday's husband, the famous TV writer and producer. Richard Corday had died in his sleep two years ago. And Corday had been in his late sixties, not mid-thirties like this man.

So friend of the family then, or even a relative—Lara's relative and therefore hers? It was conceivable. Gillian was tall for a woman, yet he was taller. Six-one or -two easily. Hair darker than her own light brown. His eyes were too deepset to see the color from where she stood. Still, she felt an odd shock of…something. Recognition on some instinctive level?

Or maybe it was just the mood of him as he glared at her from under his black level eyebrows that made the impact, and her sense of kinship was entirely false. Everyone was a potential relative once you learned you were adopted. You found yourself staring at faces as you walked down the street.

He crossed one running shoe over the other and slouched more comfortably against his putting iron. "You sky-dive, Gillian Mahler? Or maybe you made your approach by sea." He tipped his head toward the six pairs of French doors that formed the entire south wall.

Beyond them stretched the lawn, then the back side of the estate's unbreachable granite wall, and then the cliffs, with Newport's famous Cliff Walk meandering high above the blue waters. Gillian had strolled that path often enough these past four months, staring up at this mansion. And now she stood inside it, about to meet her mother. At last.

"You scuba?" the golfer prodded mildly. "Left your wet suit and fins out on the terrace?"

Why was everyone so intent on learning how she'd gotten in? "Helicopter, actually." She edged away from him toward the windows. *I don't want to talk to you, whoever you are. I came to meet my mother.*

"Funny, I didn't hear it. Didn't even hear the buzzer for the front gates." He straightened and ambled across the room to the sofa, then stooped with ease to peer beneath it. "You climbed over?" he hazarded idly, and swept his well-muscled arm under it for his ball. "Grappling hooks and all that?"

The ball he sought had rolled out in front of the sofa. Gillian picked it up and toyed with the notion of stuffing it into his mouth. *Would you please, please shut up?* Her whole life was about to change. Knowingly and unknowingly, she'd been coming to this encounter for almost twenty-eight years, and now, just when she needed to savor the moment, prepare for it, rehearse the role she meant to play and the first cautious words of her script, this big babbling...jock wouldn't leave her in peace. "I walked in the gates when a couple drove out, all right? They saw me. It isn't as if I snuck in."

They'd barely seen her. They'd been too busy laughing at some private joke to spare her more than a glance, their smiles fading for a moment, their cool eyes passing through her. The boy had flipped her a careless wave, then turned onto the avenue and roared away. Those two hadn't been concerned about any intruders.

"Toby and Joya," the man murmured, his trim rump in the air as he groped beneath the sofa.

"We didn't introduce ourselves." Gillian knelt and

thrust the ball under the sofa, toward his sweeping fingertips. "Here."

"Where?" His hand closed instead on her wrist—and tightened when she tried to withdraw.

She was suddenly angry out of all proportion to the act, whether he was teasing or only hopelessly dim. Their hands connecting in the dark, touch their only link—her skin shivered with the unexpected, unwelcome intimacy. "In my hand. Where do you think?"

He slid warm, surprisingly hard fingers down her wrist to trace the ball she clutched. "Oh." Then he lifted it delicately from her palm. "Thanks."

She sat upright, started to wipe her hand on her skirt, then chose a throw cushion, instead. Its silky chintz fabric didn't wipe his touch away but seemed to drive it into her bones. She bounced to her feet and retreated to the wall of French doors, scowling through the glass at the lawn beyond. Such a velvety expanse of green, a symbol of wealth more potent than a Rolls or diamonds. Why didn't he take his toys and go golf out there?

"I suppose you're here about the job," he said behind her. "We've been up to our chins in would-be companions all week. Short ones, tall ones, nice ones, crabby ones."

If *he'd* been the welcoming committee, she didn't doubt the crabbiness! Gillian swallowed and gripped her elbows. For some reason she hadn't thought there'd be many applicants for the job. Somehow she'd seen it as…fated. Earmarked for her and her alone. But if there'd been that many applicants… And her qualifications—she was really reaching to think they'd do, but somehow she'd thought…

Wished. *If wishes were horses, beggars would ride,*

her aunt Susan—her adoptive aunt, Gillian corrected herself—had always said. She'd been foolishly wishing...

"Funny," the pest said behind her. "You don't *seem* very companionable."

Could he possibly be coming onto her? "Companion to a woman was the job description, I believe," she said coldly, without turning.

"Companion/personal assistant to a businesswoman" was the actual wording of the ad in the *Newport Daily News.* Responses to be directed to Mrs. Lara Corday, Woodwind, Bellevue Avenue, Newport. There had been no mention of the celebrity who lived at that address, who presumably required the assistant. That Mrs. Lara Corday was actually Lara Leigh, star of the long-running soap opera *Searching for Sarah,* was one of Newport's best kept secrets. The locals might know it, but they were used to bumping into movie stars at morning coffee, presidents on the harbor launch, princes at the post office. To stare or to show yourself impressed was to mark yourself an out-of-town yokel, a tourist. And the locals didn't tell secrets to tourists.

"Getting a bit stuffy in here, isn't it?" A big hand slipped past Gillian's ribs, reaching for the door's brass handle. His tanned forearm rubbed along her waist. She gasped and shied to her right. And stumbled over her heels.

"Hey, *easy!*" His other arm hooked around her waist to steady her, then draw her upright again. "Sorry. Didn't mean to startle you like that. You could have jumped right through the glass." His arm tightened around her for an unbelievable, outrageous moment, pulling her backward. Her hips bumped his crotch.

"I'm fine!" she snapped, jamming one elbow into his ribs. *"Perfectly—"* He let her go instantly and she whirled around. "F-fine."

Or not. He hadn't withdrawn one inch. Standing toe to toe with him, she was trapped by the door at her back. A pair of broad male shoulders filled her entire horizon. He wore his white golf shirt unbuttoned, showing her a curl of dark hair at the V. She tipped back her head and found him smiling.

"Sorry," he said again, too softly. "I didn't mean to…"

Right. She sidestepped along the wall, careful to give him no excuse to "help" her again. He opened the first pair of doors, then the next, heading her way. She shied off to the center of the room and scowled at his back. *Could* that have been an accident?

"You don't need to be so nervous," he said, swinging open a third pair. The whisper of distant surf filled the room. "It's just a job like any other."

"I'm not—" She stopped and shrugged. Did it show that much? Being on edge, maybe she had misread his actions.

Dark against the brightness silhouetting him, he turned back to study her. "I suppose you're a local girl, a Vod-islander."

That mockery of the upstate accent marked *him* as hailing from other parts, she thought absently. "No." His expectant silence at her one-word response dragged more words from her. "I've been here since the spring." She'd meant to stay only a day or two, a week at most. Still wounded by Lara's letter of rejection, she'd intended only to catch a glimpse of her mother, see her in the flesh once, then go.

Oh, she'd seen Lara Leigh a hundred times or more by then watching reruns of *Searching for Sarah*. But she'd felt no sense of reality, no connection. That beautiful, mobile, weeping or laughing face on the TV screen hardly seemed a real person, much less a person connected to her as no other.

"Living here in Newport?" he prodded.

"Yes." Her first week, she'd stayed at a bed-and-breakfast a quarter mile down the Cliff Walk. Had haunted that stunning path morning and night, sure somehow that if Lara was any relation to her, then this was where they would meet. Her mother would love the cliffs, too. Living so near, she'd be bound to stroll there, drawn by the cry of the gulls, the cool breeze off the glittering ocean, the rumble of the waves grinding the rocks below.

And her certainty had proved right—proof more clinching than any DNA test, to Gillian's mind, that they were of one blood. Walking the cliffs on a misty dawn, her third in Newport, she'd looked eagerly toward Woodwind, its tall chimneys slowly taking shape through the fog. Looked—and had seen a slim figure step out through a wooden door hidden among the wild rugosa rosebushes that hedged the cliff side of the high estate walls.

The figure set off at a long-legged, floating run and vanished around a bend in the path. Gillian caught her breath and jogged after. *Wait, Lara! Wait for me!*

If the runner was her mother. Gillian rounded the bend and glimpsed silvery hair the same shade as Lara Leigh's. Then more rosebushes intervened, black against the pearly mist.

But no hurry, she told herself. She was fifteen years younger and a runner herself. She could overtake Lara whenever she chose. Cliff Walk edged the ragged peninsula jutting out into Rhode Island Sound for another two miles or so. She had plenty of time.

Mist dewed her face, beaded in her lashes, as she ran. A loon called its weird laughing cry from the gray waters below. Gillian came to a set of mossy stone steps and bounded up them, then down another set, her ears straining for footsteps ahead, hearing instead the rip of a wave combing down the black pebbles of the shingle beach fringing the base of the cliffs, some seventy feet below. The path skirted the very rim of the drop-off, and here someone had built a waist-high chain-link fence to keep unwary sightseers from stepping out into echoing space. Wild white daisies softened the craggy soil, trailing downward from rock to rock. Elephant-high clumps of rugosas pressed in from both sides of the Walk now. Blossoms of magenta and white brushed her shoulders as she ran. Through gaps in the bushes Gillian snatched glimpses of the black silhouette of a lobster boat idling in toward a line of pots laid along the cliffs. On a clear day you could see twenty miles out to the islands, but not this morning, when visibility was measured in yards.

And somewhere ahead…Gillian stepped up her pace. She passed a trail that led up between the mansions on her right toward the avenue, but somehow she knew Lara wouldn't stray from this path. A woman who lived most of her life in the public eye would surely treasure this gorgeous solitude.

And what do I do when I catch her? Glance sideways? Say something inanely pleasant, as runners often do when they pass each other—*Nice day, huh?* Or should she run a little farther, then wheel and confront her? *Mother, it's me,* she could say, *Sarah.* But she never would dare. Not after that savaging letter. Gillian pulled up the hood of the orange sweatshirt she wore till it covered her hair. Tightened the string at her throat to keep the hood in place. There was no reason to think that Lara might recognize her, but still…

Mind focused on the bow she was tying and on the coming encounter, she rounded another bend and shied violently sideways, grazing the bushes, thorns plucking at her sleeve. For all her fascination with vistas, she had a healthy fear of heights, and this was a spot she never liked. Just as the path passed a wide gap in the bushes, it dipped, then tilted subtly toward the cliff edge. Here, water ran off from the hillside above, carving a notch in the cliff. Someday the path would be entirely undermined; the hillside would cave in and fall. Cliff Walk, Gillian had learned, had been crumbling for time out of mind, the sea taking the land inch by inch, the soft slate cliffs eroding year by year. The path was perfectly safe, but still, you could feel the abyss calling. Three wincing steps and she was by the gap, looking ahead again.

Lara? The path sloped downward; the highest cliffs were behind them now. The surf sounded louder and the fog was thicker, as if it had chosen this low spot to crawl onto the land. Gillian looked down, picking a route around a puddle in the path, looked up—and Lara burst out of the mist. Retracing her steps, homeward bound already.

No time to think at all. As their strides carried them closer, their eyes met and locked. Hers were a gray so light as to seem silver, fringed by lashes as dark as Gillian's own. Lara's lips parted, Gillian opened her mouth to speak, but the only word that sprang to mind was *Why? Oh, why?*

Gillian slowed, her steps faltering, her mind stumbling. *That's her!* Near enough to touch! Near enough to question—if only she dared.

She didn't. Not this time, anyway. So instead she ran on, reliving the moment, trying to hold that startled, questioning face in her memory. Seeking from it some likeness to her own.

Finding none—

CHAPTER TWO

A HAND WAVED BEFORE HER face, then dropped as she focused on it. "Do this often, do you?" inquired the man. His lopsided smile was whimsical; his eyes missed nothing.

They were hazel, she noticed for the first time. "Do what?" She'd entirely forgotten he was in the room! For only a minute or so? It might as easily have been an hour.

"Vanish down a rabbit hole. Not a very nice one, by the look of it."

"I…was trying to remember if I'd turned off the stove."

He didn't buy it, but he cocked his head obediently, then one eyebrow. "Don't hear fire engines."

Newport wasn't large. Whenever the trucks turned out, the whole town heard the racket. "I believe I did turn it off after all."

"Ah." He'd jammed his hands into the pockets of his chinos. Eyes fixed on her face, he strolled around her. She suppressed an urge to spin warily with him, and let him instead inspect her profile, then her backside. Clenching her teeth, she tipped back her head to study the chandelier above. She'd thought meeting her mother would be the ordeal of the day. Now she looked to Lara for rescue. *Somebody deliver me from this…this…whatever he was.*

Bad news, that's what he was. Elegantly packaged bad news, from his sexily too-long, razor-cut dark hair, to his runner's shoes, which probably cost more than her monthly rent. With all stops in between just as scenic. Not handsome exactly, but something more potent, topped off with a whiff of…unpredictability. Not a trait she cared for in someone who was shaping up to be an opponent.

"You know she's been ill," he said idly from somewhere behind her right ear.

Ill? That was hardly the word Gillian would have used to describe a fall off the Cliff Walk.

Shattered? her mind supplied, and she shivered suddenly. It had been two days after their encounter before she'd heard. She'd picked up a day-old *Daily News* in the Waves, the town's favorite coffeehouse, and sucked in her breath at the headline: Woman Survives Fall From Cliff Walk! Somehow she'd known what had happened even before she'd read about it. "I heard she had…an accident," she murmured, picturing for the hundredth time the stumble—a shoelace perhaps coming undone, or Lara catching the tip of a toe. Then the horrified nosedive, the frantic snatch at the brush on the rim, a flailing cartwheel into space, the rocks rushing upward, the ice-cold sea…

The article said the woman had been lucky, unlike others over the years. She'd fallen at half tide, when a few feet of water covered the jagged beach. Luckier still, a lobsterman tending his pots had seen her from his boat, and rowed frantically over in time to save her from drowning.

The woman had a fractured skull, the article went on to note, and broken bones. She'd been rushed to Rhode Island Hospital in Providence, where the most critical cases were sent. Her name was being withheld pending notification of relatives.

Like me? Nobody told me!

Checking the date of the paper and counting backward, Gillian deduced the fall had occurred the morning of her encounter with Lara, probably within minutes after they'd passed each other. "Name withheld" was a dead giveaway. It took money and power to keep a person's name out of the papers, especially when that person was a celebrity.

The newspaper had been circumspect, but still the rumors had made the rounds. Gillian had heard them from the women in her aerobics classes at the YMCA, heard them murmured over cups of coffee at the Waves. It was Lara Corday—you know, *that* Lara—who'd fallen—

She glanced up as a humming came from somewhere overhead. The crystal pendants on the chandelier trembled and a shard of rainbow danced across the ceiling.

"The elevator," the man said at her elbow.

At last! Gillian swallowed and glanced desperately around the room. Her mind had gone utterly blank; all her endlessly rehearsed words had flown through the open doors and out to sea. There was a carriage clock on the mantel, she noticed, showing the time as ten-thirty. *Half an hour, she kept me waiting.*

But why should that surprise her? A woman who'd discarded her newborn baby like a worn-out shoe, who'd apparently made her climb to the top her highest priority—why should a woman like that worry that she kept others waiting? Whose time but her own would she value?

The door opened behind her and Gillian turned, dimly aware of the man beside her turning, as well.

"Darling," he said warmly, and went to meet the woman framed in the doorway.

So that was his place in this household, Gillian realized at last with an odd jolt of dismay. The boyfriend. A virile courtier to replace the aging husband Lara had outlived. It explained his supreme confidence, his proprietary air. He put a hand to Lara's elbow and led her into the room.

She barely spared him a glance. Her silvery eyes locked on Gillian, and it was the Cliff Walk encounter all over again. An awareness like a path of silver light, a moonbeam tunnel down which they both drifted, until only a few final feet divided them. "Do I—" Lara Corday smiled and shook her head. "I don't know you, do I? My memory these days…" She gave a tiny, rueful shrug.

"Maybe you do," suggested the man at her side. He'd advanced with her, one hand resting at the small of her back. "Newport's a small town. You bump into everybody once a week or so." His voice was tender, almost coaxing. His eyes flicked to Gillian and she could feel them bore into her.

Let him stare. It was Lara's gaze that held her. "I don't think so," she answered cautiously. *Oh, do you know me?* But how could she? One of the few facts Gillian had pried from the lawyer was that Laura Lee Bailey had signed the relinquishment papers two days after Gillian's birth. *You saw me once or twice, maybe—that was it.*

"Oh, well." Lara smiled, dismissing the notion. "I know your name, of course, from your application,

Gillian. I assume you and Trace have introduced yourselves?''

''More or less,'' he said dryly. ''Trace Sutton.'' He clicked the heels of his running shoes and gave her a mock-formal nod.

A charmer when he wanted to be. Gillian didn't trust charm.

Lara touched her elbow. ''Come sit down and tell me all about yourself.''

I'm taller than she, Gillian realized for the first time, as they moved toward the two couches that formed an L facing the French doors. By five inches or more. It was a measure of Lara's presence that she hadn't noticed till now. *I'm too tall, with different hair. My eyes are light brown and hers are gray. Why, we're nothing alike!* What if she'd gotten it wrong somehow? A birth date and a photo—what did they prove? She'd wanted more than paper proof. She'd wanted resemblance, a physical explanation of who and what she was manifest in an earlobe, the shape of a chin, *something…* Instead all she had was this elusive sense of…connection.

''You said on your résumé that you're working right now at the YMCA, teaching fitness,'' Lara said gently, an actress nudging a forgetful understudy back toward her lines.

''Ah. Yes. I've been there since May.'' She'd applied for the job the same day she learned of Lara's accident. Somehow the accident—or perhaps their encounter on the cliffs—had changed her plans. She'd meant to stay in Newport no more than a week. After the accident she could not leave. Not till she learned that Lara was out of danger, she'd told herself.

But one month had slid into the next, and here it

was September. "I taught aerobics, tai chi, weight-shaping classes while I worked my way through college. It was a good way to earn money and stay fit." She'd thought it best to stick to the truth wherever possible. "So when I saw the opening here…" She let her words trail away. *I grabbed it. A foothold in your town.*

"But I've also worked as a secretary, through a temp agency," she hastened to add, not mentioning she'd been less than a rousing success in the clerical world. What else to say? She should be selling herself, not simply staring. Lara had cut her hair since she saw her last, Gillian realized suddenly—or no, perhaps they'd shaved her head in the hospital. It was boy-short, making her lovely eyes seem enormous. Purple shadows smudged the delicate skin beneath. Her gaze also seemed shadowed, with pain or worry.

"That's *excellent,*" Lara said. "I'm looking for someone to deal with my mail and other paperwork, but if you're athletic, as well—I'm *so* out of shape—we could train together. An exercise buddy would get me off my duff, get me moving. Can you lay on the guilt? I'm *hopelessly* lazy!"

"Oh, I can guilt-trip with the best of them." Gillian laughed. "I learned from an expert—my mom." Her laughter jammed in her throat, turned to a fit of coughing that brought the tears to her eyes. *Mom, how could I?*

But it was true. Her adoptive mother, Eleanor Scott—her Real Mother any way you counted—had wielded that parental weapon with surgical deftness. Gillian couldn't recall a single spanking in all her childhood years. A few well-chosen words of reproach, or one look of loving despair, was all it had taken to make her toe the line. She glanced up to find her own sorrow reflected in Lara's eyes.

"You love your mother," she said softly.

"Yes." Gillian rubbed her lashes. "She died two years ago." *Why am I telling you that?* Perhaps because that had started it all. After the funeral they'd found the key to the safe-deposit box. And the letter waiting there for Gillian, which had turned the first twenty-six years of her life into a lie. She wasn't— never had been—who she thought. So who was she?

Only Lara knew, and in one savage letter she'd closed off all possibility of Gillian's ever asking.

"I'm sorry," Lara said. "I understand what it's like to…miss somebody."

She was nice! Gillian had expected anything but niceness. How could this woman have written that soul-crunching letter?

She's an actress, she reminded herself. And a fine one, if winning an Emmy signified anything. Give her a role and presumably she could make it live. But still—

"You went to college. Where?" Trace Sutton cut in briskly. As if he'd heard enough emotional female meandering and it was time for some facts.

"University of Texas at Austin," she answered in kind. "A double major—art and education."

"So you should be teaching art in a public school," he challenged. "Why earn a poor living doing jumping jacks at the Y?"

She could really dislike this man! "I…don't have the temperament for teaching." Not at the high-school level anyway, where she'd tried for three years, then resigned. She had no taste for the profession's disciplinary side, and the paperwork had been a nightmare. "I hope to illustrate children's books someday." The truth again, though she'd turned the clock back. She already had three children's books to her credit, was contracted to finish a fourth by Christmas. That didn't pay her whole way, but supplemented by the exercise classes, she made do. "For now…" She shrugged. "I'm enjoying traveling around, seeing new parts of the country."

"So you wouldn't plan to keep this job long," Sutton suggested gently. *Drifter,* his eyes jeered.

He really, really didn't want Lara to hire her. Why? "On the contrary." She gave him a look of limpid sincerity. "I've fallen in love with Newport. If I could find an interesting job that allowed me to stay here…"

"Then I doubt this position would suit you. Lara lives in New York whenever she's acting."

"But that won't be for months, probably not this year at all," Lara interjected. "They've written me out of this season's scripts. My doctor doesn't think I'm quite ready to—" Her shrug was apologetic, as if she'd willfully chosen her horrific fall in a fit of selfishness. Then she brightened. "Still, all this fan mail keeps pouring in, piling up in corners, and I *really* need to get back in shape, so when do you think you could start, Gillian?"

Trace Sutton coughed and bumped Lara's shoulder.

She bit her lip. "If I decide to hire you," she added like a good child reciting a lesson. A tinge of pink brightened her pale cheeks.

"I could start right away," Gillian said promptly, refusing to even glance at the overbearing brute. "That is, if you don't mind my juggling this job around my aerobics classes for a few weeks till the

Y can find a replacement. I think I could swap some of my day classes with a woman who teaches nights and—''

"That sounds *perfectly* satisfactory." Lara laid a slim hand on Trace's arm as he stirred again. "Gillian, is there a phone number on your résumé I can reach you at? Good," she continued decisively when Gillian nodded. "Then may I call you later today with my decision? I'm afraid it's time for my physical therapy session at the hospital."

"Of course." But Gillian knew the verdict already. A lover's word carried all the weight in the world. She searched her mind for something to prolong the interview, but short of crying *I'm your daughter! You really ought to give me a chance this time!* she could think of nothing to do.

Except swear to herself she would never *ever* forgive Trace Sutton for wrecking her best, probably her only, chance to learn the truth about her origins. Inwardly raging, she maintained a stony silence as he escorted her not only out of the house but all the way down the long, curving driveway to the front gates of the estate. What did he think—she might hide in the bushes, then pop out at Lara's car when it passed?

"I figured you'd appreciate a boost over," he said gravely as they arrived at the gates, an eighteen-foot barricade of ornately curlicued wrought iron topped off with vicious spikes.

He could joke while he snatched a job away from her? Maybe he didn't realize what this meant to her, but still, for all Sutton knew she might desperately need employment. *Terminally selfish, that's what he was!* All she could conclude was that he wanted Lara to himself. No doubt he'd make sure she hired some grim-faced old bag who typed a hundred and fifty words a minute.

"Or if you don't want to climb," Sutton continued when she refused to smile, "you walk between this electric eye and that one." He nodded at two knee-high metal posts implanted at intervals along the driveway. "They decide you must be a car heading out and—voilà." The gates swung majestically open. "Goodbye, Gillian," he added gently. "And…don't get your hopes up."

"I—" She spun and stalked off, tears of rage gathering in her eyes. *So close, so close!* All but for that selfish…brute.

CHAPTER THREE

HANDS JAMMED IN HIS pockets, a reluctant smile quirking his lips, Trace Sutton watched her go.

Most people tightened up with rage. Gillian swung off on those long, long legs like a woman on a mission—a tiger to shoot or a city to sack. As if she'd just heard about a summer sale on silver platters. *She needs one for my head,* he acknowledged ruefully.

He leaned against the bars of the gates to keep her in sight as long as possible and crossed his arms. After a moment he noticed he was rubbing his right forearm. It still tingled where he'd snugged it around her waist. With a grimace, he shoved his hands back into his pockets.

She hadn't been toting; he was reasonably certain of that. A weapon tucked in her waistband had been the logical assumption since she'd worn a loose, gauzy overblouse that hid the top of her skirt. But his lightning frisk had found no gun, no knife—only vibrant, willowy slenderness, a feminine shape that fit his arms as though molded to his personal specifications.

Given her skirt, there was only one other place Gillian might be packing. He'd pictured himself smoothing his hands up the inside of her long, honey-colored thighs—strictly searching for a shiv or a gun taped in place, of course. But try as he might, he hadn't come up with an excuse for doing it that the lady would buy.

Except that I'm an oaf, and she thinks that already.

Far down the street, he noticed, she reached a corner and turned left. Which checked out. That was the most logical route back to the address she'd given on her résumé.

He'd thought it was too damned convenient to Woodwind when he'd first noted her street. But Newport had a layout unlike most cities, where the rich lived on one side of town and the poor on the other. Situated on a long, meandering ridge that encircled a harbor, Newport divided its social classes not by horizontal miles but vertically. The "summer cottages" built at the height of the Gilded Age graced the top of the ridge, while the bungalows and triple deckers that had once housed the Irish maids, the gardeners and cooks and stable hands who had serviced those mansions occupied the lower slopes.

So in itself the proximity of Gillian Mahler's place to Woodwind was no grounds for suspicion. Still... "Something doesn't fit," he murmured aloud. She'd looked like a winner to him, and that didn't jibe with the profile.

But looks and manner aside, there was the fact that she'd drifted here from afar. And she lacked a steady, full-time job.

Which describes just about every kid in the city, he reminded himself. Newport had a well-earned reputation as a good-time town. The young swarmed here from all over the country, even from abroad, to work the summer jobs at the hotels, restaurants and bars. After hours they partied the night away, then spent their mornings drowsily perfecting their tans at the beach, before it was back to work again.

So explain away Gillian's rootlessness and still he had that look she'd given him when he'd stopped Lara from hiring her. If looks could kill. And rage was definitely part of the profile.

Maybe she just needed the job. He squared his shoulders, shrugging off that twinge of guilt. He had one goal here and one goal alone, and nothing would deflect him from it.

So, put her on the shortlist?

His list was damned short. Twenty-seven applicants so far and he had only three candidates, losers all, but not one he'd bet his money on.

So, Gillian? Profiling was hardly an exact science. And those emotions he'd sensed once Lara had joined them… They'd raised the short hairs on the back of his neck.

Powerful, inappropriate emotions were definitely part of the profile—though oddly, he couldn't quite swear which woman had been transmitting.

Or both? *Did I miss something? Or add something that wasn't there?* Usually he trusted his instincts in these matters. This time, something seemed to be jamming the signals.

An image of long graceful legs, of smoldering lioness eyes, drifted across his mind. Trace grimaced. He didn't like to think of sexual attraction crossing his wires, but he'd seen it happen to so many men in his business he'd be a fool to consider himself invulnerable.

And a greater fool to let it interfere with his job.

Well, the solution to that problem was easy. *Keep her at a distance.*

But put her on the shortlist, he decided also, and headed up the driveway. *Maybe even the top of his shortlist.*

LARA HAD GONE UPSTAIRS, Trace found when he returned to the mansion. He took the steps two at a time—she really did have a physiotherapy appointment within the hour. He entered her unlocked bedroom without knocking, then paused. "Lara?"

His pulse jumped a notch when she didn't answer. His eyes swept the big sunny suite, half bedroom, half sitting room, then the balcony beyond, with its magnificent view of the sea. Nothing out of order. Nothing smashed or overturned. Lucy, the downstairs maid, had told him Lara was up here, but maybe she'd—

He sensed a presence and turned to find her standing in the doorway to her dressing room. Silent and unsmiling, she gazed at him for a moment, then withdrew.

So…he had offended her. She'd been so docile and subdued since her fall, he'd grown used to taking the lead. Surprised when she'd gone her own way during the interview this morning, maybe he'd brought her back into line a little too smartly.

"We need to leave in ten minutes," he said, coming to stand in her dressing-room doorway, wondering whether to apologize or let it ride. The little room, lined with mirrors and louvered doors that hid her wardrobe of stunning simplicity, was empty. Lara had retreated all the way into her bathroom, a room that by unspoken agreement was off bounds to him. But the door was open and today wasn't just any day, since they so rarely disagreed.

"Lara?" He stopped in the doorway to her bathroom. She stood brushing her hair before her mirror, a gesture that would have expressed her irritation beautifully four months ago, when those silvery locks had been a foot longer. In her imagination, they probably swirled around her shoulders still.

In reality, short as her hair was now, it stood up in silky tufts, then fell softly as the brush passed. She looked like an outraged downy fledgling. He had to work not to smile. "We'd better go."

"I wanted that one, Trace," she said with fierce determination, staring at herself in the beveled glass.

"You know it's not in the plan." He desperately needed a second person to spell him. Backup hadn't been a problem those first two months after her fall, while she'd stayed in the nursing home. He'd brought in three capable private-duty nurses and alerted them to the danger. Whenever he'd left her bedside, he'd known she was in good hands and he could rest easy.

But these past two months back at Woodwind… There was too much ground here. Too many people for one man to cover. Even for a low-profile assignment, this was ridiculous, as he'd tried to tell her from the start.

A typical shift in his business was twelve hours. He was doing twenty-four, day after day after day. His concern wasn't exhaustion so much as growing stale. No one could live at the pinnacle of alertness without stand-down time.

"So let's *change* the plan," Lara muttered.

Trace breathed in, held for a count of three, breathed out. A centering exercise in karate: achieve serenity first, then take action. "What was wrong with number seven?" he asked finally. "Liz Galloway?"

Galloway wasn't a member of his own security firm, Brickhouse, Inc., but she'd come with the highest recommendations. To maintain her cover, she'd applied for the job in the same way as all the genuine applicants.

The brush paused midstroke. "She…intimidated me."

Trace snorted. "Don't be silly." Lara was one of the bravest people he'd ever met, man or woman. The pain she'd endured without whimpering, those first few weeks after her fall… He remembered looking down at those big haunted eyes set in that swath of bandages and wishing she *would* cry out, complain, weep—anything but lie there bleakly accepting, as if pain were only her due.

"I'm not! I felt as if she was measuring my neck for a collar and leash. As if she'd expect me to heel every time we went out for a walk. Well, *no,* thank you. It's bad enough having you—" Lara stopped, carefully set the brush aside. Reached for a bottle of lotion and fidgeted with the cap.

"Having me…?" he prompted mildly, though he knew what she'd say. It was the perennial problem between bodyguards and their clients, almost always the reason a bodyguard's contract was terminated prematurely. Along with protection came loss of freedom. Spontaneity. Privacy. Once the client's original fear diminished, resentment inevitably followed.

"Having you living on top of me," Lara mumbled without meeting his eyes. "If I was stuck with Liz, as well, I think I'd go…" She shrugged. "Nuts."

"I'm sorry. I try to not cramp your style." Yet the requirements of the detail made it all but impossible.

He was here under cover, and only one role allowed him to plausibly stay by her side day and night.

"Oh, Trace, I didn't mean it that way! You've been—" She turned and smiled up at him. "I'm *very* lucky to have you—I can't believe how lucky. But if I can't have my privacy, at least I want to be…comfortable with the people around me. And besides," she hurried on as he opened his mouth to argue, "we agreed that whoever was hired, she'd have to really function as my personal assistant. Liz Galloway just didn't have the—the warmth or the tact the job requires. Some of those fan letters are so *silly,* the people who write them so—so desperately needy… The job takes somebody with sensitivity. A sense of humor."

"Ouch, poor Liz!" But he could see what Lara meant. The ex-policewoman wouldn't score high on the warm-and-fuzzy scale. "All right, then. I'll see if I can find somebody else." Inwardly he groaned. Female BGs were rare, and therefore in demand, and of the few available not just anyone would do. He'd hire only the best for Lara. And for himself. A partner he couldn't trust was less than useless, endangered everyone.

Laura shook her head. "Don't bother, Trace. I want her. Gillian."

"Out of twenty-seven women you've interviewed, why her?" The one who worried him most.

Laura shrugged. "I don't know. She…" She shrugged again. "I liked her."

"Okay, well, let me tell *you* why not. For starters, Mahler's not a bodyguard." And that was only for starters.

Lara tipped her head in a tiny gesture that meant,

"So what?" She reached for his wrist and turned it, making a comic face at the time on his watch, then nudged him ahead of her out the door—as if he were the one who'd been delaying them. "Does it ever occur to you," she said lightly, following him into the bedroom, "that four months have passed since anyone tried to...hurt me?"

"I haven't exactly given anyone a chance," he reminded her. And if she hadn't snuck out onto Cliff Walk without him that morning in May, no one would have laid a hand on her then. "But aren't you forgetting your pen pal?" She'd received two letters since her fall, five before, for a total of seven.

Those disturbing letters, with their effusive admiration, their seething frustration, ominously mounting expectations, coy allusions to death and violence, had been sent by a fan who signed herself Sarah XXX, and had persuaded Lara to consult him in the first place.

Lara looked stubborn. "I'm not so sure they're connected to...Cliff Walk."

This was an old, old argument between them. "I'm not sure they're not. And even if we do have two separate problems—*two* crazies—that only strengthens my point. You need another bodyguard, not a ditzy aerobics instructor."

"If I'm to stay cooped up indefinitely at Woodwind, I'm more in danger of losing my girlish figure than my life! Gillian would be a big help there."

"Any competent BG can train with you, if that's what you—"

"I don't want a *drill* sergeant, Trace. I want a—" She paused, tears gathering suddenly in her wonderful eyes, then blew out a big gusty breath and gave him a wavering smile. "I want a friend, okay? All my real friends are back on the set in New York, you know. Nowadays I only have you, and you're *useless* for the girl stuff."

"Thanks, I think." He ushered her to the door of the suite, stepped out first and glanced both ways. She made her usual face at him. More and more she was considering him a worrywart, his precautions a nuisance. They walked down the hall to the tiny elevator installed in a dumbwaiter shaft and he waited till the elevator door had closed behind them. "Look, Lara, you hired me to protect you. Well, it's my considered professional advice that you still need protection."

She mulled that over while they walked through the house, out through the kitchen door to the carriage house that served as a garage. She waited obediently at a safe distance while he inspected, then started the car—he didn't expect bombs with this kind of situation but why take the chance?—then she settled onto the front seat beside him. "You know, it…wouldn't have happened if anyone else had been there to witness it or to scream. I mean, that was the act of a coward, wouldn't you say—jumping out from behind me like that and…?" Her voice trailed away.

He nearly took her hand where it lay fisted on the seat between them, then suppressed the impulse. *Brave girl,* he applauded her silently. This was the first time she'd broached the fall of her own accord. Every other time, he'd had to lead her through it, word by halting word.

He didn't agree with her assessment, though. Someone had jumped out of the bushes behind her as she jogged or had overtaken her silently. Had—in broad daylight!—gripped Lara's hair with one hand, close to her nape so she couldn't look back. Had grasped the waist cord of her sweatpants with the other hand, then forced her, step by struggling step, over the cliff edge. To his mind, the act took nerve, determination—and terrible hatred. It wasn't the act of a coward, however it might comfort her to think so. It was the act of a risk taker.

Worse yet, a well-organized, premeditated risk taker, who'd chosen his or her place of ambush with intelligence and care—a gap in the bushes, a spot where the path skirted the drop-off, where twists in the trail blocked the view at both ends.

"Gillian's a big girl," Lara went on when he didn't speak. "If she'd been there with me, no one would ever have dared..."

Yes, Gillian was a big girl—five-nine or -ten. And despite her slenderness, if she taught aerobics, tai chi, she'd be strong for her size... Strong enough to shove a smaller woman off a cliff? Definitely.

"How about a compromise?" he said, instead. "It may take me a week or two to find a female BG you can live with. In the meantime, why don't you hire one of the other applicants—"

"*No.* I want to hire Gillian."

As the gates swung ponderously inward, he studied her exquisite profile. Her chin was tipped in defiance, her arms crossed tightly across her chest. He swore to himself, then pulled out onto the avenue and stepped on the gas. For weeks he'd been silently rooting for her, hoping her spirit would mend along with her bones. But why did she have to regain her spunk today of all days? "Is there something you're not telling me about Mahler?" he asked as they passed the Newport Casino, which had the oldest grass tennis courts in America. "You're sure you've never met her before?"

"I…" Lara shook her head finally. "It's f-funny, because that's what it feels like, but no…I'm sure not."

Under stress, she had a charming hint of a stutter. The question was what was he missing here? "Then why her, Lara? You didn't even ask her how fast she types, whether she's computer savvy, if she can—"

"I think she'd be good for me."

Said with ominous finality. You could give a client advice, but you couldn't make her take it, Trace reminded himself. The cardinal rule of his profession and the most frustrating. He could push no further. He *could* give Lara an ultimatum: insist on Gillian, and you'll have to get yourself a new bodyguard. But he wasn't ready to do that. For one thing, hiring Gillian Mahler might be no more than Lara's harmless whim.

Or it might, just might, prove suicidal.

Either way, he'd stayed too long on this assignment to quit now. He meant to see it through till Lara was freed from danger. Unlike most security firms, the Brickhouse credo was that they solved the client's problem; they didn't just make their money off it.

And if Gillian was the problem?

Well, he'd meant to investigate her anyway. He just hadn't expected his prime suspect to be dropped in his lap. Trace smiled at the image—couldn't help himself—then glanced at Lara.

"All right. You're the boss, boss."

The smile she gave him was a fair trade—more than fair—for all the headaches this whim was bound to cost him in the end. They didn't speak again until he turned into the parking lot across from the Newport Hospital.

"You asked me to tell you if I ever remembered anything else about that morning," Lara murmured. "And something did come back to me a little while ago while I was brushing my hair. The runner I saw that morning out on Cliff Walk?"

The unidentified runner, sex unknown, wearing a hooded orange sweatshirt, who'd passed Lara only minutes before her attack. Trace's best bet for her assailant. It would have been easy to spin around and follow Lara back through the fog, catch her just as she passed the fatal gap... "Yes," he said without inflection. *Come on, Lara. Give me the goods and I'll nail the creep.*

"I told you I thought it was a college sweatshirt, with University of something with an M—Michigan, Minnesota, Montana?—printed on the chest."

"You did."

"It was University of Miami."

"You're sure of that?" he said quietly. Her recall of the last few minutes before the accident was piecemeal and fuzzy, a result of either head trauma or sheer terror.

"Absolutely."

He parked the car and turned to look at her. "So what brought it back to mind?" Sometimes the association that sparked the memory was more telling than the clue itself.

"D-don't know. It just came to me."

CHAPTER FOUR

Dearest Lara-Mommy,

Something told me that today I'd be SURE to get a letter from you!! I went to my mailbox four times—one, two, three, FOUR—but it never came. At least, the man behind the counter said it didn't come. I'm starting to wonder about that guy. Could he be stealing my mail?!! He stares at me every time I come in now. But maybe that's just because he thinks I look EXACTLY like the famous TV star Lara Leigh? People are always, I mean ALWAYS, staring at me on the street and thinking that. I stopped and gave one woman who was staring my autograph the other day. She thought that was *so* NICE of me to give it to her without her even asking.

But then, I'm not conceited like some people we know. And all *I* want to know is, WHY do I have to keep asking you for a letter? Asking and asking and asking and ASKING for one…CRUMMY…LETTER—what kind of mother makes her daughter beg for just the scraps—any old scrap—of her love? Just a crumb of attention? I guess the same kind of mom who sells her baby to finance her way through med school, huh?

Well, I'm getting very, very tired of asking. Tired of walking to my mailbox, then home again, then back again, then— I know every line in the sidewalk on the way to my mailbox. I play Step on a Crack and You'll Break Your Mother's BACK. Do you remember that game? It's a children's game. If you'd been there for me, Lara-Mommy, instead of devoting all your selfish life to your lousy CAREER, we could have played it together. And maybe then, if you'd been there to guide me I'd have amounted to something. Is that it? Is that why you won't answer my letters anymore? Because you're ashamed of me?

I promise you won't be when we meet. Soon. It's time for a mother and daughter reunion, don't you think?

But till then,
WRITE ME, YOU *BITCH!* (HA-HA—Just kidding!!!) your loving Sarah XXX

WITH A SHUDDER of disgust, Trace dropped the letter on his desk. He stood, switched off the lamp, then moved to the window and leaned out, greedily breathing in the sweet night air, as if the letter's cloying brew of need and hatred had contaminated his lungs as well as his mind.

His office looked out on the front grounds of Woodwind. Even with his thoughts elsewhere, his eyes roved automatically over the darkened lawn below, seeking movement, any shape that departed from the normal outlines of the lush landscaping. Nearly midnight and not even a skunk waddled across the lawn in search of grubs.

He glanced back to his desk. He'd been combing through Sarah XXX's letters for the past hour, searching for any clue he might have overlooked. That letter was number four of the collection—rather, a copy of number four, since the original was filed with the Newport police. The stalking case against Sarah XXX had to be meticulously documented so that if—*when,* he corrected himself—Trace finally tracked her down, they could prosecute.

Like all the other notes, number four was a textbook example of the kind of mash note celebrity stalkers sent the objects of their twisted affections. Whatever the words, the underlying theme was the same: terrible, unappeasable neediness. The echoing emptiness of a person who has no identity in the normal sense of the word. Because for whatever pathetic reason—neglect, abuse, psychological dysfunction?—the typical stalker possesses no self.

Like Dorothy's Tin Man, who realizes he lacks a heart, the stalker is still human enough to know he lacks something. Even if he can't describe the problem, still he senses the void within—the black hole that in a normal person is filled by a sense of selfhood. *By a soul.*

And the stalker knows he needs to fill that void. Yearns most horribly to fill it. Believes with unshakable faith that to ever be happy, to ever be normal, he *must* fill it.

So just as the Tin Man set off to ask the Wizard of Oz for a heart, the stalker goes bumbling through life, searching and searching outside himself for a solution to the problem that lies within.

Until one fine day the answer comes to him. He has a black, sucking hole where his identity should be? He'll fill it with someone *else's* identity! *Someone else's soul.*

And since the void is so big, he'll need a big identity to fill it. Somebody important, however the stalker defines importance.

A generation ago, importance was a politician. Today, importance is most often a celebrity. So one day, the stalker flips the pages of a magazine—and sees a photo. Or turns the TV channel just as a certain actress walks into a room—and wham!—there it is. A person staring into his eyes, seemingly speaking to him and him alone, promising him the solution to his whole rotten, lonely life. Promising recognition, belonging—identity.

All he has to do is win that person's love, the stalker thinks. Except he doesn't know what love is. His underlying urge is darker, deeper. He doesn't want love; he wants possession. Wants to merge with. Become. Seize that soul and swallow it whole. *To eat it.*

Trace switched the lamp back on and sat again. So with zombies like that wandering the world, what does Richard Corday do for his new, beautiful young wife?

Already the creator of five hit TV shows, Corday sets out to create a showcase series for Lara. The perfect wedding gift for an actress, he must have thought. *A role to die for.* Like a master jeweler crafting the perfect setting for a matchless diamond, he creates an evening soap opera called *Searching for Sarah.*

In which, for the past thirteen years, Lara had played the part of beautiful young Dr. Laura Daley, who has a secret sorrow. At the age of seventeen,

Daley sold her illegitimate baby in a black-market adoption and used the payment to finance her way through college, then med school. Lara had assumed the role when she was thirty—at that age, she could still play the part of a teenager—and she'd been playing it ever since. The role had evolved over the years, with Dr. Daley changing from career-driven girl, to brilliant med student, to sexy resident, to glamorous pediatric surgeon in a big city hospital. She needed only one thing to make her life perfect: reunion with her lost, never forgotten, deeply regretted daughter. Because, since episode three of the show, Dr. Laura Daley had realized her dreadful mistake. She'd been frantically searching for Sarah for thirteen years now.

The premise was guaranteed to speak to every wacko in the country—at least every female wacko, and doubtless some of the males. What could be more seductive to the loser nobody needs than a TV diva who needs you and you alone? For somebody lost to know that lovely Dr. Laura Daley is frantically searching for you?

Searching for Sarah was like a Help Wanted ad, broadcast one night a week for thirteen years. The one part waiting for an actor to fill it was the role of the missing, longed-for daughter.

Was it any wonder Sarah XXX wanted the position? The only wonder was that Trace didn't have a dozen—a hundred—wannabe Sarahs to contend with. Lara had been damned lucky to escape a serious stalking as long as she had.

How serious a stalker was Sarah XXX? That was the question.

Six days after Sarah XXX mails this letter from Boston, promising—threatening—a mother-daughter reunion, somebody pushes Lara over a cliff. The simplest explanation wasn't conclusive, but Trace firmly believed in starting with it first: one wacko, not two.

So all I have to do is find Sarah XXX.

And maybe he had. He reached for letter number five, then selected, instead, the top page from a thicker stack of papers. Gillian's résumé.

He paused as the buzzer tucked in his pocket quivered soundlessly against his thigh. Lara. He waited, eyes unfocused, breath deepening, preparing himself for action if this was a call for help—then let out a little sigh of satisfaction when the buzzer stopped vibrating after three seconds. Good. *And good night to you, too, Lara.*

Buzzers were a bit of proprietary technology that Brickhouse used in any case where physical attack was a possibility. The client was instructed to wear a special locket on a chain around his or her neck at all times. Press the button concealed in the locket's design, and a silent buzzer would alert the Brickhouse bodyguard that he was needed—and needed *now.*

He glanced at his watch. Midnight. Which meant it was nine in Seattle, not too late for his night-owl younger sister. He picked up his phone and dialed.

"Mmm, 'lo?" a drowsy voice murmured in his ear.

"Asleep already?" he said easily. "Lazy bum."

"Dozing," Emily insisted. "I'm lying here on the couch with Duncan on my chest." Duncan was one of her four tomcats, the surly orange one. "And he's emitting sleep rays. I was fighting valiantly, but—"

"Well, throw him off and go look at your computer." Trace had scanned Gillian's résumé into his computer, then e-mailed it to Emily an hour ago. "Got somebody I want you to check out for me."

His younger sister was not a partner in Brickhouse, God forbid, but an associate. They farmed out much of their research to her, especially anything that could be learned over the Internet.

"Rush job or in my own sweet time?" she inquired around a yawn.

"Like *prontissimo.* I want it yesterday."

"So my—lemme go, you cockleburr!" On the far side of the continent, something heavy hit the floor—twenty-two pounds of cat, Trace assumed. "So my brainstorm worked?" Emily continued. She'd suggested Trace run a want ad seeking a personal assistant for Lara, because if Sarah XXX had come to Newport in May, then maybe she'd stayed.

That wouldn't be untypical—the stalker's life spiraling inward in tighter and tighter circles around her target as her obsession grew. And if she'd stayed, then she'd be frantically seeking some way in past Woodwind's unbreachable walls. "So offer her a way in," Emily had urged. "Run a want ad with the Woodwind address and see who applies."

"I don't know if it worked," he said, "but it turned up a few possibles. And this is the one I want you to start on."

"Gillian S. Mahler," Emily murmured, reading Gillian's résumé on her screen.

"N. Mahler," Trace corrected absently. "The first thing I want you to check out is—"

"S," Emily interrupted, know-it-all kid sister to the end. "That's an *S.* And I'd say your Gillian's a leftie, correct?"

"*S*…" Trace stared at the spiky, backhanded letter. He'd taken it for a *N* in running script, not an *S* practically lying on its back. "By God, I believe you're right!"

"That's significant?"

"That, duckie, might be point, set and game. Okay, in that case here's what I need from you, and I need it as quick as you can. What does the *S* stand for?"

"And if it's Sarah?"

"Then bingo! I've found my pigeon."

THREE DAYS LATER, on a morning as bright as her mood, Gillian leaned out her car window to study the device that apparently controlled Woodwind's gates. Topping a metal post at a height convenient to the driver, it was an intercom of some sort, with a keypad and a speaker. Printed below the keypad was the instruction Press * To Call. She pressed the star sign, then waited.

"Yes?" the speaker said after a moment, in a metallic imitation of Trace Sutton's voice.

It would be him, playing gatekeeper. "It's G-G-Gillian. I'm here." Lara had called her two days ago to say she was hired, and could she please report for work on Monday. So here she was at last, with all the possessions she'd acquired in Newport packed into boxes and suitcases that filled the trunk and back seat of her car. Because along with the job came an unexpected, quite wonderful bonus: a carriage-house apartment on the Woodwind grounds. Given Gillian's recent problems with roommates, she might have accepted the job on those terms alone. Considering that the job and the housing gave her round-the-clock access to Lara, she couldn't have asked for a better chance to get to know her.

There was no welcoming comment from Sutton,

but slowly the gates swung inward and Gillian steered her ancient Toyota up the winding driveway. At the top of the low hill, the road divided. The right fork curved off grandly to lead front-door callers to the mansion's covered portico. The left fork wound around back, past concealing shrubbery, to the carriage house built to one side of the mansion and a bit behind it.

On the raked gravel before the carriage house, Trace Sutton stood waiting, a sardonic half smile on his face, his hands jammed into the pockets of a pair of impeccable white tennis shorts. The very picture of a gentleman of leisure.

"That's the door to your apartment." He indicated a human-sized entrance to the left of the five garage bays.

She parked before it and stepped out. "Good morning."

"Is it?" he said pleasantly.

Well, it was for me till now. Why did he dislike her so? She glanced past him toward Woodwind. "Where's Mrs. Corday?"

"She's not up and about yet. She had a bad night." As he spoke, he opened the rear door of her car and lifted out a box. "So meantime I'll show you your apartment and help you get settled."

"Oh, that's really not necessary!" She reached for the box, but he didn't relinquish it. "If you'd just give me the key, I'm sure I can…"

But he'd already stepped around her and started off. "Nonsense. It's no trouble at all."

"But—" She didn't *want* him intruding on her new space or on her new-job excitement. Fuming, she grabbed a couple of smaller boxes and followed him up the covered staircase that was built on the outer wall of the carriage house, then through a door at the top of the stairs. "Oh!" The slanted ceiling was set with skylights.

"Nice, isn't it?" Sutton said from the far end of the long room, where he waited in a doorway. "I used to live here myself."

"You did?" Perhaps that accounted for his proprietary air. Still, Gillian didn't like it. He rubbed her wrong; the vibrations he'd left behind would bother her, too. Frowning, she followed him into the bedroom, and stopped short in delight.

The end wall was mostly glass, a gigantic Palladian window that looked out on the side lawn, then over the distant back wall. Beyond that all was blue—robin's egg sky, a slash of aquamarine sea.

"Yes, I rented this place for a month this spring, before I moved in with Lara."

So their relationship was quite new. Must have blossomed almost overnight, given that Lara had spent most of her spring and summer in hospital. One of those sickbed romances—he'd wooed her when her resistance was at its lowest, chocolate and flowers and reading to the invalid? "I see," she said evenly. He'd set her box of clothes down on the bed. The top flaps, which she'd interlocked, had somehow come undone. She dumped her own boxes beside it. "What did you mean by 'a bad night'? Pain?" She straightened to find his eyes locked on her face.

"Nightmares," he said bluntly.

"Oh." Yes, she could imagine that. She shivered, and watched him note it. Why was he staring like that? The memory of his arm sliding around her returned abruptly. She'd put any notion that he might have been making a pass aside after his obvious attempt to block Lara's hiring her. Rationally, one action didn't follow the other. If Trace was attracted, then why would he object to her working at Woodwind? He wouldn't. Since he *had* objected, therefore that fumble at the windows had not been a pass.

Now, with his eyes lingering on her mouth, she wasn't so sure of her logic. "Er, there's lots more in the car." She ducked out the door.

They brought up a second load, Trace in the lead again. He swung her suitcase onto the bed, then opened a sliding door to reveal a closet. "There're plenty of hangers. Why don't you hand me your things and I'll hang them up."

Funny, he didn't look in the least domestic. "Thanks, but I'd rather do it myself." Later, without an unblinking audience.

Her words hung between them in the small room, a little too emphatic, a little too prim. Maybe she was wrong to take offense. Maybe this was no more than the kind of service a slightly younger man grew used to giving an older, richer woman. She found herself wondering for the first time what Sutton did for a living.

His smile deepened at the corners, but he didn't rush to fill the uncomfortable silence. So she did. "It's just that I've been living crunched into a tiny apartment with too many roommates." When she'd taken the place back in May, she'd signed on to share a two-bedroom apartment with its original tenant. Then Debbie had lost her job. To pay the rent, she'd taken in another two girls, college sophomores in Newport to party for the summer. "Dirty dishes in the sink, people coming and going at all hours or, worse, declaring parties at all hours. Laundry hanging all over the bathroom.'' And Michele, who'd decided she preferred Gillian's clothes to her own and who borrowed without asking. ''It's been too much togetherness by half. So it'll be heaven doing for myself for a change.''

Trace cocked his head. ''Let me guess. You're an only child.''

One minute he doesn't like me, the next he wants to know all about me. She was tempted to brush him off, but she didn't need an enemy at Woodwind. Lara's desire to hire her had overruled her lover's opposition. Still, Gillian didn't know by what margin. Better to play it safe. Try to win him over, too.

''Not quite,'' she said lightly, leading him out of the bedroom and back toward the stairs. ''I have a brother.'' By adoption. ''Chris. But he's fourteen years older than I.'' And when her adoptive parents had divorced back when Gillian was eight, Chris had gone with his father. She had stayed with Eleanor Scott—her adoptive mother—and had wondered for years why her father, Victor Scott, had dropped out of her life so completely.

Because I was never his in the first place! Because it was Mom who wanted to adopt a child, not him— he had Chris by a previous marriage and Chris was quite enough. So many mysteries of her childhood had come clear when she opened that safe-deposit box.

''And Chris lives back in Houston along with the rest of your family?'' Trace prodded, coming down the stairs at her heels.

Houston. She hadn't told him she came from there. *He read my résumé,* which listed Houston as her previous residence and the location of her last two jobs. "Oh, he's here, he's there, he's everywhere," she said with a smile over her shoulder. "He's a delivery captain. Moves other people's yachts around."

There wasn't much family beyond that to claim, in Houston or anywhere. Aunt Susan, Victor Scott's sister out in San Diego. And Ed Mahler, the lovely loony man who had married her mother when Gillian was fifteen and had adopted her, never knowing she was adopted already. He had been as thunderstruck as she at Eleanor's deception. Ed was an engineer in the merchant marine, and after her mother's death, he'd signed on for a regular run on a tanker between Kuwait and New Jersey.

Reaching the car, Gillian found herself still smarting at Trace's invasion of her privacy. It was silly to be so irritated. Perhaps he'd helped Lara cull all the applicants, deciding which were worth an interview. Still, his big hands on a paper that described her life...she didn't like it. "So what about you?" she said recklessly as she opened the trunk. "Any siblings?" Two could play the prying game.

She looked up to find a distinct frown on his face. *You'd rather question than be questioned?* Good. She cocked her head at him inquiringly. *I bet you're the youngest brother, with two older sisters. You're comfortable hanging around with older women. Pleasing them.*

Trace accepted her challenge with a wry smile and said, "Three. A younger brother and two even younger sisters."

So much for her betting instincts. "Then that makes you the responsible, conscientious one," she observed. And it would account for his air of command. The eldest was always the kid left in charge. "And what is Trace, a nickname your family gave you?" Might as well keep him on the run once she had him there.

He pulled her portfolio and the big wooden box she used for a paint kit out of the trunk. "It's short for Tracy," he said amiably, and turned to face her. "And what does the *S* stand for—your middle name?"

Touché! she thought wryly. He wasn't one to run far. *S* stood for two names in one. Sarah and Scott. But Sarah was the name Lara had given her at birth—Gillian knew that from the papers her adoptive mother had bequeathed her—and then apparently her adoptive parents had retained it. Simply because they liked the name Sarah? Or as some sort of salute to Lara's wishes?

Scott was the surname of her adoptive parents at the time of Gillian's adoption. The name she'd refused to give up in a fit of teenage defiance when her mother married Ed Mahler.

So Sarah Scott was how she'd signed her letter last year, when she first wrote to Lara asking if they might be related. And Gillian had no intention of risking exposure by giving it now. Probably she should have changed the S to something else on her job application, but all her ID showed her as Gillian S. Mahler.

She met Trace's eyes and realized that her hesitation had stretched for a minute or more. That he stood motionless, his face as intent as a cat's at a mouse hole.

"My middle name?" She smiled. "*S* stands for Seymour."

CHAPTER FIVE

"Now, TAKE A DEEP BREATH," Lara laughingly advised, as she paused, hand on a doorknob. Despite the nightmares Trace had mentioned, she seemed in fine spirits this morning. Trace and Gillian had collected her from her bedroom suite, where she had taken a late breakfast. She'd led them on a leisurely tour of the public areas of the house, the high point of which, to Gillian, had been an exercise room, complete with lap pool, in the basement that she might use whenever she pleased. The conclusion of the orientation was Gillian's new office, located upstairs in the same wing as Lara's suite, all the way at its western end. "And remember," Lara continued as she opened the door, "it isn't as bad as it looks."

"It's worse," Trace lazily assured her. Apparently having nothing better to do, he'd tagged along on the tour and Gillian wasn't sure if she was grateful or annoyed. On the one hand, his presence diluted the intensity of her first extended interaction with her mother, so that she wasn't constantly "onstage," having to pick and choose her words every minute. But on the other hand, his presence prevented her from connecting with Lara on a more intimate level.

"Hush," Lara commanded as she opened the door.

"If this is *bad*," Gillian murmured, following her into the office, "I don't know if I could stand good.

It just might kill me!'' The large room ended in a gigantic, three-sided bay window, with tiny stained-glass diamond panes trimming its upper reaches; at eye level, half-moon expanses of plate glass framed the outrageously splendid view. A long cushioned seat was built in below each facet of the window; a coffee table was placed in the alcove thus created. Gillian could see the tops of the rosebushes that edged Cliff Walk peeking above the estate walls, then 180 degrees of ocean glittering in the noonday sun.

''It is gorgeous, isn't it?'' Lara agreed. ''This used to be Richard's—my husband's—office. I never did understand how he could write here. But then, he used to sit with his back to the view.'' Her smile wavered for a moment. She swallowed, tipped her head in a movement that seemed to say, *Oh, well,* and contin-ued. ''It was Joya—my stepdaughter—who turned the desk to face the windows last year when she took over.''

Her stepdaughter! Somehow Gillian had thought, if she hadn't been told by now, that Lara had no chil-dren.

''Up until last year, I'd had the same assistant for nine years. But when Beckie left to be married, Joya asked for the job...'' Lara went on, glancing around the room with a faint frown.

''And you can see what a good job she's been do-ing,'' said Trace, nodding at the boxes lined along one wall.

A dozen boxes at least, Gillian estimated, filled with— ''Yikes! Is that all—''

''Fan mail,'' Lara said with a look of comic guilt. ''Still want the job?''

''Well, yes.'' More than ever. Lara wasn't like anything she'd expected. There was some mystery here that needed unraveling. "Who's afraid of a little fan mail?" And now was probably not the time to admit that she had suffered all her life from mild—okay, moderate—dyslexia. Reading required intense concentration and exacted fierce headaches. "Am I looking at a week's worth of mail or—"

"Oh, just today's," Trace assured her blandly.

Lara elbowed him in the ribs. "Sit down and hush *up* before you scare Gillian off the job, you brute!"

"Your wish, oh heart, is my…" Trace retired obediently to a window seat. He selected a catalog from a pile arranged on the coffee table, opened it, and seemed instantly absorbed.

Lara turned back to Gillian with a smile. "It's six months' or more accumulation. Joya fell behind some time before last Christmas and the poor darling never caught up again."

"Though she tried valiantly," Trace murmured without looking up. He turned a page.

"She was only working part-time," Lara defended her stepdaughter. "She and Toby—her brother—were attending college here in town, at Salve Regina…"

A brother, as well! Gillian's stepbrother, also, or was Toby Lara and Richard Corday's son? Which would mean that he was Gillian's half brother. She found herself hoping keenly for the second alternative. Her own adoptive brother had been plucked from her daily life with her parents' divorce. She would have liked a full-time sibling or two.

"What with her midterms and a paper she had to write…" murmured Lara, still defending the absent Joya. Trace rustled his catalog too loudly. Lara shrugged. "Anyway, all these letters need answering. So here's how you go about it."

She selected a letter from the last box in line along the wall, opened it and pulled out a printed get-well card featuring a doleful rabbit on crutches, his ears bent, his head bandaged. She laughed to herself and held it out to Gillian. "They're filming the fall season's episodes of *Searching for Sarah* already. Since I won't be returning for another six months or so, the scriptwriters have written me out of the story. They've decided that I had a dreadful accident while skiing in Switzerland, and no one knows if I'll ever walk again—art imitating life, but not too closely, thank God."

She lifted the card from Gillian's fingers. "Anyway, somehow *Soap Opera Digest* got wind of that plot twist and ran it as their lead story last month. Ever since it came out, half my mail is get-well cards and the other half is outraged complaints."

Either way, Gillian's job was to respond. Lara switched on the computer on the desk and showed her the various form letters. As time and inspiration permitted, she should add a sentence or two to customize the form letter, thus making the fan feel she was receiving a personal response. "I wish there were time to send each of them an answer from scratch, but there just isn't. Still I'm really grateful for their concern. For their…loyalty. Some of them have been writing me for years. Which reminds me—"

Lara showed Gillian how to check to see if the fan was new—in which case the name was to be added to a database Lara maintained, along with a code that showed which form letter she'd received—or if the fan was an old one, then Gillian should review the file to make sure a repeat response didn't get sent.

Autographed photos of Lara were stored in this drawer, prestamped envelopes in that. "And that's about it for the fan mail," Lara said at last. "Except for the...special cases."

"The reality impaired," Trace murmured.

Lara rounded on him fiercely. "They're *not* all—"

"There?" he supplied gently. "Any woman who thinks she might be Sarah? A fictional long-lost daughter of a fictional Dr. Daley, star of a prime-time soap opera? Anyone who believes that isn't playing with a full deck, Lara."

Gillian had wondered herself, of course. Dr. Laura *Daley* was fiction. Lara's maiden name was Laura *Bailey.* Both women, the fictional one and the factual, had sold their babies—one for the money to go to med school, the other for a red sports car. And it was Lara's own husband who'd created the Dr. Daley character. *Why?* The story was just too juicy to pass up? But how could Lara have allowed Corday to use her own life as fodder for a soap opera?

On the other hand, people did it all the time, selling their real-life tragedies or scandals to TV, to be dramatized as a movie of the week. *So why couldn't Lara sell her own story—sell me—all over again?*

"They're a little confused," Lara admitted, regaining her good temper. "So we try to straighten them out gently, pointing out that *Searching for Sarah* isn't based on reality."

Except that it is. Almost. Gillian found herself nodding to hide her confusion.

"I have a form letter for the special cases," Lara went on, "but those I handle personally. If you run across any letter where the fan thinks she might be Sarah, you bring that *right* to me and I'll deal with it, okay?''

Straightening them out gently, she'd said. Except that when Gillian had written Lara a year ago to say that maybe, just maybe, she might be Lara's birth daughter, Sarah Scott, Lara's response had been ferocious, not gentle: *If I didn't want you when you were born, why would I want you now?*

"*Laaaara.* Lara-darling?'' The owner of that caroling soprano paused in the office doorway. Gillian recognized the blonde in the Range Rover, who had coolly nodded her through the gates on the day of her interview. This morning she radiated warmth. "Oh, there you are, darling!'' Her blue eyes switched to Gillian and widened. "And you must be my poor, poor replacement!''

"Gillian, this is my daughter Joya,'' Lara said, and completed the introductions while the girl glided across the hardwood floors to offer her hand. Her palm was marshmallow soft, her grip fashionably limp; her inch-long mauve fingernails made shaking hands a bit of a hazard. Gillian could see why she'd gotten behind in her paperwork.

"Did you need something, sweetie?'' Lara asked.

The girl turned a dazzling smile upon her. "Just your car for a little bitty while? Stupid Toby took the Range Rover back to the dealer. He says it's lost its new-car smell and the dealer should have some sort of spray to make it smell new again. I mean, I ask you, so it smells like it's three months old instead of three days? Who cares? Anyway, I told Duffy and Pooh I'd meet them for lunch out at Bailey's Beach, so could I pretty, pretty please take your—''

"No," said Trace from the window seat. "I may need it."

Sunshine gave way to storm clouds in the blink of an eye, as Joya whirled to face him. "Well, too bad! I asked first!" She glanced over her shoulder at Lara. "Didn't I, darling?"

Lara bit her lip, glancing from one to the other. Trace shook his head slowly and Joya caught the movement from the corner of her eye. Her head snapped around.

"You stay out of this, Trace! It's none of your business."

"We could drive you, I suppose," Lara said. She put a soothing hand on the girl's arm.

Joya shook it off and backed away. "I don't *want* to be driven to lunch like a snot-nosed child. I—"

"Then stop acting like one," suggested Trace.

Joya stamped her foot. "You shut up!"

Gillian drifted back a step…another, then turned. If there had been some way to creep out of the room she'd have taken it gladly. Next best option was to act as though this ugly little scene wasn't happening, go about her business. She stooped by the last box in line and examined its contents.

Behind her, Trace's voice overrode Lara's placating murmur. "If these so-called friends of yours can't be bothered to drive a mile out of their way to pick you up, then call a taxi. You can afford it."

"Trace—" Lara interposed on a note of pleading.

"At least *I* pay my own way here," Joya declared in a vicious singsong, advancing on him. She snatched up the catalog he'd set aside, flipped its pages at random. "Unlike *some* of us who just lounge around, preening and *flexing*—"

Trace laughed aloud. Gillian chose a letter from the box at random. This one was a manila envelope and seemed to contain something thicker than a letter. A gift from an admiring fan? She could ask Lara to show her what to do in cases like that. Lara looked as if she'd welcome a distraction, but Gillian hadn't the nerve. Joya was standing over Trace, her hands clenched as though she wanted to smash his upturned, gently smiling face but didn't dare. Frustrated as the girl appeared, she might lash out at the next person who spoke or moved.

"Flexing and preening and sucking up to older women. Getting Lara to buy you goodies. What are you shopping for this time, Trace, another set of custom golf clubs? Or were you a *very* good boy last night? You deserve a gold Rolex this morning?"

"Joya, that's enough!" Lara said sharply.

Gillian stood, opened the envelope. Any distraction was better than this.

"Enough? It's not half enough," Joya snarled. "It's time somebody said something! If Daddy could see this—this big lapdog who's taken his place. I bet he's spinning in his grave! Spinning and puking!"

The package held something wrapped in several folds of a plastic bag. Pulling it out and unwrapping it, Gillian drifted to Lara's side. From the bag she removed a mottled white-and-brown card, folded loosely around some oblong object. "Mrs. Corday, excuse me, but this letter contained some—"

"If you don't mind, honey," Joya snapped, "you can wait your turn! I'm—"

"Stop!" called Trace, lunging to his feet and swinging Joya out of his way—just as Gillian shook the item free of the card and into her hand.

Her gasp feathered out, loud in the sudden silence.

White fur...the hardness of bone beneath...the stench of rotten meat. Trace caught her wrist and turned it, flipping the object off her palm and onto the desktop.

"Oh, gross!" cried Joya.

"Oh," said Lara, as she sank onto the office chair.

LARA'S "GIFT" WAS THE FOOT of some small animal. *Rabbit's foot,* Gillian thought with revulsion. But not a commercial, sanitized rabbit's foot you could buy on a key chain. Horrible as she thought those were, this was much worse. A homemade job, it looked like, with dark stains on the soft fur.

She became aware that Trace still held her wrist. Warm and oddly comforting, his fingers curled around her. She could feel her own pulse, slamming against the base of his thumb. And his slower, heavier beat, like an answer you could depend on.

"You're not going to faint on me, are you?" he asked absently, looking up from the rabbit's foot into her eyes.

"Of course not," she said, though she did feel— detached. Floating a few inches off the floor. As if she could tip forward and fall into his deep hazel eyes—pools of slate green spangled with gold and gray. Aware, also, that even if her knees did buckle, he was strong enough to hold her upright.

"Of course you're not," he murmured on an odd note, something almost with an edge to it. "And what have you got there?" He reached and caught her other wrist and lifted it, scowled at the bloodstained card she still clutched. "Drop it."

The wrapper fell to the desk and he released her at

last. She stood, rubbing her wrists. Trace used the eraser ends of two pencils off the desk to push open the curled card and pin it flat to the blotter. Lara wheeled her chair up beside her to watch. Joya also crowded closer.

On the inner surface of the bloody card were printed the words:

Lara-mommy! I saw this and thought of YOU. You could use some luck—maybe more than you know? See you SOOOOOOON. Your loving SARAH XXX.

"Gross!" Joya repeated. She sounded more excited than repelled.

"I'm sorry," Gillian said, glancing at Lara's troubled face.

"Why?" Trace snapped.

"What?" Swinging to face him, she found his eyes had gone darker, the pupils expanding like those of a cat when it sees a bird.

"*Why* are you sorry?" he demanded softly.

Bewildered by his intensity, she shrugged. "Of all the letters I had to choose…"

A two-heartbeat pause, then Trace looked down again. "Most unfortunate," he agreed smoothly.

"I'll say!" Joya sniggered. "First day on the job and the girl hits a home run! Way to go, Gillie."

"It's hardly Gillian's fault," Lara protested. "Not her fault at all! If anyone ought to apologize, Gillian, it's me. I should have warned you. Once in a blue moon you'll get a fan who's a little…"

"Or a lot," Trace observed wryly. He was using

his two pencils now to maneuver the manila envelope across the desk to his side.

"Oh, pick it up, for Pete's sake!" Joya reached for it. "Ow!" she yelped as he rapped her knuckles with the eraser end of a pencil. "Did you see that?" she demanded of Lara. "I'm supposed to put up with this crap?"

"Fingerprints, darling," Trace murmured, bending to study the envelope. When he straightened again, there was a stillness about him that hadn't been there before. "This envelope came from which box, Gillian?"

"Th-the one on the end." Whatever Joya might think, this man was nobody's lapdog. Gillian had met rottweilers with kinder eyes. "Why?"

"This is today's mail. Postmarked Saturday in Boston. So today, Monday, is the first day it could have been delivered. So who brought it up to the house?" His eyes swung to Joya.

She squirmed, shrugged, looked up at him with an odd defiance. "Okay, so I did, so what? When Toby and I came in from breakfast, it was there in the mail-box, so I brought it up—brought it here to the office. So what?"

"I believe we had an understanding, Joya. *I* bring up the mail."

"You think that's all it takes to earn your keep around here?" she jeered, backing away from him toward the door.

"Joya!" Lara protested.

"Oh, spare me. I don't want to hear it, okay? I'm late for lunch. Gillie, call me a cab and tell it to meet me at the front gates." Joya stalked out of the room without a backward glance.

CHAPTER SIX

AT SEVEN-THIRTY IN THE evening, a rosy light still lingered in the western sky. Standing at his office window, Trace could see, beyond a hedge of lilacs, a shadowed stretch of the service driveway. "Come on, Gillian." She'd told Lara that she taught an eight o'clock class at the Y Monday nights. Women's weights, she'd said. "Get a move on." She'd have to leave the carriage house any minute now to make it on time. And he couldn't move till she did.

Just one more roadblock in a day filled with frustrations.

After that ugliness in the office, Lara had gone straight to bed. She'd claimed a raging headache and Trace didn't doubt it. Since her fall she was subject to those, and stress looked to be a trigger. But it wasn't just pain troubling her, he'd thought, when he brought her her lunch on a tray.

The lady was blue, it struck him, in spite of her brave front. Not frightened, which seemed the more reasonable response to such a blatant threat, but deeply depressed. And not willing to talk about it— at least not with him. Not till he'd apologized for thwarting Joya.

But Trace had no intention of apologizing to the silly brat. He'd explained to Lara that he didn't want her car out on the street unsupervised, where it might be sabotaged. But he couldn't say that to Joya, since she and Toby lived in a state of blissful ignorance, unaware that Lara was being stalked. Or that their stepmother's "accident" on Cliff Walk was no accident. Only the chief of Newport police and his top detective, Jeremy Benton, were privy to that secret. Lara had wanted to avoid publicity. And Trace felt he had a better chance of nailing her assailant if no hue and cry was raised.

Since the last few minutes, even hours, before a traumatic head injury were often wiped from the victim's memory, whoever had pushed Lara off the cliff had good reason to hope she'd forgotten the assault. Let him or her think so, Trace had urged. *The better to catch you, you freak!*

For the same reason, he lived at Woodwind under cover, with no one but Lara and his police contacts knowing his true role in the household. Because he didn't want to deter a threat—postpone Lara's troubles till he'd gone. He wanted to lull the stalker, lure him or her into his reach. *Look, here's poor little Lara, protected by no one but her bumbling gigolo. Come and get her!*

Or be gotten.

TRACE STRAIGHTENED as headlights blossomed beyond the lilac leaves, then wheeled downhill toward the gates. Gillian's little Toyota. He breathed a sigh of relief. Action at last.

He left the mansion by the kitchen door, checking that it locked behind him. Barbara Heath, Lara's longtime cook and housekeeper, and Maureen, the upstairs maid, had both retired to their third-floor apartments. As had Harriet, Woodwind's perpetual houseguest.

The resident layabouts, Toby and Joya, were out for the evening. If they followed their usual pattern, they wouldn't return till the bars closed at one o'clock. Or later, if they found an after-hours party.

And his client was locked in her impregnable suite with his locket buzzer around her neck. He didn't like to leave her, but it was Lara's choice to hire only one bodyguard. There was only so much he could do.

Nail Sarah XXX and he could stop worrying.

Trace circled the noisy gravel of the courtyard, then approached the carriage house through a flower bed on the downhill side. The copy of the key he'd made two days before—without telling Lara—fit sweetly into the lock and turned. At the top of the stairs, he glanced at his watch—7:55 p.m. He'd give himself till 9:00 to toss the place. It took longer when you meant to leave no signs of a search.

Inside, he paused, listening to the silence. Smelling it. Already the air carried a suggestion of Gillian. Lemons? New-mown hay? The same sunny, subtle perfume that clung to her tawny hair. He'd noticed it that first time he held her. Must be imagining it now, surely.

He padded into the room. After he'd disposed of Sarah XXX's latest offering, Gillian had spent the rest of the morning working on the fan mail. In the afternoon she'd retreated to her apartment. To unpack and settle in, she'd said. Noting a vase of wild roses on the table in the window nook, Trace smiled in spite of himself. Whatever else she might be, she was all girl.

His smile faded. *Whatever else she might be.* He didn't want Gillian to be his psycho. Found it almost impossible to imagine she could be. But if she was?

Then the odds are very good that the lady owns an orange University of Miami sweatshirt, he reminded himself. Find that, and his search was over. Trace headed for the closet in the bedroom.

"GOT A NOTE TO YOU FROM your class," said the front-desk attendant at the Y. "One of them called it in."

Gillian unfolded it on her way up to the locker room:

Gillian, we forgot to tell you that it's Jennifer's BIG FORTY tonight. She opted for champagne instead of tummy crunches, so we're carousing at Yesterday's. Join us, why don't you, and bring the rest of the class. The Rat Pack.

Gillian laughed and shoved on into the dressing room. The Rat Pack were five women friends who'd signed up together for her weight class. A good time was always their first priority; shaping their figures with small free weights ran a distinct second. With those five truant, she'd have only two students tonight.

She'd changed to her exercise togs before leaving the carriage house, but she stopped by her locker to drop off her thigh-length cotton sweater. "Well, blast!"

"Blast?" inquired Bobbie, the sixth member of Gillian's class, sitting down on the bench behind her.

"I'm missing a sweatshirt and I was sure I'd left it here." Her favorite orange sweatshirt, which her brother, Chris, had sent her years ago, when he was attending the University of Miami. She'd looked for it this evening to wear to class and not found it. But if it wasn't back at the carriage house, wasn't in her car and wasn't here in her locker, then— *Michele!* "One of my roommates has struck again. She puts meaning on the word 'borrow' that would make a burglar blush. I'm down three pairs of earrings, a baseball cap, two T-shirts and a pair of 501 Levi's, at last count. And now my favorite sweatshirt." Gillian slammed the locker, then checked the clock on the wall. "Well, ready to hoist some metal?"

Bobbie glanced around the room. "Where are the others?" Two swimmers chatted quietly as they toweled off, but otherwise the place was empty.

"Birthday party for Jennifer at Yesterday's, to which we're invited after class. And looks like Nancy is a no-show tonight. So you get my full attention, kiddo."

Bobbie responded with a wan smile and a shake of her head. "You know what, Gillian? I almost didn't come tonight. I'm having cramps... Would you be hurt if I weaseled out on you and sat in the sauna, instead?"

"Not at all!" She'd be delighted to call it a day herself.

LEANING OUT THE WINDOW of her car to reach the keypad, Gillian punched in the code to open Woodwind's gates. Lara had given her the number that morning, and a good thing, since the mansion was dark. Eight-thirty and everyone had gone to bed? Lights in Lara's suite, situated on the oceanside of the house, wouldn't show, though, come to think of it.

Bed sounded inviting. The day had been a long one, crammed with too many impressions, too much emotion. That horrible letter. *If that's life as a celebrity, Lara can have it!* She shuddered and put the letter from mind while she parked the car.

After entering her apartment, she turned to lock the door, turned back—*"Oh!"* She flinched against the door, one hand to her stuttering heart.

Standing at the counter in her kitchen, Trace Sutton glanced over his shoulder. "I'll have to buy you a decent corkscrew." He held up the simple bartender's device he must have found in her utensil drawer, then jabbed it into the cork of a wine bottle.

Her wine, she realized, recognizing the label. Her heart was still stampeding, but fright was giving way rapidly to rage. How *dared* he simply walk in like this? "Wh-what d'you think you're doing here?"

The cork popped softly. He poured the bardolino into two glasses.

"Well?" she demanded, throwing her sweater on the couch and stalking toward him. The creep had kept a key to her apartment—that much was obvious!

He lifted the glasses, began to walk toward her—and stopped, his eyes dropping to her legs.

Which were bare below her nylon gym shorts. As were her arms, since she wore a sleeveless T-shirt. She swerved toward the sweater she'd abandoned too hastily, then stopped herself. *Show no fear.* With the thought, a twinge of alarm skated along her nerve endings. He was very large and already he'd proven he didn't respect normal boundaries.

"I thought your first day at Woodwind was a little…rough and you deserved a drink." Trace handed her a glass.

"Of my own wine?" If she dashed her drink in his eyes, would that slow him down enough? The distance to her door was twelve steps at least, and then she'd have to throw the dead bolt. Remembering the speed with which he'd crossed the office that morning, she abandoned the notion as soon as it formed.

"I'll do better next time," he assured her.

There won't be a next time, buddy! Was he that vain that he thought he could simply barge into a woman's apartment and be welcome? That with one smoldering look she'd fall into bed with him? Granted, no woman could deny his appeal, but still…

And what about Lara? God, she'd forgotten Lara! Trace wasn't just a sexy lout; he was *Lara's* lout. Too angry to speak, she took a gulp of the wine. And rattled as she was, she tipped the glass too far.

A drop dribbled past her bottom lip and fell. "Damn!" On the slope of her breast, a blood-red spot stained the white cotton.

She looked up to find his eyes aimed at her heart, his pupils gone wide and black as gun bores. His eyes lifted to hers, then slowly one of his dark eyebrows rose in a question. *Well?*

As she imagined his lips on her breast, his hands clamped on her waist, the pressure of his mouth bending her backward, a wave of raw heat washed through her. A tingling awareness spread from the back of her shaky knees and climbed. It didn't matter that he was a vain and faithless brute—in his mind he was kissing her breast and in *her* mind she was responding helplessly. She turned away—felt his eyes caressing her hips and spun back again. "Get out!"

She stalked past him to the sink. Found a dishcloth and dabbed furiously at the spot. A useless effort, of course.

He came to lean on the counter beside her, so close

she could feel the heat of his big body. Stood sipping wine and watching. "Seltzer?" he suggested huskily at last. "That's what my sisters always use."

Sisters, seltzer and spot removal. The sheer domesticity of the images banished fear. And there were rules at play here, even if she didn't understand them. Trace wanted her, that was clear enough, but he wouldn't use his size to take what he wanted—he'd have done so by now.

He expects me to give of my own free will? Oh, he was unspeakably vain! She threw down the dishcloth and wheeled. "I said, get *out*."

He tipped his dark head in mocking acquiescence, then said, "May I finish my wine first?"

May I. Her sense of control grew with the question, and after a moment of icy silence, she nodded. She wanted him out—meant to have him out—but she didn't need to make an enemy. Because faithless or not, Trace was Lara's lover. She'd seen who won the battle over Lara's car this afternoon. Trace had the clout at Woodwind. He could persuade Lara to fire her, if he really wanted to; of that she was certain now. *So I walk a tightrope here.*

He took another savoring sip. She watched his strong brown throat move as he swallowed. Another sip. He had a beautiful mouth, though very masculine. She could see why a woman might want him hanging around. Why he'd expect a woman to want him. Did Lara know he was unfaithful? Or was that simply an accepted part of the celebrity life-style? Maybe Lara didn't care. Not everyone valued fidelity as Gillian did.

"You know, you've been worrying me," he said softly, rousing her from her trance.

"Oh?" Her ever-ready sense of guilt came alive. She didn't want to worry anyone at Woodwind. She'd come here to be the fly on the wall. To silently see all, then fly away. Bluff it out, she told herself. She lifted his empty glass from his fingers and set it emphatically on the counter, then tipped her head at the door and moved purposefully toward it.

He pushed off the counter and padded alongside her with the loose-limbed grace of a sleepy tiger. "I've decided that someone who..." He paused and let the silence stretch.

"Who...?" she prompted evenly. He'd noticed some discrepancy on her résumé? Or maybe— Reaching the door, she flipped the dead bolt and opened the door wide. Stood waiting for him to take the hint and go.

He moved one step into the doorway, then swung back, much too close to her. His hand rose slowly.

So this was another pass after all, nothing more. She narrowed her eyes in warning and raised her chin. Watched his beautifully carved lips quirk at the corners with amusement.

Trace lifted a lock of her hair off her shoulder. "Who looks like you..." He gazed at the curl, rubbing it thoughtfully between thumb and forefinger. "Can't possibly be what she seems...."

God, he did know something! What?

He stared deeply into her eyes. "You can't be a Seymour."

Oh...a stupid joke. She breathed again, then tossed her head. Her lock of hair slipped through his fingers.

"So what's the S really stand for, Gillian?"

Or was it a joke? He wasn't smiling now, not with

his mouth, not with those hunting-cat eyes. Could he know?

He could not. Bluff it out, she told herself again. She sniffed. "Did I say Seymour? How silly of me. It's Sylvester, an old family name." End of discussion! She swung the door around till it bumped his track shoes, and smiled meaningfully at him through the remaining gap. *Beat it, buddy.*

"So...I guess this is good night?" he said on a note of quiet laughter.

"I guess it is." He had charm; she'd give him that. "Oh!" she cried as he retreated a step. "I forgot. You know what's worrying *me?*"

Solemnly he shook his head.

"Apparently you have a key to my apartment. So—" she held out her hand "—give."

He surrendered the key without a protest. Dropped it into her waiting palm—and touched the soft skin of her wrist with one lingering fingertip. "G'night, Gillian."

She stood staring into the shadows where he'd been, counting two of her heartbeats for each of his footfalls down the stairs, then she closed the door. And locked it.

"GOT CAUGHT WITH MY HAND in the cookie jar," Trace admitted a short while later. Lemon cookies hot from the oven. He could imagine what her skin would taste like.

"Oh?" Emily said encouragingly out in Seattle.

He'd called to ask how her research was going. And to talk. He'd been under cover too long. You had to touch base with family—and through them yourself—occasionally or you risked confusion. A blurring of your undercover role and your real identity.

Leaning back in his office chair, he told her about the snafu: Gillian's unexpected return, his frantic scramble out of the bedroom, his covering story of an impromptu housewarming.

"And she bought it?"

She bought that I was a jerk, yes. "Seemed to."

"How far had you gotten in your search?"

Far enough to determine she didn't own an orange sweatshirt.

"Not anymore, anyway," Emily murmured. "She might have dumped it after the Cliff Walk attack."

"Might have." But he couldn't see Gillian shoving Lara over the cliff. Couldn't see Gillian as his stalker at all. Yet she'd found the rabbit's foot letter—chose it unerringly out of a box of thirty or more. Go figure those odds. And her middle name started with *S,* plus she'd given two patently ridiculous versions of what the *S* stood for…

"You didn't see anything else that would tie her to Sarah XXX?"

"No." He'd just sat down to the papers in her desk when her car pulled into the courtyard. A pity. Papers always left a trail. "Speaking of Sarah XXX, her eighth letter arrived this morning." He told Emily about the rabbit's foot.

"The heartless bitch!" Emily's voice rose half an octave. She loved animals, had filled their family home in New Hampshire with hamsters, stray cats, half-fledged nestlings, throughout her childhood. She was the protector of anything that crawled or flew. "She chopped up a *bunny?*"

"Maybe it was roadkill," he lied. Stupid of him to

tell her the details. He had some notion from time to time that if Emily was to work for Brickhouse, she'd have to toughen up, but he always regretted any effort to harden her.

"Not if it was white," she said grimly. "Did you phone the local pet shops?"

"Spent all day on the phone." Calling every pet shop within twenty miles, urging sullen or harried employees to try to remember if they had sold a white rabbit last Friday or Saturday—at least, a rabbit with white paws.

Not an easy task when he couldn't see their faces, judge if they were making an effort to remember or simply brushing him off. "Nobody recalls selling a bun." Of course, the luckless rabbit might have been purchased at one of the farms out toward Second and Third Beach.

Or purchased in Boston. Trace grimaced. No, he wasn't going to find Sarah XXX that easily. "So that brings me back to you. What does the *S* in Gillian's middle name stand for?" *And don't you tell me Sylvester.*

Emily sighed. "You know Harry S. Truman?"

"As in President Truman?"

"The very same. Do you know what *S* stood for in his case?"

"What's that got to do with—"

"It stood for *S,* Trace. He didn't *have* a middle name, just an initial to puff himself up. There's absolutely no law that says you must have a middle name. Or that you can't have five."

Here lay the disadvantage in hiring your sister: you couldn't swear at her. "You're telling me Gillian doesn't have one?"

If she had, Emily had yet to find it. It didn't appear in the credit-card databases, the magazine mailing lists. The registrar at the University of Texas, Austin, knew her only as Gillian S. Mahler. So did the phone company in Houston, Texas, the electrical and gas companies. "Maybe it would show on her driver's license, but Texas has instituted antistalking laws like California, you'll be pleased to learn." Emily understood how he hated stalkers. "So I can't tap into those records. You wouldn't happen to know where she was born, would you?"

"No, and I doubt she'd tell me." She was hiding something; he was sure.

"Too bad. If I could find out that, I might be able to get a copy of her birth certificate, now that I've got her social security number off her credit data. That would show it."

"So what now?" His years as an agent with the FBI had spoiled him. The agency had computer jocks who did nothing but track down data upon request. And the government had sources that private investigators couldn't easily access. Still...

"If you'd like to finance a little road trip to Houston—all expenses including cat sitter—that might be the most efficient way. I got her family's address from the UT registrar. They've moved away—I've checked that already. But if I could run down her high-school girlfriends...or a preacher if her family were churchgoers. Or the district where she registered to vote. With some scratching I'm sure I can uncover something."

"Do it. Can you fly tomorrow?" SOOOON, Sarah XXX had promised. "I've got to know her name soon."

HOURS LATER, SOMETHING woke him. Staring into the darkness overhead, Trace lay listening, orienting himself. Lara's bedroom. Slowly he turned his head to the left. He could see moonlight shining through the tall French doors that led out to her balcony. He'd checked them before retiring, and they stood now as then—securely latched.

And no one could have entered through the corridor. He'd hardened the entire suite his first day on the job. Had chosen the locks for her door and the locksmith to install them.

The soft, incoherent sound came again, and he lifted himself on his elbows to look over the back of the sofa.

Lara, talking in her sleep. "Cloudy..."

He scowled and sat up. *Weather reports at 3:00 a.m., Lara?*

"Cloudy?" More sob than word this time. "Cloudy, I t-tried."

He scrubbed a hand through his hair. Whatever was haunting her dreams, she needed hugging. If she'd been his woman, he'd have taken her in his arms and held her. Kissed her awake.

But she wasn't. He'd drawn the line clearly the first day, and he'd never once stepped over it. You don't boff the clients was rule number one at Brickhouse. They'd all seen too many bodyguards come to grief over that one, and had voted a man out of their partnership last year for breaking that rule.

"Cloudy, she—" Not so much sobbing as keening—a heartbreaking, tiny wail, torn ragged by each indrawn breath, then resumed.

He kicked off the covers and stood. Padded to her

night table and poured a glass of water. Sat on the edge of the bed. "Lara?"

"Sh-sh-she... I think she h-*hates* me."

"Who, Lara?" Sarah XXX? Or something she sensed in Gillian? Or, since dreams didn't confine themselves to the here and now, any one of a thousand women Lara had met at any point in her lifetime, from her hairdresser to a first-grade teacher?

"She..."

He put a hand lightly on her shoulder and shook. "Lara."

She jerked awake with a cry, stared at him blankly for a moment, then hitched herself up against the headboard.

He switched on the bedside lamp. "You were dreaming."

"Oh." Her cheeks were wet with tears. She swiped the back of a hand across her lashes, gave him a wavering smile and accepted the glass of water.

He let her drink, then asked. "About that letter today?"

She shuddered violently, but she shook her head. "My...husband."

Corday had been dead two years, but she wasn't a woman who'd forget a love overnight. Yet Lara had said "she." Still, it wasn't his place to interrogate the client. Trace took the glass from her hands and set it aside. "All right now?"

She nodded, looking like a drowsy, tousled little girl, lost in a bed too big for a child. He gave her a last reassuring smile and stood, flicked off the lights. "Sweet dreams, then, Lara."

"G'night, Trace. And...thanks." A deep, sorrowful sigh feathered through the dark, then he heard her snuggle into the bedclothes.

He walked slowly back to his couch and rearranged his comforter. Lay down. Stared into the blackness again. Knowing by the sound of her breathing that she stared, too. How many people all over the darkened country right now stared at ceilings, their arms as empty as their hearts?

You've been too long without a woman, he told himself wryly, and rolled over. Five months or more.

But to be with just any attractive, available woman... The thought didn't cheer him as it once would have. As soon as Brickhouse was fully viable, had made its rep and could afford to hire some more manpower...say two years, three at the outside...he'd look into that. He thought about his brother Jon and Jon's beautiful Demi...the way she looked at him, when he didn't know she was looking. *Whatever Demi sees, I want a woman seeing that in me.* But not just any attractive, available woman.

Trace curled one arm around his pillow and hauled it close. A pair of golden lioness eyes stalked him into the thickets of sleep.

CHAPTER SEVEN

SINCE LARA SLEPT LATE most mornings, Trace liked to start his day with a workout in Woodwind's basement gym. For once, personal preference dovetailed with professional duty. He could stay fit—the perpetual requisite for a bodyguard—while at the same time he polished his image as the body-conscious gigolo, a self-preoccupied lightweight, no real protection for Lara, no threat to anyone. If anybody was looking...

Gillian, for instance?

After completing his warm-up, he moved to the leg-press machine. Set the weights—he was going for a brisk workout, but not a killer, this morning—then lay back on the inclined seat, his legs straight, his feet braced against the weight board.

Releasing the safety catches, he lowered the board till his knees neared his chest, then he exhaled and pressed up smoothly. *One rep...two reps...three.* The rhythmic thrust and release of the weight freed his mind to drift...make new and unexpected connections. He could choose a problem, then let his mind wander around it at will. Consider Sarah XXX's letters, for instance. They were almost textbook samples of a stalker's mind. *Four reps.* He inhaled, brought the weight board down smoothly. Were the letters perhaps too smooth? *Five reps.* Sarah's transitions from one thought to the next. *Six.* One sentence building on the last, laying the ground for the next—hateful thoughts flowing smoothly...*Seven reps.* An educated, intelligent organization of the contents of each message...*Eight. But who says stalkers can't be intelligent?* Yeah, some of them were off-the-charts intelligent, but smooth? *Nine.* Wounded minds lunged from one concept to another without the normal, sane transitions. *Ten reps.*

Eleven. But the emotions in those letters. The progressive obssession was textbook perfect, building from the puppy-dog anxiety to please in letter number one...*twelve reps*...to the edgy requests of letter three... To the sense of frustrated entitlement of number four...*thirteen*...to the barely veiled hostility of number five, that threat of reunion. *Fourteen*...then after number five, came the assault out on Cliff Walk... *Fifteen and set the safety catches and stand.*

He rolled off the machine, breathing deeply and easily, added five pounds to the weights. Bent over straight legged, till his fingers touched the mat and held it for a count of sixty, then straightened and climbed into the machine again for his second set.

Released the safety catches and brought the weight down smoothly. *Where was I?* Smooth, the emotions reading right, the transitions possibly reading wrong—too smooth? *Make that one rep...* Smooth as Gillian's legs had looked last night...his blood warming, breath coming faster now...*two reps*...and the image of his open hand, sliding up the slim, muscled curve of her thigh... *Smooth Gillian, what are you doing here? She stares at Lara whenever she can, seems fascinated.*

But people stared at stars; he'd guarded enough to know. People stared, wondering, *how are you differ-*

*ent, what do you have that I don't? How could I get
some? Be like you?* Envy and fascination intertwined.

But Gillian had no need to envy any woman…the
way she moved…those eyes… *Six reps.* Last night,
he'd scared her, coming on to her like that. Hadn't
meant to, but on some dark, instinctive level he'd
liked that she tacitly acknowledged his superior size
and strength, the inevitable outcome if… *Down boy!
No ifs, buts or maybes here.*

He punished himself by picking up the pace, breath
hissing in and out, and kept on pushing, no words in
the mind now, not words, but images—soft lips, soft
skin, an all-over softness of spirit that reminded him
oddly of Lara. Sheer femininity, but with an entranc-
ing edge. He'd liked her toughness last night, throwing him out… *Twelve reps.* She liked nothing about
him, demanding her key, which was just as well. If
he couldn't keep her at a distance, then thank God,
she was minding her fences.

Minding them too well? *What are you hiding, Lion
Eyes? Fifteen—* Oh, crap, so much for peace and
quiet, because here came little Joya.

He locked the weights in place and rolled out of
the machine. "'Morning," he said, panting, and
turned his back on her while he added ten pounds to
the weights. She was dressed in nothing but a beach
towel, a sullen look and a few scraps of nylon—a red
bikini he hadn't seen before. She'd come to do laps,
apparently, though this wasn't her usual time. Like
her brother, Joya generally slept till eleven, then
swam, then went out to the beach club or a restaurant
for lunch, and was rarely seen again until the following day at eleven.

He glanced her way as he climbed into the machine

again for his last set and saw that she was down on a mat by the pool, stretching in a square of sunlight like a cat. Ignoring him completely, which suited him very well indeed. He had no use for selfish brats, male or female, and she and her brother were quite the pair. Both were offspring of Corday and his first wife…a film actress, he remembered, and a third-rate talent—he'd seen her in a thriller or two. She was the one the serial killer always finished off in the first reel.

Third-rate talent, first-rate face and body, which she'd passed on to Toby and Joya. But something hard went along with the beauty—a silent message that said, *Look at me. See what you can't have, sucker, and weep!* Smart guy, Corday, to trade her in for Lara, an unknown soap-opera starlet without his first wife's icy beauty-queen looks, but with something much better—heart.

Trace rolled out of the leg-press machine and stood. Now for the bench press. He added two twenty-pound weight disks to the barbell, then lay back on the bench. He grasped the bar, positioning his hands slightly wider than shoulder width, then he lifted the bar off its rack and inhaled as he lowered it slowly to his chest. Exhaled as he pushed it up. Counted *one* as his elbows locked.

"A hundred and twenty?" Joya said beside him. "Toby lifts more than that."

And two and so what? Trace could easily lift his own body weight, 180, but only a fool did so without a spotter. Pull a tendon and they'd find you with your show-off weight compressing your chest, while you squeaked softly for help.

She drifted closer and looked down at him as he

lifted, one long, beautifully tanned calf nearly touching his thigh. What the hell did she want?

"But I guess if you're, like, past your prime and that's the best you can do..." She shrugged contemptuously.

He smiled as he raised the barbell and blew out a breath. Still pouting about yesterday, he supposed. *No* wasn't in Joya's vocabulary, or her brother's, as far as Trace could tell. Their mother out in Hollywood had had custody throughout their formative years, and in Trace's estimation, she'd botched the job. Lara and Corday had taken them on at age nineteen and twenty, after they'd flunked out of school out West.

Corday had persuaded Salve Regina, Newport's one college, to admit them—with the help of a generous endowment, no doubt. But they'd dropped out again in their junior year, last spring, without even completing the semester—"to find themselves," according to Joya. Maybe in five months they'd found all of themselves there was to find? And since their inheritance from their father had just come through probate and they now owned half of Woodwind and three million apiece...*I don't see a Bachelor of Arts in little Joya's future.*

Her calf nudged his thigh. "*Are* you?"

Am I irritated? Most assuredly—he'd lost count. Call it thirteen. "Am I what?" he gasped out on his exhale. *Fourteen.*

"Are you past your prime, Trace?"

Fifteen. He racked the bar, smiled and sat up. Swung his leg away from hers and over the bench, stood and walked slowly around the room, breathing hard, shaking his arms out, rolling his shoulders, his neck. She was spoiling his workout. This was his time to center himself, the time when he did his best thinking. He couldn't let her drive him out, or she'd do it every morning for the sheer fun of it.

Returning to the bench, he found her seated—no, posed on it, her thighs spread wide, her lids lowered in almost a parody of seduction. He swallowed his startled laugh and said simply, "Move."

She flounced off the bench and started away. He breathed a sigh of relief, lay back into his position and lifted the bar off the rack. *One.*

Then she was back beside him, knee nudging his thigh. "But I s'pose you don't have to exactly be in your prime to please an old lady, do you?"

Two. It took him a moment to realize she meant Lara. He snorted. *Three.*

"After forty, I guess you take what you can get, even if you have to pay for it, huh? Does she pay you by the…piece or by the hour?"

Four and enough! Trace paused on the upthrust, elbows locked, and met her eyes. "Sweetheart, don't you worry about Lara. When she's seventy, she'll still have something you never knew you were missing."

His biceps shivered in complaint and he brought the bar down to his chest. Joya swung a leg over him and sat. *"Uhh!"*

Grasping the barbell with both hands, she leaned all her weight on it and smiled down into his face. "What did you say, studmuffin?"

A hundred and thirty pounds at least, added to the bar's one-twenty. And her hips were compressing his abdomen, making it hard to breathe. Face hovering only a foot above his own, her long hair a silken curtain shutting out his light, she smiled a slow, taunting smile. "Hmm? What's the *matter,* studly, cat got your tongue?"

He pulled a difficult breath and looked up at her. Enjoying this immensely, she was. Not just a brat but a bully. Why hadn't he noticed that before?

He could let go the bar with one hand, grab her wrist and flip her off him, but there were exercise machines to either side. If she hit her head. Hurt Joya and Lara would fire him; he had no doubt. And Lara needed him.

Joya was pressing the bar forward, as well as down. If it rolled onto his throat while they struggled... He took another labored breath, considering. *Gotta move soon.* The muscles in his arms, already taxed by his first set, were quivering with the effort to hold the bar off his chest. Spasms weren't far behind.

"*Sooo,* you want to take that back?" she invited.

Apologize? Something in her face told him she wouldn't settle for that. The kid wanted groveling, and he didn't know how. Didn't feel like learning. "Move!" he panted.

"*Ohhh,* take your time, Traciekins. *I'm* in no hurry."

But he was. Trace drew a breath—and released the bar with his left hand. As he grasped a hank of her hair, he braced his left forearm against the bar, keeping it off his throat.

Her eyes narrowed to slits. "Hey!"

"This...is what's called...a standoff," he said between his teeth. She shoved the bar toward his throat and he stiffened his arm. "Don't *do* that!" *Unless you want to be scalped.*

The sound of breaking glass caused Joya to jump

against him. They both turned their heads toward the sound.

Across the room at the edge of the pool, Gillian stood staring. "Um, I...I... S-sorry!" she muttered, and looked down at the shattered bottle at her feet. Her shampoo. She'd intended to swim, then wash her hair in the gym shower. Had walked halfway across the room before she'd seen the couple entwined on the weight bench. Joya and Trace! "Sorry," she murmured again without looking their way. And what now? Flee and leave them to it? Or clean up the glass before somebody got cut?

She detected movement from the corner of her eye and looked around to see Joya approaching. The girl's face was brick-red, her blue eyes glittering. "Sorry," Gillian said again.

"Sure you are," Joya snarled under her breath, "Miss Underfoot!" Yanking her towel off a chaise longue, she stalked out of the gym.

And Trace preferred her to Lara? Trace... She stooped hastily and snatched up the shards of glass. *Get 'em and go.* She had no desire to face the man. *Me last night, Joya this morning. What a busy guy!* She glanced sideways at him and paused.

He lay as before, and now she realized he clutched a barbell to his chest. What the—? His elbows wavered. Was he trying to lift it?

Hesitantly she moved toward him. It was really none of my business. She'd barged in enough already. His arms tensed—the muscles jumping under his taut, sweaty skin. He *was* in trouble. "Trace?" She looked down at his face, as red as Joya's had been. "D-do you need some...help?"

"Yes." One word, compressed by fury or exhaustion or both.

"Hang on!" She moved behind him, and grasped the bar outside his hands. "Ready?"

She lifted and it came up an inch—then dropped back to his chest. He couldn't help her at all. She glanced at the weights, one twenty. She couldn't lift the barbell over without his help. "Okay, let's try this."

She moved around to his side, straddled him and the bench, then grasped the bar just inside his hands. "I can lift it a few inches if you could slide beneath."

They measured each other for a moment. He'd have to slip under the bar, then between her thighs and down the bench; couldn't roll off to either side because of her bracketing legs. If she dropped the bar on his face or his throat...

"I won't drop it, I promise."

"Then go," he gasped.

She nodded, bent her knees and lifted, puffing with the effort.

Trace caught the bench on either side and squirmed down it, his rib cage brushing her thighs. Goose bumps everywhere, muscles quivering, she stood motionless. His throat passed under the deadly bar to safety and now there was only his head to go. His eyes were locked on hers. She smiled reassuringly. He squirmed an inch or two more—and stuck, his broad shoulders wedged between her knees.

She bit her lip. *This'll teach me to exercise in the mornings!* Tipping forward on the balls of her feet, she brought the bar down. It hit the bench three inches beyond his head. "*Whew!*"

"Yeah." He patted her thigh as she backed over

him down the bench, then swung one leg across—
back to proprietyville. "Thanks," he muttered, sitting
up.

"Sure." *And next time, find someplace safer to fool
around than a gym!* She backed off a step. Clean up
the glass and scram—that was her program. She'd
swim another day.

"Can you bend your arms?" she asked, as she realized he hadn't yet.

"No. Cramps, I guess. They should go in a minute."

He deserved no consideration at all, but still.
"Let's see if I can help." She half knelt on the bench
beside him and took hold of one arm. Dug her thumbs
in gently at the biceps, then slid them along the knot-
ted muscle, walking her fingertips up the back side of
his arm.

"Ahhh…" He grunted half in pain, half relief.
Then he closed his eyes and let her work on him.

She couldn't span his arm with both her hands. He
was so graceful in movement that she hadn't realized
he was quite so large. Not overbuilt, but wonderfully
hard, with gorgeous definition. She massaged her way
up his arm to his shoulder, then switched to the other
arm before it, too, seized up. He let out a long groan
of pleasure and she glanced at him warily. "You
shouldn't work without a spotter, you know," she
murmured. *Let's pretend that whatever I saw, I didn't
see it.* Not that she'd forget.

He nodded assent, and it turned to silent laughter.
"Are you volunteering for the position?" He opened
his eyes and somehow they'd darkened.

"Nope," she said primly. So much for charity.
Give this guy an inch and he'd make a pass. She

briskly slapped his shoulder once to say he was done, and backed off.

"Too bad," he said lightly.

Oversexed, that's what he was. God's gift to women, spreading the goodies around. Not her type at all. Yet her hands still tingled with the feel of him—warm velvet stretched over steel. "You might want to take a hot shower," she advised, heading back for her broken bottle.

"Or a cold one," he said softly behind her.

She hunched her shoulders and didn't look back. Next time maybe she'd leave him under his barbell.

CHAPTER EIGHT

TWO HOURS OF FAN MAIL, some writers expressing shy admiration for Lara, others demanding her photo or autograph as their rightful due, still others suggesting ways to resolve Dr. Daley's crippling dilemma—perhaps a sexy African witch doctor flown in to effect a cure? Two hours of squinting over crabbed, handwritten notes or lengthy typed epistles, and Gillian already had a blinding headache. She winced as the phone on her desk rang, then grabbed for it. "Hello?"

"Gillian." Lara's warm voice. "Trace said you might be at work already. How's it going?"

Gillian laughed and told her about the witch doctor. "Otherwise it's going fine. I haven't sealed any of my responses in case you'd like to check them."

"I'm sure you're doing beautifully, but I'll look at a few this afternoon if you like. Which reminds me. Trace is driving me to a rehab appointment this morning, but we'll be back in time for lunch. Meet us out on the terrace at one, shall we say?"

"Of course." Gillian hung up the phone and glanced toward the door. Lara's suite wasn't a hundred feet down the corridor. Surely it would have been as easy to deliver that message in person. Was Lara avoiding her? Or just bone lazy?

Either way, if she had no more contact with Lara

than she'd had these past two days, the job was going to be a bitter disappointment. She shrugged and opened another letter, maybe the worst sample of penmanship yet. Frowning, she propped her elbows on the desk and bent over the letter, stayed that way for ten minutes or so, and still the meaning wouldn't come clear. She could make out a word or two on each line, but the rest might have been hieroglyphics twisted from black wire, wires stabbing at her eyes...

"Are you all right?"

Fingers massaging her temples, she opened her eyes. Trace, standing beside her. "Oh. Sure." She sat upright. "Just a bit of a headache." The top of her head coming off, that was all.

He showed her a double handful of mail. "Today's catch. Where would you like it?"

"The end box, right-hand side." He deposited the envelopes and returned to prop a lean hip on one corner of her desk. She glanced up at him warily, then down again at her letter.

"That's a bad one," he said after a moment.

"I'm beginning to wonder if it's English," she admitted, not looking up.

"I mean that's a bad headache." Trace pressed the tip of his forefinger between her eyebrows. "You've got a little vertical line there I haven't seen before." He rotated his fingertip in a gentle massage.

The touch feathered outward across her scalp in slow, delicious waves. She wanted to lean into that soothing pressure. Instead she sat back in her chair. "It's nothing, really."

"Hmm." A sound of polite skepticism. He glanced toward the bay window. "It's too bright in here for a computer screen. If you want drapes, I'm sure Lara would be delighted to—"

"No, really, thanks. I'd rather have any headache than shut out that view."

He cocked his head and considered her, the corners of his mouth deepening. She had a vague sense she'd passed some test, but all he said was, "I know what you mean. My idea of Hell is a desk job in a windowless room. Give me your hand."

She shouldn't let him touch her. Each time he did, she felt it for hours afterward. But his hand hung relentlessly before her nose and finally she surrendered. Trace turned her hand over, then ran his thumb in slow exploration across the palm. Her skin came alive, sensations sliding warmly up her wrist to her elbow, a hot heaviness rising from there. "What are you doing?"

"Acupressure—ah, there's the spot." His thumb tip centered on the muscle at the base of her thumb, then pressed with a pressure just short of pain.

Now hot awareness climbed her arm to her shoulder, the back of her neck, down to her breasts. She liked the size of his hand, dwarfing hers, its strength... Liked it too much. "Look, I've got a lot of work to do and..."

"Hush," he said peaceably. "Just relax."

Relax? She felt as if she'd stuck her hand in an electric socket. Alternating current, resistance and desire. The tingling had spread to her stomach and lower.

He stopped pressing on her palm. His thumb slid lazily down to stroke her wrist once, then he released her. "Other one now."

"Really, you don't have to—"

"Give," he insisted, hand outstretched.

With a little growl of exasperation she laid her hand in his. The same drill again, with the sensation rippling all the way down to her toes this time, then rebounding.

"I wanted to thank you," Trace said huskily as he pressed, "for this morning. I would have been in a jam if you hadn't come along."

"It was nothing." The less said about the whole sleazy incident the better, as far as Gillian was concerned.

His slow smile gave her the lie, but he simply completed the thumb pressure with that same tiny caress across her wrist and let her go. "How's the headache?"

"Flown out the window," she marveled.

"Good." He touched the spot between her eyebrows again. "Then don't work too hard, and call me whenever your head hurts." He sauntered across the room without looking back, closed the door softly behind him.

She sat back in her chair, her body throbbing like a beaten gong. Blast the man! If Lara was really keeping Trace as Joya had hinted, well, he just might be worth every penny.

"So you're Gillian," said the beautiful young man out on the terrace. Seated beside Joya at a glass-topped table under a candy-striped awning, he made no attempt to rise. "Joya didn't do you justice." Wide and blue as his sister's, his eyes moved over Gillian in an appraisal just this side of insolence. The smile he finally bestowed upon her was all the more arrogant for its approval. "Welcome to Woodwind."

"And you're Toby, I take it?" Gillian said, choosing a seat to his right. And no half brother to herself, she was as certain as she was grateful. He could have been Joya's fraternal twin.

"The one and only." He lifted a pitcher and filled a glass with a yellow liquid. "Have a mimosa, my very own recipe."

"Thanks, but not while I'm working." She tipped a hand up to fend off the drink, but he set it before her with a smack that rang the glass.

"Oh, don't take yourself too seriously," he said easily. "For personal assistant read court jester and you'll hit the right note around here."

"Yeah, Gillie's been a load of laughs so far," Joya said with heavy irony.

And what's eating you? Gillian wondered. *Are you blaming me for walking in on your romp with Trace this morning?* "It's Gillian, actually," she said mildly. Then the thought suddenly occurred. *Are you afraid I might tell Lara? No fear there, honey.* The incident was distasteful, but it was none of her business.

Joya sniffed as Toby drawled, "So tell us a-a-all about yourself, Gillian."

She was saved by Lara's sleighbell laugh, as she stepped out onto the terrace accompanied by Trace. "Sorry to be late. You wouldn't believe the traffic in town!" Passing behind Gillian and Toby, she patted his arm. "Hi, stranger!"

"Darling." He picked up her hand and kissed it theatrically. "Were they too brutal today?"

"Not at all. I had a wonderful session." Lara launched into a comical description of herself wired up to a machine that delivered electrical stimulation to damaged muscles—the dial turned too high, the machine's attendant happily jabbering on the phone to her boyfriend across the room. "My muscles just sort of striding along with no help from me…I felt like Frankenstein's bride—would somebody please, please unplug me?"

Lucy, the maid, relayed trays of sandwiches, bowls of roasted, marinated vegetables and a hot quiche from the kitchen. While they laughed and filled their plates, the dour-faced woman who had opened the door to Gillian the day of her interview appeared and took the last empty seat, beside Trace.

"You've met my friend Harriet Bristow, haven't you, Gillian?" asked Lara, passing the latecomer the sandwich platter.

"The first day," Gillian agreed, "and I've been thinking you look familiar, but I can't…"

"See?" Lara crowed to her friend. "You say no one ever notices you! She's my surgical nurse," she explained to Gillian.

"On *Searching for Sarah,*" clarified Harriet without a smile. She hadn't smiled once since she'd joined the table. "Currently unemployed, since Dr. Daley skied off a mountain in Switzerland."

Gillian watched Lara's smile waver, then renew itself. "I am a klutz," she admitted softly, and looked down at her plate.

As if it's your fault you fell off Cliff Walk? Gillian felt like demanding. Harriet's face wore an expression of sour agreement as she helped herself to the vegetables. So Harriet had been written out of the storyline with Lara—what good was a supporting actress, without her star? It had to be rough if that particular role was her sole source of income, but still, to blame Lara?

"Speaking of familiar," Lara said, rallying with a smile, "I keep thinking I've seen you somewhere before, Gillian."

She sat transfixed, glass halfway to her mouth. *Where? In your mirror?* She couldn't see a resemblance herself, though she'd hoped for one from the very start. To find some tangible connection... It was why she stared at Lara whenever she could. There had to be *something*—an earlobe, the shape of a hand—but she'd yet to find it.

"It's extraordinary how often people's paths will cross," Trace mused. "You go on vacation and bump into your mailman in the Caribbean. So what do you think, Gillian. Have you two ever met?"

She could hear the faintest taunting in his voice, though when she met his eyes, his look was one of innocent interest. "Well, certainly I've seen Lara on *Searching for Sarah.* Who hasn't?"

"America's *favorite* pediatrician," Harriet murmured.

"But never in person?" Trace challenged.

Why did he ask? What could he know? She met his eyes squarely and held them. "I don't think so."

But she couldn't rout that level, slate-green gaze. Found herself trapped by it for one heartbeat, two, three. Then he smiled and looked down at his plate. *Oh, really?* was the unspoken message behind that smile.

"Coffee anybody?" asked Lucy, returning with a silver carafe.

"Hit me," said Toby, "and give Joya a double. I don't think she's with us yet this afternoon."

Coffee sounded like a splendid idea. Gillian lifted her empty cup and swiveled toward Toby, bringing it within reach of Lucy's pitcher.

As the maid filled the cup, a bee landed on its rim. *"Oh!"* Coffee splashed as Gillian jumped—and Toby shoved back from the table, cursing. "Oh, I'm sorry!" The bee had toppled off the rim and into the hot brew. "Oh, damn!"

"Take it easy." Trace had risen and now stood beside her. "I've got him." He dipped a fork in the steaming liquid, and the bee crawled up on it. He walked away from the table and deposited the insect on the terrace's balustrade, then returned.

"Silly bitch!" Toby said in a voice so low only Gillian could hear him. He wiped frantically at a stain on his white trousers, then looked up at her, red-faced. "It was only a wasp."

"Way to go, Gillie!" applauded Joya.

"I'm sure the cleaners can fix that," Lara said quietly. "And if they can't, then I can—"

"You can't," snapped Toby. "Not unless you want to fly to Rodeo Drive to replace them. You won't find trousers like these in this dreary town."

"I'm very sorry," Gillian said. "I'm a wimp about bees. You see, I'm allergic..."

"Really allergic?" Trace demanded across the table. "As in anaphylactic shock?"

She nodded. "One tangled in my hair and stung me while I was in a parking lot in a strip mall. I started having trouble breathing..." She swallowed, remembering that horrible sensation of her throat swelling and closing, her skin prickling and itching. "There was a doctor's office within fifty feet of my car. The friends I was with rushed me in there and the doctor gave me a shot of epinephrine…'' She shrugged. ''And then I was fine.''

''Well, you're going to love it around here,'' Joya observed with relish. ''September in Newport it's nothing but bees, bees, bees swarming around. Anything sweet you eat, they want their share of it.''

''They're wasps, actually,'' growled Toby, looking up from his pants. ''Are you allergic to wasps, too?''

Gillian shrugged. ''I don't know. Last year was the first time I was ever stung and that was by a honeybee.''

''Most probably you are,'' said Lara. ''If you're like me. The venom has the same effect.''

''You're allergic to bees, too?'' demanded Trace on a note of outrage. ''You never told me.''

Lara shrugged. ''You never asked.''

And here it was at last. Gillian sat with her eyes fixed on her coffee cup, not daring to look up. *I'm allergic to bees—and so is Lara. This came from her to me.*

She remembered that after the epinephrine took hold and she could breathe without effort, she'd been blazingly mad. A simple side effect of the medicine, the doctor had explained, but she'd known otherwise. How many other booby traps lurked out there, just waiting for her to stumble into them? she recalled thinking.

Because that was one of the things Lara had deprived her of when she'd rejected her all over again. A medical history. Just the simple facts that most people got without having to beg for them. For all Gillian knew she came from a family at high risk of breast cancer or manic depression.

There was no way to guard against risks if she

didn't know about them. And no one had a right to keep her in the dark, she'd told herself. Maybe Lara didn't want her. Well, that was fine. Still, she owed her daughter the facts.

Funny how things worked out. Now here she was, having just learned Lara was allergic to bees, too. There was a certain…sweetness to the knowledge of what they shared.

She looked up to find Trace studying her from across the table, his eyes narrowed in speculation.

CHAPTER NINE

"WHERE'S YOUR BEE STING KIT?" Trace queried Lara when they were alone at last. Gillian had headed upstairs to her office and the brats had wandered off God knows where. Sunny Harriet had mumbled something about her afternoon soaps and departed for her room, which was where she spent most of her time brooding.

Staring out to sea, Lara shrugged. "New York, I suppose. In my apartment, in the medicine cabinet."

"You're supposed to have that with you always." Death by bee sting took about three to five minutes. If you were lucky your heart stopped before you slowly strangled to death.

She gave him a rueful smile and turned back to the view. "I did for a while, but I hate carrying a purse."

He counted to ten. Then twenty. She could be so childlike. "Fine, then I'll carry it. Let's call your doctor. I want one today."

"Trace, really, calm down." She patted his arm. "I'm sorry I ever mentioned it. You're overreacting."

"You pay me to guard your life, Lara. Well, whether you like it or not, this is part of it. No bee is stinging you on my watch."

Her smile was gamine in profile, beautiful when she turned to face him. "Dear Trace…" She patted his cheek, the first time she'd ever done so. "Nobody ever told you that if it's meant to happen, it happens? If a bee stings me..." She shrugged and made a comic face.

There it was, that dark fatalism he noticed sometimes beneath her seeming cheerfulness. *What is it with you, Lara? You miss Corday so much that life isn't worth clinging to?* Or was this some depression born of her present stress, the inescapable knowledge that somewhere out there somebody hated her?

But he was here to guard her body, not heal her spirit. Wouldn't have known how to begin if he'd accepted that mission. "If a bee stings you, lady, then the next thing you'll see is me brandishing a hypodermic."

She laughed softly. "You'd really know how to use one?"

He was as well versed in emergency medicine as any professional bodyguard. Dress a bullet wound. Set a leg. Heimlich a dinner guest. Deliver the odd baby. An injection was nothing. "Piece of cake," he assured her. "Now, let's go call your doc."

"Hello-ello!" someone called cheerfully behind him.

Trace spun and stopped, his body blocking Lara, one hand reaching behind him for her shoulder, ready to shove her to the ground. "Who the hell are *you?*" Before him stood a kid about Toby's age, his wide smile just starting to fade at this welcome. "And how did you get in here?"

"By the front gate. It was unlatched." The boy stuck out his chinless chin. "I'm looking for Joya. She skipped our tennis date."

Lara removed Trace's hand from her shoulder and

leaned around his legs. "Hello, Duffy. I believe she's upstairs."

"Uh, thanks, Lara." The kid vanished into the sun-room through the French doors.

Trace sat, his heart rate gradually decelerating. "The gates were unlatched," he said grimly. If you caught the gate manually just before it closed, you could prop the latch against the lockplate. It would look closed until someone pushed on it. He'd found Joya leaving it propped open for some friend several weeks back, and had persuaded Lara to tell her to stop that. But the Corday kids took plain orders as optional.

"You'll have to speak to her and Toby again. I can't keep you safe if any clown can cruise in here whenever he pleases." It was why he insisted that Lara lock the door to her suite whenever she was within. Because he couldn't guarantee the perimeter with her brats running in and out at all hours. *Crap, if somebody really wants you, lady, I'll be hard put to stop him.* He needed at least two more guards to do the job right.

She sighed and nodded. "I'll speak to them. But it would be so much easier if you'd let me explain the problem."

Trace had covered this ground before with Lara. "I'm sorry, but I don't trust them to keep a secret." They'd find Lara's stalker an amusing morsel of gossip to chew over in the bars with their boozy light-weight friends. *We'd be reading all about Sarah XXX in the* Daily News *tomorrow.* And when all was said and done, they'd still leave the gate unlatched. Because the only thing in the world those two honored was their own convenience.

"You're awfully hard on them," she said.

And you are woefully soft, lady. But that was another thing he couldn't say to a client. He smiled. "Am I?"

She shook her head. "Sometimes I feel like I'm talking to the wall!"

A stone wall between you and whatever comes, God willing. But a wall was no help against the enemies within. Someday those brats would break her heart.

BY THREE O'CLOCK LARA still had not stopped at the office as she'd promised earlier. Forgot, Gillian supposed, or perhaps she and Trace were... She shied away from that thought and went back to work. But a slow, painful throbbing had settled in behind her eyes again and she was in the mood for a break. She completed another letter, then picked up the phone and dialed Lara's suite.

"Hello?" Lara said eagerly. She didn't sound as if she'd been disturbed middalliance.

"It's Gillian, Mrs. Corday. I have a question about a letter and—"

"And it's Lara to you, kiddo! Why don't you bring it down here? I'm bored silly."

Tapping on Lara's door a minute later, Gillian was surprised to hear the sound of a heavy dead bolt turning. *She locks herself in, in her own house?*

"Come in," said Lara, and led her to a long couch that looked out on a balcony, and had another spectacular view of cliffs and ocean. "What's the problem?"

They dealt with the matter quickly. Letters concerning any business deal, be it product endorsements, acting roles, proposals for magazine features, etcetera, should be filtered through Lara's manager in New York. "My mail goes to her first and she's supposed to pull out that sort of business plus all my bills. Then she mails the rest to me. This one she missed because with a handwritten return address it looks like a personal letter. So all you need to do is send it back to Margaret. You'll find a file on the hard drive named Manager, which will give you her address. Excuse me," Lara added as the phone on her bedside table rang.

While she spoke at length with Barbara, Woodwind's housekeeper, about meals for the next few days, Gillian glanced casually around the suite. It was a lovely, light and sunny room, with a spectacular Chinese rug in shimmering pastels, and no sign anywhere of Trace Sutton. Good. She found it hard to concentrate on Lara when he was around. She turned to study her now.

Standing in profile, the actress was totally absorbed in Harriet's wishes for steamed artichokes, Joya's demands for low fat and Toby's insistence on smoked salmon at every meal. "Yes, yes, whatever you think, that's fine," she agreed on a note of laughing exasperation as she ran a hand through her silvery hair.

Silver-blond hair, pale gray eyes. She looks nothing like me. Or vice versa. *But if I don't look like my birth mother, whose child am I? My father's? I skipped a generation and look like a grandmother I never met?* It would be so much simpler if only she could ask.

And she must stop staring. Gillian dragged her gaze away, across the big bed, with its piles of puffy pillows and a big feather comforter. Hard to picture

Trace in such a cream-puff bed. Some emotion twisted uncomfortably in her stomach and she rubbed it absently. Maybe thinking about a parent's sexuality was taboo at any age, even when the parent was a total stranger. Her eyes refocused on something orange indenting the comforter's lush center and she felt her mouth drop. Couldn't be!

She rose and walked across to the bed and picked up the stuffed tiger just as Lara cradled the phone. "Tigger!"

"That's his name," Lara agreed, smiling.

It was eerie! "I have this—this s-same tiger." Packed with the rest of her possessions in storage back in Texas. "My parents gave him to me when I was four." Or to be more correct, she'd seen Tig in a toy store and recognized her soul mate. Had fussed and whined and nagged till they gave in and went back to the shop and bought him.

"You're kidding! I've had Tigger for twenty-seven years and—" Lara's face clouded over as she figured silently "—eleven months."

Which meant, Gillian calculated, that Lara had acquired the stuffed toy roughly one month after her birth. "Someone gave him to you?" A boyfriend or a best friend? It seemed important to know that.

"Oh, no. I...bought him...myself." The words trailed away like stones falling down a deep, dark well. Lara swallowed and stared off toward the ocean.

And so we both like tigers. I guess I got that from you? Gillian stroked the stuffed toy, not quite as ratty as her own, but a fifteen-year-old wouldn't have chewed her toy the way her four-year-old daughter had. "Well..." She smiled at Lara and put Tigger back on his puffy domain. Funny that he still held pride of place now that Lara shared a bed with Trace. She'd have thought Trace would have banished him at least as far as the bedside table.

But then, if Lara paid the piper, perhaps she called the tunes in their relationship, in bed as well as out. Suddenly the walls of the spacious room seemed to subtly draw in. "You know," she said determinedly, "during my interview, you said you'd like me to help you get back in shape. And that I was supposed to nag you. So when do I start?"

Lara laughed. "Whenever you please."

"Now, then. I'm dying to go outside. How about a walk?" She'd need to learn about Lara's present condition before she proposed much more than that.

Lara bit her lip. "I'd love to, but..." She glanced toward the open windows. "It's a beautiful day, isn't it?" she murmured wistfully.

"A short walk around the grounds?" Gillian coaxed. "There's this rosebush with blossoms like I've never seen before. Maybe you could tell me what it is."

"Of course I could. I planted all the roses..." She heaved a slow sigh, then said absently, "Trace will have a cow..."

Gillian frowned. Why should Trace object, or even have a say in how Lara spent her time when he wasn't around? "Nothing too strenuous. We'll take it very slow. Oh, come out and play, Lara!"

Lara laughed. "Yes, you're right. This..." Her eyes moved around her suite. "This is ridiculous. I'll meet you on the terrace in ten, okay?"

FOR HALF AN HOUR OR MORE, they explored Wood-wind's grounds. Lara was as lighthearted as a child playing hooky from school. Gillian discovered that another trait they shared was a love of gardening. The antique roses that climbed and rambled along the granite walls had been planted at Lara's behest when she and Corday first moved into Woodwind ten years ago. She glanced back at the mansion. "It was much too big for us then, and now…it seems even larger. But Richard loved to entertain. When he was alive we always had houseguests, and the kids would visit summers. And he bribed me with the grounds—said I could plant as many roses as Napoleon's empress, Josephine, if I liked. I'm still about nine hundred varieties behind, but I've more than a hundred at last count." She stopped and pulled a high branch down to nose level. "Smell this one."

"Heavenly!"

"Tuscany, actually, a variety that goes back to the early 1800s." She plucked the rose and handed it to Gillian. "You realize you're welcome to pick all the flowers you want, I hope. The whole point is to enjoy them."

"Thanks, I will." *She's so darned nice,* Gillian found herself thinking as they wandered on. *So warm. Is she entirely two-faced and I just haven't seen the other side yet?* Apart from her glimpse in the letter.

"And this—" Lara stopped before a wooden door let into an archway in the stone. "This gate leads out onto Cliff Walk."

Yes. It was through this gate that Lara had stepped the day Gillian had first seen her and chased after her. The day she'd fallen from the cliffs.

Lara touched the door's weathered wood. "I used to love to run out there. Every morning at dawn. You start the day in such perfect beauty and how can it go wrong after that?'' She grimaced. ''Or so I thought.'' Her shoulders hunched in something that was more shudder than shrug. ''Anyway, if you ever want to go out on the cliffs, it's locked, but I always keep a couple of spare keys here.'' She toed a stone aside to reveal a plastic margarine tub, opened it and showed Gillian two keys. ''Just be sure to lock the gate behind you.''

Beyond the wall, Gillian could hear the rumble of waves hitting the cliffs. ''Feel like going out today? Or have you had enough exercise?'' she added as Lara frowned. She'd been watching her for signs of pain or limping and had seen none. Lara was quick to confess her faults, then make fun of them, but Gillian wasn't so sure she'd admit to hurting.

''I...d-don't think I'd better. But please, Gillian, you go ahead if you feel like it. It's such a gorgeous day.''

She looked so wistful that suddenly the thought occurred: could Lara be afraid of the cliffs? After her horrific accident, it wouldn't be surprising if she avoided the path forever. What a shame, though! To be shut out of one of the most beautiful spots in the world, when it existed on your own doorstep? She *hated* for Lara to lose that.

''I should go back to work—only ten boxes of letters to go, you know. But first, why don't we just take a peek. It sounds as if the surf is breaking today.''

Confronting the fear little by little—wasn't this how you cured people of their terror? She bent for the margarine tub, removed a key and rose. ''Just a peek?''

Lara stood very still, staring through the wooden door, it seemed. She nodded finally. ''Why not?''

Before she could change her mind, Gillian unlocked the gate. The cool southwest breeze off the
ocean rushed through the gap, lifting their hair, bringing the scents of wild roses and kelp, the louder rumble and thud of the waves below.

Lara laughed like a child and stepped through the
gateway, glanced back, her eyes sparkling with her
own daring. "What are we waiting for?"

"Beats me." Gillian locked the door and followed
her down the short trail through the bushes to Cliff
Walk itself.

"Well," said Lara, staring off over the water.
"Well!" She looked both ways down the path, carefully, like an intelligent five-year-old preparing to
cross a street.

There was no one in sight, in either direction,
though by afternoon tourists typically strolled the
path. "Well," said Lara, again on a note of triumph.
"I usually run this way."

I know, Gillian thought, falling into step beside her.
She wasn't sure what obstacle in Lara's mind she'd
just overcome, but the outcome seemed to be renewed
confidence and joy. *Hurrah for us!*

NOT IN HER SUITE, not in Gillian's office. Damn him
for a fool, he never should have left her! Should have
insisted she come along when he went to the doctor's
for her kit. *Who lured you out, Lara, and how?*

He could make a good guess at that, since Gillian
was nowhere in sight, either. *First time I turn my
back, she whisks Lara away.* What if she wasn't the
innocent he'd begun to think her?

He went down to the first floor to quiz the household staff, but no one had seen Lara. At Gillian's

carriage-house apartment he hammered on her door, cursing himself for giving up her key so easily. She could have Lara trapped inside, for all he knew. The door was metal; he'd need a crowbar to break it down. Maybe he should check with Harriet first. He hadn't bothered, because as loyal as Lara was to the actress, she rarely seemed to seek Harriet out. And who could blame her?

Still, he should have a look. But Harriet claimed not to have seen Lara, and Trace nudged her door far enough open while they talked to be reasonably certain Harriet spoke the truth. So what the hell?

Back at her suite he checked for notes—no notes— then used her balcony to survey the grounds. Leaning far out over the stone balustrade, looking south, he could see a stretch of Cliff Walk—and two figures just vanishing beyond the bushes. One of them wearing lemon-yellow, as Gillian had this morning. Damn her! *This is all her fault.*

Was this an innocent escapade, or was she luring Lara off to the cliffs again? One quick shove and—

Not on my watch! He spun and headed for the door. Glanced toward his dressing room, where he kept his gun hidden nowadays. Told himself, *No, not necessary.* With Gillian Mahler? Should the need arise, he could snap her like a potato chip.

CHAPTER TEN

THEY ROUNDED A BEND in the path and there it was, the place where the pavement tilted seaward, the gap in the bushes showing blue beyond. Lara stopped short, took a deep breath and crossed her arms tightly. "This is where...I...f-fell."

"*God*, Lara." Yes, this was the place Gillian had always pictured her falling. It must be low tide—she could hear the shingle beach below, the waves thundering up the rocky slope, then dragging the gravel seaward with an odd rippling growl. "Shall we go back?" She wouldn't blame Lara in the least if she couldn't walk past this spot.

"N-no...not yet." Her face was greeny pale, beads of sweat gleaming at her hairline. She wiped her brow with a forearm, then stood staring absently out to sea. "If..." The breeze whipped her soft words away. She swallowed convulsively.

Gillian moved nearer; the only comfort she could offer was closeness. "If?"

"If someone had...wrecked your life...utterly. Without hope of mending... How mad would you be?"

"Mad as in crazy?" she asked, bewildered.

A little painful laugh escaped Lara. "Maybe that, too, but mad as in angry, I meant."

Whose life had been wrecked? Lara's own, with

this fall or by the loss of her husband? Or could she be referring to Harriet, who acted as if Lara had fallen for the express purpose of derailing Harriet's career? Or...

From the corner of her eye, she saw movement and glanced over her shoulder—to see Trace Sutton approaching at a run, with a look on his face that spelled trouble for somebody. "Um, I think we're about to—" She let out a yelp as his hand clamped on her forearm and he spun her away from Lara. The edge of the cliff whirled past—for a horrifying second she thought he was slinging her out into space! Instead she found that she'd been forcibly do-si-doed. Now Trace stood between her and Lara. His hand steadied her for a moment as she staggered, then he withdrew it.

"Trace!" Lara cried.

"What the hell do you think you're doing?" he demanded in a savage undertone.

"That's *my* line, I believe!" Lara peered around his bulk at Gillian. "Gillian, are you all right?"

She nodded, feeling her face blushing crimson. Could he be so jealous, so possessive, that he couldn't permit Lara out on her own? Or out with anyone besides himself?

"In that case, would you please excuse us?" Trace said, but it wasn't a question.

"Of course." She brushed past him, aware that he loomed over her as she came even with Lara. Setting her nose away from Woodwind and toward the sea, she stalked off. What a boor! What an unspeakable, rude and possessive boor! How could Lara put up with that?

There must be compensations, a voice that sounded eerily like Joya's observed from within.

No skill in bed would make up for that kind of boorishness, in Gillian's book. Poor Lara, if she thought so! Gillian glanced back once as she reached the next bend of the path.

Lara stood toe to toe with Trace, glaring up. She looked as if she'd happily shove *him* off the cliff. Gillian blew a shaky breath of relief and marched on. *Good, don't let him bully you.*

"I SHOULD F-FIRE YOU for that," Lara exclaimed. "You big bully!"

"I may quit for that, Mrs. Corday. You hired me to do a job, and either you make it possible for me to do it or I walk. We had an agreement that you don't stir from Woodwind without me."

"We did, but—"

"No buts, Lara. Somebody wants to kill you, got that? Somebody who's close enough to scout your routine, to learn you run on the cliffs at dawn. Who's got the time and the patience to lie in wait for his opportunity, and then—*wham!* So what do you do? Soon as your bones mend, you go strolling on the cliffs with a woman you know *nada* about."

"You can't think Gillian—"

"I can't rule her out. What's her middle name?"

"What?" Her expression plainly said, *You're nuts!* Then she glanced aside.

A family of Japanese tourists, chatting happily, strolled around the bend. The mother let out a sharp cry as she spotted the gap in the bushes, and her young son, trotting in the lead, stopped and looked back. Catching his hand, she hurried him past the drop-off. Trace and Lara stepped aside, half-bowing nods were exchanged, then the tourists vanished around the next bend.

Trace drew a deep breath. "She claims her middle name is Sylvester, which is plainly absurd."

Lara laughed aloud. "That's what's worrying you? She's teasing you, Trace. Probably thought it was none of your business, and I don't blame her."

"Maybe, or maybe it's something more. What if her middle name is Sarah?"

The color seeped out of Lara's face. He caught her forearm before she fainted. "Lara?"

Her pupils were dilated, black holes rimmed in silver, staring blankly through his chest. "Lara?"

"I should be so lucky," she murmured, and shook herself. Her color flooded back. "And one thing we know for certain is, I'm not."

He turned her gently around to face the sea and the cliff edge. "Walk over there, look down at those rocks, and tell me you're not lucky." He didn't like talk like that. He needed his client's spirit working with him, not against him. Fatalism was not allowed. "You've got a first-rate guardian angel, Lara. But I'd like to give him a hand."

She made a little grimace of resignation, then smiled. "Okay, Trace. I suppose I'm being unfair. It wouldn't do your business any good if you lost a client, would it?"

"It wouldn't recommend me to my next client, no." Yet he didn't want her to play it safe for his sake, but for her own. *Show me some will to live, will you?*

"Okay," she said, turning toward Woodwind, "I'll behave. On one condition, though. No, two. First…

you don't terrorize my household. And that includes
Gillian.''

''But—''

''I mean that, Trace! How you could imagine that
girl sending me that rabbit letter…''

''All right, all right, kid gloves for Gillian.'' *Which
doesn't mean I don't watch her like a hawk.* First
chance she got, she'd led Lara right here, to the very
same drop-off. And if he'd come five minutes later?

''Second…I'm sick of this circle-the-wagons men-
tality. There's no use guarding my body if I go out
of my mind. We *have* to get out more. I'm out of
touch with my friends, I need a new pair of running
shoes, a manicure…''

''Lara, it would be wiser if—''

''That's *not* negotiable,'' she snapped. They
walked on in tense silence, then she touched his arm
in apology. ''I'm forty-three, Trace, and I don't *do*
wise. Never did. It's a bit late to learn it now.''

*Then take my advice, dammit. I'm wise enough for
both of us.* But he was tired of arguing—and losing.
''You're the boss.''

''I am,'' she agreed briskly. ''So one more condition, Trace.''

''Which makes three.''

''Why, so it does. Condition three,'' she pronounced as they reached the turnoff that led to Woodwind's back gate. ''You scared Gillian back there.
So…apologize.''

GILLIAN WALKED NEARLY TO the end of Cliff Walk,
walking hard to blow off her anger. The path dropped
lower and lower till it meandered along only twenty
feet above the ocean. It grew more and more ragged,

becoming dikes of boulders here and there, riprap laid to withstand the waves that would break right over the path in a southwest storm. She came to the first tunnel in the rock, surmounted improbably by a Japanese teahouse, the upcurved eaves of its copper green roof decorated with slinky bronze dragons. The building was a wonderful folly, over a hundred years old, belonging to one of the summer cottages lying inward from the cliffs. You couldn't enter the teahouse, but you passed under it in a long tunnel carved from the rock.

As always she stopped at the tunnel mouth, eyeing the blackness beyond. Halfway along, the passage bent in a sharp right turn. No sunlight carried from either end into its depths. She drew a breath and walked in. The temperature dropped ten degrees immediately. Cool pounded earth underfoot, rock above and around, the sound of the waves dying to an echoing whisper. She dragged her fingertips along the stones till, fifty feet in, she reached the turn and saw light ahead. Up some mossy stone stairs, then out into the sunshine, on higher cliffs again, the blue waters sparkling forty feet below. *I wonder if Lara would have made it this far.*

Lara… She wasn't at all what Gillian had expected. And Trace, what the hell was he? Lara's faithless toy boy? Or something much more offensive, a jealous lover who abused his power? It was hard to say from moment to moment who had the upper hand between those two. *Forget it. It's none of your business, really. Just feel this gorgeous day, the sunshine, the wind, the water. Just walk.*

WHEN GILLIAN RETURNED to Woodwind an hour before sunset, it was time to leave for the Y. Aerobics tonight, a class she'd traded with a fellow instructor, who'd taken her morning assignment. She was committed to teach it till the term ended in three weeks. She drove off without seeing either Lara or Trace. Which was just as well. In spite of her walk she was still upset and offended.

The class—advanced aerobics—calmed her at last. Afterward she showered long and luxuriously, dressed, then paused, looking into her locker. It was here that she kept the manila envelope with all the papers from her adoptive mother's safe-deposit box. It had seemed safer to leave them under padlock at the Y than take them into Woodwind. On sudden impulse she picked up the envelope and retreated to the aerobics room. It was deserted now, and, settling on an exercise mat, she dumped out the contents of her envelope. Would the papers look the same, now that she'd met Lara?

She lifted the single-page typed document from the lawyer who'd arranged her private placement. It described a one-week-old female child, named Sarah Cloud "Doe" by her natural mother. The baby had been born in Virginia, legally relinquished by her mother two days after birth, was in foster care and available for adoption.

Cloud. Why Cloud, Lara? On first reading, Gillian had assumed that must be a family name, either Lara's or on the paternal side. The first way she'd tried to research her past was to go to that small town in Virginia and check in old phone books for the name Cloud.

No such family had lived there, twenty-eight years

ago—or ever—as far as she could learn. *A dead end.* The first of many.

She looked down at the document again. Next her birth parents were described. The mother was a fifteen-year-old white Anglo-Saxon named Laura "Doe." In excellent health; religion, Methodist. A graduate of the tenth grade. IQ, well above average. Her ambition, to be an actress.

So you knew what you were meant to be even back then, Lara. And perhaps that explained everything. *You would never have achieved your goal with a baby on your back, any more than your fictional double, Dr. Laura Daley, would have made it through med school with a baby to look after. So you ditched the load and went on?*

The document didn't say—said no more at all in fact about her birth mother.

It devoted one paragraph to her father, describing him as an eighteen-year-old white Anglo-Saxon, name, William "Smith"; last grade completed, eleven; IQ, well above average; ambitions for his life, unknown.

Gillian sighed and slipped the paper back into the envelope. She'd also had her birth certificate to work with, which listed her as Gillian Sarah Scott. But she'd soon learned, once she entered the Alice in Wonderland world of the searching adoptee, that this certificate was an officially sanctioned lie. It had been issued to her adoptive parents at the time of her adoption, with their names substituted for the birth parents. The real facts were buried by the state of Virginia and most definitely were not the adoptee's for the asking.

Angrily she blew out a *whuff* of air, remembering the bureaucrats who'd smugly explained they couldn't release the facts of who she was or where she came from—as if she were a half-wit, dangerous child who couldn't be trusted with the truth that everyone else had by right. *Right of birth.*

After that dead end, she'd gone to the Virginia lawyer the Scotts had used to arrange her adoption. Her lip curled at the memory: the old man with his oily, stern-uncle smile, his eyes as cunning and detached beneath their weathered folds of skin as a crocodile's. He'd told her next to nothing, pointing out that his only duty lay with his clients, her adoptive parents. He owed *her*—the child whose life he had derailed—not a word, not a fact. Not legally speaking.

"And why would you want to meet her at all? That little lady didn't give a damn about you. Traded you for a car and never looked back."

"A car?" she'd coaxed, sickened by her desperate need to ingratiate herself, when she'd have preferred to shake the facts out of him. "What do you mean?"

The Scotts had paid all her birth mother's prenatal and delivery expenses, the lawyer had explained. "And as I recall, she padded the bill something shameless." He coughed. "But the straw that about broke the camel's back was that the girl demanded a car at the last minute. Said your adoption was off without it.

"So your adoptive momma brought a brand-new red Mustang to me a few days before you were born, and after that the girl was happy to sign your relinquishment papers. So why would you want to find a mother like that? Now, if you'll excuse me, I've got a court appointment in half an hour."

Gillian had pried the rest of that story out of her adoptive brother, Chris, a month later when he called her from Hawaii, where he'd stopped off while delivering a yacht from Seattle to Japan.

"You heard about the car?" he'd asked, the worry in his husky voice coming clear across four thousand miles. She'd written him an outraged letter telling him she'd learned of her adoption, demanding to know why he'd never told her, but this was the first time they'd talked about it. "That damned car, Gillian. I didn't forgive you for that for a long time. It was Mom's car, but it was the car Dad used to teach me how to drive that year. And the understanding was, when I got my full license they'd give me the Mustang and buy Mom a new one.

"But then that sleazeball lawyer called and said he had to have a car to persuade your real mother to sign the papers—and by that time, Dad and Mom had already forked over some twenty thousand in expenses to get you.

"Anyway, there was a real dustup. Dad decided we'd been had, and maybe this wasn't even legal. You can't *buy* a baby, you know, though you can pay the mother's expenses. He said we were way over that line, and it would end in trouble, not a baby.

"But Mom didn't agree. She'd come so far she wasn't quitting when she was this close to you. She stormed out of the house, drove off in her red Mustang and arrived home a few days later by cab. And two weeks later they drove to Virginia and came home with you." He laughed softly. "A damn poor trade for a Mustang, I thought at the time. Took me a while to realize what a good deal Mom had made."

She smiled, tears beading in her lashes. Dear Chris. She glanced up as the door to the exercise room opened. Mr. Sousa, the Y's janitor. He glared at her, announced, "Lights out in ten minutes, girlie!" and slammed the door again.

Gillian sighed and started to put her papers away, then paused as a photo slipped between two sheets and fell facedown onto the mat.

She turned over the picture of Lara. Clearly a high-school photo—you couldn't mistake the format. Chin lowered like a young Lauren Bacall, Lara smiled warily into the camera. But already you could see her elfin beauty. The camera loved her.

Without this photo, Gillian would be still living back in Houston, teaching aerobics and tai chi by night, painting her watercolor illustrations by day, wondering with mounting frustration who she was and where she'd come from. It was this photo that had led her at last to Lara.

On his way back from Tokyo, Chris had stopped off in San Diego to visit their aunt—Chris's real aunt, Gillian's adoptive aunt. Aunt Susan, Victor Scott's sister. During his visit, Chris had mentioned that Gillian had learned she was adopted and was searching for her birth mother.

Gillian turned over the page torn from a soap-opera digest some nineteen years ago. Aunt Susan had found the article in a magazine in a dentist's office and recognized Lara's photo. It was the same school photo that Susan's sister-in-law—Gillian's adoptive mother, Eleanor Scott—had once shown her. But this time it accompanied an article about the promising new soap-opera actress, Lara Leigh, aka Laura Bailey, who'd grown up in a series of foster homes in West Virginia, then run away to New York City and hit the big time.

Nineteen years ago Aunt Susan had triumphantly

mailed the article to Gillian's mother—and she'd had a fit. Had made Aunt Susan promise that she'd never, *ever,* in her life tell Gillian anything about this article.

But now that I think of it, Aunt Susan had written in her letter, *I'm not sure if poor Eleanor meant never in my life, your life or hers. And since, bless her, she's gone, if you're hunting for your real mother, well, I guess this is her.*

"Lights out!" growled Mr. Sousa at the door.

"Coming, coming, I'm sorry." He dogged her footsteps downstairs to the front door, then locked it behind her.

Gillian stood on the Y's porch, staring out over Newport's vast reservoir, its swans pale, drifting shapes in the moonlight. Downhill to her left stretched First Beach, then the dark cliffs of Cliff Walk, rising beyond. Those lights about a third of the way out the headland must be Woodwind.

Traded me for a car, and ended up with a mansion by moonlight. What kind of deal would Chris call that?

CHAPTER ELEVEN

GILLIAN PAUSED OUTSIDE an open bay to the carriage house. Trace Sutton lay on a rolling cart, his head half under a car. "Uh-oh, trouble?" They were due to leave for a luncheon date with a friend of Lara's in minutes.

"You can come along and pretend to be a real lady's companion," Lara had informed her cheerfully that morning. "I'm tired of moping around the house. Meet us at the car at one?"

"Us" apparently meaning Lara and Trace, since here was Trace, half under the car. "What's up?" She dragged her eyes away from his long legs. His lightweight chinos couldn't conceal the hard planes of calf and thigh.

"Nothing," he growled. "I thought I saw an oil leak. Now, would you mind giving me some room to work?"

"Fine." *Be that way.* She stalked out of the bay and into the sunlight.

"There you are!" Lara stepped out of the flower beds and came to join her. "I was picking roses for Meagan," she said, showing Gillian a half-dozen long-stemmed buds. "She has a passion for the whites."

Trace backed the car out, then rounded its front to

open the door for Lara. Gillian reached for the rear door, but he beat her to it. "Allow me."

He was playing the perfect chauffeur this morning, except for the oddly measuring look he gave her as he closed her door. *Who are you, Trace Sutton?*

Studying the back of his dark, well-trimmed head, she pondered that all the way down the hill to the waterfront, while Lara chatted happily about the woman they were meeting, a watercolorist of some note and one of her few local friends. Trace parked the car in a parking lot before a waterfront restaurant, the Moorings, then, to Gillian's disappointment, accompanied them inside. She'd half hoped he might leave the three women to dine alone, that he'd rather wander along the docks and wharves, admiring the yachts lying alongside. But no such luck.

"SHE'S DELIGHTFUL," pronounced Lara's friend, Meagan Riley, watching Gillian make her way through the crowded restaurant toward the rest rooms. "Have you seen any of her paintings?" The older woman had spoken of her own work for much of the meal, until Lara had proudly volunteered—much to Gillian's obvious consternation—that Gillian was an illustrator. After that Trace had listened with amusement while the older woman ruthlessly pried more information out of Gillian over the course of a meal than he had managed in four days of trying.

The information was interesting—he found everything about Gillian Mahler interesting nowadays—but was it useful? Meagan clearly accepted her as genuinely knowledgeable and accomplished in the art world.

The typical stalker wasn't accomplished in much

of anything, except sometimes guns and paramilitary techniques. But if Gillian wasn't a stalker, why hide her light under a basket the way she had at Woodwind? So she could someday return to the life she'd divided so neatly from the current one? *In Houston she's a budding artist, making ends meet by teaching exercise classes on the side. In Newport she drops the art, becomes a full-time fitness trainer—till she secures a job with Lara. Why? A woman who has worked all her life in the creative and physical realms suddenly develops clerical ambitions? Which give her excruciating headaches?* He smelled a rat somewhere.

And what the hell is her middle name? He'd called his sister, Emily, last night and learned that so far she'd uncovered nothing of use in Houston. The family who might know the most about the Mahlers were off on vacation and due back this weekend.

"Oh, look!" cried Lara, pointing over his shoulder at the harbor. Two awesome, moving pyramids of white cut the blue sky—a schooner sailing past the docks.

He sighed. Here he was in the sailing capital of America and he hadn't set foot aboard a boat all summer. He returned his gaze to the room. A bodyguard always put his back to the wall, kept his eyes on the directions from which danger might come.

Speaking of which, here came Gillian, swaying between the tables. His hands remembered the pliant shape of her waist that first time he'd touched her. She'd had a faint bruise on her left arm, he'd noticed, when he put her into the car. From when he'd grabbed her yesterday. *Still haven't apologized.* He didn't need Lara's prompting for that. He could if she was innocent. If she had lured Lara out of Woodwind's walls without bad intent.

And if not?

No apologies now or ever.

Her smile met Lara's, Meagan's, then faded as she met his gaze. She sat and looked away.

"Is there a line in the bathroom?" asked Meagan.

"Not really," Gillian said. "Just smokers camped out in both stalls, that's all."

Which accounted for the faint smell of cigarettes overlaying her usual sunny fragrance.

"In that case…" Meagan stood. "Lara?"

Trace put his fingertips on the table and half rose. The rest rooms stood down a hall next to the exit. Too easy for someone to slip in to the ladies' after Lara, then make a smooth getaway. He'd have to wait outside.

"I don't think so," said Lara, frowning at him till he subsided.

Gillian hadn't missed much of their interplay. And did not like it, even if she didn't understand it. She swung accusing golden eyes his way as, from over his shoulder, a ray of sunshine bounced off some bit of chrome on the docks to gild her face, turn her tawny hair to fiery bronze. Lion eyes glaring at him out of a burning field.

Something tightened inside him. *I want to bed you! See those eyes looking up at me from a pillow by candlelight.* He turned away, stared blindly out across the restaurant. Damn her, anyway! She was the last woman in the world he should want. What if she was his freak?

Then he'd see her behind bars.

He turned back to find Meagan was making her

farewells. She'd spotted a patron in the bar, a man who'd acquired five of her works so far, and she was going to go over and make nice. Talk up her latest project, a series on the local twelve-meter yachts.

Lara signed for their meal. This earned Trace another skimming glance from Gillian, which he answered with a complacent smile. *Think I'm a useless gigolo, do you? Good.*

He played his part all the way to the car, opening the restaurant door with a flourish as they left, shepherding Lara with a hand on her waist to her usual seat. He unlocked the front passenger door—and Lara said, "Gillian, you sit there."

He scowled at his client. What was she up to this time? God, he'd rather guard a man any day. Simple and straightforward. You knew what he was thinking, what he wanted or needed, before he did—or if you didn't, he told you. None of these curves that a woman threw.

"No, really, I'd rather sit in back!" protested Gillian, looking as alarmed as if Lara had proposed she sit on his lap.

"Nonsense. I'd like to return by Ocean Drive, and you'll have a better view from up there." Lara opened the rear door and sat decisively.

Trace shrugged, opened the front door wider and motioned Gillian inside. Found himself mesmerized as she sank gracefully onto the seat and swiveled into place, her slender calves kissing from knee to ankle throughout the procedure. He'd half closed her door when it hit him.

He hadn't touched the button that unlocked all four doors at once. *Yet Lara had opened the back door.* A bolt of adrenaline shot through him, raising the hairs on his nape and forearms. He spun to face her.

Gillian glanced at him in mild surprise.

He drew a shaking breath. If there was a bomb, it should have gone off by now, under one woman or the other. Probably under Gillian, since it would have been intended for Lara, who always rode in front. No bomb, thank God.

So…false alarm? With relief he felt the first hot surge of anger, the aftereffects of adrenaline. He snapped at Gillian, "Did you unlock the back door when you got out?" He'd hit the locking control as he exited the car, he was sure of that, but if she'd then unlocked it *again* while he walked around to help Lara out…

Her eyes wide with confusion, she swallowed and shook her head. "I don't think so. Or…I'm not sure. Possibly. I thought I locked it, but maybe I—"

"So what?" said Lara from the back seat. "If you did, there was nothing to steal, apart from our bridge tokens. No harm done. Come on, Trace."

No harm done this time, but, oh, lady, it's the little slips that get you in the end. Scowling at Gillian, seeing in his mind's eye a moment's lapse that ended with the dull roar of dynamite, three lives shattered, he started to close the door.

As she reached reflexively for its inner handle.

And at some subliminal level he heard it—smashed her hand up and aside before he knew why.

"Ow!" She caught her fingers with her other hand and stared at him.

"Trace!" Lara cried from the back seat as he yanked the door wide and bent down.

The buzzing rose, then fell like a tiny bomber diving out of the sky—a blur of golden brown stripes and furious motion. A bee, struggling frantically to free itself from the hollowed-out door handle.

"What is it?" asked Gillian, bending beside him, her cheek nearly brushing his.

One second more and she'd have slipped her fingers into the handle and pulled to shut the door. Her fingers would have closed over the bee.

"Oh!" she breathed as she saw it.

He turned his head and his lips nearly brushed hers. "Just a bee. It caught its leg somehow." With the help of a dab of Super Glue.

Another second and her fingers would have pressed down on the outraged insect. A second after that, its venom would have been coursing through her body. Three to five minutes till death by suffocation.

But that death was intended for *Lara*, who now leaned impatiently over the front seat. "Don't touch it—don't move. I'll be back," he said to Gillian, as he opened the back door. "Let's go, Lara!" He almost dragged her from the car and marched her across the parking lot toward the restaurant, his eyes roving all points of the compass, his nape icy, as if he could feel a crosshair lining up on it. Whoever had done this might still be out there, crouching among the parked cars. Might make a more direct attempt, now that his nasty little trick had failed.

His? Hers. This had a woman's indirectness and subtlety, to his mind.

"Trace!" Lara protested, trotting at his side. "Dammit, have you gone mad? What are you doing?"

"I'm sending you home in a cab, Lara. Let me call it, then I'll explain."

"I DON'T SEE WHY GILLIAN can't come with me,'' Lara fretted. They stood waiting for the cab in the Moorings foyer, looking out through the glass doors. Gillian no longer sat in the car, though Trace couldn't see her.

She was down on the docks, he told himself. Or perhaps she'd lost her nerve finally and split?

"I'd be safer with her along than alone,'' Lara insisted.

Would you? That all depended on who had glued the bee to Lara's door. Trace's best guess was Gillian. "The police may want her statement, since she's the essential witness,'' he said, instead. The minute Lara was safely away, he meant to take the car to the police. Have the bee photographed. It was the star exhibit in the case he was building. All he needed was a perpetrator.

He straightened as a yellow cab pulled into the parking lot. "Now remember, don't stop anywhere on the way home. Have him drive you all the way to the front door, then make some excuse and let the maid escort you to your suite. I'll be back as quick as I can.''

She nodded unhappily. "You really think this was an attempt…on m-me? It's not some mistake—the silly bee snagged its foot or something?''

"I wish I could say so.'' He walked her to the cab, gave her an encouraging smile and her address to the cabbie. "Fast as you can,'' he added, handing him a ten. He didn't like leaving her on her own, but he couldn't be two places at once. He waved her off. When he looked around, Gillian was hurrying up the ramp from the dock.

"Where's Lara going?''

"Home. She isn't feeling well. But she asked you and me to do some errands," he added immediately. *No sneaking off to Woodwind while my back is turned.* "Get in." He nodded at the car.

"Um…" She bit her bottom lip and studied the ground, then looked up under her lashes at him—a move of such incredible unrehearsed femininity it stole his breath away. "W-would you…do something about the bee? It's still trapped. That's why I didn't…" Her voice trailed away. "But don't hurt him," she added.

"Of course not." Okay, now what? If she was innocent, she was only being reasonable to request that he deal with the bee. If she was guilty, she was as cunning as a snake—she was asking that he destroy the evidence.

"All clear," he called a few minutes later. He held the passenger door for her, but she paused, frowning down at the duct tape that now lidded the door handle and muffled the indignant buzzing that sounded from within.

"It's in there?"

"We'll need a pair of tweezers to free its leg without yanking it off. Since you told me not to hurt it…" He shrugged.

She edged away from the door. "Maybe I'll sit in back."

"Coward!" he taunted softly. Suddenly, would-be killer or no, he wanted her sitting beside him. A clear case of testosterone poisoning, but there it was.

She tipped up her chin, gave him a stormy glance and swung into the car.

All the same, he noticed when he sat behind the driver's wheel, she'd slid over to the left side of her seat. He smiled at her and she edged outward three inches, then stopped. Trapped between a rock and a hard place.

But he was in no mood to enjoy her dilemma. In the confines of the car, he could smell cigarette smoke in her hair. *If I wanted to keep a bee still while I glued its legs, say, to a door handle, I'd stun it with cigarette smoke.* The way beekeepers stunned hives of bees when they wanted to take the honey.

From the waterfront to the police station was a mere five minutes. He passed it by, drove down Broadway, then parked in front of Kelly's, a bookstore where he'd picked up several interesting histories. "Lara asked that you buy her a half-dozen books or so. She likes mysteries, the cozy sort with a vicar, an eccentric English lady, poison in the tea."

Her face lit up. "I like those, too."

Swell. Make my day. "Pick her out several of those, plus any biographies of movie stars you can find," he said gravely. "I have to run to the hardware store. I'll be back in twenty minutes."

"SHE COULD HAVE CAUGHT IT in a jar anywhere in the gardens this morning," said Trace, while Jeremy Benton adjusted his lights on the bee. Trace had parked in the cops' lot, behind the station, where Gillian wouldn't see him even if she strolled down the street.

"She could have carried it in her purse—the one she had today was large enough." Then while Jeremy shot a roll of film, Trace described how Gillian left the table at the Moorings for a good ten minutes. "It wouldn't take ten minutes to nip outside, stun the bee by blowing smoke into the jar, then glue it in place. She left her back door unlocked to gain entrance.''

The detective straightened, set the camera aside and removed his lights. ''Nasty and neat. I haven't seen better in a long, long time. If it had worked, how could you have taken it for anything but an accident? The bee would have been crushed when the target grabbed it. The glued leg would have torn free as she dragged her hand away. She'd have flipped the bee off or maybe even stomped him.

''And you'd have had no time to consider—either you'd have been racing for the hospital or you'd have been busy injecting her. Later on, who'd have thought to go back and count the bug's legs? Hell, I don't know how many it *should* have. And who'd have noticed a drop of glue no bigger than a pinhead, with one bee leg embedded in it, on the inside of your handle? Neat. You've got a sharp one here.''

''Too damn sharp.'' Studiously ignoring Benton's raised eyebrows, Trace removed his knife from its ankle sheath. ''Done with the bee?''

''You're gonna do the poor bastard?''

''Nope. I promised Gillian I wouldn't hurt it.'' He bent over the door handle, then paused, hearing his own words.

Benton laughed. ''And that's who you make for this—a woman who's deathly allergic to bees but who doesn't want the little creep crunched to kingdom come? Does that add up?''

''Nothing adds up.'' Slowly he slid the blade along the handle. Minus a toe or two, the bee shot up and away. Would probably be home, warning the other bees, before they'd finished dusting the car. ''On the other hand, with stalkers it rarely does.''

"Yeah, that kid that shot the TV actress point-blank a few years back. What was she—twenty-one? I love you to death—*bang!* Stupid freaks." He motioned the print technician, who'd been lounging in the shade by the station's back door, over to the car. "Outside and inside of this door, 'specially the inner handle." Trace and Benton wandered away, hands in their pockets. "Who else knows Lara Corday is allergic to bees?"

Trace told him about the lunch on the terrace yesterday, and Benton whistled. "Fast response! And nice improvising. But not much patience, if somebody learned about Corday's allergy yesterday, then used it against her today. Who at that table isn't softhearted and *is* impatient?"

Two blond, sulky faces came instantly to mind. "Her stepbrats, Joya and Toby. And possibly Harriet Bristow." He told Benton about the sour supporting actress. "The maid, Lucy, I don't know, but she seems a nice kid. She'd be the last on my list of all of them.

"And of course, there's always the possibility of an outsider—that Gillian isn't Sarah XXX but that Sarah XXX *is* in town, shadowing Lara. That she noticed the car door was unlocked . . ."

"And she just happened to have this bee in her pocket?" jeered Benton.

"Unless she already knew that Lara was allergic to bees," Trace insisted, playing out the scenario. "She might have come equipped with a jimmying tool, may have used it—it doesn't leave a mark. Maybe Gillian hadn't locked the car in the first place. She couldn't say."

"Okay, it's not likely, but it's possible. But how

would Sarah Kiss-kiss-kiss know Corday is allergic to bees?''

Trace shrugged. ''Beats me, but believe me, I'll ask.'' They'd made a circuit of the fenced lot and were now back at the car, where the technician was wiping his powder away.

''Here's one more thing that maybe you haven't considered,'' said Benton. ''What if someone wanted to kill *Gillian?*''

He didn't like even the thought of it, those golden eyes swelling shut, that long slender throat closing, still… After a moment he shook his head. ''Lara always rides in front.''

Benton laughed under his breath. ''Except this time she doesn't. She insists Gillian sit in front. So maybe your boss wants to kill Gillian?''

''Hey, thanks for clarifying matters!'' They shook hands. ''And let me know if anything turns up on the fingerprints.''

''Will do.'' The detective spun on his heel and sauntered toward the station, then swung around. ''And Trace? Whoever it is, the freak's got a hate on, and you're the guy standing in the way. Watch your back.''

CHAPTER TWELVE

GILLIAN WAS STILL HIS first choice, Trace reflected as he drove to the bookshop. Two incidents since Lara hired her—the rabbit's foot, now the bee. Make it three if you counted girls' day out on the cliffs, which might have been an aborted attempt.

That story at lunch yesterday about an allergy to bees. Possibly Gillian wasn't allergic at all but had some reason to think Lara might be. Wanting to check out her facts, she'd spun a tale that elicited an admission from Lara that she was allergic?

Another thing to consider: whoever had glued that bee in place had assumed Lara didn't carry a bee sting kit. That a sting would be fatal. But in fact, as of yesterday afternoon one kit now lived in the glove compartment. And he carried a second kit in his pocket and would do so for the rest of this assignment.

So the question was: had Lara told anyone he'd shot off to the doctor's yesterday to get her a bee sting kit? If so, strike that person off his list of suspects. Nobody would have risked sneaking into Lara's car in broad daylight and gluing the bee if he couldn't reasonably hope for the big payoff.

Gillian…he wished he could rule her in or rule her out. He could search her purse. It should contain a pair of tweezers to handle the bee, a tube of Super

Glue, an empty jar, matches or a lighter and maybe a pack of cigarettes. *Yeah, try to get your hands on her purse without a search warrant.* And if she was really smart—and one look at those lion eyes told you she was—she'd have dumped her tools before returning to the restaurant. *Call Benton,* he decided. *Ask him to assign a suit to do some Dumpster diving this afternoon in the parking lot, the ladies' and down on the nearby docks.*

He parked two spaces up from the bookstore, then saw her, seated on a bench outside the shop, beside a foot-high stack of books. She slung her purse over one shoulder, gathered the books into her arms and came to meet him.

His day brightened, as if the sun had stridden out from behind the clouds and for a moment he was simply a man walking toward a woman he wanted. "Here, let me carry those!" He reached for her load.

She shook her head. "I can manage."

With the gesture, her hair brushed her shoulders and he smelled cigarettes. The day darkened again as he pictured her lighting a fag, inhaling, blowing into the jar containing the bee… "I'm sure you can," he agreed huskily, stopping directly before her.

"Then wha—"

He held her shoulders and lowered his mouth to hers—caught her in midword, her lips parted. She froze, then gasped, and for a moment he forgot his reason for doing this. Then found a better one—her warm, startled softness…a silky dampness enticing him deeper…the barest flutter of a response? His hands tightened on her shoulders, drawing her closer—

Ten pounds of books cascaded over his feet. "Ouch, dammit!" He let her go.

"Y-y-you're—" She tossed her head, at a loss for words, and swept past him toward the car. "Unspeakable!"

He looked down at the books covering his shoes and found he was smiling. That his heart was bounding along, the blood zinging through his veins; that the sun had swaggered out from the clouds again. Because Gillian tasted of the chardonnay she'd had with lunch, melded with an undefinable taste that was the woman herself—honey and sunshine and musk. But no taste of cigarettes, at all, at all.

Doesn't prove a thing, his mind protested. Maybe she'd lighted the cigarette and simply stuck its burning end in the jar. His "test" didn't mean a damn thing.

Tell that to the rest of him.

IF SHE HADN'T BEEN WEARING heels, she would have walked back to Woodwind. Gillian sat stiffly, with arms crossed, scowling straight ahead as Trace turned the car uphill toward Bellevue Avenue. She couldn't just let this pass, pretend it hadn't happened. Not with her lips still buzzing, waves of heat rolling through her. "If you ever do that again," she said finally, "I'll..." *What?* she asked herself.

"Do what?" he inquired politely, turning to glance at her. "Tell Lara?"

Oh, he had her there and he knew it! *If Lara has no idea what you are, I'm not going to be the one to tell her.* "I'm not a snitch." Besides, apart from the hurt she might inflict if she told Lara, there was always the chance that Lara would let *her* go. When it came to choosing between a personal assistant and a lover, the choice was obvious. Especially a lover who could kiss like Trace Sutton.

"Good for you," he said quietly. "So what *will* you do?"

"Slap you cross-eyed to Sunday if you ever try that again."

"Ah." He stopped for a red light. "Might just be worth it."

"HAVE YOU HAD ENOUGH OF MY fans yet?" Lara's laughing voice inquired over the phone. It was the following day, nearly noon, and Gillian sat at her desk, letters stacked on all sides.

She had her usual splitting headache. "Well..."

"Say yes, you're sick of them," Lara pleaded, "and come down to my suite, would you? I need moral support."

"I'm doing a photo album," she explained, when Gillian reported for duty. "The perfect rainy day project, I told myself, but it's turning into a bear. I've never done one before." She gestured at two large cardboard boxes. "I've always just kept everything in heaps, but now..." Her smile flickered, then renewed itself. "Lying there in that hospital the first half of this summer, I got to thinking of all the things I hadn't done. That I shouldn't leave undone, if something ever..." Her voice trailed away and she shrugged. "Anyway, I've already made a good start." She gestured across the room to an arrangement of photographs laid out in front of the French doors. It straggled a good ten feet or more along the rug.

"Yikes!" *Gold mine,* Gillian thought. Here was

what she'd come for at last. If that was Lara's family history laid out on the floor, then it was also her own.

"Of course, if you'd rather not…" Lara said anxiously. "Lots of people think albums are bores, I know. Especially other people's."

"Oh, no! No. No, I love albums. "Mom was a fanatic album keeper—scrapbooks, too." *But with the real facts tucked away out of my sight.* "So where do we start?"

"How's it go—" Trace paused in a doorway to what must be his dressing room. He was clothed, but his hair was still wet from a shower. "Gillian." He nodded, not trying to hide his irritation. Eyebrows raised, he turned to Lara.

"I decided I needed some help." A note of defiance underlay Lara's cheeriness.

"In that case, maybe I'll—" He swerved toward the couch, but Lara scurried to block his way.

"*No,* Trace, go on to your office. We don't need you moping around here. I'm fine."

"Lara…" His eyes flicked to Gillian, then back to the actress.

What? Gillian wondered. *Are you afraid I'll rat on you about that kiss yesterday?*

"I'm fine," Lara repeated.

"Okay." He didn't look at all convinced. His hand strayed to her collar and he plucked at a chain hanging around her neck, pulling a silver locket into view. "You know where I'll be if you need me."

ONCE HE'D GONE, they settled to work. The first order of business, Lara declared, was a rough sort. "We need to lay out everything in somewhat chronological order. Then we'll see if I can figure out the exact year each picture was taken.''

''I'm afraid I won't be much of a help, not knowing your family.''

''Of course you will. You already know Joya and Toby. Here they are the first year I met their father. Weren't they adorable? They were eight and nine. So if you'd put this one over there...'' She pointed all the way to the left. ''About a foot from the end. Right there, perfect.''

Not perfect at all, Gillian realized, staring down at the start of the time line. ''You look about twenty here.'' She held up a photo.

''Twenty-five,'' Lara said, digging into her box.

''So...where're the early years?'' In her teens, Lara had been raised by foster parents, Gillian had learned from by reading that first article her aunt had torn from *Soap Opera Digest*. Her later research had turned up only variations on that fact, as if it were the only thing known. But before that? *What did you do with my grandparents? Did you have sisters and brothers? Where's the picture of you behind the wheel of your shiny new red Mustang?*

''The...early years?'' Lara murmured, then shrugged. ''They were nothing to speak of. Life begins in your twenties, I always say.''

Recorded life, anyway.

For the next hour, they sorted and arranged every photo in the first box. There were pictures of actors and actresses and backstage people from Lara's early years in soap opera, then later came the *Searching for Sarah* crowd. ''And this is...was...my Richard.'' Misty-eyed, Lara sat smiling down at a photo. ''I don't have many pictures of him. For some reason he was terribly camera shy.'' She passed over a shot of a thin-faced, thin-haired man in his late forties, intelligence shining out from behind a pair of wire-rimmed spectacles, a shy and kindly smile. ''This was the year I met him. He saved my life.''

''Careerwise, you mean?''

''Every which way and wise. I was running with a bad crowd. Had been since I dropped out of high school. I'd forgotten there was any other kind till Richard came along and reminded me.'' She rubbed a hand through her silvery hair. ''And yes, I never would have made it in show biz without him. I was working for the caterer who served lunches on the set, when he noticed me. Got me my first bit part.

''After that he coached me till I could halfway act. He taught me how to talk, how to walk, how to dress. How to think. Made me remember how to feel...'' She sat, head averted, throat convulsing, her hands cradling the photo. ''Sorry...''

''Oh, don't be silly!'' Gillian protested warmly.

''That's me. Silly's my middle name...'' She rose and walked over to the coffee table before the sofa and set the photo of Richard aside. ''Think I'll have a blowup made of that one.'' She pulled a tissue from the box on the table, blew her nose and wandered back, sat on the rug and delved into the photo box again. ''Speaking of middle names,'' she said casually, shuffling photos, ''what's *yours?* Gillian's so pretty. I wondered what your parents paired with it.''

Were they speaking of middle names? Gillian carefully squared one picture with its neighbors. *Trace put you up to this, didn't he?* Lara had stopped shuffling, had fixed her silvery eyes upon her with an almost fearful intensity. ''It's...'' God, she didn't like lying to this woman! "S-Susan. They named me after my aunt Susan." The kernel of truth in the lie, that she really had an aunt by that name, was the barest of comforts.

Lara blew out a long, sighing breath. "I like that. Gillian Susan…"

But you named me Sarah Cloud. Why Cloud, Lara? Why give me such a lovely, poetic name, then give me away?

There was no way to ask, with Lara's rejection engraved on her memory: *If I didn't want you when you were born, why would I want you now?*

Why indeed?

They worked for another hour, till there was less than an inch of pictures left in the second box and their photo train stretched for nearly twenty feet around the room. They broke for lunch—Lucy brought up a tray of soup and sandwiches—then on they slogged. "You don't have half enough space in your photo album," Gillian pointed out. "Joya and Toby alone would fill one."

There were pictures of Lara's stepchildren swimming at Bailey's Beach, sailing their dinghy in junior regattas at Ida Lewis Yacht Club. Of Joya competing in a horse show. Toby behind the wheel of his first car, a Porsche. Pictures of them in evening dress with Richard, at the Emmy Awards ceremony. Gillian plucked an early photo out of the box that was almost an eerie foreshadowing of that one—Toby in a child's tuxedo, Joya in a floor-length gown much too sophisticated for a girl of eight or nine. The two of them flanked Richard Corday, his buoyant smile contrasting oddly with his children's stony stares.

"That was at our wedding," Lara said, peering

over Gillian's shoulder. "They were supposed to take part in the ceremony, ring bearer and flower girl, but at the last minute Joya wouldn't and—" Her laughter was soft and rueful. "Somehow Toby lost the ring. We never did find it."

She shook her head slowly, remembering. "Richard was living in New York and their mother in Hollywood when I met him. The marriage was over in all but name, but the kids didn't know it. Wouldn't have it. They blamed me, of course." She set the photo in its place among those of the early years, then straightened, and stood staring down at it. "Took me forever to win them over…"

Jealousy plucked at Gillian's sleeve. *You wanted them but not me. Wasn't I good enough?* She stirred the remaining photos. "Another inch to go, plus this envelope." It lay at the very bottom of the box, a big tattered manila one, closed with a brass hasp. She turned it over—and Lara almost snatched it from her fingers.

"Oh, don't bother with those!"

"W-why not?" The envelope was dingy from years of handling. It was all she could do not to grab it back. *That! That's what I came for!*

"It's just some old junk…doesn't belong with the rest of this."

"Your childhood?" Gillian asked bluntly.

Lara grimaced, looking down at the envelope. "Such as it was."

"Show me," she coaxed in almost a whisper. *Please, please, please show me.*

"It's nothing much…" Lara's fingertips traced the bent clasp, drifted away from it, while Gillian clenched her teeth and held her breath. "Haven't looked at it in years…"

Oh, Lara, show me!

Her mother's slender fingers lifted the clasp, the tattered flap, reached in and drew out a photo. A young man and woman stood next to a worn old Chevy from the fifties. Whoever held the camera had backed far away, so that the entire car was visible in the photo—which meant the faces of the couple were tiny. The man wore a hat that shaded his upper face, but you could see his wide grin. His long bony arm was draped in casual possession over the shoulders of the tiny, white-blond, beaming woman in the flowered sundress.

"My parents," Lara said as softly as if she and Gillian sat together in church. "The day Daddy bought his new car. He was *so* proud of it."

The car might have been new to him, but this photo must have been taken in the mid-sixties, since Lara had been there to see their pride. Gillian's eyes stung. Such pride, such young hopes. "Where…" She swallowed; she could guess the thrust of the inevitable answer, if not its details. "Where are they now?"

Silently Lara pulled a yellowed newspaper clipping from the envelope. Flood Claims 7, proclaimed a mid-size headline. Bridge Washes Out In Storm Of Decade, it continued in smaller caps. She set it to the far side of her.

Gillian swallowed and nodded. *And so you ended up in a foster home. Or series of homes,* as the magazine article had put it. "How old were you?"

"Twelve." Lara pulled out a high-school photo— a copy of the same photo the lawyer had sent Gillian's adoptive parents so many years ago. "Here's me at fourteen, ninth grade."

And within a year this child was pregnant with me. Would buy herself a stuffed tiger after she'd given me away. A more suitable toy than a baby for this big-eyed, delicate child with the wary smile.

"The photographer was having the darnedest time getting me to smile," Lara remembered. "Finally he told me he'd bet I'd grow up to be a model someday, and that was so ridiculous I had to laugh—and he snapped this one."

"He wasn't far wrong," Gillian observed huskily.

"You could say it's all his fault," Lara agreed. "When I finally ran off, I needed *some*where to run to. And I guess becoming a model had stuck in my mind. Everybody knew you went to New York to be discovered." She smiled and set the photo aside. "But nobody in West Virginia knew you had to be five foot ten before they'd even let you in the agency door. I pounded mile upon mile of pavement before anybody bothered to set me straight."

"You grew up in West Virginia?" It was one of the many mysteries Gillian had yet to solve. She'd first learned that fact from the *Soap Opera Digest* article. She'd assumed Virginia, since her own birth certificate was issued by that state and her adoption decree was granted by a court of Virginia. So that was where she'd looked for her parents when she first started searching. *No wonder I didn't find any trace of you!* Could that muddling of facts have been intentional—perhaps by the lawyer who'd arranged her adoption? Change a state here or a date there and the link between parent and child was effectively broken.

Lara nodded. "I was born and raised in the mountains, yes. Coal country."

"Do you...still have family there?"

Staring into the mouth of the envelope, Lara shook her head. "Nobody."

So... Gillian sat, folding and tucking away her hopes of aunts, uncles, cousins, grandparents, like outgrown but still treasured clothes. *Well, I still have Chris. Sort of. He was such a traveling man that theirs was a phone-and-letter relationship more than a tangible, hugging one. A birthday present arrived every September without fail—one should be arriving any day, come to think of it—and he'd phoned her every Christmas since their parents divorced. That's more than lots of people have,* she reminded herself.

Lara pulled a card from the envelope, a homemade affair with a graceful sketch of a tree in black ink. On its trunk was drawn a heart, with the inscription *W. M. loves L. B.*

L.B. was Laura Bailey, of course, Lara's maiden name. But *W.? As in William?* That was her birth father's name, according to the document the lawyer had sent her adoptive parents. Gillian sat, her hands painfully clasped. "Beautiful sketch," she said finally. Her throat had almost closed on her and the words came out in a croak.

"It is," Lara agreed, setting the valentine on her far side. "He could draw anything."

And so can I! Could this be where that talent came from? A valentine proved nothing, of course, nothing at all; still, the blood hammered in her temples. *So close...so close...*

Lara lifted another photo from the envelope. Her eyes glistened as she stared at it, then she laughed in soft bewilderment. "He's so young and I...I got old."

"Who is he?" Gillian leaned in to stare at the young soldier. He looked...familiar. Something in the slant of his eyebrows or the shape of his face. *Could it be?*

"My first true love," Lara murmured. "He flunked out of high school—he was so smart, but he couldn't read to save his life. I used to do his homework for him." She smiled, lost in some long-ago sweet memory.

"What happened to him after that?" *Tell me. Oh, tell me!*

"He found some recruiter who helped him lie about his age, joined the marines. They shipped him off to Vietnam a few months later." Her smile faded. "He came home after training to say goodbye. I never saw..." Lara gulped, shook her head at the words that wouldn't come, then spun in relief as the telephone rang. She set the photo gently on the carpet and went to answer the phone.

Gillian stared down at the picture. *Never saw him again? Why, Lara? He died in the war, or he never came home again, or he found another girl?* She could imagine a dozen reasons. Eyebrows that seemed familiar... She longed to take the photo to the nearest mirror and compare it feature by feature with her own. *Is this my father? Flunked out of school because he couldn't read. And now here am I, a woman who scrambles her alphabet, who confuses numbers with letters, when she reads.* She'd never thought of dyslexia as a gift before.

CHAPTER THIRTEEN

"WHAT NEWS?" TRACE demanded when Jeremy Benton came on the line. "Any word back on the prints?"

"Yeah, I got word," Benton said, " for all the good it did me. Had to call in some favors to get it this fast."

"I owe you, Jeremy." Favors were better than cash in the pocket, in their world, and the tally of who owed whom was scrupulously kept. "No matches, huh?" He wasn't surprised. Stalkers weren't your normal felons, who, starting in their teens or even earlier, served long apprenticeships in crime or violence or both and collided at regular, well-documented intervals with the law. Some stalkers suffered only one obsession in a lifetime. Others cruised from celebrity to celebrity. But unless and until they crossed the line from obsession to murderous possession, they didn't appear on the police officer's radar screen. "Well, thanks anyway."

"And as to the Dumpster diving down at the Moorings—the guys turned up zip. No glue tubes, no matchbooks or lighters, nothing. You've got a cute one there." Hearty male laughter sounded in the background, and Benton murmured, "Yeah, yeah, I'm coming," then asked hurriedly, "what about your end?"

"Lara told no one I ran out and got a bee sting kit. So that means anybody at that lunch day before yesterday who knows she never carries a purse would have had good reason to hope a bee would do the trick."

Benton grunted. "You warn her not to tell anybody from now on?"

"I did." Much better to leave the stalker thinking the bee trick might work next time than to have the person seeking a new method of attack.

"Good. You realize that if your Gillian babe isn't the freak, then whoever it is may not know for sure you spotted the bee. It could have torn its own leg off and flown away, or maybe it's still stuck in place and died of a heart attack, for all Sarah XXX knows."

"Or maybe she was watching and saw it all." The waterfront parking lot was open on three sides, with crowds of tourists strolling past. The stalker could have hidden there in plain sight. Trace rubbed his nape where his hair bristled. "And here's another thing. You asked me yesterday if a fan would know that Lara Corday is allergic to bees. The answer is probably not, *but*—hang on to your hat—Dr. Laura Daley, the character Corday plays in the soaps, is allergic to bees."

"What the hell, Sutton?"

"Yeah. Lara's husband had a habit of borrowing from real life to enrich his fictional characters, she tells me. So he borrowed his wife's allergy, tacked it onto her character and wrote an episode a few years back where Dr. Daley is stung by a bee during a hospital staff picnic. And guess who saves her life by doing an emergency tracheotomy with a pocketknife and a straw?"

"No. I don't wanna hear this."

"Oh, yeah. Dr. Daley's faithful surgical nurse and best friend, aka Woodwind's perpetual houseguest—Harriet Bristow."

Benton let out a sigh of disgust. "You got a butler over there by any chance?"

"Nope."

"Okay, so the butler didn't do it. He's the only one in the whole wide world we don't suspect. But it looks like it could be either of her stepkids, her personal assistant, her actress buddy. Or it could be a nutcase—one of ten—twenty?—million viewers who's confusing Corday with her TV role. We'll catch Sarah XXX someday and find out she's a fruitcake who hates all *doctors!* Meantime, I've got a hot date with a steak and pepper grinder across the street."

After cradling the phone, Trace sat scowling into space for a while, then dialed again.

"'Lo?" his sister snapped.

"How's it going, kiddo?"

"Ho—so glad *somebody* asked! Let's see. I'm stuck on a freeway—the wrong freeway, headed God knows where—someplace on the north side of Houston. Pre-rush-hour rush hour, apparently. I've been sitting here for forty minutes now, and the air conditioner croaked twenty minutes ago. And it's a hundred degrees in the shade, except there isn't any. Nothing but concrete and kudzu as far as the eye can see. Five minutes more of this and I leave the key in the ignition and walk."

"Stay calm, Em."

"I *am* calm. Five more minutes and I calmly walk!"

This was why you didn't hire relatives. "Fine. Before you go, tell me your latest, okay? What's Mahler's middle name?"

"Scott."

As bad as Sylvester. "Scott is a guy's name," he said with exaggerated patience. Unless it was a last name? Her maiden name? Meaning Mahler's her married name? His stomach did a nasty triple gainer off a high board. Gillian married. It made sense. Any man looking for a wife would—

"According to her next-door neighbor, Mahler's mother was married twice. She was a divorcée named Eleanor Scott, with a daughter named Gillian Scott in tow, when she arrived in Houston. Then she met a man named Ed Mahler, married him, and Ed adopted her daughter—"

"Who became Gillian Scott Mahler. Got it." He let out a long breath of relief. Not married. Even better, not Sarah. His eyes narrowed. So why had she lied?

"*Aaaand* the crowd applauds," Emily teased, "The sound is deafening. Wait, the're all getting to their feet! It's a standing o—"

"Good job, kiddo. Well done. Thank you very much."

"*Ohhh,* you're entirely welcome. You'll receive my invoice tomorrow. Now, can I *please* go?"

"Not quite yet." He ignored her yelp of anguish. "So Gillian Scott Mahler used to be Gillian Scott. What was her middle name back then?"

"I don't care! I want to go home."

"Emily, if you work for Brickhouse, it's a job, not a hobby. You stick till it's done or go find something softer. Research librarian maybe?" She'd quit that job last year after feuding with the head librarian about whether *The Hitchhiker's Guide to the Universe* was appropriate children's literature.

"Creep."

"The creep who's paying your bills this month. Mahler's original middle name, and I need it on the double. We had another attempt on my client yesterday."

"Why didn't you say so?"

"You were too busy whining." He told her about the bee, to a background of hooks and revving engines, till all trace of temper and tears had left her voice.

"Okay," she said humbly when he'd ended. "Mahler's original middle name coming up, ASAP."

"You could try to find the court in which Ed Mahler adopted her. Might be on record there. Or maybe you can think of some way to trick it out of her parents."

"'Fraid not. Her mother died two years ago—cancer. And Ed Mahler sold his house and went to sea. He's a merchant marine."

A family existed—a family blown away like dust. He and Emily were luckier than most. They were two of four children, with happily married parents thriving up in Vermont. He could go home anytime and find his high-school letter jacket hanging in his bedroom closet, his rock posters still tacked to his bedroom walls. But Gillian couldn't. She'd had not one but two families fall out from under her.

How much does it take, he wondered, to push a sensitive person over the edge? How much loneliness and dislocation does she suffer before something snaps—and she sets out in search of somebody to belong to who'll never let her down? Someone who can't really die because she never really existed? Someone like a TV mother searching for her daughter?

And when her TV mother rejects her?

"TWO MORE ALBUMS SHOULD do it," Lara decided, thumbing through the album they'd completed. "Or let's say three to be safe."

"We could run down to the photo shop in the Brick Market," Gillian suggested. "They should be open for another hour."

Lara glanced at her watch and let out a groan, just as a key turned in the door to the suite. Trace Sutton peeked in. "Twenty minutes till your rehab session."

"I just realized! Darn, I wanted these off the rug today." She looked down in dismay at their train of photographs.

"That's why you hired a personal assistant," Gillian reminded her. "If you could drop me on your way, I'll buy them."

"Terrific. Or better yet, why doesn't Trace drop *me* off, then he can drive you around to the shops?"

"No!" Gillian and Trace protested as one. Startled, Gillian swung to meet his scowl, then turned away. "No, thanks," she said briskly. "It's stopped raining and I'd like a walk."

Head cocked to one side, Lara stood very still. Then she smiled and shrugged. "Of course."

AFTER SHE'D PURCHASED Lara's albums, Gillian wandered back toward Woodwind, following Thames Street south along the harborfront. The storm clouds had cleared out, leaving the old town bathed in a rosy glow as the sun sank beyond the bay. Lovely light for painting. She'd been too long away from it. There just wasn't time, between Lara's assignments and her classes at the Y. But she was storing up images.

She stopped to peer down one of the ancient cobblestoned wharved toward the water. Old two-story shops leaned in from either side. At the far end where the wharf jutted into the harbor, the dark masts of sailboats striped a pink sky. She jumped as a car horn blared close behind her. She turned to see a black Range Rover, Joya smirking at her from the open passenger window, her brother, Toby, at the wheel. The sports ute cut off a gaggle of tourists venturing timidly out onto the crosswalk and sped on down the road. *I guess you could call that progress,* Gillian told herself. Usually, Lara's stepbrats either ignored her or patronized her when they crossed paths at all. A honked acknowledgment was a definite advance. Not that they'd bothered to stop and ask if she'd like a ride home.

Even if they had, she preferred her own company. Especially this afternoon, two days before her birthday.

For the past twenty years, Gillian had celebrated a ritual with her mother—her real mother Eleanor Scott—window-shopping together two days before her birthday. Eleanor would point out objects she thought Gillian might like for a present. Gillian smiled, remembering. *Isn't that beautiful? Oh, honey, what do you think of this bracelet?* Gillian would dutifully admire them or express tactful reservations, then they'd wander on to the next shop. At the same time, she'd keep a sharp eye out for a present for Eleanor—whose birthday was—had been—in October. Because her mother generally pointed out objects that pleased her own eye.

At the end of the excursion, they'd eat supper in some special restaurant—a carefully considered treat in itself. The following day, they'd sneak back separately to the shops to make their purchases. And the day after, Gillian's birthday on September 12, she'd receive the object she'd most admired, beautifully gift-wrapped and lovingly presented—and she'd express delighted astonishment. *Dear Mom.*

Last September, her first birthday without her mother, she hadn't been able to make herself shop. But this year, two days before her birthday, Gillian thought she could continue the tradition. Maybe she wouldn't buy, but at least she could admire, and listen for her mother's ghostly remarks at her shoulder. *Yes, Mom, it does match my eyes, but how often do I wear a scarf. Now, this hat...*

Still, she surprised herself by finding an irresistible pair of Victorian earrings in an antique shop that specialized in estate jewelry. Baroque pearls edged with garnets. She shouldn't—it would cost a week of the salary Lara was paying her. She bought them anyway. Who else would be gifting her this year?

Well, there was Chris; his birthday present arrived every September without fail. Which reminded her. She should stop by her old apartment, see if there was mail. She'd filed a forwarding address with the post office, but so far they didn't seem to be forwarding.

On her arrival she rang the bell for the upstairs apartment—it felt odd to no longer have a key—then heard footsteps clattering down to meet her. Michele, one of the two sophomores Debbie had added to their household to make ends meet. About Joya's age and rather like her, Gillian thought, looking up at her, poised uncertainly on the third stair.

"Oh, it's you." Michele decided to brazen it out. "I was just leaving."

"Not in my sweatshirt, you're not." Gillian made no move to step aside. Her favorite orange University of Miami sweatshirt, a Christmas gift from Chris when she was fourteen. She held out her hand. "Give."

"This is yours?" Michele caught a pinch of fabric and stared down at it, as if someone had slipped it over her head while she slept and she'd only just noticed. "I thought it was Debbie's."

"It's mine and I'll take it now, please."

Michele tossed her blond curls. "But I was just going out."

Was I ever this young? Gillian settled herself more comfortably against the doorjamb. "Oh? Well, you may want to find something warm to wear. It's getting chilly."

An hour later, arms now loaded with Lara's albums and a plastic bag stuffed full of her own missing clothes, Gillian cut uphill to Bellevue Avenue. Less than half a mile to Woodwind, she assured her feet. *And a treat when you get there,* she reminded herself. Apparently the package she'd expected from Chris had arrived this morning. Debbie, it seems, had delivered it to Woodwind on her bicycle, and had met Harriet just exiting the front gates.

"You know who she is, don't you?" Debbie demanded. "She plays that bitchy nurse on *Searching for Sarah,* and I guess she's typecast. I told her I needed to see you, but she claimed you were too busy working to entertain visitors. That she'd give you the package. She didn't?''

''She was still out when we left. Lara said she went up to Providence to talk to some theater director.'' But she ought to be back by now and Gillian smiled in anticipation. Chris gave wonderful, whimsical presents, often picked up on his wanderings around the world. Seashells, carved coconuts…a pareu from Bali one year— A horn honked and, still smiling, she turned.

''What perfect timing!'' Lara cried from the car window as Trace pulled over. ''Hop in.

''We're taking a short detour,'' she added as Gillian settled into the back seat and the car swung off the avenue. ''I remembered I needed something.'' Trace threaded through back streets with silent skill, while Lara admired the new photo albums and told Gillian about her rehab session. ''The therapist says I should be able to do anything I want to from now on. Just as long as I don't try to push through any pain.''

''Excellent. I've been meaning to suggest we start doing tai chi together, if you're interested.'' They settled on a time for their first lesson, then Gillian looked up as Trace parked the car in front of a small market that catered to the carriage trade. ''I think I'll just sit,'' Gillian said quickly, as Trace opened his door and walked around to Lara's.

Mr. Possessive, dogging Lara's every footstep. Having a man follow her everywhere like that would drive her wild. *How can Lara stand it?* Remembering his kiss yesterday, she supposed there were compensations. She ran a finger absently back and forth

across her lips, then grimaced as she realized what
she was doing.

A car pulled in off the street and edged into the
one remaining space near the market's door. Red...its
make came to her slowly, then Gillian sucked in her
breath. A Mustang from the early seventies, clearly a
collector's car. Not that vintage cars were unusual in
Newport, where only last month they'd held a parade
of antique Rolls-Royces that had stretched for more
than two miles along Bellevue. This was a town
where people came to strut their stuff.

A red Mustang. Like the car Lara had demanded
before she'd sign the relinquishment papers. Hardly
aware she was doing it, Gillian opened her door and
stepped out, as if the Mustang were a magnet, hauling
her home. She stopped when her outstretched fingertips touched the Mustang's shiny flank. *Lara traded
me for one like this.*

She glanced aside as the door to the market opened
and Trace and Lara walked out. Laughing softly,
Trace stopped beside her. "I see you like sports
cars."

"This one anyway," she murmured, her eyes fixed
on Lara. "Such a lovely color."

Expressionless, Lara walked past her to the door to
her own car. "Don't you think so?" Gillian added,
coming to join her. "It's a beauty, isn't it?" she
asked. *Am I turning the knife? I suppose I am.*

"Is it?" Lara said. "I wouldn't know. I've always
hated Mustangs." Huddled into herself, she didn't
speak again all the way home to Woodwind.

CHAPTER FOURTEEN

"I LEFT IT ON THE hall table," said Harriet.

Gillian frowned. Lara's reaction to the Mustang had driven all thoughts of Chris's package from her mind. She'd run upstairs to her apartment on their return, gulped down a bowl of yogurt and changed for the aerobics class she was scheduled to teach at 7:00. On the way down to her car, she'd remembered and dashed up to the mansion. "Are you sure?" she asked now. The table in the front hall was the logical place to look, since Trace left all the family's mail there excepting Lara's. "I've checked and—"

Harriet bridled. "Of course I'm sure." She glanced angrily around the terrace at Toby and Joya, who were lounging on the balustrade, sipping one of Toby's alcoholic concoctions—apparently they were dining at home this evening—then at Lara, who sat beside her, as if to summon their support.

Trace glanced up from his golf club in mild interest. "Maybe you left it in your car, Harriet." He tapped the ball at his feet. It rolled twenty feet across the terrace and missed his crystal vase by an inch. "Damn."

"I didn't." Harriet stuck out her chin. "Go back and check again. It's there."

"Maybe Lucy moved it when she dusted," drawled

Toby. "What's the big deal anyway? Somebody sending you some special dope, Gillie?"

"It's just a package I was expecting from a friend," she said stiffly, absurdly near tears. Here she stood among uncaring strangers, blocked from contact, no matter how tenuous, with the only person left in the world who loved her. *I want my birthday present!*

"I'm sure it will turn up," Lara said quickly. "I didn't notice it when we walked through the hall. Did you, Trace?"

He shook his head. "Why don't we ask Lucy and Barbara? Somebody must have put it away for safe-keeping."

"Never mind. I'm late for my class already," Gillian said, trying to be gracious. "I'll look for it afterward." The last thing she saw as she turned away was Joya's Cheshire-cat smirk.

HOURS LATER, SHE THOUGHT of the package again as she parked before the carriage house. She glanced over her shoulder, but this side of Woodwind was dark, excepting the window on the second floor that, she had learned, marked Trace's office. Should she go up and look?

It was nearly midnight. Three women in her class had practically shanghaied her off to a bar, for a drink and what had turned out to be an attempt to pair her with the brother of one of them. She'd been flattered but the image of Trace Sutton had intruded. When had he become her standard for comparison?

And what about my package? she reminded herself. The day after tomorrow was her birthday, so she wouldn't, by her own rule, open Chris's gift even if she found it. Still, not knowing its whereabouts made her uneasy. She'd be happier with it sitting safely on her table, giving her two days to shake it and anticipate its contents. Trace was right, she told herself. She'd find it tomorrow, on the floorboards in Harriet the Grump's car.

She opened the door to the staircase, then paused, looking over her shoulder. To the east a full moon was rising over the trees. A lovely night for a walk. She'd yet to do Cliff Walk by moonlight.

But she was tired. Tomorrow night the moon would be nearly as full. She flicked on the light, trudged upstairs—and stopped short. "Son of a gun!" A package leaned against the wall beside her door. "Were you there all along?" Had she overlooked it this evening, going upstairs with her arms full of the clothes she'd retrieved from Michele? Or did Trace find it for her and bring it up? The man might have all the sexual fidelity of a tomcat; still, she could see him doing that. He was such a puzzling mixture of aggressiveness and consideration.

Whatever. She swooped up her gift and carried it into the apartment, over to the coffee table—and frowned. A wide flap of brown wrapping paper dangled from the bottom. Upending the parcel, she found that one end had been neatly wrapped and sealed with duct tape. The other end had once been finished in the same fashion, but at some point in the package's travels, the folds had come loose and been torn. She grimaced. Post-office sorting machines, no doubt. Someone had patched the shreds together with clear tape, then sent the package on.

She turned it over and studied the return address: Christopher Scott, Yacht Malay, Tahiti. "Lucky dog!'' she murmured affectionately. He'd been in Hawaii last time she'd heard from him back in June. He'd called her to urge once again that she give up her quest, forget about learning anything about her birth parents.

Because her adoptive brother was the only person she'd told about that horrible letter of rejection, and from that moment, Chris had despised Lara on her behalf. *You don't need a reunion with a selfish bitch like that,* he'd pointed out. *She's the past, Gillian. You need to get on with your future. You need nothing from her.*

If you could meet her now, Chris, would you still think that, I wonder? That car today at the market... *I don't know what to make of her.* Chris had always been a shrewd judge of character. *I wish you were here.*

He almost was. Always a letter came with his present. She turned the package again and picked at the torn flap. *Hope you didn't send me something fragile.* Could the post-office brutes have broken it? She shook the package, yet nothing rattled.

Two days to her birthday, but there would be no celebration this year. The only other person who knew the significance of September 12 apparently didn't care. Had never cared.

She hugged the package to her breast. *Why am I so blue, all of a sudden?* Still embracing it, she drifted to the window overlooking the courtyard. Beyond the fluttering leaves of an elm, she could see the light was still on in Trace's office. He was working late.

On what? She hadn't a clue. She ought to ask him sometime.

She wouldn't. He was Lara's man. The less she

messed with him, let herself think about him, the better. The light blurred for a moment, and blinking, she let out a startled laugh. *Hey, what's the matter with me?*

Antidote time. Immediately. She sank onto the sofa, balanced the package on her knees and attacked it. Let Chris drive the demons out. This year she was celebrating early.

Inside the wrapping paper, she found a much-battered cardboard box, which was taped with clear tape. She frowned, a vague sense of...uneasiness pricking at the back of her mind. She rose to find a knife with which to attack the tape, then paused, glancing toward the courtyard windows. A feeling of intrusion, of being watched, was growing slowly within her. *Don't be absurd.* Even if someone stood down below on the gravel, looking up, he couldn't see her from that angle. But still...

She sliced the knife through the tape, then raised the box's lid. And looked down at a book, dark blue with an exuberant design of S-curves and curlicues in gold. With a tremulous laugh, she traced the familiar pattern. She hadn't seen this book in twenty years, but still she remembered it. Tears trickling down her cheeks, she opened the birthday card that lay on top of it.

"I found it at last," Chris had written. "It was up in Dad's attic, and he said of course you should have it, when I reminded him."

Hans Christian Andersen's fairy tales, an edition printed in the 1890s, with wonderful art nouveau illustrations. Her mother had read her a few pages of a tale every night before bed from the time she was three till she grew old enough to read for herself.

They'd reach the end of the book then start over again. Somehow it had been left behind when her parents split households, but she'd never forgotten. Had mentioned it wistfully to Chris only last year.

"I remember how much you loved the illustration of the dog with eyes the size of saucers," his note continued. "I can still see you, lying on your stomach by the fire, your feet waving in the air while you pondered that picture."

He then went on to tell her about the yacht he was delivering to New Zealand, a wonderful old tub, with every comfort in the world aboard, but he could have reached the islands faster by swimming. "Meantime I worry about you," he wrote. "Have you achieved any kind of reunion with your mother? And if so, was it worth it? Or at least, have you pried the real story out of her?

"I wish you'd leave well enough alone, but you were always a stubborn brat. And curious as the cat. Please keep in mind what they say about kitties who insist on answers."

"The only thing that might be hurt is my feelings," she assured him. She finished the card, folded it and sat smiling for a moment. The blues hadn't quite departed her door; still, Chris had driven them back to a respectful distance. She set the letter aside and opened the book. Paged slowly through it, pausing to admire the illustrations for the Ice Queen, Hansel and Gretel and the Dog with Eyes— Her gasp feathered out into the silence.

Between two pages of text only a ragged stub remained—one paw of the dog and a bit of delicate background. Whoever had ripped out this illustration had done so carelessly, with malice, intending to destroy, not steal, leaving the tattered page like a mocking signature. *I passed this way and I wrecked it!* With a shudder, Gillian glanced up at the courtyard window.

Darkness pressed its face against the panes.

"CLOUDY," SAID LARA distinctly.

Instantly awake, Trace blinked at the darkness overhead. *Damn, here we go again.* Her third nightmare in a week. *What's bothering you, lady?* All this anguish about the weather? And why now? Even in the hospital, the first days after her fall, she hadn't dreamed like this.

"It's all my...stupid, stupid, *stupid*...oh, Cloudy, I...she's gone and I..." A keening, tiny sound of unappeasable, unending grief.

Time to get up and wake her. Maybe he should let her sleep, let her work it through, but no one with a heart could allow such pain to continue uncomforted. He swung his covers aside and sat.

She swore, one sudden, crystal-clear word, coarse and brutal. He'd never heard her curse before. He padded toward the bed.

"He'll never drive that car again," Lara muttered. "Never! And *I'll* never..." Anger shaded into wordless, murmuring heartbreak.

Moonlight flooding in the French doors helped him find the decanter on her bedside table. He poured a glass of water, started to sit on the edge of her bed, but suddenly she rolled over. Hugged her pillow and let out a long, shuddering sigh.

He stood, waiting while her half-sobbing breaths deepened and slowed. *Good,* he told her silently. *Sleep, Lara, go to sleep. Sleep and don't dream.* She sighed again and burrowed her face in the pillow. He set the glass down and backed off from her bedside. *Good…*

He waited for almost five minutes, but the nightmare didn't resume. Good for Lara, but now *he* was wide-awake. He shrugged and padded into his dressing room, set into the opposite end of the suite from hers, then to his bathroom beyond.

When he came out a few minutes later, she was sleeping as peacefully as a child. He glanced at his watch. Three in the morning. No chance of sleep for him once his mind started spinning. And it had plenty to spin about.

Gillian Scott Mahler. *Why lie about your middle name, Gillian?* Could Lara have been right? *She took offense when I first questioned her. Were her lies ever since simply teasing?*

No, his instincts told him it was more than that. Lion eyes, with something moving in their depths. She stood always on the edge of things here at Woodwind, watching, waiting… *For what?* A chance to belong or a chance to strike?

The Mustang at the market this afternoon—what was that about? For that matter, what about Lara's reaction? He remembered once, back in his FBI days, someone had tried to shoot him at close range and he'd barely deflected the gun. For two days after, his left ear heard nothing but ringing. This was like that. As if urgent conversations filled the air around him at Woodwind, but he could see only moving lips.

Lara and Gillian, then Lara again—shopping for food at the market, baker's chocolate and walnuts. He'd lived with the woman since May and not once had she shown any interest in cooking. He'd tried to question her in the store and she'd brushed him off with a joke about craving chocolate. But baker's chocolate is unsweetened. No chocoholic would buy it for eating, not when the market also sold the finest Belgian varieties. So that was a lie. Gillian and Lara both lying...why?

He prowled to the French doors, moonlight diffusing through the diaphanous sheers that covered the floor-to-ceiling panes. Unlocking one door, he smiled as the sound of the sea rolled into the room. Better. He walked out onto the balcony. A full moon riding high. What a shame to stay inside on a night like this.

He leaned on the stone balustrade, breathing deep, looking out over the moonlit lawn bounded by the pitch-black slashes of the surrounding walls. Something flickered in the shadows and his eyes homed in on the movement. Something pale—the gate in the wall swinging open, then closing again. *Son of a bitch!* He straightened, waiting. *Come on, Sarah XXX. Here I am. It's high time we met.*

A minute pulsed by, two heartbeats to each second, but no one stepped forth from the shadows. Was the watcher standing perfectly still? Could the watcher see him? Or—it hit him. He'd just seen someone *leaving* Woodwind, not entering! His eyes swept beyond the walls, out onto Cliff Walk, and for a moment, he thought he detected movement where the path twisted—someone heading south. He raced into the suite, ticking off his needs as he went. His sweats, his shoulder rig to hold his gun, his running shoes. No way was he missing this chance to end the whole maddening masquerade. If Sarah XXX walked the cliffs tonight, she was his!

TWO HOURS OF TOSSING and turning had convinced her she wouldn't sleep tonight. She might as well get up, go out, see if moonlight and the ocean could drive this sickness from her heart. Dressed in a T-shirt and running shorts, a light cotton sweater slung by its sleeves around her neck, Gillian unlocked the gate in the wall, locked it behind her, then pushed carefully through the rosebushes onto Cliff Walk. Starlight tipped the dark waters with diamonds; the sea sighed against the rocks far below. She drew a deep breath— roses and kelp—and broke into a jog, heading out the peninsula toward the ocean. She had the whole night to herself.

Running through moonlight felt more like floating, her loosely curled fingers flickering dark, then milky before her as the bushes shrouded her in shadow or broke to show the glittering waters beyond. The growl of waves dragging down the shingle beach; the soft thud of her running shoes on damp stone—up a flight, across a stony flat, then down again. Then the gap in the bushes, the unnerving seaward tilt in the path— the spot where Lara came to grief. Gillian held her breath as she passed the drop, let it out in a grateful puff and ran on, fleeing from the knowledge, feeling it loping at her heels like a black dog. A dog with eyes the size of saucers…a dog that was no more.

Chris, did you look at that illustration before you sent me the book, or did you only recall it from our childhood? Maybe someone had torn it out years and years ago—past malice, not present hatred. Perhaps her adoptive father in a fit of rage, just after the divorce, twenty years ago.

No. Victor Scott had never bonded with her, but neither had he hated her.

She quickened her steps, but she couldn't run fast enough to escape the conclusion: Someone had torn open the package, not caring that she'd notice, then opened the box inside.

And read Chris's loving note. Shuddering as if bony, claw-nailed fingers stroked across her skin, she ran faster. The path sloped downward, speeding her flight; her feet jarred against the concrete, resisting gravity. Read Chris's message, so he or she knew what Gillian loved—the dog—then wrecked him. But why?

The towering chimneys of the Breakers reared against midnight-blue. Out to her left stretched a reef of black stones, the waves breaking white on them to give the mansion its name. *It could have been any sickie between Tahiti and Rhode Island. It doesn't have to be anyone I know...*

But she knew better. She would check with her ex-housemate tomorrow, ask Debbie if the package had been ripped when she'd delivered it, but already Gillian knew. *Someone here at Woodwind hates me....*

The same person who had removed the package from the front hall table. Or maybe Harriet lied and she never put it there at all. Ripped it open in the privacy of her car. Maybe she never meant to deliver it. Wouldn't have if Gillian hadn't asked for it. Harriet seemed to hate almost everyone. But why single me out? What have I done to her?

Come between her and Lara?

She'd reached the riprap. Not slowing her steps, she leaped from rock to rock. One misstep and her foot would slip into a gap; she'd break a leg for sure.

Didn't care. The malice behind her was what she feared tonight. *Joya...* Joya could have noticed her name on the package on the hall table. She could picture Joya reading Chris's note, see her searching the beloved book for the dog, laughing as she tore him out. But why?

Or perhaps the question with Joya was why not? Had it been a simple, malicious thrill, done merely because she *could* do it, the way a child torments a fly, pulls off a wing to see what happens next? *When she smiled at me on the terrace I thought she was enjoying my dismay about my missing package.* But maybe that had been a smirk of triumph. Of gloating. *I know something that you don't, Gillie.*

Up another flight of stone stairs as the cliffs rose again, Cliff Walk climbing with them to overlook a smaller cove, with the clatter of rolling shingle and an eerie phosphorescence where the waves raked the beach. Roses and the high walls of the mansions were on her right, empty moonlit space to her left, though not so scary here—the drop-off was only forty feet or so. More intimidating by far was the tunnel ahead, looming like a yawning mouth, surmounted by the Japanese teahouse… Copper dragons leering at her from its winged rooftop as she neared, her steps slowing to a faltering jog. Should she turn back?

Back to where somebody hated her? She couldn't, not yet. Catching her breath, she slowed to a fast walk and plunged into the tunnel, right hand grazing cold stone, not a ray of moonlight piercing the black. Twenty halting steps…thirty…forty. And now the faintest echo of waves, coming from up ahead, the palest moonlight promising the exit above. And then a velvety buttermilk sky, the moon a gigantic glowing pearl rolling westward.

Higher cliffs now and more riprap, more gaping

cracks between the stones. She took the boulders at a run, as if the mouth of the tunnel might suck her back inside. *Lara, Lara, Lara, could it be you?* Couldn't…could it? Chris had printed his name on the return address. She hadn't thought to warn him, had never dreamed that Lara might someday see a letter from her adoptive brother, with his telltale name of Scott.

Nine months before, when she sent Lara that shy letter of inquiry, she'd signed herself Sarah Scott.

So if Lara didn't know my adoptive parents' name when she relinquished me, she's known it ever since my letter. Could have spotted it on the package when she walked through the front hall this evening. Could have taken it up to her room to open it. *No, please, not Lara!*

But then who?

The face that was never very far from mind loomed in her thoughts, a face that called her, mocked her, disturbed her always. *Trace Sutton, who else?*

Because who else, the logical part of her mind demanded, was, despite his infidelities, fiercely protective and possessive of Lara? *If Trace knew that my name was Scott?* He'd only come to Woodwind in early May, she'd learned from Lucy. So he hadn't been living there when her letter arrived nine months ago. But if Lara had told him about it and then he'd noticed Chris's name on the package? Trace wouldn't be slow to put two and two together.

But to do this? She couldn't imagine it. The man might be her opponent, might see her as competition for Lara's affections and time, but the more she knew him, the less she could imagine him sneaking or conniving. *If he's my enemy, it wouldn't be behind my*

*back. He'd tell me, show me, perhaps pick me up by
the scruff of my neck and fling me through the gates
of Woodwind, but he wouldn't mangle my book. No,
whoever hates me, I can't believe it's Trace.*

Safely over the riprap, she'd come to the second
tunnel. A less-fearsome one this, a corrugated steel
pipe, burrowing under craggy rock for forty feet in a
straight line. The light at its far end beckoned you as
you entered it. Steps echoing, she flew through, then
out the far side. From there to the end of Cliff Walk
a mile south lay a wilderness of tumbled boulders, the
path breaking down entirely in places where storms
had washed it out. It ran only ten feet or so above
sea level, straggling along the base of the crumbling
cliffs. Because it was a wild and private stretch, very
few tourists ever ventured this far, and none at night.

Gillian slowed to a walk, panting. No, whoever it
was that hated her, surely it wasn't Trace. But then
who?

She halted, looking down at a horseshoe of soft
sand and powdered seashells encircled by massive
boulders. She'd waded off this tiny beach once or
twice this summer, though the big icy waves of Rhode
Island daunted a Texan used to the bathtub-warm
Gulf of Mexico waters. A few times at dawn she'd
come here to do tai chi.

With that memory, she realized—she wasn't fleeing from but to. No trouble was so black that the
ancient rituals of tai chi couldn't transcend it. She
jumped from ledge to ragged ledge down to the sand.
Stopped to unlace her shoes and set them aside. She
walked to the water's edge. Stood facing the sea, the
waves licking her toes, inviting serenity.

After a measureless time of slow breathing, she
bowed to the moon and began.

CHAPTER FIFTEEN

WHOEVER SHE WAS, she was young and in superb condition. Trace had caught glimpses of her flying shadow from half a mile back, but he hadn't yet managed to overhaul her. Each time she vanished around a bend, he had to follow with caution. Every time he passed a side trail, he scouted up it a ways, assuring himself that she hadn't cut between two mansions up to the avenue. He had to scan every pathside boulder or clump of brush for fear that she might have spotted him following her, might now be crouching under cover, hoping that he'd pass her by, so she could double back on her trail. So Trace took his time. He didn't mean to lose her. Catch her tonight and this detail was done at long last. Once Lara was freed from danger, he could go home with a fat check and a clear conscience.

The thought didn't give him the satisfaction it would have even a month before. Home was nothing but a place, an apartment in San Francisco, comfortable surely, filled with his books and music. But home wasn't a person, as it was for his father or his brother Jon. He ran lightly, leaping from boulder to boulder as he hit the riprap, smiling grimly at the thought. *I need a woman.* Something about chasing this one through the moonlight had set all his instincts howling. *Finish this assignment and I could go find one.*

One came instantly to mind. Lion eyes, a soft vulnerable mouth, slender waist he could almost span with his hands, she'd bend like a willow. *Forget it. Pay attention.* Lose his quarry now and he was going nowhere but back to his lonely couch at Woodwind.

He slowed to a half jog when he came to the teahouse tunnel. The perfect place for an ambush. If his runner had looked over her shoulder and seen him, here was where she'd lie in wait. He considered drawing his gun, then dismissed the notion. Whoever Sarah XXX was, so far all her murderous tricks had been low-tech, another reason he was sure she was a woman.

Hugging the right wall, he stepped into the darkness with no show of fear. Ten feet in, he crouched and cut over to the left wall. Hands upraised to chop or protect his head, he padded on, left shoulder brushing stone, ears craning for any sound ahead, hearing nothing but the faint echo of waves off the tunnel walls.

When his outstretched fingers found the turn, he stopped. Listened. The logical place for an attacker to wait was just beyond, with a stone or a knife at the ready. *Come on, come on, make your move!*

Nothing but the faintest susurration of the waves. Slowly he stooped, brushed the damp earth with his palm, found a pebble. He cracked it hard against the far wall.

No reaction. *Nobody here but me and the boogeyman.* Or a cool and intelligent opponent who knew a feint when she heard it. He shuffled on, found the stone steps with his toe, rattled up them—he'd lost too much time in the tunnel, dammit!

Burst out into moonlight again, eyes scanning the

far end of the cove, the path curving above it. Nothing. *If I've lost her...* He broke into an all-out run, leaping from stone to stone along the riprap like a broken field runner. *Wait for me, Sarah, you bitch!*

He paused, panting, at the next tunnel, but no one was silhouetted against the milky oval of sky beyond, so he plunged on through, footfalls echoing off steel, to halt just inside its far end.

Nothing and no one moved out on the path. He cursed silently. *Lost her.* Perhaps she'd simply lurked on the far side of the teahouse tunnel and let him bumble past her, then doubled back the way she came.

Or maybe Sarah XXX crouched behind one of the thousands of boulders in the half mile ahead. If so, it would take an army to winkle her out of hiding. He should turn back; his place was by Lara. But, too stubborn to call it a night, he pushed on.

Passing a boulder the size of a house, he glanced down at the pocket beach beyond it—and saw her. Dancing with the ocean. One foot upraised, he froze.

Hands sweeping across the sky, limber body on tiptoe, a soft lunge onto one foot, then the dancer paused. His heart beat once, twice, three times and he realized. Not dancing exactly, but the flowing movements of tai chi.

And his quarry was Gillian. He should have known. After days of covert watching, her shape and way of moving were tattooed on his brain by now, but darkness and distance and his own hunting lust had confounded him. He padded off the trail and uphill to sit on a rock above the natural amphitheater. *You've lured me into the night, woman. Now dance for me.*

Silently, gracefully, seemingly mesmerized by the

night and the ocean, she danced, one flowing motion merging into the next, then a graceful stance held, while a wave washed in and the moon rolled across the sky. He could feel the ease of her muscles as if he moved with her. Feel his heart pumping steadily, the warm blood surging. His own discipline was karate, but these moves were similar, if softer. His body knew them all. He could have wrapped his body around hers, limb for limb, and moved as one with her, dancing…

Gillian, fey mystic woman, I need to know you. Mean to know you. There was no use denying it any longer.

And if you're the enemy? Lara's and therefore mine?

He couldn't believe it. Would not. A woman who danced with the moon and the waves? She was celebrating beauty out here tonight. Creating it. Whoever and whatever she was, she wasn't a person who could push another off a cliff, not and move like that, too.

Cobras are graceful, his inner cynic reminded him.

He wouldn't believe she was a stalker. Could not.

Because you can't believe it and have her, the coolly objective half of his brain pointed out.

Whatever secrets she was hiding, they couldn't be hurtful ones.

With a client's life in jeopardy, all secrets are dangerous. To be distrusted.

Then he'd make her secrets his own.

He sat and watched while the moon sank into the west. While the tide rose and his desire with it, dragged up by the moon and Gillian's flowing grace.

Higher than all those that had come before, a wave washed in, wetting her to her knees. She laughed, completed a final sequence—and turned. He saw her head snap up as she spotted him, then her hair fly out in a silken bell as she spun toward the rock. She froze. With him waiting at the top of the path, she was trapped and she knew it. Another wave washed in around her ankles. Deliberately she turned to face him, chin up, shoulders squared.

He stood, rising up out of the shadows thrown by the cliff. "It's Trace, Gillian."

"Oh…" She flattened a hand to her breastbone. "I thought…"

"I'm sorry. I didn't mean to scare you."

"Oh, *really?*"

He deserved her anger. He'd invaded a ritual as private as bath or prayer. But no man would have done otherwise. She turned around and bent over, hunting slowly along the rock. Another wave swept in. The sand would be entirely covered at high tide. "What are you looking for?"

"My…" She turned back, retracing her steps. "My shoes. I thought I left them over…" Another wave washed in and she whirled to the water. "Oh, *no!*"

He laughed in spite of himself. "Oh, yes. Tides do that."

One of her shoes was still visible, about thirty feet out, a jaunty boat heading off to sea. She took a step toward it.

"Don't even think about it," he advised, coming to the edge of the path, prepared to stop her if need be. "The currents are nasty, and sharks hunt at night."

"Oh, thanks," she said bitterly. She shrugged and started up the rock, her arms outstretched sideways for balance.

He climbed halfway down and caught her hand as she wobbled. "Easy!" His voice was husky with amusement and delight. Two miles of ragged rock back to Woodwind and not a cab in sight. He'd have thrown a kiss to the waves if she hadn't been frowning at him.

She stepped up wincingly onto the path, which wasn't paved this far out Cliff Walk. "Coming home now?" he asked rhetorically. There was no other place she could go. The last mile would have cut her feet to shreds, and it led farther out the peninsula, away from town.

"Yes, I..."

He could almost see the wheels spinning inside her head. Did she dare ask him to run two miles back to Woodwind to fetch her a pair of shoes? Theirs was a prickly relationship at best and whatever else Gillian was, she was both self-sufficient and proud. Joya would have blithely issued an order and expected him to hop to it. Gillian wouldn't ask.

And it was too early for him to point out the obvious. Instead Trace slowed his steps to match her halting progress. Ten wincing feet and his amusement started to fade. She stumbled and her hand flew up and he caught it. "Careful there!"

"You should go on," she muttered. "I plan to take my time."

"I'm in no hurry." He placed her hand on his forearm, covered it with his own, pressed insistently on her slender fingers when she would have withdrawn.

She let out an exasperated breath but stopped resisting. After a few more halting steps, she leaned some weight on him.

Her hand on his bare skin...he'd wanted this since

the first day when he'd frisked her, wanted it more after she'd lifted the bar off his chest, then massaged his cramped muscles. He'd thought of little else since he kissed her outside the bookstore. Her thigh brushed his and a flurry of goose bumps stampeded across his skin. *Oh, woman, what you do to me!*

They hobbled along for another twenty yards, Gillian in grim silence, Trace pondering, *Why this woman?* Take her feature by feature and she wasn't extraordinarily beautiful, but take her as a whole— Some inexplicable instinct simply cried, *This one.* Now. No compromise, no substitutes acceptable. *This one.*

Might as well tell the tide to back off.

No, the only way out was straight through. Once he'd possessed her, the desire would surely fade to manageable proportions. He'd be his own man again.

They reached the first tunnel. It was too narrow for a couple to go abreast, so reluctantly he let her precede him. The path was crushed rocks the size of a fist; she took it without a whimper.

How could a woman be so stubborn? His own pride was starting to kick in. Did she think he couldn't carry her? Wouldn't? Or was it something more fundamental—an essential, physical distaste? That would have stopped him cold, but somehow he didn't think that was the problem. As often as his eyes had sought her out these past few days, he'd found her watching him.

They exited the tunnel and Gillian drew a shaky breath. "I think I'll stop here awhile."

"Sure." He stopped beside her, his arm brushing hers.

She rounded on him. "Trace, will you just go *on?* I'm fine. Really."

"But I'd rather limp along with you." He brushed his knuckles down the side of her upturned face, along the corner of her mouth and felt his heart surge as he did so. "We've got all night." *Let's not waste it.*

"Dammit, I—" She sounded halfway to tears, half laughing. "What am I supposed to do, I can't—"

"You can." *I'm yours to command.* "Is there something I can do for you?"

She let out a little growl of frustration. "*Yes!* You could go get me a pair of shoes."

"There's a simpler solution." *Ask me.*

She shook her head fiercely.

Laughing under his breath, he touched her cheek and waited for it. *Come on, give up. Give in. Give yourself to me.*

"C-could I…" She drew a deep breath. "Could I have a ride?"

"Thought you'd never ask!" He swept her up, all long coltish legs and slender arms—she wasn't heavy, not with a bolt of pure male energy shooting through him, swelling his muscles, stiffening his spine. When he straightened, he felt half a foot taller. The night brightened around him, as if the moon had pulsed. Gillian in his arms, a perfect fit! Memory intruded gradually on stunned delight, reminding him that he'd offered to carry her, not simply hold her. He moved out, their bodies rocking warmly together with each stride.

"I…meant ride on your back," she murmured, sounding breathless.

"Oh? Call me old-fashioned, but I've always pre-ferred face-to-face." Her eyes gleamed brighter. By God, she was blushing! He wanted to laugh aloud, whirl her around and around and kiss her senseless. Instead he strode soberly along, half his attention on the path ahead, the other half enthralled by the sunny scent of her hair and skin, the softness of her left breast pressing against his chest, the feel of her heart beating against his. *What a night!*

"Did you follow me?" she asked after a while.

The sane half of him couldn't help responding to the guilt in that question. "Why would I do that?"

"I—" She started to shrug, then froze as her breast moved against him. His arms tightened reflexively and she gasped. "I don't know, but—"

"I couldn't sleep," he said to let her off the hook. "So I came out for a walk. And you?"

"The same. I was sad, and this place…takes that away."

I could take that away. "Why sad, Gillian? He could have dipped his head and kissed her.

"I…" She shook her head, willing to share her feelings, but not her thoughts.

Her left arm was hooked around his neck, her right hand locked onto her left wrist. Gradually she'd relaxed as she realized he wasn't going to drop her. Her hand smoothed across the breadth of his shoulder, almost a caress, then stopped. "What's that?"

You ass! he cursed himself. He'd been so hot to hold her he hadn't thought once of his shoulder harness, the gun tucked under his left armpit. It wasn't pressing against her thigh, not quite, but still. "That? Just my suspenders. The waistband's gone on these sweats. Fiddle with that and they'll probably drop."

"Oh!" She snatched back her hand. It hovered uncertainly, then settled around his neck. Careful to hold her legs out from the gun, he hitched her a little higher. "You're getting tired," she said anxiously.

"Nope." Harder than a rock, but never tired. After another hundred yards, though, he had to admit he needed a break. Trace glanced around, looking for a likely place to sit. Nothing, but they were coming to the teahouse tunnel. Maybe beyond it?

"Kinda spooky, isn't it?" Gillian murmured at his ear.

"It's those dragons," he agreed. "Each time I pass I'd swear they've moved."

"Brr!" She laughed huskily. "I never noticed that. It's the darkness, and what might be hiding in it, I think about."

"Well, you're safe tonight." *Except from me.* He paused at the top of the stone stairs leading down.

"Really, I can walk," she assured him.

"No need." With deliberation he descended, feeling his muscles pump with the effort. Halfway down the stairs, the darkness closed around them entirely. Gillian in his arms in the dark—with no premeditation at all, he sat. "Just a breather," he assured her.

"You can put me down." Her voice had dropped to a whisper, barely louder than the distant echo of waves off stone.

"Can't," he lied. "I've stiffened up." Had he, indeed. "I think it's better if we stay this way." Better? No, the best, with her warm trim bottom resting on his thighs, her heart stampeding against his chest. *Keep talking, Sutton. Distract her.* Considering the way she was distracting him, it was only fair. "What scares you in the dark?"

"*Ohhh…*" She let out a slow breath. "The dog

with eyes as big as saucers…?'' Her statement lilted like a question.

''Yow! If you'd told me about *him*…'' He snuggled her closer against his chest, couldn't help doing it. ''Saucer eyes. Do they glow in the dark?'' He dipped his head, feeling the warmth of her face radiating against his own, her breath on his cheek. *Stop me if you're going to, Gillian. Surely you know what I want.* She had to feel his runaway pulse where her arm encircled his neck. *Say something, if you don't want what I want.*

''I…don't know. I never thought…'' She laughed shakily. ''Probably.''

''Yours do,'' he half whispered. *Lion eyes!*

''Do *not*.''

''They do. I can see them. Here's *one*…'' He dipped his head and kissed her eyebrow. She drew in a feathering breath as he brailled his lips slowly across her forehead, to find her other eyelid, closed now, a warm velvet curve. He brushed his lips through her quivering lashes. ''And here's the other. Like spotlights.'' Shining straight into his heart. She shuddered and his arms tightened. His lips traveled down the side of her smooth cheek, slowly, giving her time to protest, but her arm tightened around his neck, molding them closer.

Go slow, go slow, he warned himself, sensing the resistance in her body even as she sighed. His lips going slow, his heart in overdrive, his body starting to shake with desire. Oh, Gillian! His lips found her mouth—closed, but soft and trembling, not clamped. He traced the tender triangle with the tip of his tongue. *Open, for me, darling.* She moaned deep in her throat, a sound of protest, but it must have been her own actions she was protesting—she opened her mouth and stroked a hand up into his hair.

Groaning with delight, he plunged into her before the invitation could be withdrawn. Honey and sunshine and musk and twining, vibrant strength. He dipped his right shoulder to bring her down; he needed to be over her, in her; he dragged his mouth from hers, spoke her name against her lips, "Gillian!" Kissed her chin, her throat, a place beneath her ear till she squirmed and cried out, his tongue lapping greedily at her pulse, urging it higher.

Her hands tightened in his hair. "Trace…" There was a note of dazed, drugged pleading in her voice, a woman pulled two directions at once.

But he was of one mind only, and until and unless she told him otherwise… He lipped the side of her neck, lingering at that sensitive corner where the tendons run shallow beneath velvety skin. His teeth closed on her gently—she gasped and convulsed in his arms. He found her mouth again and she shuddered and took him deeper, tongue dancing with tongue in the honeyed darkness, an endless plunging celebration that might have lasted minutes or hours—he was losing all sense of time. Of himself entirely. There was only Gillian, like a golden moon at the center of his consciousness, drawing him down and in and down, a wandering astronaut caught in a field of gravity he was powerless to resist. Wandering no more, homing straight in…

She tore her mouth away and moaned as he traced the delicate rim of her ear with his tongue. "S-stop…" she gasped.

"Mmm?" She could not possibly mean that. He rubbed his face through her fragrant hair.

"We've got to stop," she insisted, but without conviction.

"Who says?" He kissed the tip of her nose. *Don't do this, Gillian!*

She framed his face with both hands and held him off. "Stop!"

"You don't want to stop. I don't want to stop. So we're stopping?"

"Yes." She'd said the word softly but there was no compromise this time.

He sighed and lifted her upright, resettled her bottom against his thighs, stifled a groan. "Mind telling me why?"

She laughed incredulously. *"Trace!"* He could feel her shake her head. "Look…" She rested her hands on his shoulders. "In a word? Lara, that's why."

He swore silently, viciously, then tipped back his head to consult the invisible rocks above. *Let me explain!* Except that he couldn't. He couldn't break cover while there was one chance in a million Gillian was untrustworthy.

And he wouldn't have even if he *was* entirely sure of her. Being undercover meant you lived the part, night and day, till you were done. He'd learned that first as an FBI agent, then relearned it as a bodyguard. People died when you broke that rule.

Which meant he could come to Gillian only as Trace Sutton the faithless gigolo, not Trace Sutton the heart-free bodyguard. He blew out a frustrated breath. "Are you…sure?" And now *he* was torn. He wanted her to have character, but oh, God, couldn't she please have it later?

"Yes." She sighed and rubbed her palms along his shoulders, a frustrated caress. She brought them down his chest, then paused. "What's..." Her right hand settled over the butt of his gun just as he grabbed her wrist. "Ow!"

His move was sheer reflex to stop someone from drawing your own gun against you. He gentled his grip. "I'm sorry." Lifted her wrist to his mouth and kissed it. "Didn't meant to—"

"What the hell is that, Trace?" she insisted, struggling to sit up.

He stood, the best way to stop that. "Just my gun." Leaning slightly against the left wall, he carried her down the last steps to the tunnel floor.

"Your—put me down!"

"It's wet in here and there are probably snails." He kept walking and smiled to himself as her squirming stopped abruptly. Ah, snails. They'd worked to keep the girls in line when he was twelve and they worked still.

"Why are you wearing a gun?"

"The same reason I golf and play squash. Shooting's an ancient and honorable sport of gentlemen." Dammit, he didn't want her thinking of him as a feckless idiot, one of those gentlemen blowhards you met around Newport in their Breton-red yachting slacks. They thought they were at the top of the feeding chain, but take away their polo ponies and their platinum Visa cards and dump them in a jungle with nothing but a pocketknife and see if they walked out again... "I'm a crack shot," he couldn't resist adding quite truthfully.

She snorted. "If you shoot like you golf, Trace? I haven't seen you sink a putt yet."

Hey, I miss on purpose! He bit down on the words, reminding himself that more covers were blown over wounded pride than for any other reason. "I shoot better than I golf."

"Even if you do, what were you planning to shoot on Cliff Walk? Seagulls?"

"A gun's very handy for self-defense," he insisted. "You never know who you might meet out here. Gangs, druggies…"

"Ravening tourists," she said dryly, "or someone walking a vicious toy poodle? I've lived here just four months, Trace, but noise violations from the bars are the only crime I've heard about. This is tame country compared with Texas."

"Even so…" he said peaceably. The worst of his frustration was ebbing with movement, but with the scent of her hair in his nostrils, the supple weight of her in his arms, desire still rolled like a river through him. *Gillian, Gillian, what am I going to do with you?* If she thought she could end what they'd started back there with just a word…

But they'd ended for the night. The night was ending, for that matter. He paused and turned back to look at the moon, gone from silver to saffron as it drowned in the sea. She sighed against him and automatically he tightened his arms.

"Here's where it…happened," she murmured.

He refocused, and realized they were standing at the spot on the path where Lara had been ambushed. His mind stirred uneasily. "How do you know that?"

"Lara told me."

"Ah." He probed her face, homed in on her pupils, which were nicely expanded with darkness—and desire, he hoped. "About her…falling?" he asked, and watched. Then drew a breath of relief. They hadn't contracted as he pronounced the lie. Or maybe sexual arousal canceled out that response. Reading pupils was an art, not a science.

"Mmm," she agreed, sounding sleepy.

He wanted most urgently to kiss her. Walked on, instead. His arms were starting to ache along with the rest of him, but it wasn't far to the gate.

One last argument when they reached it. She wanted to be set down. He insisted, quite truthfully, that the ground had to be littered with rose branches. She managed to pull her key out of her running shorts and unlocked the gate while he held her.

He shoved it shut behind them with his hip, then leaned back against the wood, fresh out of excuses. He could think of no good reason Gillian shouldn't walk across Woodwind's velvety lawn on her own, though he'd rather have carried her to her door.

Rather have carried her on up the stairs, to the big bed in her bedroom.

Soon, he promised himself. Somehow.

"Thanks for the ride," Gillian said gravely.

"My pleasure." A painful pleasure, but then most of the best ones were, one way or another. He set her gently on her feet, then steadied her when she wobbled. His hands tightened on her arms and he swayed her against him. His hands slipped to her waist and yes, he nearly could span her.

"Trace—" she said on a note of alarm.

Yes, but he couldn't help himself. He kissed her on one cheek, then the other, then rested his brow against hers. "Good night, Gillian. Or I suppose it's good morning." He could imagine starting a lot of mornings like this one.

She shivered in his grasp and stepped backward. "Good night." She turned it into a mournful farewell.

No need, darling. It's not for long. Still, it took a conscious effort to straighten his fingers and release her. To stand there watching her go across the dewy grass without a backward glance. His heart skipped a beat as her stride broke for an instant—she was having second thoughts?—then gradually resumed its rhythm as Gillian squared her shoulders and walked on.

No matter. He had second thoughts enough for both of them. *Later,* he promised himself, promised her. She vanished beyond the corner of Woodwind, headed for the carriage house. He let out a sigh and turned his attention to the rest of the world.

Up on Lara's balcony, a curtain swayed. He'd shut and locked that door behind him—hadn't he?

CHAPTER SIXTEEN

GILLIAN SAT IN HER OFFICE, elbows braced on her desk, her aching head propped on her hands, her thumbs pressing the soft hollows below her brow bones till purple spots filled her inner vision. Lara had seen them this morning! She was all but certain.

Feeling Trace's eyes upon her like a physical caress, she'd focused her attention behind her when a movement ahead, up on Lara's balcony, had broken his spell. Her eyes had refocused on a form drawing back through the sheer curtains. Lara. No one else would be standing there.

And if she stood there, then she must have seen us. Seen Trace kissing me. Seen me, hardly resisting that kiss.

She grimaced and pressed harder against her brow bones, as if to gouge out that image. *We were standing very still, up against the wall. The sun hadn't yet risen.* Maybe Lara had overlooked them, had been looking, instead, far out to sea.

Dream on!

How *could* she have let Trace kiss her?

Could I have stopped him? she asked herself wryly.

But she couldn't weasel out of her guilt by blaming Trace, though his passion had carried her along like a surfer on the crest of a tidal wave. Still, in spite of his desire, he'd made it clear that she held the final word, that he'd stop if she insisted. He *had* stopped, once she'd found the will to stop him.

Lara, I never, never meant to hurt you. Yes, she'd come in anger to Woodwind, still aching from that letter of rejection, righteously intent on stealing her own history despite that repudiation. But stealing her own life story was one thing, stealing her mother's lover something else entirely.

So now it's over. Just as she and Lara were coming to know each other, to even like each other, just as she was laying her hands on the first few pieces of the jigsaw puzzle that was their shared history. Yet there was so much still to learn—why Lara hated Mustangs, when by all rights she should love them; if the young man in the uniform was Gillian's own father; why Lara had let her go… *You stupid, greedy little fool, trading Trace's kisses for all that!*

She ran the tip of her tongue over lips still swollen and bruised from those kisses. She could say goodbye to Trace, too, when Lara fired her. Tears stung at the back of her eyes. *It's all over.* No doubt Lara would be phoning her any minute now from her suite—she couldn't imagine Lara would fire her in person.

Or maybe she'd send Trace to tell her to pack her bags. Showing both of them at once who held the real power at Woodwind. She made a little sound of anguish deep in her throat. Better to quit this minute than wait for—

"Now that's what I call a righteous hangover." Two hands descended on her shoulders, began massaging her tension-taut muscles.

She glanced up to find Toby's face overhead, grinning down at her.

"And here Joya and I thought you were a straight

arrow, Gillie." His thumbs found her spine, dug into the muscles on either side, traced small circles up toward her nape. "Where do you go when you party?"

She shrugged, but he didn't take the hint. Clever and insistent, too intimate, his hands rode the movement. Her body was craving a touch, but not this one. "Cut it out, Toby. This isn't a hangover." Or maybe that's precisely what it was—a moral one. Whatever, he wasn't helping. She caught his wrists and tried to lift his hands from her shoulders, but he resisted with surprising strength.

At least his fingers stopped moving. "If it isn't a hangover, then you're wasting the Newport experience. You should come out and let me show you the town. It doesn't start rocking till midnight."

Gillian sighed, clamping down on her irritation. *What is this?* He and his sister had shown no inclination to seek out her friendship. So why now, just as she was leaving? She remembered for the first time in hours—her mutilated book. Could this invitation be connected to that? Toby's way of an apology? He and Joya were practically joined at the hip. If Joya had opened her present, Toby would have found out, sooner rather than later. And now this?

"What about it?" His fingers rotated again. "Say tonight?"

"Thanks, but I'm not much of a drinker. And I have a class to teach tonight," she added as she remembered it.

"Then tomorrow night," he said, turning the question into a statement.

"Maybe." By tomorrow she'd be gone. She twitched her shoulders, but again he ignored the hint.

"Gillian?"

She looked up to find Trace filling the doorway—as Toby's fingers moved seductively on her shoulders. "Yes?" Trace's eyes dropped from Toby's face to her own, and his dark eyebrows lifted. She felt her face pinken. Only hours ago, it had been Trace touching her. She wanted to smack Toby's hands aside, but if she humiliated him in front of the older man, she knew instinctively he'd never forgive her.

"Lara wants you in her suite, at your convenience."

Here it came. "Right away," she said evenly, then winced as Toby gave her back a hearty clap—his finishing benediction.

"When the boss says frog, we all jump," he said cheerfully. "Right, Trace?"

She'd never noticed how hard he could look when the mood hit him. As if he could have thrown Toby through her closed bay window and not bothered to watch him hit ground. She blinked and the expression was gone, or maybe she'd imagined it.

"Right you are," he said amiably, then turned and went.

SHE FOUND HIM WAITING for her outside Lara's door a few minutes later. They studied each other in silence. She couldn't read his mood at all, but it didn't seem much cheerier than hers. Perhaps he'd been enduring tears and tantrums all morning. Because somewhere within Lara was the woman who'd written that savage note to her own daughter nine months ago. Maybe Gillian was about to meet that side of her mother at last.

"She's still in bed," he said, unlocking the door

for her, then inclining his head when she hesitated. "Go on."

He didn't follow. The door closed softly behind her; the bolt turned. Locking her in with Lara. She wouldn't be able to retreat with dignity, if need be. Cautiously she moved into the room. "Lara?"

Lara lay in the center of the king-size bed, propped up on a heap of pillows, one arm hooked around something small and orange. Her stuffed tiger. She gave Gillian a wan smile. "Hi."

She looked about twelve, except for the purple shadows under her silvery eyes, the hollows that had deepened under her high cheekbones. Gillian's fear turned to dismay. She thought *she'd* looked bad, when she studied her face in the mirror this morning, after a night out on the cliffs. But Lara! *I did this to her. Trace and I…* "H-hi yourself."

"I know, I know," Lara said ruefully, answering her expression rather than her greeting. "I look like something the cat dragged in." She pulled Tigger onto the comforter over her stomach and clasped her hands on him. "It wasn't much of a night for sleeping." She patted the edge of the bed. "Sit down."

Reluctantly Gillian sat. Lara must have lain awake all night, wondering where Trace was and with whom. *And I didn't think of her once.* "I'm sorry." *So sorry.*

Lara shrugged slim shoulders. She was dressed in pajamas, with her silver locket dangling around her neck. "Happens. Sometimes I get…bummed. I guess today's going to be one of those days. Tigger and I just pull the pillows over our heads till it passes."

"Anything I can do?" If Lara had trusted Trace—however naively—and Gillian had shattered that trust, it was irreparable. There'd be no way she could take back the harm she'd done. She swallowed around a lump in her throat. Unable to hold Lara's level gaze, she glanced around, noticed the scrapbook near the foot of the bed, reached for it with relief.

"Thanks, but no. I just have to wade through it. I think I'll give a pass on my tai chi lesson, if you don't mind. Maybe tomorrow?"

Gillian had forgotten—they'd scheduled the first session for noon today. "Oh, of course, that's fine." Her hands smoothed restlessly over the cover of the scrapbook. This was the first one they'd filled, containing Lara's earliest pictures. "May I?" she murmured at last.

"Wouldn't exist but for you." Lara hooked a finger under its cover and flipped it open.

Gillian sat, staring hungrily down at the photo of the young soldier. *My father, perhaps?* And most surely Lara's first love. *And now I've ruined her latest—maybe her first love since her husband died. How could I?* A wave of self-loathing washed through her and she shut the album abruptly. "I think I should quit." Lara was too nice to fire her, she saw now. But how could Lara ever feel at ease, ever hope to repair whatever kind of relationship she had with Trace, if she feared that her personal assistant and her lover were meeting in dark corners? *She's been nothing but kind to me. I owe her this much.*

"What?" Lara cried. "But why?"

Gillian drew a nervous breath. *Don't make me say it.* It was better for all of them if they pretended it never had happened. If Lara simply accepted her resignation as the apology it was intended to be and let her slink off. Her eyes filled with tears as she pictured it. She'd lose everything she wanted if she left Wood-wind. But if she hurt Lara by staying…

"*Why?*" Lara demanded. "Have I been working you too hard or I'm not paying enough or—"

"No!" Gillian laughed shakily. "I just…" She'd spoken on impulse and she had no arguments at hand, aside from the truth she couldn't speak. "I just think maybe I…should go." It got harder each time she pictured it. She'd be throwing away her last chance at family if she turned her back on Lara. Chris, much as she loved him, was a brother in absentia. "Don't you think?" she added weakly. *Help me out here. I'm trying to be brave for you. Don't make it harder.*

"No!" Lara shook her head vigorously. "I don't!"

"Oh…" Gillian swiped at a tear rolling down her nose. "I thought maybe…"

"It's Trace, isn't it?" Lara demanded. "Is he…pressuring you?" She tugged a hand through her silvery hair, leaving it standing in soft spikes, which made her look like an exotic, indignant bird. "I would have sworn he was a gentleman, but…" She shook her head disgustedly. "Is that it?"

"*Ahhhh…*" Gillian found her mouth hanging open and shut it. "Um…"

"Because believe me, he'll back off if I tell him to—that or he's fired," Lara declared imperiously, sounding for the first time since Gillian had met her like the star of the soap opera. "I won't tolerate a molester!"

"He didn't molest me," Gillian said faintly, still scrabbling for some sort of reality under her feet. "Not at all."

"I didn't think so. I didn't mean to spy," Lara added hastily. "I was out on the balcony, since I couldn't sleep, and suddenly there you two were. You appeared to be enjoying yourself, I thought, but if I was mis—''

"Fired?'' Gillian repeated. Trace seemed to be a man of no visible means—she'd assumed he was a gigolo. But was that considered employment by the parties involved?

Lara clapped a hand over her mouth. "Oops,'' she said from behind her fingers.

Gillian cocked a head at her, then an eyebrow. And waited.

"Look…'' Lara said after a moment. She gazed at her stuffed toy, scooped him up, brought him nose to nose with herself. "Would it…change anything about your leaving if I told you Trace and I were just…friends?'' she asked, apparently addressing the tiger.

Gillian's eyes dropped helplessly to the enormous bed. *Friends who sleep together?* No, that didn't make her feel better. Casual sex was fine for those who wanted it. As for her… Maybe she needed to leave Woodwind for her own sake, not Lara's.

"Platonic friends,'' Lara enunciated with precision. "Not even kissing cousins. Tigger and I get the bed— Trace sleeps on that couch.'' She gestured across the room.

"Oh,'' Gillian said blankly. A sun was rising somewhere inside her, along with an almost irresistible sense of the absurd. "D-d-do you mind my asking why?''

"Yes.'' They stared at each other, Gillian with utter mystification, Lara with embarrassed defiance, then all of a sudden it was too funny for words—they burst out laughing.

DEAREST LARA-MOMMY,
If they electrocute fifteen-year-old murderers
And you as good as murdered me
What do you think you deserve?
What do you think you'll GET?
A BIG shock!!!!!!!!!HAHAHA. Ha.
See you Soooooooooooooooooooooooon,
your (and you better not try to deny it) Sarah
XXX

Feet on his desk, Trace sat tipped back in his chair,
holding a copy of Sarah XXX's latest filth in his lap.
He'd discovered the original this morning when he
collected the mail, and bad as the message was, its
manner of delivery was worse. The letter had been
hand-delivered rather than mailed. He'd found it
taped to the estate's mailbox, for which only the post-
man and the occupants of Woodwind had keys. No
Boston postmark on the envelope this time. No postmark at all. Sarah XXX had walked right up to the
gates sometime between sundown last night, when
he'd last driven through with Lara and Gillian, and
this morning at eleven, when he'd gone for the mail.

Actually he could narrow that gap. The mailman
delivered at roughly ten. He was, thanks to Trace's
instructions, already on the lookout for questionable
packages, as was the main post office. If he'd noticed
an envelope taped to the outside of the box, no doubt
he'd have called up to the house.

*So she strolled up bold as brass between ten and
eleven this morning and taped it in place.* He could
picture a faceless hag, all elf locks and frumpy
clothes, fixing her hate-filled message in place, then
standing for a moment, grasping the gate with nail-

bitten hands and peering through the bars. Eyes bloodshot and wide-open, showing whites all around.

A chill skated down his spine and he shivered—the chair creaked ominously. He brought his feet down from the desk. *Sure, if Sarah XXX is your typical stalker, she'll look something like that.*

But if she's really a mask for an insider, as he'd begun to wonder after the bee attack? *Where was Toby at ten-thirty this morning? Or Joya? Or Harriet the Glum?* Or the maid or housekeeper, for that matter?

Or Gillian. He found himself shaking his head even as he thought it. No, absolutely not. Not Gillian. There wasn't a mean bone in her delectable body. He stared into space for a moment, lips crooked into the faintest of faraway smiles, then gave himself a mental kick in the pants.

If his FBI instructors could see him now, ruling out a female suspect because his gut told him she was innocent! Instincts might serve a man well when the quarry was male, but once you threw sex into the equation, then feelings were automatically suspect. *Give us the facts to clear her, and nothing but the facts,* they'd insist.

The fact was, Gillian had had the same opportunity every other one of his inside suspects had for delivering this message undetected. Because between ten and eleven this morning, he'd been napping here at his desk with a goofy smile on his face.

Yet another reason not to mix romance with duty. A man had only so much energy and he shouldn't divide it. Stifling a yawn, he realized he was bone-tired and glanced at his watch. Nine o'clock. A long

day, considering he'd barely slept the night before.
And not a happy one since dawn.

He'd returned to find Lara in a dismal mood. She'd
clearly not slept well, and had stayed in bed all day,
silent and withdrawn. Gillian had succeeded in cheer-
ing her around noon, but she'd relapsed to near tears
within the hour. He'd tried the direct approach—asking her why she was sad—and received sighs and
shrugs and damn-all else. Woman problems, he'd finally concluded, though she'd never showed this kind
of moodiness before.

Reminding himself that he was her bodyguard, not
her therapist, he'd left her to it and devoted his day
to Sarah XXX's letter. First he'd arranged for Jeremy
Benton to meet him down at the gates and pick up
the original, which was now being fingerprinted—
with the usual fruitless results, no doubt. Any doofus
who watched TV knew you had to wear gloves to
write a poison-pen letter.

He'd tried to discreetly check on the whereabouts
of all his insiders between ten and eleven this morning, and now knew any—or *every*—one of 'em had
the opportunity to post that message. Toby and Joya
had returned from brunch during that time period.
Gillian, Harriet and the household staff had all been
on the grounds. Any one of them could have strolled
down to the gates, then reached through to put the
message in place. All it would take was masking tape
and nerve.

Headlights swept across the wall above his desk.
He rose and went to the window. Gillian in her little
Toyota, returning from her weight-lifting class. Leaning out over the windowsill, he smiled, imagining her
in her gym shorts, her skimpy tank top, a stern and

serious expression in those big golden eyes as she lectured her women lifters. He'd like to be a fly on that wall, or watch her lead an aerobics class. She'd bounce in all the right places.

He heard her quick steps across the gravel, then the sound of the door opening and closing. Mentally he followed her up. *I could drop in, say hello. If she invited me in…?*

Down, boy. She had to be whipped after last night, then her class tonight. Besides, she'd told him to go chase himself. Or at least, Lara.

It would be a pleasure dissuading her of that notion one of these days. *First, all you have to do is catch Sarah XXX,* he reminded himself. Frowning, he picked up the letter again.

If they electrocute fifteen-year-old murderers…

Why fifteen years old? Just a random choice? Or maybe Sarah had read something in a newspaper or heard some news on radio or TV? Had there been anything about a fifteen-year-old, anyplace in the country, going to the electric chair? He'd ask Emily to do an Internet search, keying in the appropriate words. Maybe that would give him some clue.

Better yet, he'd skim yesterday's *Newport Daily News* for such a headline. Sarah XXX could have sat down at the Waves, sipping coffee and reading the paper, while she composed her letter.

And you as good as murdered me…

How did Lara nearly murder you, Sarah? Is it all in your poor twisted mind? Or is there the tiniest nugget of truth, no matter how distorted, that would point the way to you, if I could only pan it out of this dross?

He'd have to show Lara this message. Trace scowled and shifted in his chair. All his instincts told him to shelter his client from pain and fear, but if she could help him in any way... Dammit, showing her this note—now that would cure her blues!

For all their sakes, he had to crack this case soon.

Soooooooooooooooooooooooon, Sarah kept promising. She was coming closer and closer, knocking at their gates now. He had to catch her soon. Before her next attempt.

She's clever. Too damned clever. A sick but first-rate mind, an odd combination.

Cleverer than me? He clenched his teeth. *No way!*

But then, she didn't have to be, when she held all the aces. The assassin got to choose the time, the place, the method. He had to defend against all possible variables, couldn't miss a trick. Ran himself ragged, trying to cover all conceivable possibilities, while Sarah XXX had only to focus on her one attempt.

He needed reinforcements. A backup. Another pair of eyes. Given two BGs, one could scout the town while the other guarded Lara.

But all four Brickhouse agents were out on assignment. And Lara had chosen Gillian over the subcontractor he'd had in mind. By now he wasn't unhappy with her choice—far from it—but still...

He was going around and around here. Time to give it a break. He glanced at his watch. Eleven, and Lara still hadn't sent him her good-night buzz from her locket, which was his normal all-clear to enter her suite.

She fell asleep, he told himself. Barring a trip or two to the bathroom, she hadn't left her bed all day. Not good. The client's morale was crucial. He needed her alert, ready to fight or flee if need be, with an unambiguous desire to survive. If she didn't perk up tomorrow, he'd drag the reason out of her. He didn't like secrets on the job.

Standing at the door to her suite, he glanced right toward the elevator, left toward the stairs and the corridor beyond that led to the other bedrooms. All quiet. Unlocking the door, he entered.

The bedside lamp showed him the tumbled bed-clothes, an open picture album lying on top of the comforter, her toy tiger glaring at him with glassy eyes.

"Lara?" He stood listening, dread curling in his stomach, all his instincts crying that there was no one here to answer.

CHAPTER SEVENTEEN

SOME TEN MINUTES LATER, he found her in the kitchen. Ten minutes that had probably sheared ten months off his life. Trace leaned panting in the doorway, too angry even to consider speaking, sick to his stomach with the aftereffects of his own adrenaline. Reaching inside the windbreaker he'd thrown on, he resettled his 9 mm in its holster under his armpit, then zipped the jacket. *What the hell, Lara?*

Oblivious to his presence at the end of the room, she leaned over the big kitchen table, her hand moving from a small box to whatever object was blocked from view by her body. She worked with the fierce concentration and painstaking movements of someone compensating for a drink or two. A bottle of wine sat half empty across the table. The kitchen smelled of chocolate. *Baker's chocolate,* he reminded himself. *We bought it at the market yesterday.*

She reached for another oblong box, fumbled, gave a soft exclamation of disgust, then came the *scritch* of a match lighting—a tiny flame underlit her face. The flame vanished beyond her body, but a warm glow pushed back the darkness, edging her in wavering gold. *She's lighting candles.* The smell stirred old memories of his own mother working in the kitchen. His younger brother, Jon, had always demanded a chocolate cake for his birthday.

Lara dropped the spent match on the table, then sat, contemplating her flickering shrine. "Happy birthday to you... Happy b-birthday to you..." She sang in a tiny, breathless, barely audible soprano. A tender secret song blurred by tears.

Trace swallowed around a lump in his throat. *Who do you sing for, Lara? Richard? Is today your dead husband's birthday?* That would explain today's inconsolable sorrow.

"Happy birthday, dear S-S-S-Sarah..."

God! It was what you didn't know that would get you in the end. Trace started grimly across the kitchen.

"Happy..." The song quavered away into the gulping beginnings of a sob. Her head dropped into her hands.

Pulling out a chair, Trace sat beside her. He rested a hand on her shuddering shoulder.

She jumped violently and turned to look at him. "Oh..."

Staring down at the birthday cake with its half-burned candles, he patted her absently. *Talk to me, Lara.*

She swallowed audibly and turned back to the cake. Silently they watched as the pink candles wept wax, drooped, then puddled. The flames flickered, then died, one by one. *Who should have been here to blow them out, Lara?* He counted the blackened wicks. Twenty-eight candles. "Tell me," he said finally, voice low and uninflected.

"I n-never have..." she said in a wondering monotone. "Nobody, except Richard..."

But now I need to know. "Sarah," he said uninsistently. "Who is she, Lara?" Or should he have said *was?*

She drew a breath that would have sucked the air out of the candles if they hadn't burned out already. "S-Sarah was...*is*...my baby. Sarah Cloud Bailey."

She's twenty-eight today. But Lara was only forty-three!

"Her father was my true love, William McCloud." She smiled, tears trickling. "His friends called him 'Cloudy.'" She knuckled her lashes, but more tears fell. "He came home on leave after basic training. We went to a New Year's party and then—" Her wistful smile glowed like a thousand candles. "I loved him so, and he was bound for Vietnam..."

Trace sat, aching for her as she built the story word by halting word. Two months later she'd learned she was pregnant. They'd been exchanging love letters all that time, but this was the test of their love. And McCloud hadn't flinched. He sent her one last letter, in which he pledged his devotion, promised her that he'd be home as soon as he could arrange leave with his commanding officer to marry her, that he couldn't be prouder or happier. Two weeks later his family received notice of his death in some futile, nameless skirmish in the jungle.

"What happened then?" She would have been maybe fourteen, living with foster parents by then, she'd told him once. No, she was fifteen! he realized, a chill raising the hair on his arms. *You're the fifteen-year-old murderer, Lara? But how does Sarah XXX know?*

"It...it took me years to piece it all together." Lara stood, picked up the cake plate and tipped her head toward the kitchen door. "Come with me?"

Trace followed, punching the code that disarmed the burglar alarm, then preceding her out the door. Bearing the cake before her, she headed for the seaside of the estate. Trace unzipped his windbreaker as he scanned the moonlit lawn. All clear.

"My foster father began to have money..." Lara said as they walked. Carter, a drunken, brutal layabout who lived off the child-support payments his downtrodden wife earned by keeping foster children. Suddenly Carter had enough money to buy an enormous color TV set. To drink in bars, rather than swill moonshine on their swaybacked front porch. Enough money even to take Lara to a doctor several times in her pregnancy. "He was always yelling at me not to lift things or run. I couldn't understand it—he called me 'little slut' every chance he got, yet he was so considerate." She laughed bitterly.

Twenty-eight years ago, Trace calculated coldly. The bastard was probably beyond his reach, gone on to his well-deserved reward, which was a pity.

"The last week, before my...baby came, he drove home in a red Mustang car. Claimed he'd won it gambling, but, oh, he smirked at me when he said that."

He sold your baby, Trace realized, and found his fingers caressing the butt of his gun. You heard the rumors from time to time of baby brokers, lawyers usually, who sought out young, presentable pregnant girls through ads in newspapers. Who arranged the sale of their babies to the highest bidder. Private placements were legal, and the adoptive parents could legally pay the girl's prenatal expenses. If those expenses were outrageously inflated and the lion's share of the money vanished into the pockets of the lawyer and whoever delivered the girl to the lawyer, who was to know or care?

They'd reached the gate onto Cliff Walk. Trace unlocked it, checked outside for any lurkers, then escorted Lara south along the path, his heart as saddened tonight as it had been shouting with joy the night before, though the moon was as brilliant as ever.

The birth hadn't been easy. Lara was tiny and the contractions started too soon. The baby hadn't turned. Carter had been in a drunken lather, frantically cursing her, ordering her to wait till they reached the hospital. She traveled the whole nightmarish way lying down in the back of his car, then had been rushed into Emergency and up to a private room. She'd been delivered of her baby by cesarean, one minute before midnight on the eleventh, as her stepmother told her later.

"God, Lara." Fifteen, with nobody in the world on her side. They reached the place where someone had pushed her. Trace moved between her and the cliff edge, though that put her on his right, in the way of his gun hand. Once they were safely past, he reversed positions.

She'd had two days to adore her baby. Two days to nurse her, cuddle her, sing to her, tell her that her name was Sarah Cloud. To tell her all about her brave father. "She had blue-gray eyes just like Cloudy, and she was the sweetest child. Not a cry or a whimper." To tell Sarah of the wonderful life Lara was determined to make for her. Someway. Somehow.

But you were only a baby yourself.

On the third day her foster father had arrived along with the breakfast tray. He'd made her take medicine from a bottle, spooning it down her in spite of her weak protests, insisting that the nurse had told him to give it to her. She'd begun to feel funny almost immediately, then had fallen asleep.

In her weakened, postoperative condition, any kind of codeine-based cough syrup would have done the trick, Trace figured.

"When I woke up—" her voice wavered "—there was a strange man in the room with my foster father. Very official-looking, white jacket, clipboard, stern and brisk." Carter stood with his back to the door—guarding it, she realized years later.

The stranger had presented her with a form on the clipboard and told her to sign it—so the health insurance would pay for her operation, he explained.

Lara had drifted to a halt, hugging the cake plate to her stomach. "I was so stupid, stupid, stupid, so *stupid!* I tried to read it, Trace, but he was leaning over me, breathing garlic on my face, telling me to hurry up—it was just a simple formality—talking and talking and talking at me. I couldn't concentrate, was sick to my stomach…"

Drugged…tranquilized. Trace clenched his hands to fists.

"So I signed it and he went away." Slowly she started walking again. "I…I slept most of the day." A doctor came to examine her in the afternoon and told her what a brave girl she was, what a good decision she'd made. She hadn't known what he was talking about, was too shy to ask.

Then a nurse arrived with a wheelchair and helped her into it, telling her she was going home. When Lara asked where her baby was, the nurse clucked, patted her shoulder and told her she'd have to ask

"Doctor." In the corridor, she'd handed the wheel-chair over to Carter.

Who assured Lara that his wife was collecting Sarah from the nursery. That she'd bring the baby to the car, meet them there. "We got to the car..." Lara said in a flat little voice. "I was hurting from my stitches, sitting up. He put me in the back seat, gave me some more medicine—for the pain, he said. I asked where Sarah was, and he told me to be patient, that it took a long time to check a baby out of a hospital. I f-f-fell asleep, Trace. So stupid, stupid, *worthless* and stupid! If I hadn't fallen asleep..."

"It would have ended the same, Lara." What chance did a kid have, when the adults who should be protecting her betrayed her, instead? Betrayed her profoundly, ruthlessly, with such single-minded greed?

"No!" She shook her head fiercely. "No, I could have done *something*. B-but when I woke up, we were speeding along, my foster mother driving, Carter sitting with me in the back seat. I asked where my baby was and he said she was in the front seat, to shut up, I'd wake her. I tried to sit up, and he kept shoving me down. I finally realized—somehow I knew—Sarah wasn't there. I started screaming, trying to sit up." She'd struggled till she fainted. When she awoke, she was home in her own bed.

She stopped. They'd come to a spot where the path dipped within twenty feet of sea level with a rough path leading down to the water below. She turned and started down it.

"Let me carry the cake, Lara."

"No. I do this every year."

Teeth clenched, he followed at her heels, prepared

to grab if her feet slipped from under her, but she made it safely to sea level.

Where a series of flat boulders led out into the sea—an eroded dike of slate, a giant's stepping stones to nowhere. Lara leaped lightly from the shore to the first boulder. He shouldn't let her do this, didn't dare to stop her. Trace leaped after her. Luckily the sea was glassy calm.

Balancing along the mossy ledges, leaping from stone to stone, they made it to the end of the dike. The ocean heaved and sighed at their feet. Lara put the plate down on the rock, stood staring out to sea. They'd kept her locked in her room for a week, she told him without emotion. During that time, Carter told her she'd signed papers that gave up her baby to the state. That the state knew she was too young to keep a baby, too wicked to deserve one, so they'd find Sarah a good home.

As soon as her stitches allowed it, she'd climbed down the tree outside her bedroom window, had hitched into town to the hospital. "But…" She shook her head helplessly. "It took me all day to hitch and walk there, some thirty miles, since we lived up in the mountains. B-but when I got to the hospital, it didn't look quite the way I remembered it. And when I demanded my baby, demanded to know where my baby was, they said they had no record of me or Sarah. That we hadn't been patients there. I insisted we *had,* they told me to get lost and I…" She drew a breath. "I started smashing windows. Smashing and smashing and *smashing* every piece of glass I could reach, till they called the security guards." Who'd turned her over to the police, who eventually remanded her to her foster father.

For a few more months she tried to find Sarah. But she never was able to locate the hospital where she'd delivered her baby—there were three towns within driving distance of Carter's house, each with its own hospital. Carter might have even driven her over the state line into Virginia or Pennsylvania, for all she knew. The more she wandered through emergency rooms, the more her original pain-blurred memories merged with the new places. The insides of hospitals looked much alike, and she'd been in no state to notice the architecture of the building, either coming or going. And she began to think that all the doctors and administrators were lying to her. "They could see I didn't deserve a baby. They weren't going to tell me where Sarah was, even if they knew."

At last she'd despaired. She'd been a little goody-goody before she became pregnant, trying to please her foster parents, working hard at school. Afterward, she ran with the wild crowd. She'd lost Cloudy's baby—stupidly signed the papers that let the state take her away. "Sarah was the last of Cloudy, his last chance to live on, have a daughter who'd speak his name, hang his picture on her wall, tell her own children someday about their brave grandfather…" Lara stood, tears streaming. "I let Cloudy down, so I deserved nothing. Was worth nothing. Which meant that any boy who wanted me could have me, I didn't care."

"Oh, Lara…"

"Yeah, I know." She wiped her nose. "But that was how I felt. Nothing mattered. I was numb." Until one night when she was seventeen. Carter, drunk as usual, had slapped his wife around—no novelty there—then had roared off in the Mustang, not so shiny or new now, to drink in town. Half-drunk herself, bitter and humiliated, Mrs. Carter told Lara the truth at last, while Lara washed the blood from her face. That her worthless husband had sold Lara's baby—the Mustang was his final payment.

"After she fell asleep I sat and thought for a while," Lara murmured. "I knew I'd never be able to make Carter tell me where my baby was. He was as stubborn as he was mean. And I knew if I stayed there I'd kill him, that if I did, then I'd go to prison and never find Sarah." Her hope of recovering her child hadn't quite died after all, she realized that night. So she'd packed her clothes in an old backpack. She'd stolen Mrs. Carter's pitiful stash of money, which she kept hidden from Carter in a can in the freezer—Lara hadn't forgotten that no matter how unwillingly, Mrs. Carter had conspired with her husband to sell Sarah.

She'd waited until Carter returned home and staggered into the house. Fell asleep on the couch in the living room. Then she'd slipped out the kitchen door, stopping only to fill the Mustang's gas tank with a five-pound bag of sugar. "I didn't want him to ever have another minute's pleasure in selling my baby." And then she had walked off into the night.

She stooped to the cake, rearranged it on the last ledge above the sea, where it was invisible from land. "The seagulls will eat it in the morning," she told him. "Maybe they'll fly off to Sarah, tell her I'm still searching."

She'd run off to New York City, she told him as they made their way back to shore. Some ridiculous notion she'd had that she might be a model. Instead she'd found a job waitressing, then working for a caterer—who catered for a soap opera production company, where she'd met Richard Corday, the lead writer. "If he didn't save my life, he saved my soul," she said as Trace helped her up the rocks to the main path.

"And he wrote *Searching for Sarah,*" Trace prompted her.

"Yes." After their marriage, Richard helped her search. But twelve years had passed since Sarah's birth; the trail was obliterated. Carter had drunk himself to death, and his wife had moved away. Lara and Richard never succeeded in finding her. Two of the three nearby hospitals had merged, reorganized, then closed their doors forever. If they had ever possessed records of Lara's admission and Sarah's birth, they had lost or destroyed them. The state of West Virginia steadfastly maintained it had never taken custody of a child named Sarah Cloud Bailey. "We finally realized that most of what Carter had told me was a lie. That I'd never know how much of it, or what part of it, was lies, and what truth. In all likelihood, Sarah had been purchased on the black market, perhaps by someone who'd lost a child, who'd then given her that child's identity. That if she'd never been adopted legally through the courts, then there was no record anywhere that would allow us to trace her.

"I signed up with the matching registries anyway. You give them your baby's date of birth, the state where she was born and the town if you know it. If your child ever...wants to find you and enters the same information with the registry, then they contact you."

Wants to find you. The words echoed between them as they walked. "And the soap opera, *Searching for*

Sarah, was that just Corday using life to make art?"
As he'd done with Lara's bee sting allergy.

Lara shook her head. "That was Richard's gift to
me. His idea of a way to reach Sarah. Like a nation-
wide Help Wanted ad, he always said. Wanted—one
daughter named Sarah, lost from birth, missed and
loved always by a mother named Lara. He changed
some of the facts—he didn't have complete artistic
control and the coproducer wanted my character to be
a doctor. But enough of the real story remained that
we hoped...thought maybe someday..."

That an adoptee name Sarah Cloud would come
knocking. A thousand-to-one shot, but if that was the
only hope you had... Except that the premise would
appeal just as strongly to any neurotic with delusions
of grandeur. If you can't be the reincarnation of Po-
cahontas, why not discover you're the long-lost
daughter of a prime-time celebrity?

They reached the spot again where Lara had fallen,
and automatically Trace glanced over his shoulder,
then scanned the bushes. Nobody. The one good thing
about this expedition was that it was a complete break
from their routine. It was hard to set up an inpromptu
killing, harder still to do it safely. "So have you had
any applicants for the position over the years?" Besides Sarah XXX.

"About one a year," Lara said, then laughed painfully when he swore. "Come on, Trace, we discussed
that the first time I showed you Sarah XXX's letters."

"Yes, but you didn't tell me... Was there any
chance that any of those applicants was the real one?"
Sarah Cloud, a pretty name. He pictured her with
Lara's platinum-blond hair, like a cumulous cloud,
and gray-blue eyes, five-two or -three like her mother.

"No." They'd reached the gate and he unlocked it for her, checked the far side, then ushered her through. "No, they were always too old, or too young, or born somewhere out west, or they had brown eyes or...no."

"And Sarah XXX?" He stopped, staring up at the unlit bulk of Woodwind. A long way from a loveless shack in the West Virginia mountains.

"I don't know, Trace. You've seen all her letters. She deals in emotions, not facts."

Red-hot emotions, resentment forging itself to a brighter and sharper point with each letter.

"She never gave me any address so that I could respond to her. Try to calm her down. Ask her questions that would help me to know."

"But you think there might be a chance." *God help you if that's so, Lara. You don't need a child like that.*

"I..." Lara shook her head, and kept on shaking it slowly. "The child I imagined all these years? Cloudy's daughter? He was the most sensitive, the kindest... To think that his daughter could cut the leg off a rabbit and mail me the bloody stump..." Her arms flew around herself and she shuddered. "But, Trace, I don't know what happened to my baby. Who got her, what they did to her...who she became..." Her head drooped till she stared at the ground. "What...she thinks of me. Maybe she *hates* me for giving her away. For not being there for her. I hate myself. Why shouldn't she? God knows why she thinks I did it..."

So this was the ambivalence he'd sensed at Lara's core, the resignation in the face of danger rather than vigorous indignation. *Half of her wants to meet Sarah*

XXX, however warped she may be…half of her thinks that if Sarah XXX is the damaged remains of her beautiful baby, then she deserves whatever punishment her child decides to mete out. God, we're in trouble here.

CHAPTER EIGHTEEN

YESTERDAY AFTERNOON, after she'd left Lara, Gillian had spent the day dancing on clouds. Trace wasn't Lara's lover! Never had been!

Which meant, at the very least, she needn't feel guilty for their wonderful night out on the cliffs. Better than that, it meant she was free to learn what that night had meant to him—just a passing impulse born of a warm, willing woman in his arms, the moon and the silver sea? Or a deeper, more personal attraction?

Dazed by Lara's admission—by its implications—she'd felt no hurry to seek Trace out. First, she needed to think.

She'd left Lara's suite with strict instructions to take the day off—Lara pointing out that if *she* intended to spend all of September 11 in bed, then her personal assistant should goof off, too.

She had. She'd gone back to her apartment and crashed till almost five, then had risen, pottered luxuriously around the place with a drowsy, dreaming smile, then driven off to her weight class at the Y. She'd returned home, contentedly exhausted, at nine and gone straight to bed.

She'd risen this morning, the twelfth—her birthday!—to clouds and rain. And dreadful doubts. So Trace was a free agent—so what? That didn't mean he was free for the taking. She'd been building castles in the air, on the most ephemeral of foundations—a few passionate kisses out on the cliffs? A week of meaningful glances? *Get real, woman!* Looked at like that, her hopes were pathetically feeble. *And aren't you forgetting that steamy little scene you witnessed in the basement, Joya and Trace entwined on the weight bench?*

She'd seen no interaction since that would lead her to think they were involved. Joya always fixed Trace with a smoldering stare when he entered her presence, but it seemed more akin to resentment than lust. Still, Gillian didn't pretend to understand Joya. For all she knew, they could be having a volcanically passionate affair.

Compounding her doubts was a niggling uncertainty born of ignorance. If Trace was just Lara's friend, why was he sleeping on her couch? *Maybe it's one of those unrequited relationships: she considers him just a friend; he loves her madly. Till she comes to her senses, Trace patiently waits on her couch?*

But if he's crazy in love with Lara, what was he doing night before last kissing me senseless in the teahouse tunnel?

Try another theory: maybe Trace was some sort of promotional gimmick, dreamed up by the public relations staff of *Searching for Sarah* to enhance Lara's image as a sexy celebrity. Wasn't it true that a generation ago the Hollywood studios had forced some of their gay male stars to marry to protect their box office image as superstuds? Maybe Trace had been hired to make Lara look sexily satisfied now that she was a widow?

It didn't *quite* wash, and why wouldn't Lara have explained, if that was the reason?

Or maybe he's just what she said and no more—a

friend. Come to sleep on her couch—why? *Because he's a friend in need, and Lara needs him right now?*

Or perhaps Trace needed *Lara's* protection.

She couldn't make it out, and not knowing made her uneasy. Wary. Uncertain how to proceed, or if she should proceed at all. Worse yet, she could see no way to learn the truth. Lara had made her promise she wouldn't tell Trace she now knew they weren't lovers. *What is this, a soap opera?* And wasn't Lara's concern that she not tell Trace weird in itself?

Once she'd shoved all her doubts into the back cupboard of her mind and locked its door for the moment, the blues had stepped forth. As she'd sloshed through the puddles up to Woodwind, she'd reminded herself, *Today's my birthday.* September 12. Barring last year, when she'd endured it alone, September 12 was always her favorite of days. Her mother had always made a fuss of her birthday. *All those years of cakes and parties, Mom, I was happy as could be, feeling loved and cherished. But what were you feeling, all alone with the knowledge that the one birthday we hadn't shared was my first one?*

Was it an uncomplicated day of joy for you, as it was for me—or something more poignant, tarnished by the lie you lived alone?

How could you have ever dreamed I would have loved you the less because we weren't of one blood? Didn't you trust me? Gillian stood before the kitchen door, transfixed by that terrible thought, wishing she could unthink it.

Gray clouds stormed up over the cliffs, to scrape the wet treetops. The wind moaned through the tossing branches. Leaves flew on the gale, some green, a few golden—autumn approaching on leaden feet, months before it would arrive in Texas. A chill hung in the air, which hadn't been present there yesterday. There was no way to unthink a thought. She shivered and pushed on into the house.

Harriet the Glum sat at the kitchen table, a spoonful of cereal halfway to her downturned mouth. "Did you ever find your package?" she demanded.

"I did." *Did you open it?* If Harriet had, she'd never admit it.

"I told you it was there," Harriet said smugly. "Hope it was worth all the fuss."

Are you hoping the book mattered to me? No way would Gillian give her that satisfaction. "Oh, it was just an old book someone sent me. Nothing important."

By the time she reached her office, the blues had settled in to stay. Kneeling on the window seat, Gillian pressed her nose to the glass and stared out at a gray, rumpled sea. Born twenty-eight years ago today, thanks to a woman who was still, in spite of her efforts, a stranger. She still didn't know why Lara had written that horrible letter.

If I didn't want you when you were born, why the hell do you think I would want you now?

Gillian could certainly understand a fifteen-year-old not wanting to keep a baby—how could Lara have hoped to raise her? But it was one thing to give up a child with tenderness and regret, for the good of them both. Quite another to relinquish a child with rage and resentment, as her letter seemed to suggest.

Which was it, Lara? I'd really like to know.

Maybe that was why she was so blue. Today was the acid test. There was no way that Lara could have forgotten the significance of September 12. No way in the world. *If she's grieving today, I could take that as a sign that she wishes she'd never given me away.*

Or at least that she remembers me with fond regrets. That she might someday be open to a reunion, in spite of last year's letter.

But if Lara was happy today, then that proved she felt nothing but relief. That casting her baby off had been the right thing to do. That she did not look back with regret.

In which case, maybe it was time to respect Lara's wishes?

Just when their friendship was blooming and Trace was suddenly an unanswered, tantalizing question? Gillian sighed and turned away from the glass. *I don't know, I don't know!*

To drive out the demons, she dug into the fan mail. Despite her reading headaches, she had made excellent progress this past week. Working backward from the present, she had only four boxes to go to reach the point where Joya had abandoned the job last spring. Once she'd caught up, it should be easy to keep up with the half dozen or so letters that arrived every day. *But will I be the personal assistant who benefits?* She had a feeling today that something was drawing to a close. The season turning outside her windows perhaps, or that she was—overnight—a year older? She jumped as the phone rang, then swooped it up. "Hello?"

"Hard at work," Lara observed with a warm chuckle. "Are you ready to take a break? Teach me some tai chi? It's noon, you know."

Gillian bit her lip. "I was w-wondering if you'd still want to. You seemed to be feeling so down yesterday…" The test, oh Lord, here came the test!

Lara said briskly, "Well, that was yesterday, kiddo, and yesterday's gone. I feel fine today. Why don't you throw on some sweats and come on down."

THE RAIN HAD STOPPED and a few streaks of blue showed beyond the clouds, out on a gunmetal gray horizon. Gillian gave her first lesson out on Lara's balcony.

Whatever mood had been troubling Lara, it had vanished today. Lara wasn't cheery so much as she was serene, looking determinedly forward instead of back, Gillian would have said. They discussed a training program to put Lara back in television shape by Christmas—weights, walking and tai chi.

So that's that, she told herself as she executed a series of movements while Lara watched. *Lara doesn't care about her lost child—about me—at all.* She meant what she said in that letter: *Go get a life! And stay the hell out of mine!*

Now it was up to Gillian to accept that. *If I could just learn the name of my father—if that photo is of my father. Maybe I should settle for that and go?*

"Wait, stop, do that again!" Lara cried, laughing.

After the lesson, Gillian suggested a walk outside. The sun should be breaking through any time now and the temperature had turned almost summery. Lara looked wistful. "Let me ask Trace if he has any plans, okay?"

Gillian stayed out on the balcony while Lara went in to call Trace on the house phone. *And why doesn't she simply unlock her door and cross the hall?* It wasn't twenty feet to his door. Gillian was coming to the rueful conclusion that Lara was bone lazy—not a trait she'd inherited, she hoped.

"I guess I'll pass," Lara told her, coming to the door, looking mildly ruffled. She sighed. "Trace has some errands to run and I...I guess I'll hang around here and finish a book I'm reading."

Your just a friend has errands to run, therefore you don't think you'll take a walk. I don't get it, Lara.

But Lara wasn't explaining. She suggested good-naturedly that Gillian take the afternoon off, as well. But Gillian thanked her and declined. The tai chi had cured her headache. She might as well earn her salary.

AS LARA LOCKED THE SUITE door behind her, Gillian stood staring at the door to Trace's office. *What does he do in there?* On impulse, she crossed the corridor and knocked.

Within the room, she heard the creak of a chair, then footsteps. The door opened to reveal Trace's inquiring gaze, higher than she expected to see it—he was always a little taller than she remembered. His smile curled slowly. Her skin tingled wherever those beautiful, masculine lips had brushed her only two nights ago. "Um, hello." This was the problem with impulses, she'd nothing planned to say.

"Hello yourself." He stroked a skein of hair off her cheek with the backs of two fingers. "I've been thinking about you."

"Oh?" Her breath feathered out like silent, shaken laughter. Just like that, one touch and he'd chased her blues away! "I...was just being n-nosy. What do you do in there all day, anyway?"

His fingers returned to her hair. He captured another lock hanging on her shoulder and studied it gravely, rubbed it between his fingers. "I'm writing the great American novel."

"Why do I not believe you?" He was pulling on his prize now, a gentle teasing tug that sent ripples of awareness spreading across her scalp, shivering down her nape. At this moment, she would have followed him anywhere he cared to lead her.

Eyes dancing, he shook his head solemnly. "Beats me. Don't you trust me?"

About as far as she could have thrown the man, all 180 or so sexy, muscular pounds of him. "Nope. So why not show me?"

"Sure. When it's published." His forefinger rotated lazily, winding her hair around and around its tip, gradually reeling her in.

He was lying. *Teasing,* she amended. *What do you really do in there? Play computer games all day?*

"That's too long to wait," she protested.

"I'll say!" The timbre of his voice had lowered and roughened.

She couldn't help smiling. "I'm talking about your so-called novel. What's the first sentence, then?"

His spooling forefinger had reached the level of her mouth. Now he stroked her bottom lip. "The first sentence?" he murmured absently. "'She had lion eyes. They glowed in the dark of his dreams.'"

"Sounds...racy."

"I sincerely hope so!" His fingertip found her lips again, traced the deepening curve between, coaxing entry.

Not here in the hall, where anyone could wander past! She smiled and turned her head aside, turned back again as he tugged on her hair. "I was thinking...would you feel like a walk later today? Out on the cliffs? You could tell me the plot to your novel."

"I'm afraid I can't." No excuse, no explanation.

One moment she felt utterly confident in his company, certain he felt what she was feeling. Then the next—like this—she was dangling, no sure ground beneath her feet. "Oh," she said flatly. *I thought...* She was making far too much of this. Just because a man enjoyed flirting with a woman, that didn't mean he wanted to come closer in any meaningful way. "Sure, well, some other time."

"Like tonight?" he said quickly. "I have to go into town, but I should be back about seven."

So he hadn't been brushing her off. "Come out for a drink, then?" she suggested—and remembered. *It's my birthday!* An evening with Trace would be a fine gift indeed.

"Can't go out, actually." He frowned abstractedly over her shoulder. "This business associate might call and I need to be near a phone."

Thoroughly frustrated, she gave up. He led her on—then slammed the door in her face each time she tried to enter. "Hey, well, never mind." She caught his wrist and began to unspool her hair from his finger. *One minute he's an author, the next he has business.* To heck with this man of mystery routine!

"I could…invite you to supper in," Trace proposed, his eyes not missing her hurt. "As I recall, you have an excellent kitchen. And I make a mean *steak au poivre.* I could pick up the fixings while I'm out."

"You cook?"

"All the men in my family do. Mom's a police officer. It was cook or starve, most days."

He was opening up to her the tiniest bit. *Tell me all!* Maybe he would tonight. "Sounds heavenly," she said in all truth, smiling again. "Okay. See you at seven?"

LARA'S LAWYER KEPT HIM waiting for almost half an hour after Trace's six o'clock appointment. And when he finally ushered Trace into his office, it was to face a briskly skeptical cross-examination. "Jeremy Benton vouches for you, of course," Dudley said, cleaning his wire-rimmed spectacles. "And I spoke with Margaret Feinstein, Mrs. Corday's business manager in New York, after you called. She tells me you come with the highest recommendations, that it was she who hired you for Mrs. Corday in the first place. But no one has explained why you want to see Mrs. Corday's will without her knowledge or permission. Although Feinstein has limited power of attorney and so may request this, ethically speaking this situation makes me...uneasy." He positioned his glasses precisely behind his ears. "Of course, Jeremy and I go back—all the way back—so..."

"My mandate for this assignment is twofold," Trace said easily. "First, I protect Mrs. Corday from direct harm." *Which means, you pompous pencil pusher, that I need to get back to Woodwind ASAP.* She'd promised him she'd stay safely in her suite, but still... He took a calming breath. "The second objective of a Brickhouse agent—always—is to solve the problem. Which in this case means find the stalker and see her convicted."

"Laudable. Laudable. But how would learning the terms of Mrs. Corday's will aid you in that?"

"Certain...facts that I've recently uncovered lead to the possibility that this isn't a conventional celebrity stalking. That there might be an underlying profit motive."

"I see," said the attorney. "Follow the money."

"Precisely." *So could I please have the damned will?* Trace clasped his hands loosely in his lap to keep from drumming them on Dudley's desktop.

"Seems a reasonable theory to explore," murmured Dudley. "But why withhold this from Mrs. Corday? I'd be a lot happier if she knew."

"Because that's all it is at this point—a theory," Trace said patiently. "And though reading her will may narrow my list of suspects, it may not eliminate some entirely innocent people. I'm not here to do harm but to cure harm. Raising suspicions in Mrs. Corday that some of her nearest and dearest might want to kill her…" He shrugged. "Trust is a fragile emotion. Hard to rebuild once the question has been raised. Better not to raise the issue with her at all unless and until I have some proof." He looked pointedly at the folder resting by the lawyer's right hand. "But if her will *leads* me to that proof and a cessation of the threats against Mrs. Corday's life…" *Will you get out of the way and let me get on with it?*

Dudley nodded. "Discretion is what I'd hoped for. Very well." He flipped open the folder. "Shall I summarize?"

"No, thanks." Trace held out his hand and kept it extended till the lawyer grimaced and surrendered the document.

TEN MINUTES TO SEVEN by his watch, Trace noted, standing third in line at the market's meat counter. Damn Dudley anyway for all his delays! He needed to check in with Lara, tell her he'd be across in the carriage house this evening. Extract a stern promise from her that she'd stay in her suite. And he'd wanted to take a shower before presenting himself at Gillian's door. *Call her,* he told himself, and pulled out his portable phone. He dialed her Woodwind extension as he stepped up to second place.

No answer. He snapped the phone shut. Out in the gardens, perhaps. Or showering, herself? His heart gave a funny little lurch at the image of beads of bathwater like diamonds on hot, velvety skin. Hang-

ing like crystal in her long lashes...Gillian... He
didn't know why she'd changed her mind about coming between him and Lara, and at the moment he
didn't care. *She feels it, too.* There was such a right-
ness between them, such an inevitability. He was
hardly a novice with women, but this feeling was all
new. Would have to be explored in-depth. Hopefully
tonight. Yes, most definitely a shower...

"Are you going to just stand there grinning, or
would you like something?" the blonde behind the
counter inquired, adjusting a curl behind her ear.

TRACE WAS FIFTEEN MINUTES early, Gillian thought,
as he rapped on her door. No matter. She was ready,
after spending the past hour showering, then dithering
over her clothes, changing outfits three times before
she settled on a burgundy silk shirtwaist blouse—it
matched the garnet-and-pearl earrings she'd purchased two days before—and a pair of olive green
tailored slacks. Keep it simple, for Pete's sake. They
were only eating in.

But her heart was cutting a complicated little fan-
dango as she hurried to the door. *Oh, Trace!* "You're
early," she laughed as she opened it—to find herself
gaping at Toby.

He looked her up and down and grinned. "It's
never too early to howl. You look wonderful."

But not for you! She'd forgotten he'd asked her out
for a drink, the day before. "Oh, Toby, I'm *so* sorry.
I h-had a change in plans. Trace is due any minute
now and..." *And would you please just go?* She
smiled at him apologetically.

He smacked his forehead. "You mean Joya didn't
tell you? That silly bitch! She said she'd stop by on
her way out. Must have forgotten."

"Forgotten what?"

"Trace called a little while ago. He asked Joya to tell you that something had come up and he was unaccountably delayed. Wouldn't be back till very, very late."

"Oh." She stood motionless, all her hopes for this evening popping like bright-colored birthday balloons. She'd gotten beeswax candles for her table, picked half an armful of the most fragrant roses, bought a special bottle of wine and salad makings in case Trace forgot, had chosen music to play—Brazilian guitar, light but not too romantic. For pity's sake, she'd even painted her toenails! *You silly, pathetic little fool.* The height of her anticipation was now the depth of her fall.

"Stood you up, did he?" Toby observed, staring over her shoulder at her table already set with crystal and china. "The rat."

She couldn't agree more. She'd sensed Trace's ambivalence this morning, when she kept proposing timid dates and he kept refusing. Well, apparently he'd had second thoughts about this evening. Fine. She wasn't going to sit home and cry about it. "Does that offer for a drink still stand?"

BY SEVEN TRACE WAS STUCK in traffic, waiting for the light to turn onto Bellevue. He should have taken a back route—had been so intent on his goal he'd taken the straight line approach to it without considering what lay between. He swore and whipped out his phone. Dialed and again got no answer. *Maybe she's up at the big house, looking for me.* Or maybe she was working late in her office. Well, ten minutes more and he could apologize in person.

Drumming his fingers on the steering wheel, he

forced his mind back to Dudley's office and what he'd learned there. It was just as he'd expected, only worse. Much worse, with the bombshell Dudley had dropped on him at the end.

Reading the will, Trace had been startled at the size of Lara's estate. Her own residuals from *Searching for Sarah* plus her recent inheritance from her late husband added up to roughly ten million dollars. Add to that a fifty percent share in Woodwind, with Toby and Joya owning the other half of the estate, plus an apartment on one of the classier streets of the East Side in New York, which Lara owned in its entirety—a gift from her husband while living. Value of her liquidated estate? Dutton estimated it at fourteen million. *That might be worth a murder or two...* He stepped on the gas as the light far ahead turned to green, hugged the bumper of the van in front—then swore as the light turned yellow and the van stopped short. "Come on!"

Roughly one-tenth of Lara's fortune went to charities—a foundation for aging, penniless actors and several funds for orphans here in the States and abroad. Then there were the minor bequests—a hundred thousand to Barbara Heath, the housekeeper who'd cared for the Cordays since they'd purchased Woodwind. A hundred thousand to Lara's friend and colleague Harriet Bristow. Smaller sums to the present maid, a former one now retired, a doorman down in New York, a teacher back in West Virginia, a makeup artist and a hairdresser from Lara's soap opera company. These sums were chickenfeed compared with the major bequests, but that didn't mean he should eliminate Harriet and the housekeeper from his list of suspects. A hundred thousand would tempt some people to murder.

And if a hundred thousand could inspire bloodshed, consider the remainder of Lara's estate, worth roughly twelve million. It was divided into three blocks, two quarter shares worth about three million apiece, plus one half share of roughly six million dollars. Serious money any way you reckoned. Seriously scary money, from the point of view of a bodyguard. *Why couldn't you leave it all to the SPCA, Lara?*

The light changed to green and he stepped on the gas, chasing the van around the corner and into the stop-and-go traffic of Bellevue.

Instead of the SPCA, Lara had willed the two quarter shares to her stepchildren, Toby and Joya. Who were already millionaires from their father's estate, Dudley pointed out. He'd estimated they'd inherited roughly three million each from Corday, with the rest of his estate going to his wife, Lara.

So if either Toby or Joya killed Lara—and escaped detection—they'd double their take. Some might call that greedy, but he couldn't swear Lara's stepbrats were among them.

It was the six-million-dollar bequest, though, that had raised his hair on end. If and when Lara died, six million would be put into a trust fund in the name of Sarah Cloud Bailey. The interest accruing from that fund would pay for detectives, hired by the fund's trustee, to search for her lost daughter and keep on searching. The fund would stay intact for sixty years; then, no daughter having been found, the money would be donated to a scholarship fund for orphans.

All Sarah Cloud Bailey has to do to earn six million dollars is kill her own mother. There were usually bonds of affection, all sorts of emotional taboos, that forbade matricide, no matter how much the offspring might be tempted. But in a case where the two women were essentially strangers? If shoving a stranger off a cliff earned you six million dollars? And how much easier would it be to shove a stranger you resented? Whom you felt had brutally rejected you as a child— and by doing so had somehow wrecked your life?

Arriving at the gates to Woodwind, he punched in the code to open them, sat watching their ponderous inward swing.

The will also made provision if any of the heirs died before Lara. If either Toby or Joya predeceased their stepmother, the surviving sibling would take the other's share, inheriting six million instead of three.

And if anyone could ever prove that Lara's lost child had died *before* her mother, then Sarah Cloud Bailey's six million would be divided equally between Toby and Joya, if and when Lara died.

So there he had it—three people with million-dollar reasons to kill Lara. Two more who'd earn a hundred thousand by doing so. And then Dudley had dropped his bombshell.

Trace wasn't the only one who'd been checking out the terms of Lara's will.

CHAPTER NINETEEN

BIG MISTAKE, GOING OUT with Toby. Gillian sat at a table out on the veranda of the Inn at Castle Hill, one of Newport's swankier watering holes, surrounded by half a dozen of Toby's tipsy friends. Newport's chosen, they clearly considered themselves, not townies but from the top of the hill. Their hooting, self-conscious laughter had risen to a level where patrons at the surrounding tables were giving them cool and cooler glances.

In spite of their gaiety, Gillian found them a mean-spirited bunch, whose conversation consisted mainly of back-biting gossip about members of their clique not present. Suki was pregnant for the second time this year, the slut, and of *course* she was getting an abortion, at that private clinic in Paris that everybody used. She'd come back with some decent clothes, at least. Buffy had bought—would you believe?—a Lexus. Turn thirty and you might as well be dead. Next thing you knew, he'd be going off to Manhattan to work at his father's brokerage! Had anyone else noticed that Pooh's nose was getting pinker and drippier by the day? The girl didn't have a hobby—she had a habit! (Hoots all around.)

Gillian smiled gently, rose and walked to the railing. At least the view was spectacular. The Inn was built on a high headland that overlooked the mouth of Narragansett Bay where it met the ocean. To her north arched the two-mile curve of lights that was the cross-bay bridge, connecting the eastern shore of the state with the western. Around the shoulder of the headland, Newport's lights bleached the sky. Some five miles away from where she stood.

She'd assumed Toby would take her for a drink downtown, on the harbor, an easy walk back to Woodwind. She could have had one drink for politeness, then bolted, taken herself out to a solitary birthday dinner at one of the waterfront restaurants. Instead, here she was, marooned out in the fashionable wilderness with a bunch of shallow, drunken brats.

The contrast with the company she'd hoped to keep tonight was brutal. And the beauty and romance of this place tore at her heart. If Trace had been there they could have strolled down the long sloping lawn to the cliffs that overlooked the water and watched the sailboats gliding downwind back to port, their wings spread to the moonlight like gigantic moths. Could have stood down there and drunk their fill of that beauty and kissed. Could have talked in half whispers of things that mattered. *What do you believe? What brings you joy? Where are you going? Who are you?* Instead—

"There you are, Gillie!" Toby loomed up beside her and smacked a tall glass on the railing. "Now, this you've got to try. Ever had a Pimm's Cup before?"

"No, but I think I've had enough, thanks. Why don't you drink it and I'll get an orange juice." And then she was out of here if she had to walk.

In high heels, she reminded herself, with no Trace to carry her home when she went lame. Her eyes suddenly blurred and she tossed her hair angrily. This was what came of building castles in the air! At her

side, Toby was insisting that he'd bullied the bartender into making it especially for her, that she really
must try it. She shrugged and took a sip, then kept
the glass in her hands until one of the girls at the
table shrieked and called for Toby's assistance, and
she was able to pour the rest of it over the railing.

"Joy*uh! Joyuh!*" two of the boys at the table bel-
lowed, turning the name into a jungle mating chant,
which the rest of the pack took up. Gillian saw Toby's
sister breezing along the terrace toward them, a
haughty blond amazon flanked by two lesser blondes.
Toby reached out and caught his sister's hand, and
she leaned down so he could whisper in her ear. Then
her wide blue eyes swung around to find Gillian—
and she smiled.

As SOON AS HE PARKED the car in the carriage house,
Trace sprang up the stairs. He'd apologize, explain he
had to run up to Woodwind for a few minutes, ask if
she could hold out for half an hour more. Then a
quick shower and change, and let the evening begin.
He rapped on her door. *It's me, beautiful.*

Shifted impatiently from foot to foot, then rapped
again. Cocked his head this time to listen, then
frowned. No sounds of her light footsteps as she hurried to greet him. He knocked a third time, held his
breath, then let it out slowly. So…

He'd dated more than one woman—usually very
beautiful women—who refused to wait for a man, to
cut him any slack. One had had a strict fifteen-minute
rule, he recalled, after which she walked. He'd let her
keep on walking. But Gillian—he wouldn't have
thought she had that kind of brittle princess edge.
Maybe she's up at the house. Yes, that was much

more likely. He was only twenty minutes late. He rattled back down the stairs.

Half an hour later, after a tour of the mansion, a casual word with Lara—Trace wasn't about to explain why he was asking, but had she seen Gillian?—then a circuit of the grounds, he had to face it. She'd stood him up. Must have walked into town, since her car was still parked before the carriage house.

Biting down hard on his disappointment, he carried his steaks to the kitchen and threw them in the freezer, then slapped together a cold chicken sandwich and took it up to his office with a beer. So he'd struck out in love. All the better to focus him on business. He picked up his phone and dialed.

"'Lo?" HIS SISTER ANSWERED absently.

"About damn time! I've been trying to reach you for two days now. What's wrong with your phone?"

"*I'm* fine, and how are *you?* Jeez, I never thought of it before, but Mom didn't perfect her socialization techniques till after the first kid or two, did she?"

"I suppose you, being the fourth, represent a culmination of all Mom's hard-earned child-rearing wisdom? To say nothing of Dad's."

"You suppose right, my little cabbage. Now, as to your question, day before yesterday I forgot to turn on my phone. Yesterday I was flying all day and not wishing to disrupt my pilot's navigation systems, antigravity systems, etc., etc., I—"

"You're back in Seattle?" He swung his legs onto the desktop and pulled the plate with his sandwich onto his stomach.

"I wish! I'm out in L.A., hot on your Gillian's trail. I found her father, Victor Scott. Well, almost." She'd struck out with learning Gillian's original middle name in Houston, Emily told him. But she'd found a helpful secretary at Gillian's elementary school, who'd dug up her record of enrollment there in fourth grade. An annotation on the card stated she'd last attended a school in Los Angeles. "So I called every Scott in L.A., Abelard to Vanya, and eventually I hit Victor Scott's second, well, latest wife."

"You always were a stubborn brat." Still, he felt his pulse ticking faster. "So what's Gillian's middle name?"

"Mrs. Scott didn't know and couldn't care. And I'm afraid I made a botch of explaining who I was or why I wanted to know. Halfway into it, she shut me down and said I'd have to ask her husband, who's due back tomorrow. I decided I'd make a better show in person—don't bother to correct that notion—so here I am."

"That's wonderful, Em, but I wish you'd checked with me first. Gillian Mahler's no longer our number-one priority. I'm now more interested in a woman named Sarah Cloud Bailey—that's Bailey with an *i* and an *e*."

"Oh, swell! That's just perfectly swell." This outburst was followed by an extended indignant silence. Time enough for Trace to down a couple of bites of sandwich. Then she said suspiciously, "Bailey. Isn't your client's maiden name Bailey?"

"This is her daughter, given up for adoption at birth."

Emily let out a long, appreciative whistle. "And she's only just told you?"

"That's right." He didn't elaborate and he didn't bother to remind her that anything he told her was to be held in strictest confidence. She was good that way.

"And you think this daughter might be Sarah XXX, come back with some very hurt feelings?"

"Looks like a possibility. She turned twenty-eight yesterday—September 11. Born somewhere in West Virginia. If she favors her mother, she'll be about five-two or -three, weight about 105, hair platinum."

"*If* she favors her mother," Emily pointed out.

"True. The one fact I have for sure is that her eyes are blue-gray."

"Terrific. So I'm supposed to track down every twenty-eight-year-old female in the country with blue-gray eyes?"

"I hoped you might think of something. A Lexus/Nexus search with all variations of that name, to start with, I'd say. Then the magazine subscription databases, with an emphasis on subscribers to soap opera fan mags and magazines for adoptees searching for their parents."

"Gotcha," Emily said quietly. "And if those come up blank?"

"Then we'll see how stubborn you are. Go to your phone databases and find the number for every hotel and bed-and-breakfast in Newport and start calling. She dropped a letter off here at our gates yesterday. My guess is she's staying somewhere in town. Describe her to every desk clerk you reach. She might be using the name of Sarah or she might not. Ask, also, for S. Cloud, and Sarah with any last name starting with *X* or *E-x.*"

"And dare I ask how many hotels, etcetera, there are in Newport?"

"A couple of hundred, at a guess," he said blandly over her groans. "If you find anything that sounds like a lead, call me. I'll keep my phone switched on."

She let out a long, put-upon sigh. "Okay." Comfortable with each other's silence, they said nothing for a minute, then Emily asked, "What would Sarah Cloud inherit if her mother was to die? Have you thought about that, Trace?"

"Way ahead of you, kiddo. She'd clear about six million, and guess what, somebody obtained a copy of Lara's will back in May—three days before she was pushed off the cliff." He told her about Dudley's sheepish revelation. That on a night back in May, the building security guard had entered the lawyer's office by the front door—and heard the back door banging shut. A search of the suite of offices had shown the copying machine was on, when it should have been off. And in the copier was the last page of Lara Corday's will, though the rest of the original was safely in its folder in the proper file cabinet.

"I've done that one myself," Emily said thoughtfully, "when I *wasn't* in a panic. I suppose whoever it was heard the guard coming, had just enough time to clean up, cover his tracks but forgot the last page."

"That's how I see it," Trace stated. "Dudley assumes somebody bribed one of his secretaries or paralegals to obtain a copy. Since he knows that they know he'd fire anyone he caught doing that, he didn't bother to question them. Besides, no one would ever admit it. And since he assumed the briber must be one of Lara's heirs being greedily curious, no more than that, he decided it was smartest to let sleeping dogs snore."

Emily snorted. "And three days later somebody pushes his client off a cliff! That didn't embarrass him the teeny-weeniest bit?"

"Since we've kept that under wraps, he didn't know."

"Ah." She thought for a minute. "So this isn't really about stalking, is it? It's about money."

"If our premise is correct," he reminded her. "Or maybe it's about hatred plus money." An even deadlier combination.

"Or something even subtler," Emily murmured. "Hatred with money being the excuse your killer is giving herself."

"Possibly." If she hadn't been his kid sister, and therefore never to be risked, he'd have recommended Brickhouse hire her as a field agent. Her brains were first-rate, her instincts better. "Whatever, let's find her first, then we'll ask her. I need a full-court press on this one, Em."

"Mmm," she agreed, then added, "why are we ruling out Gillian?"

Because I think I might love her. He blinked, as if the phone had sent a jolt of electricity ear to ear. Where had that come from? "Um," he intoned, a sound to cover a temporary cerebral overload. *No way! No way at all.* He was happy single—had scheduled at least two more years of putting Brickhouse on a solvent footing, before he could consider a change in status.

"She's the right age," Emily was saying persuasively. "You sent me her job application, you know, and she's twenty-seven. If a woman were to lie, she'd reduce her age rather than add a year. So maybe she's really twenty-eight?"

"She has the wrong color eyes," he reminded her with a rush of relief. "Whiskey colored." Lion eyes.

"You never heard of tinted contact lenses?"

Gillian was sane; he'd bet his last dollar on her.

A person could be legally sane—*and* rapacious as a piranha, his inner cynic observed. He'd spent nine years in the FBI; he knew that too well. *But not Gillian.*

"What about contact lenses, Trace?" prodded his relentless sister.

"I don't think so." But every time he'd gazed deeply into Gillian's eyes, he'd looked as a lover, not Lara's bodyguard. "I'll check it out, however." Tonight. His pulse quickened with the resolution. He'd gaze into those big golden eyes tonight. See if he could make them glow in the dark.

"TOBY!" GILLIAN PROTESTED as he swung the Range Rover abruptly off Ocean Drive onto an unpaved side road leading down to the water. A sign posted in the shrubbery proclaimed this King's Point Park, closed from sunset to sunrise, except for those with fishing licenses. "Where are we going?" The wheels bumped over unpaved potholes, a ridge of rock. He stopped the car on a bare, sandy ledge overlooking a tiny crescent of beach, with flat boulders stair-stepping down into the sand.

"We're taking the scenic route home, Gillie. Ever been here?" Toby got out of the car and went around to lean against the hood.

"Dammit," Gillian muttered. She should have called herself a cab instead of accepting Toby's offer to take her home.

"Oh, *relax,* Gillie," Joya said cheerfully from the back seat. She got out, too, and joined her brother.

Gillian watched them through the windshield, talking quietly, their cheeks almost touching—then the two broke apart with a burst of almost hysterical laughter. Joya stepped away from the car, flung out her arms like a child and, head thrown back to stare up at the stars, whirled around and around. *"Whoo-eee-eee-eee!"*

Gillian groaned and climbed out to join them. The black of the night folded around her like a velvet shroud. The ocean sighed on the sand. Stars spangled the sky overhead. The moon that had smiled on Trace and her would rise much later tonight. She stared eastward along the ragged coast, over small craggy peninsulas of stone thrusting out one after another into the water. Walk two miles along the shore drive and she'd reach Cliff Walk. Another three miles along that and she'd come to Woodwind. *Trace, are you home yet?*

"Panoramic to die for, huh?" Toby murmured, dragging something from his hip pocket. He uncapped a silver flask and offered it to her.

"No, thanks, and you shouldn't, either." If she had brought her license tonight, she would have insisted on driving. She didn't know how many drinks he'd taken, but his mood was definitely affected. He seemed alternately reckless and morose.

"Shouldn't, shmoodn't. Who appointed *you* our big sister?" He tipped back his head and drank. Coughed. Staggered comically. "You!" Then handed the flask to Joya, who also took a hearty swig.

I practically am your big sister. Or stepsister, anyway, though she'd just as soon claim neither of them.

"This is our favorite beach in the whole wide world," Joya proclaimed with childish enthusiasm. "Didya ever swim here, Gillie?"

"No." It looked no better than a dozen coves she knew along the shore. And it was too close to the road for her taste, she thought, as a car's headlights swept around Brenton Point in the distance and prowled their way, zigging and zagging as the road followed the tortured coastline.

"Well, come on, then! It's the perfect night—calm, warm."

Lousy company. Now, if Trace had been proposing a skinny-dip... "I don't think so, thanks."

"Oh, don't be such a party pooper!" Toby hooked an arm around her waist and started toward the beach. "Come on, just a quickie. You'll love it."

"No!" She dug in her heels, tripped as he kept moving, then staggered on alongside him. "Toby, I'm not in the mood. Cut it out!"

"Hey!" said Joya tensely, in an entirely different sort of voice, as she spun toward the road.

Headlights turned the wild roses edging the road to black filigree, then burst into the clear to illuminate the Range Rover. A black-and-white police car glided past it like a two-tone shark.

"Shit!" Joya said, her knuckles at her mouth.

The black-and-white circled, then braked, its headlights playing full upon them. A car door opened, and a tall, backlit figure stepped out of the passenger seat and swaggered toward them. "Fishing tonight?" the officer inquired easily.

"Uh, no," Toby muttered sullenly. He stepped away from Gillian, and from the corner of her eye, she saw him struggling to stuff his flask into his back pocket.

"What have you got there, son?" The officer held out his hand. "Give."

"Damn, damn, damn, oh damn!" Joya swore in a vicious undertone. "Of all the filthy luck in the world..."

"Open liquor container in a public place," noted

the officer, recapping the flask. He hooked a thumb at the Range Rover. "Who's driving?"

"She is!" cried Toby and Joya together, pointing at Gillian.

Their timing was so comedically perfect she laughed. "I am not! I don't have my license tonight, Officer, and it's not my car."

"Then who's driving?" he demanded.

She bit her lip. Much as she was starting to dislike the younger Cordays, she didn't care to tattle. "I really couldn't say."

He seemed to grow half a foot in the headlights. "Who's got the keys? Who owns the car? Somebody tells me now or all three of you win a ride to the station."

"My brother owns it, Officer," said Joya in a huskier voice. "He's a bad, bad boy, and you're absolutely right, he ought to be punished." Hips swaying seductively, she approached him and reached into the bosom of her low-cut dress. "If I paid his fine right now, plus something for your, um, trouble, could we forget all about this?"

The cop was shaking his head, more incredulous than disapproving.

Gillian clutched her head in her hands and clamped her teeth to keep from laughing again. *This is how they do it in Beverly Hills, Joya?* She'd just earned them a ride to the police station for sure.

CHAPTER TWENTY

NOW THIS WAS A BIRTHDAY to remember, Gillian told herself, half an hour later as she unlocked the door to her apartment. Or to forget. The cops had given her a ride as far as Woodwind's gates. Would have probably dropped Joya off there, too, with a well-deserved lecture, but she'd insisted on riding down to the station, where they meant to book an increasingly belligerent Toby on everything from drunk driving, to trespassing, to obstructing an officer in the course of his duty. Being a mouthy brat didn't go down well with the police.

Once inside she switched on a lamp, then headed straight for the shower. Something about the whole evening needed to be washed away. The last part of it especially—Toby's drunken insistence that she swim with them, his arm around her waist forcing her onward... A silly incident, with an inexplicably nasty edge to it. She shivered, stripped off her clothes and stepped into the tub. *Forget it.* Forget the whole sorry day.

She scrubbed herself under the hot spray, letting her muscles and her mind loosen, till the water ran cool. Then she stepped out, dried her hair, wrapped another bath sheet around her body and wandered into the living room. And heard the insistent knocking on her door.

"Who is it?" she called through the paneling, but

already she knew. It wasn't an impudent knock like Toby's but a solid demand.

"Trace." His voice was as uncompromising as the two inches of oak it penetrated.

"So you came home at last." And now what, apologies? She wasn't in the mood.

"What? Open the door, Gillian."

She let out an exasperated breath and rested her forehead against the barrier. She didn't need this.

"Gillian?"

Swearing silently, more at herself than him, she unlocked the door and tipped her head around the edge. "What?"

After all that racket, suddenly he had nothing to say.

She opened the door an inch wider, the better to glare at him. "Well?"

His hand drifted up. His fingertips came to rest along her temple; his thumb stroked across her lashes, sending a shower of raindrops down on her cheeks. "You were in the bath?" he asked huskily.

She nodded, feeling heat climb from the towel she held clasped with one hand at her breast all the way to her cheeks. She shouldn't have opened the door.

His hand curled around under her wet hair to clasp her nape. A simple, compelling act of possession.

She wouldn't surrender that easily! But her hand, of its own accord, opened the door a foot wider. "So you finally came home," she said spitefully, then felt another wave of heat wash up her body. That sounded as if they shared a home!

"Me?" Trace took a step nearer, his shoulders wedging into the gap of door and doorjamb, then stopped, making his desire to enter clear, while still he waited for permission. For surrender, because that was what it would be if she let him walk through her door. "What are you talking about? I've been here all night, waiting for you."

"Joya said—" And then she realized. Her own lack of confidence was what had fooled her! That and the fact that willful, blatant lying was something she didn't expect from anyone. "Toby said that Joya took a message from you, canceling our date. That you wouldn't be back till late. So I went out." She shoved the door wide.

"Son of a bitch," Trace said quietly. "I'm going to have to do something about those twerps." He took the last step to close the gap between them and stood looking down at her. "I was twenty minutes late, and I apologize for that, but wild horses couldn't have made me break our date."

The wild horses had gotten into her blood somehow; her pulse thundered like racing hooves. "Oh," she said softly, beginning to smile. "That's...good."

"I'm starting to think so." His hand at her nape threaded up into her hair, caught hold and tugged gently.

In unquestioning obedience she lifted her face to his. He groaned against her lips, then his tongue was inside her; his other arm hooked around her waist, pulling her up on tiptoe against him. She shuddered violently and wrapped her arms around his hard waist, then thought Oops!, as the towel began to slip.

But she didn't care—cared only that his tongue danced with hers, that she could feel his heart hammering against her breasts crushed to his chest, that he was whispering her name again and again as he laid a chain of kisses up the side of her face, across her eyelids... That they were turning in a slow dance of enchantment across the floor, her towel falling around their feet and Trace kicking it aside. They kissed again, then another turn, and now they were at her couch and sinking onto it, Trace drawing her down on his lap without a break in their liquid, honey-eyed, heart-stirring kiss.

As if the weight of her kisses bore him down, Trace toppled sideways onto the couch, taking her with him. Arms braced on his broad chest, she broke apart to breathe and laugh. "You're really good!"

"With you, I am." His hands, warm, pleasantly hard, smoothed up her back, then down again. He'd recognized her sudden hesitation and he slowed the pace accordingly, his fingers soothing and cherishing, tacitly showing her that his control was hers to command. At least so far. His body trembled beneath hers.

Of course he was good, and practice had made him so. But she shoved the ghosts of all his women aside. *Tonight he's mine.* It was her birthday and he was the gift. She lowered her mouth to his and, asking, received a hundredfold, kiss after kiss after kiss—tender, playful, passionate, one mood unfurling into the next. His hands stroked down her damp shoulders; she moaned and pushed herself up from him so they could explore lower. He cupped her breasts and gave a hum of delight—answered a second later by hers two octaves higher as his thumbs rubbed back and forth across her nipples.

Yes, oh yes, Trace! She twisted around to stretch her legs out along the couch and he swung his up from the floor, so they lay finally entangled, pressed together from thigh to mouth.

Clasping her waist, he held her up at arm's length in the air above him. 'You are so beautiful!'' He brought her halfway down, his lips claiming her breasts, while she twined her hands helplessly through his thick hair in wordless, rapturous joy. He brought her down, then rolled with her, and she felt his whole weight upon her for the first time.

Glorying under his muscled length, she tugged impatiently at his shirt. "I want to feel you!" Skin to skin, not this damned shirt; she hated his shirt—wouldn't have it. She fumbled feverishly with the buttons, while he laughed and tried to help her. An easy job if he could have sat up and away from her, but neither of them could bear that parting.

Trace got it unbuttoned at last, and she rubbed her lips across him, hairy and hard, with a wonderful, indefinable smell that was his and his alone. "Oh, Trace..." She wanted more of him, wanted all. Now she tugged impatiently at his belt. He laughed breathlessly and undid it for her, and it sailed off into the dark. "The rest of you," she demanded imperiously.

"I'm yours."

She cherished him, inch by hard silky inch as he found the strength to stand, strip the rest of his clothes away, before falling into her arms. *Trace.* All of him for all of her. The best, the only gift she'd ever need. The gift she'd been born for.

DEEP IN THE NIGHT they awoke to find they'd been making love in their sleep. They coupled with the drowsy, dreaming tenderness of longtime lovers, something sweeter and stronger than passion, bodies and spirits merging without boundaries. Two hearts to make one whole. Afterward, Trace held her in place on his chest, cupping her face in the dark. Their lips met one last, liquid time and she sighed and fell toward sleep. He whispered words inside her.

"Mmm?" she murmured dreamily.

He kissed her eyelids and whispered them again. "I think I love you…"

"*Ohhh,*" she said, a word like one note of a golden bell. And fell asleep smiling.

SHE WOKE UP TO SUNLIGHT, to find Trace propped on one elbow, smiling down at her. "Lion eyes," he said softly, and brushed a lock of hair off her cheek. Resting his forehead on hers, he stared deep into her eyes. "They really do glow in the dark. All of you glows."

That's just my heart shining out through my skin. She drew his fingers down to her mouth and kissed them. He dropped his head and took her lips in a lingering, coaxing kiss, and when they broke apart to breathe, he tipped an eyebrow. "Mmm?"

She laughed and shook her head. "Uh-uh. Not before breakfast. I skipped supper last night, you know." She'd yet to tell him about her night out with the brats, she realized.

"Deal. Let me cook, since I didn't make supper." He rose, stretched magnificently, grinned—a little embarrassed at her unabashed admiration, and retreated to the bathroom.

She lay, too happy to move. *I'm twenty-eight and a day.* If the rest of the year continued like this…! She hugged herself and stared up at the ceiling, a memory flowering in her mind—or had it been a dream? Could he have really said— She rolled off the bed to go ask, realizing as she sailed through the bathroom door that she couldn't possibly. But maybe she could read the answer in his eyes.

Trace stood peering into her medicine cabinet. She stopped short as his head swung around a little too fast. He blinked, changing from guilt to bland in the wink of an eye. Maybe she'd imagined it? "Did you need something?"

"The toothpaste." He shut the mirrored door.

"It's here, silly." In plain view, balanced on the toothbrush holder that stuck out from the wall.

"Why, so it is," he said a little too casually.

So he's nosy, she told herself as she adjusted the hot-water faucet and stepped into the shower. How could she blame him, when she wanted to know everything, from his shoe size to the name of the first girl ever to send him a valentine? Not that she didn't know the most important things about him already, she thought as he joined her. *Gentle. Kind. Intelligent. Sexy as the devil himself.* He took the soap from her fingers and turned her around, lathered her back with heavy, intimate strokes, as if molding a piece of wet marble. She purred her delight. Purred louder as he cupped her breast and kissed her nape. "We really have to eat first?" he growled in her ear.

"We do," she insisted, though she shuddered against him and backed up to rub against his hardness.

"Torture," he complained good-humoredly. "Save me some cold water, in that case."

They soaped and teased each other till they were long past squeaky clean, then Gillian slipped out and left him to it. Wandering into her bedroom, she noticed for the first time that it was chilly this morning. What to wear? Nothing restrictive or difficult to take off again, she decided. Skipping a bra, she slipped into her favorite orange sweatshirt, the one she'd rescued from Michele, then a pair of black silk bikini panties for contrast. The sweatshirt covered them and brushed the tops of her thighs. *Let him wonder if I'm wearing any at all.* She smiled, thinking of after breakfast and wandered into the kitchen.

She was breaking eggs into a bowl when she heard him come out of the bedroom. "How hungry are you, Trace? Three eggs or four?"

No answer. She looked over her shoulder to find him dressed in his jeans only, standing frozen in the bedroom doorway, staring. "Trace?"

He shook his head as though shaking off a fly and walked toward her silently. Something in his face made her think of a tiger, the way the muscles had clenched along his jaw. "Trace?" He reached her and gripped her shoulder—too hard. Turned her. "What is it?"

His eyes were fixed on her chest. "Where did you get this?" His finger traced one letter of the emblem across her breast, then he snatched his hand back as if the fabric had scorched him.

"My brother, Chris, gave it to me years ago. Why?" What was the matter with him?

He shook his head again, that same shaking-a-fly-off motion, shaking something unpleasant aside. "I...I used to know a woman who went to the University of Miami. That's all."

She swallowed. "Oh." *That's not all!* Whoever the woman had been, she'd meant something very special to him. Dammit! Should she go change? No, that would make too much of this. "So three eggs in your omelet or four?" she asked briskly.

"Uh...you know, I don't think I'm hungry yet."

"Oh." Something was seriously wrong. He was avoiding her eyes. "Coffee?"

He shook his head. "I don't think so. Not yet..."

"Then..." What? From easy intimacy and laughing tenderness to this. She stood stranded in her kitchen with a frowning stranger. Feeling suddenly naked with her bare legs exposed, which was absurd, considering what they'd shared.

He turned without a word and walked across to the couch. Found his shirt they'd abandoned the night before and slipped it on; returned, buttoning it. She read the answer in his face before he spoke, and braced herself for it.

"You know, Gillian, I think maybe I'll skip breakfast, if you don't mind. Hit the gym, instead. It's going to be a busy day and…"

And you won't be a part of it. He might as well have shouted those words.

"Of course," she said around the lump in her throat. "I understand." *Nothing.* How could he change this fast?

"Thanks."

Thanks? She could have slapped him. Thanks for nothing! He leaned down to kiss her cheek—her cheek, not her mouth—and she closed her eyes. "Bye," she whispered. It really was goodbye; there was no mistaking it. What the hell had she done? Or not done?

But she was damned if she'd ask, and he wasn't saying.

"Bye," he said. She opened her eyes to find him at the doorway, shifting from foot to foot.

"See you around," she said wryly. *But not if I see you first.* What a fool she'd been! Castles in the air, crashing down around her. *Little fool, giving yourself to a stranger!*

He shifted his weight one more time, then realized she'd dismissed him and he could go. She turned her back so she didn't have to watch him walk out her door. Stood, head high, listening to the door shut, the soft sound of his retreating feet.

When the bottom door closed, she dumped the eggs into the sink and took a step toward the bedroom. But her bed would smell now of him. Of them. She sank down at her table, dropped her head on her arms—and cried.

"WHUH?"

"Wake up," Trace said rudely. *I need your help.*

"Trace?" His sister yawned. "Whuh'suh matter?"

"Did you fly home to Seattle yet?"

"Do you have any clue what *time* it is out here?" Sleep was rapidly giving way to annoyance. "It's—jeez, you brute—it's five in the morning!"

"Out where, dammit? Seattle or L.A?"

"L.A.," Emily said sullenly. "I didn't fly yet."

He breathed a sigh of relief. "Good." He wouldn't have to tell her to get herself back on a plane. "I've changed my mind. Forget the hunt for Sarah Cloud Bailey for the moment. I want you to talk to Victor Scott. Like yesterday."

"I was going to anyway," she growled around a yawn. "Why else would I still be here? I checked that job application you sent me. Did you notice what she put for a birth date? October 12. Almost a month to the day from September 12. That seems too much of a coincidence to me."

"Why not October 11?" he mused, momentarily diverted.

"Beats me. 'Cause she's crazy?"

Gillian, eyes of a lion. She was anything but crazy. But then, neither were lions when they dragged a gazelle down into the dust. He rubbed his aching eyes.

"When can you talk with Victor Scott?"

"Not till late this afternoon. His wife said he's coming in from Chicago around five."

"Then meet him at the airport, if you can figure out which flight. I have to know, Emily."

"What happened?" she asked quietly.

She tore a strip off my heart, that's what. Nothing he'd share with a sister—or anyone else, for that matter. Only with one woman, and her he couldn't ask, *I love you, but by any chance are you a murderer?*

"What about her eye color?" Emily continued when he didn't speak. "Did you check that?"

"She doesn't wear contact lenses." With the sunlight slanting in her bedroom window this morning, he'd made sure of that just before he kissed her. He touched his lips, then scowled. And he'd checked her medicine cabinet to be doubly certain. No lens solution, no lens case, but— "But I found the red sweatshirt. You remember that the runner Lara saw on the cliffs—the person I think pushed her—wore an orange University of Miami sweatshirt? Well, Gillian has one." Draping her long slender body, which he'd made his own again and again last night. To give her up now, when they'd only begun, was to tear out his own heart.

"Aha! I knew it! That's why I stayed here to see Scott. I got to thinking about her eye color."

"What about it?" He rubbed a forearm across his face. God, he was tired. *Let me sleep and wake to find that last night was real, this morning a nightmare.*

"What color are Risa's eyes?"

Their niece, Jon and Demi's baby. "Dark brown," he said absently. Like her spectacular mother's. Demi was a quarter Egyptian, a quarter French.

"So your client, Corday, told you her baby's eyes were blue-gray. But the last time she ever saw her baby was on the second or maybe its third day. What color were Risa's eyes when you held her at the hospital, Trace?''

"Blue-gray," he said faintly.

"Like lots of babies. They change color around the second month. Your client never knew that?''

A motherless fifteen-year-old when she gave birth? And since then, how many babies had Lara held? He could imagine her shying away from that experience. How could she bear to hold another woman's child when she'd lost her own? Or even to talk about babies. "I guess not. Quite likely not."

"So there you go," his sister said triumphantly. "I think your Gillian heads the suspect list. I mean, she's there. She sought out that job."

"So did some twenty-six other applicants."

"But how many of them own a University of Miami sweatshirt, huh? Huh? Am I right?''

He felt his temper jolt upward and he took a breath. It wasn't her fault in any way; it was his, because he led with his heart, not his head. "You may be. Talk with Scott and find out, then call me immediately, Em. The minute you know, okay?" *And meantime I'll pray.*

AFTER HE HUNG UP he glanced at his watch—8:15 a.m. Too early to stumble into Lara's suite and disturb her. God, he hated this job. No bed even to call his own—he'd never take another detail like this one. Bed…there was only one he wanted, one woman in it. He shook his head abruptly and rose as he heard a car's engine outside. He strode to the window— Gillian leaving?—but no. It was Toby's black Range Rover, coming up the driveway. The brats, straggling home from another night on the town. For some people life was nothing but party, party, party. *They have*

three million apiece from their father and no incli-
nation to work at all. Wonder how long that will last
them. He glanced at his watch again—hours till Emily
would contact Scott. Hours before he could know.
Hours he wanted to murder. He sank down at his
desk, put his head on his forearms and—saw eyes that
glowed in the night. He drew a shuddering breath and
followed them into darkness.

CHAPTER TWENTY-ONE

KNOCK, KNOCK, KNOCK. "Trace, are you in there? Trace?"

Gillian calling him—he bolted upright at his desk.

"Trace?"

Not Gillian, but Lara, calling half an octave above Gillian's range, but still, there was something about the voice quality. *And they both have that tiny stutter! Why had he never noticed before? Proves nothing, he told himself,* as he rubbed his face with both hands. *Wait for the proof from Emily.*

"Trace!"

"Sorry," he said, opening the door, "I was asleep." And it hit him. "Hey, I thought we had an agreement that you wouldn't—"

"Would stay in my box like a good puppy? Do you realize I've stayed cooped up in my suite since yesterday *afternoon?*" Lara glowered at him. "This is how you bodyguard me? Why don't I just rent myself a safe-deposit box and camp out there till this blows over?" She stamped her foot. "I'm sick of this!"

He could have pointed out that she should have let him hire a second bodyguard, that it was she who'd wanted a minimalist, low-profile detail. "I'm sorry." Trace glanced at his watch. It was past twelve. No wonder she was ripping! "I'm really sorry, Lara, I..."

She tipped up her head and appraised him, and the corners of her mouth twitched upward. "When you didn't come to bed last night, I worried about you. I thought maybe something…bad had happened."

It did. He nodded glumly. *I've been derelict in every way.* He'd had no intention of spending the night with Gillian, even though he'd known that Lara was safe in her impregnable suite, but once he'd touched Gillian, kissed her… *Was I sleeping with your enemy?*

He didn't know that yet. Didn't know it for sure.

"And where's Gillian?" Lara asked shrewdly— nothing wrong with her radar. "She's usually in her office by now."

"Um, she might be sleeping late."

"Might she indeed," Lara said with a wicked smile, which gradually faded when he didn't return it. "Trace, what's the matter? She's all right, isn't she?"

Remembering the stricken look in her eyes when he left her, he didn't know. Couldn't say. He shrugged.

"I'd better call her!" Lara spun and headed for her suite and he caught her arm.

"Lara, leave her alone. Please? We're all adults here."

"Some more than others, it seems!" she snapped. But she nodded, and he let her go. "Fine, you two settle it among yourselves. I'm warning you, though, Trace. I don't want her upset or unhappy with this job. She's a gem and I mean to keep her."

The first time Lara had met Gillian there'd been an affinity, he remembered. Gillian had reminded her of someone, though she hadn't known who. Some instinctive recognition? *You bonded twenty-eight years ago, and your subconscious knows her at the emotional level, even while your brain insists that her eye color won't do?* He nodded. "Understood." God, if Gillian was the one who'd pushed Lara off the cliff... *You don't deserve this!* He could guard Lara's body, but how to protect her heart once she learned that? *And I'll be the one who has to tell her. Your baby came back for your money, Lara, not for you. You shouldn't have searched for Sarah.*

"Just as long as you do," Lara said darkly, crossing her arms. "And now, in case you've forgotten, I'm due at the hospital for my rehab appointment in twenty minutes. Would you care to shave, or is it bodyguard au naturel this week?"

AFTER LARA'S APPOINTMENT, she wanted to go shopping. Trace had to drive her to a mall, then sit patiently while she tried on two dozen pairs of jogging shoes, before she found a pair that suited her. *Here I'm guarding Lara,* he thought grimly, as she solicited his opinion on the fit, *when the one person in the world who means her harm is probably still curled up in bed, sleeping off our night together.*

There's more than one way to keep a client safe, he told himself grimly, but the joke was sour. Hands in his pockets, he glowered at the passing shoppers and wished one would make a move. He'd like to punch somebody's lights out.

The closest he came was a couple of women, autograph seekers, who pounced on Lara once they moved on to a boutique. But Lara wasn't annoyed in the least. She accepted their giggling adulation with her usual self-deprecating grace, signed their shopping bags, assured them she'd be back on *Searching for Sarah* in the following TV season, then waved

them on their way. "I'd almost forgotten how nice
that can be," she murmured, taking his arm. She nodded at the men's side of the store. "And now, my
dear, what about you? We're stepping out on the town
tonight. Medium dressy. Do you have what you need
at home, or shall we get you something?"

A night out, and said with a determined glint in her
eye. She was paying him back in spades for his neglect. "A Brickhouse agent is always prepared," he
said equably. "Tuxedo to wet suit, with all stops in
between. Where are we going?"

"Providence—a play at Trinity Rep."

The famous repertory theater upstate, where Harriet
had offered her talents only two days before and been
politely rebuffed, according to Lara. The actress had
been in a foul mood ever since. "I see," he said neu-
trally. "What are you plotting?" He would have expected her to shun the place while her friend was
smarting. So if she wasn't…

Lara looked guilty, then defiant. "I phoned my
manager, Feinstein, in New York and found out she
has some connections to Trinity's director. She made
a call or two, and now Harriet and I have an invitation
to dine with him, just a light meal before the show,
and a bit of business discussion. Then he offered us
all seats for tonight's performance. That'll give me a
chance to look over his style—ooh and aah in all the
right places."

*You mean you're going to throw your weight
around on Harriet's behalf,* he realized. Maybe make
the director a deal he couldn't refuse—a reigning soap
opera queen, plus her supporting actress, for the price
of one? *You're very, very nice, Lara Corday.* She deserved nice things in her life, like a daughter who
loved her.

"I hope Gillian will come along," Lara added, as if reading his mind.

"Don't ask her," he said automatically. It was half personal dread, half professional. You don't walk your client into the lion's den and then plan to protect her there. A pro didn't take chances.

"Trace," Lara said with steel in her voice. "If you two can't get along…"

Then I'm a goner, he realized. Might as well stand between a mama bear and her cub. But then, that was his job, to take the bullet if need be. "Don't do it."

"Why don't *you* stay home tonight and I'll take Gillian," she suggested waspishly.

"If you invite her tonight, I'll have to resign." *And then tell you why.*

"Dammit!" She stamped her foot at him. "Why do I put up with this? Do you realize there's been no…no attempt on me since that bee, and I'm still wondering if it didn't just catch its leg in a crack. What am I paying you for? Reminds me of that old joke about snapping your fingers to keep the elephants away."

He smiled—couldn't help himself—and delivered the punch line. "Then if you don't see any, I guess I'm doing a pretty good job, aren't I?"

She laughed, but she didn't back down. "Are you?"

"Give me a few more days and I'll let you out of your box. I promise." *By tonight even, with any luck.*

Luck? Imagining Jeremy Benton taking Gillian away in handcuffs, he felt as though one of Lara's elephants had sat on his heart.

SOMETIME AFTER NOON, Gillian crawled off the couch. Her wet hair had dried all bizarre. She show-

ered again, then blew it dry, dressed and threw some
things in a shoulder bag. She ought to report in to
Lara, but she couldn't face Woodwind, take the
chance of encountering Trace. She hurried down the
hill and out the gates, hunching her shoulders as she
fled. Was he watching from his office window? Not
that he'd care if he saw her go.

Too blue to settle, she wandered the town, staring
in shop windows at tourist T-shirts, trudging the
docks, passing million-dollar yachts without a glance.
She bought a cookie and a coffee—breakfast or was
it lunch?—and sat on a bench on Bowen's wharf. And
fed the cookie to a seagull that strutted over the cobblestones to demand it. Somebody knew what he
wanted, anyway. But what did she want?

Trace. She wanted Trace back—the Trace of last
night and early this morning, with a smile in his eyes,
a body that worshiped hers. What had she done? She
closed her eyes to hold the tears in and listened to
tourists wander past, to whining children, giggling
newlyweds; it was still too early for the serious party
animals, Toby's crowd.

She could go back and ask him, but the parting this
morning had been so brutally final. *He used me, then
when he'd had enough he was out of there. What's
to ask about?* Men did that to women all the time.

No one had ever done it to her. She'd never let any
man this close, before. Though "let" hadn't come
into it—Trace had vaulted over her hesitations and
simply claimed her, as though someone had given
him the deed to her heart in a previous lifetime and
that was that.

He had it still.

So…she opened her eyes to find the seagull standing before her. Sitting as she was, hunched over her

knees, they were almost eye to eye. "I've made a botch of things," she told it. The gull blinked one merciless golden eye, then turned its head to study her with the other one. "So what do I do now?"

She'd come to Woodwind for Lara's sake and nothing had changed there. Maybe that was part of her blues, as well—nothing had really changed. She had glimpsed a photo of a man who might be her father, had befriended Lara, but she was no closer to knowing why Lara had written her that awful letter of rejection. She'd told herself that she was coming to Woodwind to steal her life history, but she'd found that was easier said than done. *What else can I learn without first confessing?*

And if she confessed, would Lara turn against her? Throw her out?

Once those gates closed behind her, she'd never see Trace again. Never have the chance of a family. Tears gathered slowly on her lashes. Not a family from her past, and not a family for her future. Last night when he'd said— "You dreamed that!" she cried aloud. Must have, or else how could he have changed so by morning?

The gull tipped up its beak, stretched out its neck and screamed, a savagely mocking *awk—awk—awk— AWK!*

"You think so too, huh?" She stood and it waddled hurriedly away, then flapped off, gliding low over the cobblestones, then out past the docked fishing boats to the harbor beyond.

Maybe I should fly away, too. The thought of staying, passing Trace in the halls of Woodwind, watching him avoid her eyes as he had this morning...*I couldn't bear that.* But the thought of going, never seeing him again, never seeing Lara...?

SHE SPENT THE DAY DREARILY pondering her dilemma. She could see that the logical solution was to leave, but she hadn't the strength to embrace the decision. Maybe tomorrow... Trudging back to Woodwind, she heard the firemen's six o'clock horn blast over the town—and remembered. Her last aerobics class of the term was tonight at seven. *Skip it,* she thought wistfully. But no, not with her students depending on her. She groaned and broke into a trot.

THROWING HER GYM BAG into her car, she climbed in and backed in a rasping circle over the gravel, started forward, then heard a cry.

"Gillie!" Toby hurried across the courtyard, flung himself at her open window and caught hold, panting. "Where...are you going?"

"The Y. Got a class tonight, Toby, at seven." She tapped his wristwatch, which read 6:40.

"I...I wanted to apologize for last night. Those miserable pigs...a hell of an ending to a wonderful evening. I...want to make it up to you."

"No need." *Besides, you lied to me,* she remembered. Why? Simply to cut Trace out?

"There certainly is! Come out tonight and let me show you a proper time. The Black Pearl for a late dinner, say?"

She shook her head. "I don't think so, Toby, but thanks. Don't worry about it." Toby and Joya were the least of her worries. Her eyes flicked to the carriage house and she realized for the first time that the bay that usually held Lara's car was empty. She couldn't resist adding, "Where is everybody, anyway?"

"Oh, they've all gone up to Prov to see some dreary play. Won't be back till late. Sure you won't come out for just a drink after your class? I feel wretched about last night.''

He didn't look so much wretched as impatient. And she couldn't understand his sudden yen for her company. She wasn't remotely his type. Maybe it was male competition—he'd noticed Trace's interest in her and reflexively set out to beat him. In which case, Toby's interest would soon die a natural death when he realized Trace was out of the running. ''Gotta go, Toby.'' She stepped on the gas.

THE PLAY MADE NO SENSE to him, possibly because he wasn't hearing one sentence in ten. Trace sat between Lara and Harriet—the director had given them the best seats in the house—and stared blankly at the posturing actors onstage. They were anxious about something, he'd noticed that much, or perhaps he was projecting. *Gillian, what are you doing right now?* Surreptitiously he turned his wrist and consulted his watch. Nearly eight. Did she have a class at the Y tonight? He couldn't remember, could remember only the magic of their lips moving together, the shape of her, trembling in his arms. Her smile when she woke in the morning. Her hurt when he walked out on her. He moved restlessly in his seat, earning himself a sour glance from Harriet.

Gillian as his perpetrator didn't feel right, didn't feel right at all, yet everything pointed her way. The orange sweatshirt—how many University of Miami sweatshirts could there be in Newport? The initial *S* for a middle name that she wouldn't reveal. Her fascination with Lara—she was as drawn to Lara as Lara was to her.

Still, it didn't feel right, a woman who danced with the moon, who'd laughed in his arms last night? She seemed vulnerable, not hard. Loving, not hating. *Don't think, don't feel, simply wait for the facts. Emily, where the hell are you?* It was five o'clock in L.A. and if Victor Scott had flown in late this afternoon—

He jumped violently as the phone vibrated in his pocket. Yes! He drew it out and flipped it open. "Hold on." Harriet had turned to glare her outrage. Lara was smiling and shaking her head at him—probably thought it was Gillian calling. The couple in front turned to stare as he stood. "Back in a minute," he muttered, and worked his way past a dozen outraged drama lovers. His seat *would* have to be the middle one of the row. He bolted up the aisle and into the lobby and clapped the phone to his ear. "Shoot."

Silence—they'd been cut off, or he'd pressed the wrong button in the dark. Crap! He nearly threw the phone across the room, paced savagely back and forth, till in a minute it vibrated again. "Emily!"

"I was right," she crowed without preamble. "Your Gillian's middle name is Sarah!"

So. He closed his eyes and nodded. So everything he'd felt had been a lie. Everything he wanted was dust. He swallowed and said hoarsely, "Go on."

"Scott says he and his wife, Eleanor, adopted her in Virginia—not West Virginia—twenty-eight years ago, when she was a week old. They were told her name at birth was Sarah Cloud Doe and that she was born on September *12*. They kept 'Sarah' to honor her birth mother's wish and gave her a first name of Gillian. Some of the facts are scrambled, I know, but they're so close to a match. If she was sold on the black market, maybe the broker altered some facts to prevent a later search?"

"So…" he said, but no words came after. It was

over. He sat down on a bench and stared at his reflection in one of the lobby's plate-glass walls. A man alone, unsmiling. Not planning to smile for a long, long time.

"But there's also this, Trace," continued his sister. "Scott's a closemouthed, none-of-your-business type. I had to do some fancy talking to prime his pump. Had to tell him that a woman's life might be in danger."

"You shouldn't have," he said sharply.

"Judgment call and I made it, Trace. I told him his daughter might be stalking our client, that we wanted to stop her before she did anything that could send her to jail. And you know what he did?"

"No."

"He almost fell over laughing. Said that was absolutely impossible."

"That's what any relative of a criminal says." It was what he felt, too.

"Scott said that she was a sweetheart and had been since day one. He remembered her at six, giving him hell because he set a mousetrap in the house they were renting. He had to go out and buy a live trap. Each morning he and she would walk down the street to a meadow and set the mice free."

He smiled, picturing it, Gillian earnest and big eyed, defender of mice, then hardened his heart. "Gillian moved to Houston at age eight, however. Did he see her after that? She could have changed."

"He didn't. He said he's always regretted losing touch with her. I got the feeling the divorce was pretty bitter, and he married shortly thereafter, a woman with two kids from a previous marriage, and he already had an older son from an earlier marriage himself, and anyway Gillian wasn't his or even his idea.

It was his wife, Eleanor, who was infertile, who wanted to adopt. So he gave her custody. But as to Gillian's changing, I tried that on him, and he wouldn't have it. Said you see a kid for the first eight years, you know what you've got. And that Gillian was quote—'sweetheart to the bone.'''

Like her mother, Lara Corday. He felt as though a hand were slowly unclenching around his heart, but still… ''I don't know that I buy that. If something terrible happened to her over the next twenty years…''

''Scott said that although he hadn't stayed directly in touch, his real son, Christopher Scott, had maintained a relationship, and that Christopher said she'd turned out pretty wonderful. That's another quote. And Scott said he trusted his son's judgment completely. He said we're barking up the wrong tree, chasing Gillian. That it's completely absurd.''

The doors to the theater burst open as the intermission crowd poured into the lobby. Trace almost had to shout as he said thanks and farewell. He tucked the phone into his sportcoat and sat staring at the carpet. Gillian—had he figured her all wrong?

His instincts had so violently approved of her he'd refused to trust them. But in his effort to be objective, had he swung too far the other way? Convicted her simply because he was so helplessly attracted?

Victor Scott hasn't seen her since she was eight years old, he reminded himself. A lot could change in twenty years.

But what does the Bible say? Give me a child for the first seven?

Still, if she was innocent, why had she lied from the start, hidden her true identity? He had a good ear for false notes; it was no wonder he hadn't trusted her in spite of their chemistry.

Turn the problem around. Start with the given that Scott is right, your instincts are right and Gillian is a honey, whatever the hell she's up to. What does that leave you?

Two selfish brats who stood to gain three million apiece if Lara died. But— His hair stood up along his arms. My God, was this what came of guarding one person day and night for months on end—you saw everything in terms of the client? Tunnel vision. He'd read the will thinking only of how it endangered Lara. But there hadn't been an attempt on Lara since the bee. What would happen if Toby and Joya learned somehow who Gillian was?

If Lara's long-lost daughter died *before* Lara, then, by the terms of her will, Sarah's six million went to Lara's stepchildren, doubling their take. *They have to kill Gillian first!* He bolted to his feet, stepped up onto the bench and searched the intermission crowd, looking for Lara.

CHAPTER TWENTY-TWO

GILLIAN WAS ALMOST stumbling with fatigue by the time she came home from her aerobics class. Talk about a low-energy last class! Well, it had been the best she could do, she told herself as she shambled up her stairs. And somewhere in the midst of the cooldown, she'd had a revelation. She'd been trying to learn the truth of her life by lying. No wonder it had all come to grief.

No more lies. Not to Lara, not to Trace. No matter what the consequences. She'd decided that the decent thing to do was pack and move out tonight, take a hotel room somewhere. Tomorrow she would write Lara, try to explain what she'd done and why she'd done it. And at some point she'd try to see Trace. *There's one truth I owe you, whether you want it or not. I think I love you.*

She dumped her gym bag before the door, reached into her pocket for her key—and saw the note tacked at eye level. She pulled it down and read the neatly printed words:

> Gillian, I have reason to believe you might be my daughter. Could that really be true? I'm too excited to sleep, so I'm walking out to the end of Cliff Walk, then back again. Want to join me and talk about it? Lara

"Oh, my...*God!*" She stood, shaking her head. *How did you learn?* It didn't matter, only that Lara knew and didn't sound angry. Fatigue entirely forgotten, Gillian turned and rattled down the stairs. She didn't realize she still held the note till she reached the gate in the wall. Folding it, she tucked it into her pocket, then found the hidden keys and let herself out onto Cliff Walk. Breaking into a trot, she headed south toward the ocean.

"WOULD YOU KINDLY PLEASE tell me what's going on?" Lara cried as Trace hit the highway, swerved into the fast lane and stepped on the gas.

The car hummed up to seventy-five and he held it there, well over the legal speed limit, precisely at the unspoken limit the drivers and state troopers of Rhode Island apparently agreed upon. One mile over and he was courting a ticket. No time for that. He glanced at his watch. Thirty minutes to Newport, he figured, at this speed.

Lara punched his arm. "Trace? I'm the boss here, remember?"

No more. He'd told her only back at the theater that they had to go. Harriet had pulled a fit and decided to stay, would take a bus back after the performance, and that suited him fine. But he couldn't leave Lara.

"*Trace!*"

He reached into his jacket, pulled out his phone and handed it over. "Gillian might be in trouble, Lara." He was explaining no more than that if he could help it. In the end the secret was Gillian's to tell, and meanwhile the last thing he needed was a hysterical mother on his hands. "Would you dial her number for me?"

"No answer," she said tensely a minute later. "What kind of trouble?"

"Would the YMCA still be open?" She shrugged, so he said, "Then get their number from information and dial it."

By the time they got to the halfway-home mark, she'd tried the Y, which was closed, Gillian's phone number in her office—no answer there—and Jeremy Benton's cell-phone number, which responded with a recorded message that the customer had traveled beyond his service area. They'd also tried the chief of Newport police, Trace's only other contact with the cops, and been told he was up at some dinner in Boston and not reachable.

Trace would need at least fifteen minutes to bring any other officer up to speed, and he didn't trust just any cop with what might prove to be a hostage situation. He eased the car up to eighty and held it there, weaving in and out through the home-going traffic. *Gillian, hang on, sweetheart. I'm coming!* ·

SHE SAW NO SIGN OF LARA for the first mile, though she peered ahead eagerly each time she rounded a bend or reached a high point. Lara could have left that note hours ago. But no, Toby had said she and Trace had gone up to Providence. So she came back early, left the note and walked. She could easily be three miles ahead, at the end of the path, turning back now to retrace her steps.

At the first dike of riprap, Gillian slowed her pace. With the moon rising later and later each night, she had only starlight to see by; the deep gaps between the boulders were a net of shadows, laid to snare her hurrying feet. *Lara, Lara, wait for me, I'm coming!*

As she rounded the horseshoe of low cliffs that led

to the teahouse tunnel she looked ahead. Thought she saw a flicker of movement at the mouth of the tunnel—someone just entering the passage? Or perhaps she'd imagined it. Trace had said the dragons that decorated the teahouse eaves moved each time he looked. Maybe one had slunk to ground level and awaited her there. Her steps faltered, then she pushed herself on. *Don't be silly,* there was only Lara somewhere ahead.

She reached the mouth of the tunnel, drew a breath and entered at a walk. *Nothing to be afraid of,* she assured herself, trailing her right hand along the cold stones. The last time she'd passed through here she'd been in Trace's arms.

In his arms she'd been safe. But without him to keep the dragons at bay... Her steps slowed, as if the darkness were a cold membrane that resisted her passage.

Don't be a baby, she scolded herself. A child afraid of the dark. Around the corner ahead were the stone stairs where he'd sat down and kissed her. Her eyes squeezed shut against the tears. *God, I want that back!* More even than she wanted a reunion with Lara she wanted one with Trace. Tomorrow, she promised herself. She'd seek him out tomorrow and demand to know what was wrong, make him tell her. Anything was better than not knowing. Her fingertips found the corner and she swung wide around it.

A light flashed directly in her eyes—she cried out and threw an arm up to shield them. A hand gripped one of her wrists, then the other.

"Be still, Gillian," said a familiar voice.

"T-Toby?" He was using the light to blind her. Three hands held her, she realized, someone using two hands to hold her left wrist, while Toby held her right. "Joya!"

"Got it in one, Gillie," she chuckled out of the blackness, her laugh rich with contempt.

"Let go!" She tried to pull away, but their grips tightened bruisingly.

"See this?" Toby tucked the flashlight under one arm, then pulled something from his waistband and held it before her nose. "A gun, Gillie, and I know how to use it. So come along nicely. We just want to talk."

"I don't believe this!" she cried, as they guided her toward the bottom of the stairs. "What are you trying to prove?"

"Up," snapped Joya.

Toby pressed the bore of the gun into her ribs and held it there. "Go on. We just want to talk."

The second time he'd said that. *He's protesting too much,* she thought, her mind whirling like a merry-go-round in the dark. They were climbing past the spot where she and Trace had sat and kissed. She stumbled as she remembered, and they jerked her upright and hustled her on.

They meant to kill her; she could feel it in Joya's excited breathing, Toby's brittle gaiety that shielded him from shame. What she'd felt last night without understanding when they'd tried to force her to swim with them. "Why?" she asked as they reached the top of the tunnel and stepped out into starlight.

"Because you came nosing around," Joya said. "Couldn't take a warning and stay away, could you, Miss Greedy-guts?"

"What warning?" Then she realized. "You mean that letter last fall—*you* wrote it!" Of course they had. She'd never been able to reconcile its pure hatefulness with Lara. Should have known better, except that taking her original relinquishment as rejection, she'd half expected a second rebuff. "So you opened my letter to Lara." Although she'd written Personal and Confidential all over the envelope. That had probably drawn Joya to it, when she'd worked as Lara's personal assistant.

"You bet I did. No big surprise to find out she had a bastard somewhere out there named Sarah Scott. Little Lara was a shameless slut in her twenties when she stole our dad away. You just prove she was a slut from the word go."

"If you'd stayed away, everything would have been fine," Toby continued as they walked. "But we were damned if we'd share the money with you. Dad never should have willed it to Lara in the first place. He earned it through his writing. All of it should have come to us."

"She'd be nothing but a penniless waitress or a coked-up streetwalker by now if it hadn't been for Daddy," chimed in Joya. "With his connections, he made her a star. That should have been enough. She's got her salary. But giving her half of Woodwind and his New York apartment? Half his interest in all the shows he ever created? What are we supposed to live on?"

Gillian jolted to a halt. They weren't talking about waiting for Lara to die, then inheriting! They were talking about here and now. "You mean to kill my mother."

TRACE POUNDED THREE TIMES on Gillian's door, without hope. He'd seen no lights on from down below. Then he scooped up her gym bag and unzipped it. *Any note for me here?* He emptied its contents onto the landing and stirred through the pile as Lara came panting up the stairs.

"Trace, so help me God, if you don't tell me what's going on…"

"Someone may have kidnapped her, Lara." He'd keep the details for later. "I hope I'm wrong, but—" But there was no reason Gillian would leave her bag outside. Either they'd taken her here or something had distracted her, called her away. What? He patted Lara's shoulder as he clattered past her down the stairs. "I'll be up at the house." He glanced over his shoulder as he ran. Gillian's car was parked in its usual spot. Toby's Range Rover wasn't in its stall. They could have taken her anywhere!

By the time Lara caught up with him in her suite, he'd changed to running sweats and stood shrugging on his shoulder harness. "Shouldn't we call the police?" she demanded.

He snatched up a pad of paper from the bedside table and scribbled Jeremy's number on it. "This is a Newport detective, Jeremy Benton. Try his number again, would you?" While she dialed, he checked the loads in his gun, holstered it. The harness carried another twenty loads, much more than he'd need. *Pray I don't need a one!* Pray that Gillian was out on the grounds somewhere, picking roses. That she'd simply dropped her bag off and gone for a walk.

His instincts, though, said she hadn't.

"Same damned message!" Lara cried in frustration. "I can't reach him."

"So go check her office," he said, as he slipped into his running shoes. "Look for a note, or anything you can think of." That got Lara off his neck for a moment. He touched the knife in its sheath at his ankle, then straightened, closed his eyes and thought. *Gillian, where are you? Speak to me, baby.*

Silence… Still, he figured he'd know somehow if she was dead. Would feel a black hole of loss inside himself. He didn't feel that, only a rising anxiety that made him want to leap from his skin. *If I were Toby or Joya, where would I take you?* Every attempt they'd made so far had been low-tech. They were the bright kids of a brilliant father, keeping it simple. Each time so far they'd tried to make it look like an accident, but if they were now feeling pushed… *And frustrated.* The short-attention-span brats at the end of their patience? *I wouldn't kill her here if I wanted to avoid police attention.* And even with most of the household out for the evening, the maid and house-keeper lived on the third floor. Why risk an accidental witness?

"Trace!" Lara wailed from down the corridor. He spun and ran.

And found her seated before the computer in Gillian's office, her hands clamped to her temples, her face greenish white by the light of its screen. "Is it true?" she whimpered. "Gillian?"

Standing behind her, he clasped her shoulders and read the words on the screen:

Dearest Lara-Mommy,

I came here to kill you. You deserve to die, you slut, giving away your own flesh and blood, a helpless baby. What kind of a mother would DO that? But God tells me it's not for me to judge (though I do, I do, I DOOOOOOOO). He said the best way I can punish you is to give you what you WISHED for. (You gotta be careful with that wishing, you know. Somebody's always watching wishers.) So you wanted your baby gone? I'm gone for KEEPS. Bye-bye, Sarah, bye-bye!!! No more searching, she drowned, you can bury the bitch if you find me. So have a loooooooooong, MISERABLE life, you selfish bitch,

Your late, loving Sarah XXX. aka Gillian Sarah Scott Mahler

(no joke).

"Trace?" Lara whimpered, biting her knuckle.

"Gillian didn't write this. Trust me."

"Then *who?* Somebody who knows I had a baby! Who is Sarah XXX?"

"Toby and Joya, I'm afraid." They'd been planning murder for months, setting up their alibi—a fictional suspect. An invisible stalker. They'd hoped to make Lara's death appear an accident, but if the police penetrated that veil, Sarah XXX was the backup plan. *Don't look at us, Judge. We didn't do it. That crazy, murderous bitch Sarah XXX is the one.*

"They're their father's children," he murmured, thinking out loud. "Spinning fiction from facts." Storytellers, liars. Corday had told his tales to entertain. They used theirs as a smoke screen behind which to operate. And as a road map to shape their future— wouldn't it be so much nicer to have nine million apiece instead of three? They had a fatal case of the storyteller's what-ifs. *What if Lara died?* It was only one short step from imagining a different reality to creating it.

What if Gillian conveniently drowned herself? Which meant they hadn't taken her away in their car—that wouldn't fit the story of a lonely, emotionally fragile woman killing herself to shame her mother, which they'd concocted here. The Range Rover was gone to serve their alibi. When nasty things happened, the brats preferred to be elsewhere.

Gillian has to drown someplace within walking distance, since she didn't take her own car.

The roughest waters in the state were at Woodwind's back door.

So one of the brats drove the sports ute to the far end of Cliff Walk, parked it, then walked east. And the other is either walking Gillian west, or following her. Once they've killed her, they'll return to their car, celebrate out on the town all night, making sure they're noticed, then come home all drunken innocence at dawn. Simple as that.

"They're faking Gillian's suicide?" Lara spun in her chair and gripped his arm. "Because that's what this is, Trace, a suicide note!"

"I think so. Somewhere out on Cliff Walk. Now, I want you to stay here, Lara, locked in your suite. Keep ringing Benton's number. If you reach him, tell him to drive to the far end of Cliff Walk and come in from there. I'm heading west from this end." He glanced at his watch. "I left at 9:25. Tell him that, too. Can you do it?"

She shot to her feet. "I'm coming with you!"

He gripped her by the shoulders and stared into her eyes, willing obedience. "No. You can't keep up, and I need you here. Call in my reinforcements." He let her go when she nodded and sank down in the chair.

"But why would they do this?" she cried as he reached the door.

He couldn't leave her in utter confusion. "They told one truth, Lara. Gillian is your Sarah."

SHE WALKED DOCILELY between them for a dozen yards or so, too dazed to take it all in. Could this really be happening? Here in the midst of this beauty, with cricket sound and the hush of the waves for background and Venus hanging in the sky ahead like a crown jewel? She was meant to live in this world, share it with Trace, not be booted out of it by two ruthlessly selfish brats. *Trace, where are you right now?*

Up in Providence, if Toby hadn't lied about that. So if she wanted to see him again, tell Lara the truth, it was up to her. *Think. Where are we going?*

The cliffs ahead were only forty feet or so and descending, not high enough for a fatal fall. It hit her suddenly. "Did you push Lara off the cliff?"

"Of course," said Toby. "We'd have done that with you, but it's half tide already and rising."

"This time he checks it," Joya muttered derisively.

"Yeah, and you thought of it last time, too!"

Good. Fight. Please do. But they stopped, so after a moment Gillian said, "I don't understand. If Lara knows you pushed her…?"

"She didn't see me," Toby assured her. "And then she fractured her skull, you know. I don't think she remembers the fall."

"Oh." They kept walking, her wrists aching where they held her. *Think.* No high cliffs ahead, but once they passed the next tunnel a wilderness of jumbled boulders stretched before them till the end of the path. An utterly private place for a killing. So they'd wait till beyond the headland. Drown her or shoot her there. *Fight them here?* But there was no real cover. If Toby knew how to use that gun… Up ahead lay all the cover in the world, if somehow she could get away.

TRACE LOST PRECIOUS minutes crawling out to the edge of the cliff they'd pushed Lara over. He peered down, trying to see past the overhang. He could see no body below. The tide was already rolling over the beach. Since it didn't work last time, maybe they'd learned?

He rose and ran, pacing himself. Figure seven minutes a mile, with no more than two miles to cover, since they'd do her someplace in the middle of the walk. Not at the far end, where lovers sometimes parked. *The teahouse tunnel!* He shot ahead—to hell with pacing himself. Gillian, Gillian, why had he ever let her out of his arms? *If I get another chance,* he prayed. *Are You listening? If You give me another chance, I won't ever let her go again.*

The waning moon sulked somewhere below the horizon behind him; there was less light than he'd expected. He ran the riprap at half speed, leaping from boulder to boulder. Break a leg here and Gillian would die. *I won't permit that!* Guarding the wrong woman. *You fool! Idiot! Don't let me be too late.* He stopped, panting, inside the mouth of the tunnel, crouched and listened. Heard nothing but the echoes of her soft moans when he'd kissed her, how many nights ago? *If I'd held on to you there. Understood I held everything I needed in my arms, right then and there.*

He leaped to his feet and ran on. Rounded the corner and paused. They ambushed her here? Somehow he thought so. He took the steps up, two at a time. If they clubbed her with a stone as she came around the corner, then threw her unconscious off the cliffs up ahead, the fall wouldn't be enough to kill her, but she'd surely drown. Chest heaving, he walked out to the edge of the cliffs and stared down, scanning the shallow cove, searching for a darker shape floating in the dark water. Seeing nothing.

If not here, then beyond the next tunnel, somewhere out among the boulders, the most private part of the trail. Trace broke into a run, hit the next stretch of riprap, twisting and leaping—and leaped six inches too far. His leading foot shot off a smooth boulder and down into a crack and his momentum carried him onward.

CHAPTER TWENTY-THREE

"BUT WHY DO YOU HAVE TO kill me?" Gillian asked casually as they approached the second tunnel.

"Because—" Joya began.

"We just want to talk with you," Toby cut in. "That's all."

Joya snorted.

Yeah, right. Gillian rephrased the question as a hypothetical. "I can't see how killing me would do you any good."

"Lara willed half her money—Daddy's money— six million—to her beloved child, Sara Cloud Bailey. That's you, isn't it?" said Joya.

"Her *beloved child?*" Gillian stumbled. "It really says that?"

Joya burst out laughing, so she turned to Toby. "Does it? Please?"

He nodded rapidly without looking at her.

"She doesn't get it." Joya snickered. "The point of the story, Gillie, is the six million, not the window dressing."

She loved me all along! Gillian glanced triumphantly from one to the other, wanting to share the miracle, but Toby avoided her gaze and Joya's shining, shallow eyes held nothing but contempt. *Love? Joya doesn't know the meaning of the word.* Gillian tipped up her head and stared at the planet hanging in the black above, a blazing jewel. Such beauty, so much to live for, Lara's friendship waiting back there to be claimed. *And Trace…* most of all Trace. Glancing back over her shoulder, she saw the red rim of the moon rising over the jagged horizon. The same moon that had smiled on her and Trace only three nights ago. Toby and Joya pulled at her arms, forcing her onward, and she turned ahead, to see the mouth of the second tunnel gaping wide.

HE'D BROKEN HIS FALL with his right wrist and broken it doing so. Teeth clenched, Trace tried to rotate it and felt the bones grind. He knew the sensation well; he'd busted this same wrist years ago skiing. With exquisite care, breath hissing between his teeth, he shoved himself one-handed to his knees. Worked his left foot free from the gap between two boulders. His ankle was ballooning over his shoe already. Sprained, he thought, which could be more incapacitating than a break. *You moron, you fool!* he swore at himself as he struggled to his feet, then stood, listing to the right. Great.

So move it. Wincing, he shambled on, his teeth clamped in his lip. *Gillian, hang on, I'm coming.*

There were perhaps a hundred yards to the next tunnel, and one of them might be standing sentry there, guarding their back trail. He stopped to catch his breath—limping took more out of him than running—and pulled his gun. Awkwardly, since it was placed for a right-handed draw. Better to do it now at his leisure than later when he might not have a second to spare. He limped on, doubly careful of the cracks between the boulders now, after the harm was done. Clumsy fool!

Chest heaving, he stopped after another twenty yards to stare at the tunnel mouth—could see no

movement there—then back over his shoulder. The
moon was rising. No friend to him now. He could
shoot left-handed but not with right-hand precision.
He'd need to be much nearer to risk a shot. On two
good feet, under cover of darkness, he could have
padded up close enough to tap Toby on his shoulder
or snap his neck. But now?

He needed all the help he could get. Darkness. Also
a crutch, he decided, would help him move more quietly, though the time he'd lose finding one tore at his
nerves. A clump of brushy trees grew uphill from the
riprap; he headed that way. Stepped up onto the slope
above the boulders—and slipped on a patch of gravel.

"Crap!" Twisting frantically to land on his good
shoulder, he hit and rolled onto his back—and slith-
ered downhill on a rattling cascade of pebbles, clawing frantically with elbows and his good hand at the
hard slope.

He fetched up sideways against a boulder with a
grunt and lay there, swearing breathlessly at the stars,
assessing damage. Barring his wounded pride, there
wasn't much more damage than before, he concluded
after a minute. Some abrasions on his back, but— *The
gun!* He flopped over onto his stomach and stared
uphill—didn't see it. God, the gun! With him half
disabled, he needed it. Toby outweighed him by ten
pounds at least. Nothing to worry about normally, but
tonight— *Where's my damn gun?*

He found it lying between the piled boulders and
the side of the hill above it. Down a crack, five foot
deep, six inches wide. As unreachable as if it had
fallen down a well.

No time to waste cursing his criminal clumsiness.
There was only Gillian. He limped up the slope again
and vented his rage on a tree—tore it limb from limb

till he held a piece some five feet long, with a fork at its upper end. Tucking that under his left armpit, he gimped on, faster now, the pain in his arm and foot only a spur. *Wait for me, lion eyes. I'm coming.*

THEY HAD TO WALK THROUGH the steel-pipe tunnel sideways, Toby in the lead, drawing her onward. She suppressed her own urge to fight them. She'd never break free in this enclosure, and she wanted them to think her cowed, dazed by her coming fate. She hoped they thought her state reflected her terror, not her growing resolution.

Beyond the tunnel, Joya glanced at Toby. "What time is it?"

He lifted his left hand along with Gillian's to look at his watch: "Nine-fifty."

"It's getting too late. I think we should shoot her."

Toby's fingers clamped down brutally as Gillian flinched. He shook his head and kept walking. "We've still plenty of time. The play finishes at nine-thirty, the box office said. They're standing around telling the director what a genius he is right now. If they start for Newport at ten o'clock, then they won't be home before ten-forty, an hour from now, at the earliest. And there's no reason anybody should go into her office and see the message before morning. We've all the time in the world."

But she hadn't. They were passing the beach where she'd practiced her tai chi with Trace watching. Gillian swallowed and stared at the boulder where he'd sat and waited, as if his ghost might be sitting there still, ready to rise and come to her rescue. But no Trace. *Think. Think!*

"You're just being squeamish," Joya complained.

"Look, we can't afford any more mistakes. Shoot her."

"Where would I have gotten a gun?" Gillian asked in a voice of desperate rationality. "The police will check that, you know."

"It's Daddy's," Joya said impatiently. "Toby stole it years ago and kept it hidden in the carriage house. We'd forgotten all about it. You must have found it poking around."

That was barely plausible. "They'll know it's murder anyhow," she insisted.

"Wish on," Joya sneered. "You walked out here and shot yourself in the head. They'll buy it."

"That's not in our script," Toby protested. "She said she'd drown herself."

"I didn't!"

Joya leaned around her to scowl at her brother. "So she changed her mind and decided to shoot herself, so what? She's crazy, remember? The cops won't think twice once they've read all her letters."

She'd never considered before, yet given the choice of water or bullets, she'd take her chances in the sea. But as they nudged her off the trail and out onto a smooth, house-size slab of granite rearing some ten feet over the water, Joya seemed to be winning the squabble. Or maybe her demise could be a compromise scenario; she'd shoot herself in the head, then topple into the water.

"The cops won't think twice," Joya insisted. "Do it."

Gillian found her tongue at last. "They'll think twice when I shoot myself with the wrong hand!"

There was a weighty pause while they stared at each other, then her. "You're right-handed," Toby said on a note of doubtful challenge.

"Am I?" She was trembling from head to toe, but still she smiled.

THEY WERE ARGUING, all three of them, it looked like, Gillian pinned between them on the end of a rock overlooking the sea. He'd have to cross a long, clear space with no cover, and Toby was holding a gun. Trace paused and leaned down painfully to pull his knife from its sheath. Left-handed he was a lousy thrower. He grabbed a stone for backup, jammed it into his pocket and straightened. *Keep talking, Gillian.* Whatever she was saying, she held their attention.

"SHE'S LEFT-HANDED," scoffed Joya. "She sat to your right, Toby, next to you out on the terrace and you bumped elbows three or four times, remember?"

Damn. What else, what else, what else to say?

"Hell, you're right," Toby agreed. "So guess what. That means *you* have to shoot her. She's got to be shot from the left." He laughed in relief.

"Trade places with me," demanded Joya.

"Huh! This is your idea and you can do it. Here."

Now, Gillian prayed as he passed the pistol behind her back. Joya let her go with one hand to reach for it—and Gillian spun, wrenching down on the wrist Toby held as she leaped for the sea, shoving a screaming Joya before her.

COLD! HOW COULD ANYTHING be this cold? She writhed underwater, entangled with Joya, frantically pushing her clawing limbs aside, and rose with a desperate gasp—to find Toby taking careful aim from above. "Don't!" she cried, and threw up a hand.

"Don't!" shouted a voice from the path.

Trace? Or was she dreaming? Treading water, Gillian swirled backward from the rock and saw him some thirty feet behind Toby, leaning on a stick.

"Don't," he said quietly, and limped forward as Toby spun to face him.

A few feet to Gillian's right, Joya also treaded water, while she cursed and wiped the hair from her eyes. "Shoot him," she said flatly.

"It's over." Trace limped on, closing the gap to twenty feet, fifteen...

"*Shoot* him, Toby!" screamed Joya. "Shoot, you *stupid—!*"

"That's too many bodies to explain, kid," said Trace, limping on. "Forget it. Put the gun down."

"Don't listen to *him*—listen to me, Toby, you *jerk!* Shoot him!"

Toby's arm straightened and—as Gillian screamed her heart out, he spun to jab the gun at Joya. "Shut up, shut up, shut *up!* And you, too!" The gun stopped, pointing at Gillian. "You come a step closer, Sutton, and I'll waste her—I really will, so help me God!"

"Well, do it!" cried Joya.

A rock sailed out of the darkness and thumped Toby in the thigh. He swore and wheeled in its direction.

"You put that gun down right...*now,* Toby Corday!" Finger pointing, Lara stalked down the path, sounding like nothing so much as an outraged mother.

His gun rose and centered on her small, unflinching form. "It really was you we wanted to kill..." he said in a wistful voice, his arm slowly extending—as Trace's crutch came scything out of the night at knee level to cut him off his feet.

TRACE SENT THE TWO WOMEN on ahead, while he limped along as the rear guard. Not that he was really worried. They'd left the brats to fend for themselves, Toby nursing a shattered knee, while Joya wept out her rage and frustration.

Trace would dearly have loved to haul them in, see their fresh-scrubbed faces behind bars, but Lara had insisted she wouldn't press charges.

He had no intention of marring her joy in Gillian with the hard truth tonight, but this wasn't a soap opera, where the heroine could forgive all at the end of the episode. Once Trace and Jeremy Benton laid the facts of the case before the district attorney, that official would prosecute—for assault, if not attempted murder.

Meanwhile, the bubbling talk of two blissfully happy women drifted back on the wind—laughter, exclamations. He thought he heard sobs once or twice. They walked with arms wrapped around each other's waists, occasionally stopping and smiling back at him. And each time he'd wave them on. They had twenty-eight years to fill in.

When he reached the teahouse tunnel, they stood waiting for him, each with her head cocked slightly to the same side. "I don't know why I didn't notice sooner," he said. "So many of your gestures are the same. I suppose it's the difference in coloring and height." And not knowing there was a missing daughter to be discovered.

"I figured out who she looks like," Lara said triumphantly as they closed in on each side of him. Gillian took his crutch away and slid under his left armpit, while Lara supported him as best she could on the right. They descended the stone stairs with care. "She looks like Cloudy's older sister. I only met her once or twice—she'd already left home. Gillian has her eyes and hair. And Cloudy's height.''

Gillian laughed happily and he felt his heart contract. *This is what she wanted. What she came looking for. A mother, a family, her place in the world. She doesn't need a lover right now. She needs Lara.*

Well, he'd told himself he didn't want a wife for another two years. Two years now seemed like two hundred. He turned his head to sniff the hair at her temple, but tonight she smelled more of saltwater than sunshine. Lion eyes. All that really mattered was that she lived. Anything else he could handle.

At the far end of the tunnel, Lara eased out from under him. ''I think I'll go on ahead now, Trace.''

''Don't do that,'' he said automatically.

But she just smiled and stood on tiptoe to kiss his cheek. ''It's over now, Trace, thanks to you. I'll be all right.''

''But—''

''No buts.'' She backed away from him laughing. ''I can't tell you how nice it is after five months to walk alone.'' She backed another step. ''See you two later.''

He stared after her small, erect departing figure with something like dismay. A feeling of loss. What a mother duck must feel watching her duckling paddle off over the horizon. Finally he smiled. ''Are you as stubborn as your mother?''

Gillian laughed. ''Oh, I hope so. She's something, isn't she?''

They stood there, unwilling to follow too closely, savoring the feel of their bodies molded together. She didn't try to draw away. He felt his heart accelerating.

Gillian reached across his body to touch his right forearm. ''You've hurt your hand.''

"It's nothing." He supposed he'd have to get it set tonight.

Slowly, leaning together, with her taking much of his weight, they started to walk. "I have to thank you," she said after a while. "Coming after me like that. You walked right into his gun." She shivered. "If he'd pulled the trigger..."

He laughed, embarrassed. "I'm a bodyguard, Gillian. That's what I do."

"But you're not mine."

He stopped and looked down at her. "Only if you say I'm not."

She stood for a dozen heartbeats, then sixty or more, head tipped, as if she could hear something he couldn't. There was just enough moonlight to see she didn't smile. "The other night...was it just last night? You said something."

"I said a lot of things," he said. *Yes, ask me that!*

"You said... If I didn't dream it, you s-said...I think I love you?"

"You didn't dream it, but I was wrong." He drew his hand over her damp shoulder, till he found her wet hair and laced his fingers into it. Tugged gently.

"Oh?" Her face tipped up to meet his; there was no question of resistance. Her eyes seemed to glow in the moonlight.

"There's no 'think' about it, lion eyes. I love you." As she started to smile, he kissed her.

Such beauty. Within—as their mouths joined and danced and Gillian's heart exulted. And without—waves whispering, the smell of wild roses. Past and the present knitting their ragged ends in the moonlight—Lara and Trace and herself, a father she'd

READER SERVICE™

The best romantic fiction direct to your door

Our guarantee to you...

The Reader Service involves you in no obligation to purchase, and is truly a service to you!

There are many extra benefits including a free monthly Newsletter with author interviews, book previews and much more.

Your books are sent direct to your door on 14 days no obligation home approval.

We offer huge discounts on selected books exclusively for subscribers.

Plus, we have a dedicated Customer Care team on hand to answer all your queries on
(UK) 020 8288 2888
(Ireland) 01 278 2062.

never known. Family—stretching from the unknowable past into the unseeable future. The ties that bind and lead us onward into joy.

"And I love you!"